A Son at the Front

"Something veil'd and abstracted is often a part of the manners of these beings."

—Walt Whitman

Edith Wharton

A Son at the Front

Introduction by Shari Benstock

Northern

Illinois

University Press

DeKalb 1995

© 1995 by Northern Illinois University Press
Published by Northern Illinois University Press, DeKalb, Illinois 60115
Manufactured in the United States using acid-free paper ⊕ ∞
This text of *A Son at the Front* follows the original
1923 Charles Scribner's Sons edition.
Design by Julia Fauci

Library of Congress Cataloging-in-Publication Data
Wharton, Edith, 1862–1937.
    A Son at the front / Edith Wharton : with an introduction by
Shari Benstock.
    p.   cm.
Includes bibliographical references.
ISBN 0-87580-203-6 (alk. paper)—
ISBN 0-87580-568-X (pbk.: alk. paper)
    1. Fathers and sons—France—Paris—Fiction. 2. Americans—
France—Paris—Fiction. 3. World War, 1914–1918—Fiction.
I. Title.
PS3545.H16S66   1995
813'.52—dc20   95-17536
                        CIP
Title page drawing by Pierre-Auguste Rénoir,
"Portrait of His Son, Wounded in the War."
Paperback cover photograph of Edith Wharton courtesy of
Yale Collection of American Literature, Beinecke Rare Book and
Manuscript Library, Yale University.

Contents

Introduction

SHARI BENSTOCK

In late spring 1918, while recovering from a heart attack brought on by overwork at her war charities, Edith Wharton began writing *A Son at the Front*. Exhausted, her spirit "heavy" with sadness, she refused to "sit still and brood" over the war's losses. "I wanted to put them into words," she would later write in her autobiography, *A Backward Glance*, "and in so doing I saw the years of the war, as I had lived them in Paris, with a new intensity of vision, in all their fantastic heights and depths of self-devotion and ardour, of pessimism, triviality and selfishness." She wanted to portray "that strange war-world of the rear with its unnatural sharpness of outline and over-heightening colour." The result was *A Son at the Front*, a novel that stands today alongside *Fighting France: From Dunkerque to Belfort*, essays based on Wharton's visits to the front in 1915, as her most important contribution to World War I literature.[1]

Wharton completed the first four chapters of *A Son at the Front* in a "white heat of passion" in 1918 and returned to it again in spring and summer 1919, when she nearly completed it. The book was destined to remain unpublished until 1922, however, due to lack of public interest in war literature.[2]

Throughout the long years of stalemated conflict, writing about the war had sold well in the United States and Great Britain, finding especially enthusiastic audiences during the weeks of the Allied advance that routed the invading German army in autumn 1918. In December of that year, Wharton published *The Marne*, a patriotic tale that captured the high-flying sentiments of the July battle in the

Marne valley, when the armies of Pershing and Foch checked the last German offensive and brought an end to the war. *The Marne* received rave reviews. Initial sales were so strong that the book appeared to be a bestseller, but a spring 1919 quarterly royalty report from her publishers revealed that sales volume had not been sustained into the new year. Commenting on readers' changed desires, Joseph Sears, vice president of the New York publisher D. Appleton and Company, wrote to Wharton: "It was almost grotesque to see the aversion which the American public had for purely war literature." She admitted to "bewilderment at finding that a public whose own sons and brothers have been in the war should already have ceased to take an interest in it."[3]

Realizing that she would have difficulty finding a market for *A Son at the Front*, Wharton declared that it was not, in fact, a war novel. She described it as a psychological study of an artist father and his son that chronicled French-American life in Paris in 1915–1916. Indeed, it is a book that explores themes of fatherhood and sonship, art and self-sacrifice, national loyalties and class privilege. Although she twice changed its title in efforts to sell it—one title, "Paris," evoked the primary setting, while another, "Their Son," suggested the familial context—her publishers remained convinced the public would see it as war fiction. They wanted a novel of manners, an updated *House of Mirth*, that would capture a large American readership.

Wharton eventually produced such a work, *The Glimpses of the Moon* (1922), an instant bestseller for which F. Scott Fitzgerald wrote a screenplay. Yet before she could write a "modern" novel—indeed, before she could write her novel of Old New York, *The Age of Innocence*, for which she won the Pulitzer Prize in 1921—Edith Wharton felt compelled to finish *A Son at the Front*. When it was completed, she asked her editors at Appleton to put the manuscript in their vault until reader antipathy to the war had abated. She then entered into complicated negotiations with her former publishers, Charles Scribner's Sons, who eventually bought the novel for $15,000 and serialized it in *Scribner's Magazine* between December 1922 and September 1923.[4]

Hoping for a bestseller, Charles Scribner's Sons produced a first book edition of sixty thousand copies. To the publishers' disappointment, it neither sold well nor received critical praise. Opinion weighed on the side represented by the *Bookman* critic, who described *A Son at the Front* as "a belated essay in propaganda," commenting that Wharton was "still too angry" about the war. Several other reviewers called it "belated," to which they added other deprecatory adjectives: outdated, egregious, obtuse, myopic, disagreeable, disappointing, and—in the words of Robert Morss Lovett of the *New*

Republic—"snobbishly blind to every point of view but that of her class." In his review, Lovett, who later wrote the first book of literary criticism on Edith Wharton, overlooked her characterization of Madame Lebel, Campton's aged, poor concierge, who loses all of her sons to the war. Madame Lebel's story provides a counterpoint to Campton's, and the scenes in which she appears are among the most poignant in the book.[5]

Generally, reviewers felt that Wharton was too close to her material. The reviewer for the *New York Evening Post* commented that the "chief value" of the book was as a "cathartic for the author's feelings." The *Times Literary Supplement* (London) predicted that the book would eventually have "permanent value among the minor documents of the war." *A Son at the Front* received better reviews in the British press than among American critics, although the critic for *The Nation* commented that D. H. Lawrence (who did not serve in the military) would probably agree that the book constituted "Post-mortem effects. Ghosts." Women reviewers were sometimes better attuned to the subtleties in Wharton's theme. Dorothea Lawrence Mann, writing for the *Boston Evening Transcript*, doubted that "anyone in any language" could write the epic of war "so truthfully and sympathetically as Mrs. Wharton has done for parents of the war."[6]

Two factors influenced the generally negative reception of the novel. The postwar climate of increased nationalistic rivalries and ideological divisions (signaled by the rise of communism and fascism) and increasing European economic instability raised the specter of a future war. Writers who had come of age during the 1914–1918 conflict had, by 1923, begun publishing testimonies of the war. To this generation of artists—which included e.e. cummings, Ernest Hemingway, and John Dos Passos—Wharton's war fictions seemed not only dated but also maudlin and full of hackneyed and false patriotic sentiments. Drawing on their personal experience as combatants, ambulance drivers, and prisoners of war, they recreated the grim reality of battle from the viewpoint of the Great War's ultimate futility—its failure to save the world from future conflicts.

Wharton knew the battlefield poetry of men who had served with the British forces. She printed some of it in her 1916 collection, *The Book of the Homeless*, an anthology of original poetry, prose, musical scores, and artwork sold to support her war charities. She might have agreed that these firsthand accounts gave a seemingly truer vision of the war than did writing by women who served, as she did, "behind the lines." Yet she wrote *A Son at the Front* in order to illuminate another side of the war—"the world at the rear." As she explained in *A Backward Glance*, this was a world she knew intimately.[7]

Edith Wharton was made an officer of the French Legion of Honor in recognition of her work to save starving refugees from the invaded regions of Belgium and northern France. She visited the Marne battlefields and delivered hospital supplies to Verdun, Ypres, Dunkerque, and the Vosges, describing conditions there in a series of essays for *Scribner's Magazine*. Yet she knew that by gender and citizenship she was distanced from the war's central drama and mystery. From the first moments of the war her sympathies were with France. She longed to be an "Ally" in the conflict, and the prolonged period during which the United States remained neutral (the situation that forms the political backdrop of *A Son at the Front*) made her feel—for most of the war—ashamed to be an American. No sooner had the United States declared war on Germany in spring 1917 than Edith Wharton began "planning and brooding over 'A Son at the Front.'" Moreover, her deeply held conviction that civilization itself was at stake in the war undoubtedly contributed to her disappointment at the delay in publishing the novel and its poor critical reception.

Wharton's war fiction has always been viewed as ancillary to her novels of New York society. Long out of print, her war novels either went unmentioned by literary historians or were treated scornfully by critics who measured the standards of war fiction by Hemingway's *The Sun Also Rises* and Ford Madox Ford's *The Good Soldier*. It was Wharton's fate to be cast in the shadow of male writers who were thought to be either her mentors or her models. In her lifetime, critics compared her writing to that of her friend Henry James, often pronouncing them to be pale imitations of his work that succeeded only in reproducing his worst faults. Twenty years after Wharton's revival in academic circles, her name is still linked to James's despite research by feminist literary historians and biographers that reveals the originality of Wharton's social criticism and the false assumptions that underlie the "Wharton-James" coupling.[8]

Until recently, Wharton's war fiction was overlooked even by scholars, and her nonfiction writing during the war (*Fighting France* and *French Ways and Their Meaning*, out of print for many years) was discussed alongside her travel writings. These slights to such a significant category of Wharton's canon resulted not from an absence of interest in the broader range of her writing but from the larger problems of categorizing women's contributions to war literature. Recent scholarship on World War I writing by British and American feminists has provided a revisionist history of women's engagement in the war, a history that challenges longheld beliefs that war, like childbirth, constitutes an unbridgeable divide in men's and women's experiences. Women's writings about World War I challenge this assumption by providing a wider definition of the war experience, one not limited to "seeing action."[9]

A central theme of *The Marne* and *A Son at the Front* is the desire of young American men to see action at the front, a theme joined to the question of the roles artists and intellectuals should take in wartime. Wharton personalized these themes, drawing her characters from among friends, family members, and colleagues in her war charities. She used as settings for *A Son at the Front* the places she knew well: her Left Bank apartment, her brother's house off the Avenue du Marigny, the Crillon hotel where she frequently stayed after the war, the military emplacements she visited as part of her charity work. As always, she cast aspects of herself in the artist figures.

Wharton dedicated both her war novels to the memory of Ronald Simmons. An expatriate painter in Paris who had served as secretary for one of her charities until United States forces joined the war effort, Simmons was recruited by American Intelligence and rose to the rank of captain. While stationed in Marseilles in summer 1918, Simmons died of the Spanish influenza that swept across Europe. Devastated by his death, Wharton described herself to friends as "paralyzed," her heart "murdered." She identified with the nearsighted, shy, and modest Simmons—a "pathetic figure"—and with his grieving mother. In *The Marne* Simmons contributes to Wharton's portrait of an artistic boy caught in Paris with his mother during the 1914 Battle of the Marne. After completing his education, the boy returns in 1918 as an ambulance driver wounded in the second Battle of the Marne. In *A Son at the Front* Simmons appears as Boylston—a fat, jolly, nearsighted Beaux Arts student engaged in war charity work. Wharton modeled George Campton, the "son at the front" to whom the title refers, on her youngest cousin, the handsome "golden-haired" Newbold Rhinelander. An army pilot, he was lost behind enemy lines in the last weeks of the war when his plane was shot down. Working through diplomatic and military channels, it took Wharton more than three months to determine his fate and to recover his body. She arranged for Rhinelander's burial and presided at the funeral in the absence of his parents. His death and Simmons's were inevitably linked in her mind, representing her greatest personal tragedies of the war.[10]

While the drama of the novel turns on George Campton's fate as an American born in Paris and subject to French army mobilization, the thematic focus of the book remains with his father, John Campton, who loves his son with an obsession that blinds him to George's own secret desires—his love for a married woman old enough to be his mother and his desire to see active combat. Guilty about this child born of a "stupid ill-fated marriage" (p. 25) that ended in divorce, Campton repeatedly paints George, his art portfolio a silent testimony to the son's place in the father's art. Indeed, Campton's most famous work is a portrait of George, which he donated to the Luxembourg

Museum in Paris (where it hung on the same wall as Whistler's Mother) to prevent Anderson Brant, a rich banker who married Campton's former wife, Julia, from buying it.

This portrait and one that Campton sketches in the novel reveal the probable artistic inspiration for *A Son at the Front*. In 1915, French painter Pierre-Auguste Renoir contributed to *The Book of the Homeless* a charcoal sketch of his son, who was wounded in the war, a portrait generally considered the most moving image of the collection. Dressed in military uniform, young Renoir looks to be a mere child, his rounded, innocent face belying the horrors he is about to confront. In a scene that foreshadows the coming tragedy of *A Son at the Front*, John Campton sketches his sleeping son on the eve of their departure for a long-awaited trip to Spain and Africa that the mobilization of troops will force them to cancel.

This scene is balanced by a later one in which Campton again sits by George's bedside, memorizing his son's features. Campton tries repeatedly in the novel to achieve emotional closeness to his son through physical proximity—planning trips, dinners, walks, and long evenings with him. Yet his sense of emotional separation from his son (a distance that widens as the story progresses) mirrors an aspect of the novel's artistic theme: to capture his subject, the painter requires distance and perspective. The longing for paternal intimacy with his son is tempered by Campton's stronger desire to turn his son into art—to memorialize him. Such thoughts come to the painter as he sits near his bed in the Crillon hotel, modeling the boy's "slim flank and legs as he lay in dreamless rest" (p. 31) and taking care not to wake him:

> "Like a statue of a young knight I've seen somewhere," he said to himself, vexed and surprised that he, whose plastic memories were always so precise, should not remember where; and then his pencil stopped. What he had really thought was: "Like the *effigy* of a young knight"— though he had instinctively changed the word as it formed itself. He leaned in the doorway, the sketch-book in hand, and continued to gaze at his son. It was the clinging sheet, no doubt, that gave him that look . . . and the white glare of the electric burner.
>
> If war came, that was just the way a boy might lie on a battle-field— or afterward in a hospital bed. Not *his* boy, thank heaven; but very probably his boy's friends: hundreds and thousands of boys like his boy, the age of his boy, with a laugh like his boy's. . . The wicked waste of it! Well, that was what war meant . . . what to-morrow might bring to millions of parents like himself. (pp. 31–32)

These morbid visions do not forecast the hellish battle scenes of the coming war (John Campton never sees the front); rather, the effigy and prone body under the clinging sheet predict the shellshocked

faces and deathly wounds that are war's primary effects. The phrase
"a son at the front" conjures up such images. Campton is frightened
by his own vision—"Just because the boy lay as if he were posing for a
tombstone!"—and recalls a painter who, in another circumstance,
"had sat at his dead son's side and drawn him, tenderly, minutely,
while the coffin waited" (p. 32). This specter causes Campton to throw
down his sketch book and leave the room.

Like the events of the Great War itself, the narrative sweep of *A
Son at the Front* is overdetermined, its conclusion projected in its
opening scenes. The war takes the Camptons by surprise, as it did
many others. Although they had lived for many years in Paris, they
felt no stake in the European struggle: "After all, we're Americans;
this is not our job," Campton exclaims when he learns that France
has declared war on Germany. It was, he rationalizes, mere accident
that his son was born in France; another accident of timing that
George's arrival in Paris to join his father for the Spain trip placed
him on French soil when mobilization was declared. Recently recuper-
ated from a bout of tuberculosis, George should be spared duty at the
front. His estranged parents join forces, working "behind the lines"
(and behind George's back), to assure his safety at a desk job far away
from the action.

Yet as the war progresses and the losses mount, George's parents
realize that their loyalties are with France. Wharton underscored this
point in the summary of the novel's themes she sent to her publisher:
"They have seen Frenchmen of all ages and classes, from volunteers of
18 to men of over 50, who have insisted on resuming their military
service." As time passes, John Campton does volunteer charity work
and donates paintings to the "Friends of French Art," a group supporting out-of-work artists modeled on one Wharton organized for un-
employed musicians. Campton's former wife, Julia, trains as a volunteer nurse. Their son George arranges to leave his depot "at the rear"
for duty at the front, and several of his Paris friends, including Boylston, keep his whereabouts secret from his parents.

For much of the novel, George is out of sight—unseen by his parents or the reader, his motives and actions unknown. The "front" is
also hidden from view, although Wharton could have described it in
detail had she chosen to do so. Her decision to keep the war off-scene,
something talked about but never viewed, was no doubt based on
artistic grounds. As recent feminist scholarship on World War I at-
tests, she gained an important measure of verisimilitude by adopting
this narrative method. Like real-life civilians, her characters receive
official news of the front through carefully worded communiqués,
which only further fuel their desire to know more about events. Dinner table conversation consists of gossip, rumor, and speculation.

Wealthy women such as Julia Brant seek out the clairvoyant Madame Olida, who assures them that their sons at the front will return safely. (Madame Olida, who for months has had no news of her own son at the front, invents letters from him to reassure her clients that their loved ones are also safe.)

Invoked by the phrase "at the front," the war occupies a space of the unimaginable in Wharton's text. On one hand, the war is described in euphemisms ("that hideous barbarism"); on the other, its savagery becomes an "entertainment" for charity events (p. 109). Campton is "pursued by visions of that land of doom"—the "Out there" of the front—but he is unable to produce a coherent view of the place (p. 103). Described in the overblown rhetoric of war propaganda and charity appeals as the "Great Struggle . . . to save the world from barbarism" (p. 109), this war is so savage that it cannot be compared to other wars.

Hearing stories of the front, Campton is relieved to think that George is safely distant from the battle: "George, God be praised, was not at the front" (p. 74). But George is never where Campton thinks he is, nor is the war ever "real" to Campton in the way it becomes for his son. For Campton (as for Edith Wharton), the war represents a great divide within history and between human beings—between those who experienced the unspeakable at first hand and those who did not. Campton concludes that George has been "plunged in secret traffic with things unutterable": "Between himself and George lay the unbridgeable abyss of his son's experiences" (p. 212). The novel closes as Campton attempts to bridge this distance by artistic means: "He pulled out all the sketches of his son from the old portfolio, spread them before him on the table, and began" (p. 223).

Wharton also turned to art in an effort to make sense of the war and its losses. She writes in *A Backward Glance* that she wanted to put her "losses" into "words." Like the painter Campton, she needed to establish a certain distance from her subject: "Before I could settle down to this tale, before I could begin to deal objectively with the stored-up emotions of those years, I had to get away from the present altogether." The four-year delay between first conceiving *A Son at the Front* and publication of the novel probably had as much to do with Wharton's need to "get away" from the war years as it did with public reaction against war fiction—a reaction that was an effort to "get away" from the war.[11]

More than seventy years have passed since *A Son at the Front* first appeared in print—a vast distance in time and human experience. We are separated from the Great War by other wars that followed it—that were engendered by it—each cutting their own divide across our collective history. Technological advances have profoundly changed how we experience war. The "front" is no longer located "out there" (p. 103), far distant from us; it is everywhere. The most fundamental change in our collective *experience* of war, however, is a truth long repressed in western culture: war—and its cultural products (literature, film, music, painting, and sculpture)—was never the sole province of men. Edith Wharton understood this truth, and in *A Son at the Front* she pictures for us the "other" side of World War I—the "world at the rear," a world composed of women, children, the aged, infirm, ill, and homeless.

NOTES

This text of *A Son at the Front* follows the original 1923 edition published by Charles Scribner's Sons and corrected by Edith Wharton. Page references to the novel, included parenthetically in my text, refer to the present edition. Wharton's letters and other writings are cited in the notes by first and last words of quotations. All unpublished letters from Edith Wharton cited here are located in the Yale Collection of American Literature, Beinecke Rare Book and Manuscript Library (YCAL), Yale University.

1. "heavy/colour," Edith Wharton, *A Backward Glance* (New York: D. Appleton and Co., 1934), pp. 368–69. Hereafter cited as *BG*.

2. "white/passion," *BG*, pp. 368–69. For the writing schedule of *A Son at the Front* (hereafter cited as *Son*), see correspondence between Jeanne Duprat (Wharton's secretary) and Joseph Sears, 21 June 1918 and 31 October 1918.

3. "It/literature," J. Sears to EW, 11 April 1919; "bewilderment/it," EW to Rutger Bleecker Jewett, 25 July 1919 (hereafter cited as RBJ). Critical reception of *The Marne*, see Shari Benstock, *No Gifts from Chance: A Biography of Edith Wharton* (New York: Scribners, 1994), pp. 346, 355. Hereafter cited as *Gifts*.

4. Changed titles of *Son*, EW to RBJ, 25 July 1919. See *Gifts*, pp. 355–56. EW's description of *Son*, see summary sent to Appleton (YCAL). Fitzgerald's script was not used for the 1922 film of *Glimpses*, see *Gifts*, pp. 370–71.

5. "a/propaganda," John Farrar, *Bookman* [England] 65 (October 1923), p. 46; "snobbishly/class," Robert Morss Lovett, *New Republic* 36 (19 September 1923), p. 105.

6. "chief/feelings," H.W. Boynton, *New York Evening Post* (22 September 1923), p. 61; "permanent/war," Anon., *Times Literary Supplement* [London] (20 September 1923), p. 618; "Post-mortem/Ghosts," John Macy, *The Nation* 117 (10 October 1923), pp. 398–99; "anyone/war," Dorothea Lawrence Mann, *Boston Evening Transcript* (15 September 1923), p. 22.

7. Edith Warton, ed., *The Book of the Homeless* (New York: Charles Scribner's Sons, 1916); "the/rear," *BG*, p. 368.

8. "Ally," EW to Mary Cadwalader Jones, 6 April 1917; "planning/Front," *BG*, p. 369.

9. Important revisionist works on women and World War I include Peter Buitenhuis, *The Great War of Words: British, American, and Canadian Propaganda and the Great War, 1914–1933* (Vancouver: University of British Columbia Press, 1987); Jean Bethke Elshtain, *Women and War* (New York: Basic Books, 1987); Jean Bethke Elshtain and Sheila Tobias, eds., *Women, Militarism, and War: Essays in History, Politics, and Social Theory* (Savage, Md.: Rowman and Littlefield, 1990); Margaret Higgonet, Jane Jenson, Sonya Michel, and Margaret Collins Weitz, eds., *Behind the Lines: Gender and the Two World Wars* (New Haven: Yale University Press, 1987); Helen M. Cooper, Adrienne Munich, and Susan Squier, eds., *Arms and the Woman: War, Gender, and Literary Representation* (Chapel Hill: University of North Carolina Press, 1989); Claire Tylee, *The Great War and Women's Consciousness: Images of Militarism and Womanhood in Women's Writings, 1914–1964* (Iowa City: University of Iowa Press, 1990); Anne Wiltsher, *Most Dangerous Women: Feminist Peace Campaigners of the Great War* (Boston: Pandora, 1985).

10. "pathetic figure," EW to Elisina Tyler, 16 August 1918; "paralyzed/golden-haired," EW to Bernard Berenson, 11 September 1918; see *Gifts*, pp. 342–43, for deaths of Simmons and Rhinelander.

11. "Before/altogether," *BG*, p. 369.

A Son at the Front

In Memory of Ronald Simmons

Book
One

John Campton, the American portrait-painter, stood in his bare studio in Montmartre at the end of a summer afternoon contemplating a battered calendar that hung against the wall.

The calendar marked July 30, 1914.

Campton looked at this date with a gaze of unmixed satisfaction. His son, his only boy, who was coming from America, must have landed in England that morning, and after a brief halt in London would join him the next evening in Paris. To bring the moment nearer, Campton, smiling at his weakness, tore off the leaf and uncovered the 31. Then, leaning in the window, he looked out over his untidy scrap of garden at the silver-grey sea of Paris spreading mistily below him.

A number of visitors had passed through the studio that day. After years of obscurity Campton had been projected into the light—or perhaps only into the limelight—by his portrait of his son George, exhibited three years earlier at the spring show of the French Society of Painters and Sculptors. The picture seemed to its author to be exactly in the line of the unnoticed things he had been showing before, though perhaps nearer to what he was always trying for, because of the exceptional interest of his subject. But to the public he had appeared to take a new turn; or perhaps some critic had suddenly found the right phrase for him; or, that season, people wanted a new painter to talk about. Didn't he know by heart all the Paris reasons for success or failure?

The early years of his career had given him ample opportunity to learn them. Like other young students of his generation, he had come to Paris with an exaggerated reverence for the few conspicuous figures who made the old Salons of the 'eighties like bad plays written around a few stars. If he could get near enough to Beausite, the ruling light of the galaxy, he thought he might do things not unworthy of that great master; but Beausite, who had ceased to receive pupils, saw no reason for making an exception in favour of an obscure youth without a backing. He was not kind; and on the only occasion when a painting of Campton's came under his eye he let fall an epigram which went the round of Paris, but shocked its victim by its revelation of the great man's ineptitude.

Campton, if he could have gone on admiring Beausite's work, would have forgotten his unkindness and even his critical incapacity; but as the young painter's personal convictions developed he discovered that his idol had none, and that the dazzling *maëstria* still enveloping his work was only the light from a dead star.

All these things were now nearly thirty years old. Beausite had

vanished from the heavens, and the youth he had sneered at throned
there in his stead. Most of the people who besieged Campton's studio
were the lineal descendants of those who had echoed Beausite's sneer.
They belonged to the type that Campton least cared to paint; but they
were usually those who paid the highest prices, and he had lately had
new and imperious reasons for wanting to earn all the money he
could. So for two years he had let it be as difficult and expensive as
possible to the "done by Campton"; and this oppressive July day had
been crowded with the visits of suppliants of a sort unused to waiting
on anybody's pleasure, people who had postponed St. Moritz and
Deauville, Aix and Royat, because it was known that one had to accept the master's conditions or apply elsewhere.

The job bored him more than ever; the more of their fatuous faces
he recorded the more he hated the task; but for the last two or three
days the monotony of his toil had been relieved by a new element of
interest. This was produced by what he called the "war-fund," and
consisted in the effect on his sitters and their friends of the suggestion
that something new, incomprehensible and uncomfortable might be
about to threaten the ordered course of their pleasures.

Campton himself did not "believe in the war" (as the current phrase
went); therefore he was able to note with perfect composure its agitat-
ing effect upon his sitters. On the whole the women behaved best: the
idiotic Mme. de Dolmetsch had actually grown beautiful through fear
for her lover, who turned out (in spite of a name as exotic as hers) to be
a French subject of military age. The men had made a less creditable
showing—especially the big banker and promoter, Jorgenstein, whose
round red face had withered like a pricked balloon, and young Prince
Demetrios Palamèdes, just married to the fabulously rich daughter of
an Argentine wheat-grower, and so secure as to his bride's fortune that
he could curse impartially all the disturbers of his summer plans. Even
the great tuberculosis specialist, Fortin-Lescluze, whom Campton was
painting in return for the physician's devoted care of George the previous year, had lost something of his professional composure, and no
longer gave out the sense of tranquillizing strength which had been
such a help in the boy's fight for health. Fortin-Lescluze, always in contact with the rulers of the earth, must surely have some hint of their
councils. Whatever it was, he revealed nothing, but continued to talk
frivolously and infatuatedly about a new Javanese dancer whom he
wanted Campton to paint; but his large beaked face with its tri-
umphant moustache had grown pinched and grey, and he had forgotten to renew the dye on the moustache.

Campton's one really imperturbable visitor was little Charlie Alicante, the Spanish secretary of Embassy at Berlin, who had dropped
in on his way to St. Moritz, bringing the newest news from the Wil-
helmstrasse, news that was all suavity and reassurance, with a touch

of playful reproach for the irritability of French feeling, and a reminder of Imperial longanimity in regard to the foolish misunder-
standings of Agadir and Saverne.

Now all the visitors had gone, and Campton, leaning in the window, looked out over Paris and mused on his summer plans. He
meant to plunge straight down to Southern Italy and Sicily, perhaps
even push over to North Africa. That at least was what he hoped for:
no sun was too hot for him and no landscape too arid. But it all de-
pended on George; for George was going with him, and if George preferred Spain they would postpone the desert.

It was almost impossible to Campton to picture what it would be
like to have the boy with him. For so long he had seen his son only in
snatches, hurriedly, incompletely, uncomprehendingly: it was only in
the last three years that their intimacy had had a chance to develop.
And they had never travelled together, except for hasty dashes, two or
three times, to seashore or mountains; had never gone off on a long
solitary journey such as this. Campton, tired, disenchanted, and near-
ing sixty, found himself looking forward to the adventure with an eagerness as great as the different sort of ardour with which, in his
youth, he had imagined flights of another kind with the woman who
was to fulfill every dream.

"Well—I suppose that's the stuff pictures are made of," he thought,
smiling at his inextinguishable belief in the completeness of his next
experience. Life had perpetually knocked him down just as he had his
hand on her gifts; nothing had ever succeeded with him but his work.
But he was as sure as ever that peace of mind and contentment of
heart were waiting for him round the next corner; and this time, it
was clear, they were to come to him through his wonderful son.

The doorbell rang, and he listened for the maid-servant's step.
There was another impatient jingle, and he remembered that his
faithful Mariette had left for Lille, where she was to spend her vaca-
tion with her family. Campton, reaching for his stick, shuffled across
the studio with his lame awkward stride.

At the door stood his old friend Paul Dastrey, one of the few men
with whom he had been unbrokenly intimate since the first days of
his disturbed and incoherent Parisian life. Dastrey came in without
speaking: his small dry face, seamed with premature wrinkles of
irony and sensitiveness, looked unusually grave. The wrinkles seemed
suddenly to have become those of an old man; and how grey Dastrey
had turned! He walked a little stiffly, with a jauntiness obviously intended to conceal a growing tendency to rheumatism.

In the middle of the floor he paused and tapped a varnished boot-
tip with his stick.

"Let's see what you've done to Daisy Dolmetsch."

"Oh, it's been done for me—you'll see!" Campton laughed. He was enjoying the sight of Dastrey and thinking that this visit was providentially timed to give him a chance of expatiating on his coming journey. In his rare moments of expansiveness he felt the need of some substitute for the background of domestic sympathy which, as a rule, would have simply bored or exasperated him; and at such times he could always talk to Dastrey.

The little man screwed up his eyes and continued to tap his varnished toes.

"But she's magnificent. She's seen the Medusa!"

Campton laughed again. "Just so. For days and days I'd been trying to do something with her; and suddenly the war-funk did it for me."

"The war-funk?"

"Who'd have thought it? She's frightened to death about Ladislas Isador—who is French, it turns out, and mobilisable. The poor soul thinks there's going to be war!"

"Well, there *is*," said Dastrey.

The two men looked at each other: Campton amused, incredulous, a shade impatient at the perpetual recurrence of the same theme, and aware of presenting a smile of irritating unresponsiveness to his friend's solemn gaze.

"Oh, come—you too? Why, the Duke of Alicante has just left here, fresh from Berlin. You ought to hear him laugh at us. . ."

"How about Berlin's laughing at *him?*" Dastrey sank into a wicker armchair, drew out a cigarette and forgot to light it. Campton returned to the window.

"There can't be war: I'm going to Sicily and Africa with George the day after tomorrow," he broke out.

"Ah, George——. To be sure. . ."

There was a silence; Dastrey had not even smiled. He turned the unlit cigarette in his dry fingers.

"Too young for 'seventy—and too old for this! Some men are born under a curse," he burst out.

"What on earth are you talking about?" Campton exclaimed, forcing his gaiety a little.

Dastrey stared at him with furious eyes. "But I shall get something, somewhere . . . they can't stop a man's enlisting . . . I had an old uncle who did it in 'seventy . . . he was older than I am now."

Campton looked at him compassionately. Poor little circumscribed Paul Dastrey, whose utmost adventure had been an occasional article in an art review, an occasional six weeks in the near East! It was pitiful to see him breathing fire and fury on an enemy one knew to be engaged, at that very moment, in meeting England and France more than half-way in the effort to smooth over diplomatic difficulties. But Campton could make allowances for the nerves of the tragic generation brought up in the shadow of Sedan.

"Look here," he said, "I'll tell you what. Come along with George and me—as far as Palermo, anyhow. You're a little stiff again in that left knee, and we can bake our lamenesses together in the good Sicilian oven."

Dastrey had found a match and lighted his cigarette.

"My poor Campton—there'll be war in three days."

Campton's incredulity was shot through with the deadly chill of conviction. There it was—there would be war! It was too like his cursed luck not to be true.. . . He smiled inwardly, perceiving that he was viewing the question exactly as the despicable Jorgenstein and the Fatuous Prince Demetrios had viewed it: as an unwarrantable interference with his private plans. Yes—but his case was different. . . Here was the son he had never seen enough of, never till lately seen at all as most fathers see their sons; and the boy was to be packed off to New York that winter, to go into a bank; and for the Lord knew how many months this was to be their last chance, as it was almost their first, of being together quietly, confidentially, uninterruptedly. These other men were whining at the interruption of their vile pleasures or their viler money-making; he, poor devil, was trembling for the chance to lay the foundation of a complete and lasting friendship with his only son, at the moment when such understandings do most to shape a youth's future. . . "And with what I've had to fight against!" he groaned, seeing victory in sight, and sickening at the idea that it might be snatched from Him.

Then another thought came, and he felt the blood leaving his ruddy face and, as it seemed, receding from every vein of his heavy awkward body. He sat down opposite Dastrey, and the two looked at each other.

"There won't be war. But if there were—why shouldn't George and I go to Sicily? You don't see us sitting here making lint, do you?"

Dastrey smiled. "Lint is unhygienic; you won't have to do that. And I see no reason why *you* shouldn't go to Sicily—or to China." He paused. "But how about George—I thought he and you were both born in France?"

Campton reached for a cigarette. "We were, worse luck. He's subject to your preposterous military regulations. But it doesn't make any difference, as it happens. He's sure to be discharged after that touch of tuberculosis he had last year, when he had to be rushed up to the Engadine."

"Ah, I see. Then, as you say. . . Still, of course he wouldn't be allowed to leave the country."

A constrained silence fell between the two. Campton became aware that, for the first time since they had known each other, their points of view were the width of the poles apart. It was hopeless to try to bridge such a distance.

"Of course, you know," he said, trying for his easiest voice, "I still consider this discussion purely academic. . . You'd better know that. . ."

Dastrey, rising, held out his hand with his faithful smile. "My dear old Campton, I perfectly understand a foreigner's taking that view. . ." He walked toward the door and they parted without more words.

When he had gone Campton began to recover his reassurance. Who was Dastrey, poor chap, to behave as if he were in the councils of the powers? It was perfect nonsense to pretend that a diplomatist straight from Berlin didn't know more about what was happening there than the newsmongers of the Boulevards. One didn't have to be an Ambassador to see which way the wind was blowing; and men like Alicante, belonging to a country uninvolved in the affair, were the only people capable of a cool judgment at moments of international tension.

Campton took the portrait of Mme. de Dolmetsch and leaned it against the other canvases along the wall. Then he started clumsily to put the room to rights—without Mariette he was so helpless—and finally, abandoning the attempt, said to himself: "I'll come and wind things up tomorrow."

He was moving that day from the studio to the Hotel de Crillon, where George was to join him the next evening. It would be jolly to be with the boy from the moment he arrived; and, even if Mariette's departure had not paralyzed his primitive housekeeping, he could not have made room for his son at the studio. So, reluctantly, for he loathed luxury and conformity, but joyously, because he was to be with George, Campton threw some shabby clothes into a shapeless portmanteau, and prepared to despatch the concierge for a taxicab.

He was hobbling down the stairs when the old woman met him with a telegram. He tore it open and saw that it was dated Deauville, and was not, as he had feared, from his son.

"Very anxious. Must see you tomorrow. Please come to Avenue Marigny at five without fail. Julia Brant."

"Oh, damn," Campton growled, crumpling up the message.

The concierge was looking at him with searching eyes.

"Is it war, sir?" she asked, pointing to the bit of blue paper. He supposed she was thinking of her grandsons.

"No—no—nonsense! War?" He smiled into her shrewd old face, every wrinkle of which seemed full of a deep human experience.

"War? Can you imagine anything more absurd? Can you now? What should you say if they told you war was going to be declared, Mme. Lebel?"

She gave him back his look with profound earnestness; then she spoke in a voice of sudden resolution. "Why, I should say we don't want it, sir—I'd have four in it if it came—*but that this sort of thing has got to stop.*"

Campton shrugged. "Oh, well—it's not going to come, so don't worry. And call me a taxi, will you? No, no, I'll carry the bags down myself."

II

"But even if they do mobilise: mobilisation is not war—*is* it?" Mrs. Anderson Brant repeated across the teacups.

Campton dragged himself up from the deep armchair he had inadvertently chosen. To escape from his hostess's troubled eyes he limped across to the window and stood gazing out at the thick turf and brilliant flower-borders of the garden which was so unlike his own. After a moment he turned and glanced about him, catching the reflection of his heavy figure in a mirror dividing two garlanded panels. He had not entered Mrs. Brant's drawing-room for nearly ten years; not since the period of the interminable discussions about the choice of a school for George; and in spite of the far graver preoccupations that now weighed on him, and of the huge menace with which the whole world was echoing, he paused for an instant to consider the contrast between his clumsy person and that expensive and irreproachable room.

"You've taken away Beausite's portrait of you," he said abruptly, looking up at the chimney-panel, which was filled with the blue and umber bloom of a Fragonard landscape.

A full-length of Mrs. Anderson Brant by Beausite had been one of Mr. Brant's wedding-presents to his bride; a Beausite portrait, at that time, was as much a part of such marriages as pearls and sables.

"Yes. Anderson thought . . . the dress had grown so dreadfully oldfashioned," she explained indifferently; and went on again: "You think it's *not*: don't you?"

What was the use of telling her what he thought? For years and years he had not done that—about anything. But suddenly, now, a stringent necessity had drawn them together, confronting them like any two plain people caught in a common danger—like husband and wife, for example!

"It *is* war, this time, I believe," he said.

She set down her cup with a hand that had begun to tremble.

"I disagree with you entirely," she retorted, her voice shrill with anxiety. "I was frightfully upset when I sent you that telegram yesterday; but I've been lunching today with the old Duc de Monthléry—you know he fought in 'seventy—and with Lévi-Michel of the 'Jour,' who had just seen some of the government people; and they both explained to me quite clearly——"

"That you'd made a mistake in coming up from Deauville?"

To save himself Campton could not restrain the sneer; on the rare occasions when a crisis in their lives flung them on each other's mercy, the first sensation he was always conscious of was the degree to which she bored him. He remembered the day, years ago, long before their divorce, when it had first come home to him that she was always going to bore him. But he was ashamed to think of that now, and went on more patiently: "You see, the situation is rather different from anything we've known before; and, after all, in 1870 all the wise people thought till the last minute that there would be no war."

Her delicate face seemed to shrink and wither with apprehension.

"Then—what about George?" she asked, the paint coming out about her haggard eyes.

Campton paused a moment. "You may suppose I've thought of *that*."

"Oh, of course. . ." He saw she was honestly trying to be what a mother should be in talking of her only child to that child's father. But the long habit of superficiality made her stammering and inarticulate when her one deep feeling tried to rise to the surface.

Campton seated himself again, taking care to choose a straight-backed chair. "I see nothing to worry about with regard to George," he said.

"You mean—?"

"Why, they won't take him—they won't want him . . . with his medical record."

"Are you sure? He's so much stronger. . . He's gained twenty pounds. . ." It was terrible, really, to hear her avow it in a reluctant whisper! That was the view that war made mothers take of the chief blessing they could ask for their children! Campton understood her, and took the same view. George's wonderful recovery, the one joy his parents had shared in the last twenty years, was now a misfortune to be denied and dissembled. They looked at each other like accomplices, the same thought in their eyes: if only the boy had been born in America! It was grotesque that the whole of joy or anguish should suddenly be found to hang on a geographical accident.

"After all, we're Americans; this is not our job—" Campton began.

"No—" He saw she was waiting, and knew for what.

"So of course—if there were any trouble—but there won't be; if there were, though, I shouldn't hesitate to do what was necessary . . . use any influence. . ."

"Oh, then we agree!" broke from her in a cry of wonder.

The unconscious irony of the exclamation struck him, and increased his irritation. He remembered the tone—undefinably compassionate—in which Dastrey had said: "I perfectly understand a foreigner's taking the view" . . . But *was* he a foreigner, Campton asked himself? And what was the criterion of citizenship, if he, who owed to France everything that had made life worthwhile, could regard himself as owing her nothing, now that for the first time he might have something to give her? Well, for himself that argument was all right: preposterous as he thought war—any war—he would have offered himself to France on the instant if she had had any use for his lame carcass. But he had never bargained to give her his only son.

Mrs. Brant went on in excited argument.

"Of course you know how careful I always am to do nothing about him without consulting you; but since you feel about it as *we* do——" She blushed under her faint rouge. The "we" had slipped out accidentally, and Campton, aware of turning hard-lipped and grim, sat waiting for her to repair the blunder. Through the years of his poverty it had been impossible not to put up, on occasions, with that odious first person plural: as long as his wretched inability to make money had made it necessary that his wife's second husband should pay for his son's keep, such allusions had been part of Campton's long expiation. But even then he had tacitly made his former wife understand that, when they had to talk of the boy, he could bear her saying "I think," or "Anderson thinks," this or that, but not "*we* think it." And in the last few years, since Campton's unforeseen success had put him, to the astonishment of every one concerned, in a position of financial independence, "Anderson" had almost entirely dropped out of their talk about George's future. Mrs. Brant was not a clever woman, but she had a social adroitness that sometimes took the place of intelligence.

On this occasion she saw her mistake so quickly, and blushed for it so painfully, that at any other time Campton would have smiled away her distress; but at the moment he could not stir a muscle to help her.

"Look here," he broke out, "there are things I've had to accept in the past, and shall have to accept in the future. The boy is to go into Bullard and Brant's—it's agreed; I'm not sure enough of being able to provide for him for the next few years to interfere with—with your plans in that respect. But I thought it was understood once for all——"

She interrupted him excitedly. "Oh, of course . . . of course. You must admit I've always respected your feeling. . ."

He acknowledged awkwardly: "Yes."

"Well, then—won't you see that this situation is different, terribly different, and that we ought all to work together? If Anderson's influence can be of use. . ."

"Anderson's influence——" Campton's gorge rose against the phrase! It was always Anderson's influence that had been invoked—and none knew better than Campton himself how justly—when the boy's future was under discussion. But in this particular case the suggestion was intolerable.

"Of course," he interrupted drily. "But, as it happens, I think I can attend to this job myself."

She looked down at her huge rings, hesitated visibly, and then flung tact to the winds. "What makes you think so? You don't know the right sort of people."

It was a long time since she had thrown that at him: not since the troubled days of their marriage, when it had been the cruellest taunt she could think of. Now it struck him simply as a particularly unpalatable truth. No, he didn't know "the right sort of people" . . . unless, for instance, among his new patrons, such a man as Jorgenstein answered to the description. But, if there were war, on what side would a cosmopolitan like Jorgenstein turn out to be?

"Anderson, you see," she persisted, losing sight of everything in the need to lull her fears, "Anderson knows all the political people. In a business way, of course, a big banker has to. If there's really any chance of George's being taken you've no right to refuse Anderson's help—none whatever!"

Campton was silent. He had meant to reassure her, to reaffirm his conviction that the boy was sure to be discharged. But as their eyes met he saw that she believed this no more than he did; and he felt the contagion of her incredulity.

"But if you're so sure there's not going to be war——" he began.

As he spoke he saw her face change, and was aware that the door behind had opened and that a short man, bald and slim, was advancing at a sort of mincing trot across the pompous garlands of the Savoneric carpet. Campton got to his feet. He had expected Anderson Brant to stop at sight of him, mumble a greeting, and then back out of the room—as usual. But Anderson Brant did nothing of the sort: he merely hastened his trot toward the tea-table. He made no attempt to shake hands with Campton, but bowing shyly and stiffly said: "I understood you were coming, and hurried back . . . on the chance . . . to consult. . ."

Campton gazed at him without speaking. They had not seen each other since the extraordinary occasion, two years before, when Mr. Brant, furtively one day at dusk, had come to his studio to offer to buy George's portrait; and, as their eyes met, the memory of that visit reddened both their faces.

Mr. Brant was a compact little man of about sixty. His sandy hair, just turning grey, was brushed forward over a baldness which was ivory-white at the crown and became brick-pink above the temples, before merging into the tanned and freckled surface of his face. He was always dressed in carefully cut clothes of a discreet grey, with a tie to match, in which even the plump pearl was grey, so that he reminded Campton of a dry perpendicular insect in protective tines; and the fancy was encouraged by his cautious manner, and the way he had of peering over his glasses as if they were part of his armour. His feet were small and pointed, and seemed to be made of patent leather;

and shaking hands with him was like clasping a bunch of twigs.

It had been Campton's lot, on the rare occasions of his meeting Mr. Brant, always to see this perfectly balanced man in moments of disequilibrium, when the attempt to simulate poise probably made him more rigid than nature had created him. But today his perturbation betrayed itself in the gesture with which he drummed out a tune on the back of the gold and platinum cigar-case he had unconsciously drawn from his pocket.

After a moment he seemed to become aware of what he had in his hand, and pressing the sapphire spring held out the case with the remark: "Coronas."

Campton made a movement of refusal, and Mr. Brant, overwhelmed, thrust the cigar-case away.

"I ought to have taken one—I may need him," Campton thought; and Mrs. Brant said, addressing her husband: "He thinks as *we* do—exactly."

Campton winced. Thinking as the Brants did was, at all times, so foreign to his nature and his principles that his first impulse was to protest. But the sight of Mr. Brant, standing there helplessly, and trying to hide the twitching of his lip by stroking his lavender-scented moustache with a discreetly curved hand, moved the painter's imagination.

"Poor devil—he'd give all his millions if the boy were safe," he thought, "and he doesn't even dare to say so."

It satisfied Campton's sense of his rights that these two powerful people were hanging on his decision like frightened children, and he answered, looking at Mrs. Brant: "There's nothing to be done at present . . . absolutely nothing—Except," he added abruptly, "to take care not to talk in this way to George."

Mrs. Brant lifted a startled gaze.

"What do you mean? If war is declared, you can't expect me not to speak of it to him."

"Speak of it as much as you like, but don't drag him in. Let him work out his own case for himself." He went on with an effort: "It's what I intend to do."

"But you said you'd use every influence!" she protested, obtusely.

"Well—I believe this is one of them."

She looked down resignedly at her clasped hands, and he saw her lips tighten. "My telling her that has been just enough to start her on the other tack," he groaned to himself, all her old stupidities rising up around him like a fog.

Mr. Brant gave a slight cough and removed his protecting hand from his lips.

"Mr. Campton is right," he said, quickly and timorously. "I take the

same view—entirely. George must not know that we are thinking of using . . . any means . . ." He coughed again, and groped for the cigar-case.

As he spoke, there came over Campton a sense of their possessing a
common ground of understanding that Campton had never found in
his wife. He had had a hint of the same feeling, but had voluntarily
stifled it, on the day when Mr. Brant, apologetic yet determined, had
come to the studio to buy George's portrait. Campton had seen then
how the man suffered from his failure, but had chosen to attribute his
distress to the humiliation of finding there were things his money
could not purchase. Now, that judgment seemed as unimaginative as
he had once thought Mr. Brant's overture. Campton turned on the
banker a look that was almost brotherly.

"We men know . . ." the look said; and Mr. Brant's parched cheek
was suffused with a flush of understanding. Then, as if frightened at
the consequences of such complicity, he repeated his bow and went out.

When Campton issued forth into the Avenue Marigny, it came to
him as a surprise to see the old unheeding life of Paris still going on.
In the golden decline of day the usual throng of idlers sat under the
horse-chestnuts of the Champs Elysées, children scampered between
turf and flowers, and the perpetual stream of motors rolled up the
central avenue to the restaurants beyond the gates.

Under the last trees of the Avenue Gabriel the painter stood looking across the Place de la Concorde. No doubt the future was dark: he
had guessed from Mr. Brant's precipitate arrival that the banks and
the Stock Exchange feared the worst. But what could a man do, whose
convictions were so largely formed by the play of things on his retina,
when, in the setting sun, all that majesty of space and light and archi-
tecture was spread out before him undisturbed? Paris was too tri-
umphant a fact not to argue down his fears. There she lay in the security of her beauty, and once more proclaimed herself eternal.

———

III

The night was so lovely that, though the Boulogne express arrived
late, George at once proposed dining in the Bois.

His luggage, of which, as usual, there was a good deal, was dropped
at the Crillon, and they shot up the Champs Elysées as the summer
dusk began to be pricked by lamps.

"How jolly the old place smells!" George cried, breathing in the
scent of sun-warmed asphalt, of flower-beds and freshly-watered dust.
He seemed as much alive to such impressions as if his first word at
the station had not been: "Well, this time I suppose we're in for it." In

for it they might be; but meanwhile he meant to enjoy the scents and scenes of Paris as acutely and unconcernedly as ever.

Campton had hoped that he would pick out one of the humble cyclists' restaurants near the Seine; but not he. "Madrid, is it?" he said gaily, as the taxi turned into the Bois; and there they sat under the illuminated trees, in the general glitter and expensiveness, with the Tziganes playing down their talk, and all around them the painted faces that seemed to the father so old and obvious, and to the son, no doubt, so full of novelty and mystery.

The music made conversation difficult; but Campton did not care. It was enough to sit and watch the face in which, after each absence, he noted a new and richer vivacity. He had often tried to make up his mind if his boy were handsome. Not that the father's eye influenced the painter's; but George's young head, with its thick blond thatch, the complexion ruddy to the golden eyebrows, and then abruptly white on the forehead, the short amused nose, the inquisitive eyes, the ears lying back flat to the skull against curly edges of fair hair, defied all rules and escaped all classifications by a mixture of romantic gaiety and shrewd plainness like that in certain eighteenth-century portraits.

As father and son faced each other over the piled-up peaches, while the last sparkle of champagne died down in their glasses, Campton's thoughts went back to the day when he had first discovered his son. George was a schoolboy of twelve, at home for the Christmas holidays. At home meant at the Brants', since it was always there he stayed: his father saw him only on certain days. Usually Mariette fetched him to the studio on one afternoon in the week; but this particular week George was ill, and it had been arranged that in case of illness his father was to visit him at his mother's. He had one of his frequent bad colds, and Campton recalled him, propped up in bed in his luxurious overheated room, a scarlet sweater over his nightshirt, a book on his thin knees, and his ugly little fever-flushed face bent over it in profound absorption. Till that moment George had never seemed to care for books: his father had resigned himself to the probability of seeing him grow up into the ordinary pleasant young fellow, with his mother's worldly tastes. But the boy was reading as only a bookworm reads—reading with his very finger-tips, and his inquisitive nose, and the perpetual dart ahead of a gaze that seemed to guess each phrase from its last work. He looked up with a smile, and said: "Oh, Dad .. ." but it was clear that he regarded the visit as an interruption. Campton, leaning over, saw that the book was a first edition of Lavengro.

"Where the deuce did you get that?"

George looked at him with shining eyes. "Didn't you know? Mr. Brant has started collecting first editions. There's a chap who comes over from London with things for him. He lets me have them to look at when I'm seedy. I say, isn't this topping? Do you remember the fight?" And, marvelling once more at the ways of Providence, Campton perceived that the millionaire's taste for owning books had awakened in his stepson a taste for reading them. "I couldn't have done that for him," the father had reflected with secret bitterness. It was not that a bibliophile's library was necessary to develop a taste for letters; but that Campton himself, being a small reader, had few books about him, and usually borrowed those few. If George had lived with him he might never have guessed the boy's latent hunger, for the need of books as part of one's daily food would scarcely have presented itself to him.

From that day he and George had understood each other. Initiation had come to them in different ways, but their ardour for beauty had the same root. The visible world, and its transposition in terms of one art or another, were thereafter the subject of their interminable talks; and Campton, with a passionate interest, watched his son absorbing through books what had mysteriously reached him through his paintbrush.

They had been parted often, and for long periods; first by George's schooling in England, next by his French military service, begun at eighteen to facilitate his entry into Harvard; finally, by his sojourn at the University. But whenever they were together they seemed to make up in the first ten minutes for the longest separation; and since George had come of age, and been his own master, he had given his father every moment he could spare.

His career at Harvard had been interrupted, after two years, by the symptoms of tuberculosis which had necessitated his being hurried off to the Engadine. He had returned completely cured, and at his own wish had gone back to Harvard; and having finished his course and taken his degree, he had now come out to join his father on a long holiday before entering the New York banking-house of Bullard and Brant.

Campton, looking at the boy's bright head across the lights and flowers, thought how incredibly stupid it was to sacrifice an hour of such a life to the routine of money-getting; but he had had that question out with himself once for all, and was not going to return to it. His own success, if it lasted, would eventually help him to make George independent; but meanwhile he had no right to interfere with the boy's business training. He had hoped that George would develop some marked talent, some irresistible tendency which would decide his future too definitely for interference; but George was twenty-five, and no such call had come to him. Apparently he was fated to be only a delighted spectator and commentator; to enjoy and interpret, not to create. And Campton knew that this absence of a special bent, with the strain and absorption it implies, gave the boy his peculiar charm. The trouble was that it made him the prey of other people's plans for him. And now all these plans—Campton's dreams for the future as well as the business arrangements which were Mr. Brant's contribution—might be wrecked by tomorrow's news from Berlin. The possibility still seemed unthinkable; but in spite of his incredulity the evil shadow hung on him as he and his son chatted of political issues.

George made no allusion to his own case: his whole attitude was so dispassionate that his father began to wonder if he had not solved the question by concluding that he would not pass the medical examination. The tone he took was that the whole affair, from the point of view of twentieth-century civilization, was too monstrous an incongruity for something not to put a stop to it at the eleventh hour. His easy optimism at first stimulated his father, and then began to jar on him.

"Dastrey doesn't think it can be stopped," Campton said at length.

The boy smiled.

"Dear old Dastrey! No, I suppose not. That after-Sedan generation have got the inevitability of war in their bones. They've never been able to get beyond it. *Our* whole view is different: we're internationals, whether we want to be or not."

"To begin with, if by 'our' view you mean yours and mine, you and I haven't a drop of French blood in us," his father interposed, "and we can never really know what the French feel on such matters."

George looked at him affectionately. "Oh, but I didn't—I meant 'we' in the sense of my generation, of whatever nationality. I know French chaps who feel as I do—Louis Dastrey, Paul's nephew, for one; and lots of English ones. They don't believe the world will ever stand for another war. It's too stupidly uneconomic, to begin with: I suppose you've read Angell? Then life's worth too much, and nowadays too many millions of people know it. That's the way we all feel. Think of everything that counts—art and science and poetry, and all the rest—going to smash at the nod of some doddering diplomatist! It was different in old times, when the best of life, for the immense majority, was never anything but plague, pestilence and famine. People are too healthy and well-fed now; they're not going off to die in a ditch to oblige anybody."

Campton looked away, and his eye, straying over the crowd, lit on the long heavy face of Fortin-Lescluze, seated with a group of men on the other side of the garden.

Why had it never occurred to him before that if there was one being in the world who could get George discharged it was the great specialist under whose care he had been?

"Suppose war does come," the father thought, "what if I were to go over and tell him I'll paint his dancer?" He stood up and made his way between the tables.

Fortin-Lescluze was dining with a party of jaded-looking politicians and journalists. To reach him Campton had to squeeze past another table, at which a fair worn-looking lady sat beside a handsome old man with a dazzling mane of white hair and a Grand Officer's rosette of the Legion of Honour. Campton bowed, and the lady whispered something to her companion, who returned a stately vacant salute. Poor old Beausite, dining alone with his much-wronged and all-forgiving wife, bowing to the people she told him to bow to, and placidly murmuring: "War—war," as he stuck his fork into the peach she had peeled!

At Fortin's table the faces were less placid. The men greeted Campton with a deference which was not lost on Mme. Beausite, and the painter bent close over Fortin, embarrassed at the idea that she might overhear him. "If I can make time for a sketch—will you bring your dancing lady tomorrow?"

The physician's eyes lit up under their puffy lids.

"My dear friend—will I? She's simply set her heart on it!" He drew out his watch and added: "But why not tell her the good news yourself? You told me, I think, you'd never seen her? This is her last night at the 'Posada,' and if you'll jump into my motor we shall be just in time to see her come on."

Campton beckoned to George, and father and son followed Fortin-Lescluze. None of the three men, on the way back to Paris, made any reference to the war. The physician asked George a few medical questions, and complimented him on his look of recovered health; then the talk strayed to studios and theatres, where Fortin-Lescluze firmly kept it.

The last faint rumours of the conflict died out on the threshold of the "Posada." It would have been hard to discern, in the crowded audience, any appearance but that of ordinary pleasure-seekers momentarily stirred by a new sensation. Collectively, fashionable Paris was already away, at the seashore or in the mountains, but not a few of its chief ornaments still lingered, as the procession through Campton's studio had proved; and others had returned drawn back by doubts about the future, the desire to be nearer the source of news, the irresistible French craving for the forum and the market when messengers are foaming in. The public of the "Posada," therefore, was still Parisian enough to flatter the new dancer; and on all the pleasure-tired faces, belonging to every type of money-getters and amusement-seekers, Campton saw only the old familiar music-hall: the look of a house with lights blazing and windows wide, but nobody and nothing within.

The usualness of it all gave him a sense of ease which his boy's enjoyment confirmed. George, lounging on the edge of their box, and watching the yellow dancer with a clear-eyed interest refreshingly different from Fortin's tarnished gaze, George so fresh and cool and unafraid, seemed to prove that a world which could produce such youths would never again settle its differences by the bloody madness of war.

Gradually Campton became absorbed in the dancer and began to observe her with the concentration he brought to bear on any subject that attracted his brush. He saw that she was more paintable than he could have hoped, though not in the extravagant dress and attitude he was sure her eminent admirer would prefer; but rather as a little crouching animal against a sun-baked wall. He smiled at the struggle he should have when the question of costume came up.

"Well, I'll do her, if you like," he turned to say; and two tears of senile triumph glittered on the physician's cheeks.

"Tomorrow, then—at two—may I bring her? She leaves as soon as possible for the south. She lives on sun, heat, radiance. . ."

"Tomorrow—yes," Campton nodded.

His decision once reached, the whole subject bored him, and in spite of Fortin's entreaties he got up and signalled to George.

As they strolled home through the brilliant midnight streets, the boy said: "Did I hear you tell old Fortin you were going to do his dancer?"

"Yes—why not? She's very paintable," said Campton, abruptly shaken out of his security.

"Beginning tomorrow?"

"Why not?"

"Come, you know—*tomorrow!*" George laughed.

"We'll see," his father rejoined, with an obscure sense that if he went on steadily enough doing his usual job it might somehow divert the current of events.

On the threshold of the hotel they were waylaid by an elderly man with a round face and round eyes behind gold eye-glasses. His grey hair was cut in a fringe over his guileless forehead, and he was dressed in expensive evening clothes, and shone with soap and shaving; but the anxiety of a frightened child puckered his innocent brow and twitching cheeks.

"My dear Campton—the very man I've been hunting for! You remember me—your cousin Harvey Mayhew of Utica?"

Campton, with an effort, remembered, and asked what he could do, inwardly hoping it was not a portrait.

"Oh, the simplest thing in the world. You see, I'm here as a Delegate——" At Campton's look of enquiry, Mr. Mayhew interrupted himself to explain: "To the Peace Congress at The Hague——why, yes: naturally. I landed only this morning, and find myself in the middle of all this rather foolish excitement, and unable to make out just how I can reach my destination. My time is—er—valuable, and it is very unfortunate that all this commotion should be allowed to interfere with our work. It would be most annoying if, after having made the effort to break away from Utica, I should arrive too late for the opening of the Congress."

Campton looked at him wonderingly. "Then you're going anyhow?"

"Going? Why not? You surely don't think——?" Mr. Mayhew threw back his shoulders, pink and impressive. "I shouldn't in any case, allow anything so opposed to my convictions as *war* to interfere with my carrying out my mandate. All I want is to find out the route least likely to be closed if——if this monstrous thing should happen."

Campton considered. "Well, if I were you, I should go round by Luxembourg—it's longer, but you'll be out of the way of trouble." He gave a nod of encouragement, and the Peace Delegate thanked him profusely.

Father and son were lodged on the top floor of the Crillon, in the little apartment which opens on the broad terraced roof. Campton had wanted to put before his boy one of the city's most perfect scenes; and when they reached their sitting-room George went straight out onto the terrace, and leaning on the parapet, called back: "Oh, don't go to bed yet—it's too jolly."

Campton followed, and the two stood looking down on the festal expanse of the Place de la Concorde strewn with great flower-clusters of lights between its pearly distances. The sky was full of stars, pale, remote, half-drowned in the city's vast illumination; and the foliage of the Champs Elysées and the Tuileries made masses of mysterious darkness behind the statues and the flashing fountains.

For a long time neither father nor son spoke; then Campton said: "Are you game to start the day after tomorrow?"

George waited a moment. "For Africa?"

"Well—my idea would be to push straight through to the south—as far as Palermo, say. All this cloudy watery loveliness gives me a furious appetite for violent red earth and white houses crackling in the glare."

George again pondered; then he said: "It sounds first-rate. But if you're so sure we're going to start why did you tell Fortin to bring that girl tomorrow?"

Campton, reddening in the darkness, felt as if his son's clear eyes were following the motions of his blood. Had George suspected why he had wanted to ingratiate himself with the physician?

"It was stupid—I'll put her off," he muttered, He dropped into an armchair, and sat there, in his clumsy infirm attitude, his arms folded behind his head, while George continued to lean on the parapet.

The boy's question had put an end to their talk by baring the throbbing nerve of his father's anxiety. If war were declared the next day, what did George mean to do? There was every hope of his obtaining his discharge; but would he lend himself to the attempt? The deadly fear of crystallizing his son's refusal by forcing him to put it into words kept Campton from asking the question.

IV

The evening was too beautiful, and too full of the sense of fate, for sleep to be possible, and long after George had finally said "All the same, I think I'll turn in," his father sat on, listening to the gradual subsidence of the traffic, and watching the night widen above Paris.

As he sat there, discouragement overcame him. His last plan, his plan for getting George finally and completely over to his side, was going to fail as all his other plans had failed. If there were war there would be no more portraits to paint, and his vision of wealth would vanish as visions of love and happiness and comradeship had one by one faded away. Nothing had ever succeeded with him but the thing he had in some moods set least store by, the dogged achievement of his brush; and just as that was about to assure his happiness, here was this horrible world-catastrophe threatening to fall across his path.

His misfortune had been that he could neither get on easily with people nor live without them; could never wholly isolate himself in his art, nor yet resign himself to any permanent human communion that left it out, or, worse still, dragged it in irrelevantly. He had tried both kinds, and on the whole preferred the first. His marriage, his stupid ill-fated marriage, had after all not been the most disenchanting of his adventures, because Julia Ambrose, when she married him, had made no pretense of espousing his art.

He had seen her first in the tumble-down Venetian palace where she lived with her bachelor uncle, old Horace Ambrose, who dabbled in bric-a-brac and cultivated a guileless Bohemianism. Campton, looking back, could still understand why, to a youth fresh from Utica, at odds with his father, unwilling to go into the family business, and strangling with violent unexpressed ideas on art and the universe, marriage with Julia Ambrose had seemed so perfect a solution. She had been brought up abroad by her parents, a drifting and impecunious American couple; and after their deaths, within a few months of each other, her education had been completed, at her uncle's expense, in a fashionable Parisian convent. Thence she had been transplanted at nineteen to his Venetian household, and all the ideas that most terrified and scandalized Campton's family were part of the only air she had breathed. She had never intentionally feigned an exaggerated interest in his ambitions. But her bringing up made her regard them as natural; she knew what he was aiming at, though she had never understood his reasons for trying. The jargon of art was merely one of her many languages; but she talked it so fluently that he had taken it for her mother-tongue.

The only other girls he had known well were his sisters—earnest eye-glassed young women, whose one answer to all his problems was that he ought to come home. The idea of Europe had always been terrifying to them, and indeed to his whole family, since the extraordinary misadventure whereby, as the result of a protracted diligence journey over bad roads, of a violent thunderstorm, and a delayed steamer, Campton had been born in Paris instead of Utica. Mrs. Campton the elder had taken the warning to heart, and never again left her native soil; but the sisters, safely and properly brought into the world in their own city and State, had always felt that Campton's persistent yearnings for Europe, and his inexplicable detachment from Utica and the Mangle, were mysteriously due to the accident of their mother's premature confinement.

Compared with the admonitions of these domestic censors, Miss Ambrose's innocent conversation was as seductive as the tangles of Neæra's hair, and it used to be a joke between them (one of the few he had ever been able to make her see) that he, the raw up-Stater, was Parisian born, while she, the glass and pattern of worldly knowledge, had seen the light in the pure atmosphere of Madison Avenue.

Through her, in due course, he came to know another girl, a queer abrupt young American, already an old maid at twenty-two, and in open revolt against her family for reasons not unlike his own. Adele Anthony had come abroad to keep house for a worthless "artistic" brother, who was preparing to be a sculptor by prolonged sessions in Anglo-American bars and the lobbies of music-halls. When he finally went under, and was shipped home, Miss Anthony stayed on in Paris, ashamed, as she told Campton, to go back and face the righteous triumph of a family connection who had unanimously disbelieved in the possibility of making Bill Anthony into a sculptor, and in the wisdom of his sister's staking her small means on the venture.

"Somehow, behind it all, I was right, and they were wrong; but to do anything with poor Bill I ought to have been able to begin two or three generations back," she confessed.

Miss Anthony had many friends in Paris, of whom Julia Ambrose was the most admired; and she had assisted sympathizingly (if not enthusiastically) at Campton's wooing of Julia, and their hasty marriage. Her only note of warning had been the reminder that Julia had always been poor, and had always lived as if she were rich; and that was silenced by Campton's rejoinder that the Magic Mangle, to which the Campton prosperity was due, was some day going to make him rich, though he had always lived as if he were poor.

"Well—you'd better not, any longer," Adele sharply advised; and he laughed, and promised to go out and buy a new hat. In truth, careless of comfort as he was, he adored luxury in women, and was resolved to let his wife ruin him if she did it handsomely enough. Doubtless she might have, had fate given her time; but soon after their marriage old Mr. Campton died, and it was found that a trusted manager had so invested the profits of the Mangle that the heirs inherited only a series of law-suits.

John Campton, henceforth, was merely the unsuccessful son of a ruined manufacturer; painting became a luxury he could no longer afford, and his mother and sisters besought him to come back and take over what was left of the business. It seemed so clearly his duty that, with anguish of soul, he prepared to go; but Julia, on being consulted, developed a sudden passion for art and poverty.

"We'd have to live in Utica—for some years at any rate?"

"Well, yes, no doubt——" They faced the fact desolately.

"They'd much better look out for another manager. What do you know about business? Since you've taken up painting you'd better try to make a success of that," she advised him; and he was too much of the same mind not to agree.

It was not long before George's birth, and they were fully resolved to go home for the event, and thus spare their hoped-for heir the inconvenience of coming into the world, like his father, in a foreign country. But now this was not to be thought of, and the eventual inconvenience to George was lost sight of by his progenitors in the contemplation of nearer problems.

For a few years their life dragged along shabbily and depressingly. Now that Campton's painting was no longer an amateur's hobby but a domestic obligation, Julia thought it her duty to interest herself in it; and her only idea of doing so was by means of what she called "relations," using the word in its French and diplomatic sense.

She was convinced that her husband's lack of success was due to Beausite's blighting epigram, and to Campton's subsequent resolve to strike out for himself. "It's a great mistake to try to be original till people have got used to you," she said, with the shrewdness that sometimes startled him. "If you'd only been civil to Beausite he would have ended by taking you up, and then you could have painted as queerly as you liked."

Beausite, by this time, had succumbed to the honours which lie in wait for such talents, and in his starred and titled maturity his earlier dread of rivals had given way to a prudent benevolence. Young artists were always welcome at the receptions he gave in his sumptuous hotel of the Avenue du Bois. Those who threatened to be rivals were even invited to dine; and Julia was justified in triumphing when such an invitation finally rewarded her efforts.

Campton, with a laugh, threw the card into the stove.

"If you'd only understand that that's not the way," he said.

"What is, then?"

"Why, letting all that lot see what unutterable rubbish one thinks them!"

"I should have thought you'd tried that long enough," she said with pale lips; but he answered jovially that it never palled on him.

She was bitterly offended; but she knew Campton by this time, and was not a woman to waste herself in vain resentment. She simply suggested that since he would not profit by Beausite's advance the only alternative was to try to get orders for portraits; and though at that stage he was not in the mood for portrait-painting, he made an honest attempt to satisfy her. She began, of course, by sitting for him. She sat again and again; but, lovely as she was, he was not inspired, and one day, in sheer self-defence, he blurted out that she was not paintable. She never forgot the epithet, and it loomed large in their subsequent recriminations.

Adele Anthony—it was just like her—gave him his first order, and she did prove paintable. Campton made a success of her long crooked pink-nosed face; but she didn't perceive it (she had wanted something oval, with tulle, and a rose in a tape hand), and after heroically facing the picture for six months she hid it away in an attic, whence, a year or so before the date of the artist's present musings, it had been fished out as an "early Campton," to be exhibited half a dozen times, and have articles written about it in the leading art reviews.

Adele's picture acted as an awful warning to intending patrons, and after one or two attempts at depicting mistrustful friends Campton refused to constrain his muse, and no more was said of portrait-painting. But life in Paris was growing too expensive. He persuaded Julia to try Spain, and they wandered about there for a year. She was not fault-finding, she did not complain, but she hated travelling, she could not eat things cooked in oil, and his pictures seemed to her to be growing more and more ugly and unsalable.

Finally they came one day to Ronda, after a trying sojourn at Cordova. In the train Julia had moaned a little at the mosquitoes of the previous night, and at the heat and dirt of the second-class compartment; then, always conscious of the ill-breeding of fretfulness, she had bent her lovely head above her Tauchnitz. And it was then that Campton, looking out of the window to avoid her fatally familiar profile, had suddenly discovered another. It was that of a peasant girl in front of a small whitewashed house, under a white pergola hung with bunches of big red peppers. The house, which was close to the railway, was propped against an orange-coloured rock, and in the glare cast up from the red earth its walls looked as blue as snow in shadow. The girl was all blue-white too, from her cotton skirt to the kerchief knotted turbanwise above two folds of blue-black hair. Her round forehead and merry nose were relieved like a bronze medallion against the wall; and she stood with her hands on her hips, laughing at a little pig asleep under a cork-tree, who lay on his side like a dog.

The vision filled the carriage-window and then vanished; but it re-

mained so sharply impressed on Campton that even then he knew
what was going to happen. He leaned back with a sense of relief, and
forgot everything else.

The next morning he said to his wife: "There's a little place up the
line that I want to go back and paint. You don't mind staying here a
day or two, do you?"

She said she did not mind; it was what she always said; but he was
somehow aware that this was the particular grievance she had always
been waiting for. He did not care for that, or for anything but getting
a seat in the diligence which started every morning for the village
nearest the white house. On the way he remembered that he had left
Julia only forty pesetas, but he did not care about that either. . . He
stayed a month, and when he returned to Ronda his wife had gone
back to Paris, leaving a letter to say that the matter was in the hands
of her lawyers.

"What did you do it for—I mean in that particular way? For goodness knows I understand all the rest," Adele Anthony had once asked
him, while the divorce proceedings were going on; and he had shaken
his head, conscious that he could not explain.

It was a year or two later that he met the first person who *did* understand: a Russian lady who had heard the story, was curious to
know him, and asked, one day, when their friendship had progressed,
to see the sketches he had brought back for his *fugue*.

"*Comme je vous comprends!*" she murmured, her grey eyes deep in
his; but perceiving that she did not allude to the sketches, but to his
sentimental adventure, Campton pushed the drawings out of sight,
vexed with himself for having shown them.

He forgave the Russian lady her artistic obtuseness for the sake of
her human comprehension. They had met at the loneliest moment of
his life, when his art seemed to have failed him like everything else,
and when the struggle to get possession of his son, which had been going on in the courts ever since the break with Julia, had finally been
decided against him. His Russian friend consoled, amused and agitated him, and after a few years drifted out of his life as irresponsibly
as she had drifted into it; and he found himself, at forty-five, a lonely
thwarted man, as full as ever of faith in his own powers, but with little left in human nature or in opportunity. It was about this time that
he heard that Julia was to marry again, and that his boy would have
a stepfather.

He knew that even his own family thought it "the best thing that
could happen." They were tired of clubbing together to pay Julia's alimony, and heaved a united sigh of relief when they learned that her
second choice had fallen, not on the bankrupt "foreign Count" they
had always dreaded, but on the Paris partner of the famous bank of

Bullard and Brant. Mr. Brant's request that his wife's alimony should be discontinued gave him a moral superiority which even Campton's recent successes could not shake. It was felt that the request expressed the contempt of an income easily counted in seven figures for a pittance painfully screwed up to four; and the Camptons admired Mr. Brant much more for not needing their money than for refusing it.

Their attitude left John Campton without support in his struggle to keep a hold on his boy. His family sincerely thought George safer with the Brants than with his own father, and the father could advance to the contrary no arguments they would have understood. All the forces of order seemed leagued against him; and it was perhaps this fact that suddenly drove him into conformity with them. At any rate, from the day of Julia's remarriage no other woman shared her former husband's life. Campton settled down to the solitude of his dusty studio at Montmartre, and painted doggedly, all his thoughts on George.

At this point in his reminiscences the bells of Sainte Clotilde rang out the half-hour after midnight, and Campton rose and went into the darkened sitting-room.

The door into George's room was open, and in the silence the father heard the boy's calm breathing. A light from the bathroom cast its ray on the dressing-table, which was scattered with the contents of George's pockets. Campton, dwelling with a new tenderness on everything that belonged to his son, noticed a smart antelope card-case (George had his mother's weakness for Bond Street novelties), a wrist-watch, his studs, a bundle of bank-notes; and beside these a thumbed and dirty red book, the size of a large pocket diary.

The father wondered what it was; then of a sudden he knew. He had once seen Mme. Lebel's grandson pull just such a red book from his pocket as he was leaving for his "twenty-eight days" of military service; it was the *livret militaire* that every French citizen under forty-eight carries about with him.

Campton had never paid much attention to French military regulations: George's service over, he had dismissed the matter from his mind, forgetting that his son was still a member of the French army, and as closely linked to the fortunes of France as the grandson of the concierge of Montmartre. Now it occurred to him that that little red book would answer the questions he had not dared to put; and stealing in, he possessed himself of it and carried it back to the sitting-room. There he sat down by the lamp and read.

First George's name, his domicile, his rank as a *maréchal des logis* of dragoons, the number of his regiment and its base: all that was already familiar. But what was this on the next page?

"In case of general mobilisation announced to the populations of France by public proclamations, or by notices posted in the streets, the bearer of this order is to rejoin his regiment at ——.

"He is to take with him provisions for one day."

"He is to present himself at the station of —— on the third day of mobilisation at 6 o'clock to 24 o'clock. The first day is that on which the order of mobilisation is published."

"The days of mobilisation are counted from 0 o'clock to 24 o'clock. The first day is that on which the order of mobilisation is published."

Campton dropped the book and pressed his hands to his temples. "The days of mobilisation are counted from 0 o'clock to 24 o'clock. The first day is that on which the order of mobilisation is published." Then, if France mobilised that day, George would start the second day after, at six in the morning. George might be going to leave him within forty-eight hours from that very moment!

Campton had always vaguely supposed that, some day or other, if war came, a telegram would call George to his base; it had never occurred to him that every detail of the boy's military life had long since been regulated by the dread power which had him in its grasp.

He read the next paragraph: "The bearer will travel free of charge——" and thought with a grin how it would annoy Anderson Brant that the French government should presume to treat his stepson as if he could not pay his way. The plump bundle of bank-notes on the dressing-table seemed to look with ineffectual scorn at the red book that sojourned so democratically in the same pocket. And Campton, picturing George jammed into an overcrowded military train, on the plebeian wooden seat of a third-class compartment, grinned again, forgetful of his own anxiety in the vision of Brant's exasperation.

Ah, well, it wasn't war yet, whatever they said!

He carried the red book back to the dressing-table. The light falling across the bed drew his eye to the young face on the pillow. George lay on his side, one arm above his head, the other laxly stretched along the bed. He had thrown off the blankets, and the sheet, clinging to his body, modelled his slim flank and legs as he lay in dreamless rest.

For a long time Campton stood gazing; then he stole back to the sitting-room, picked up a sketch-book and pencil and returned. He knew there was no danger of waking George, and he began to draw, eagerly but deliberately, fascinated by the happy accident of the lighting, and of the boy's position.

"Like a statue of a young knight I've seen somewhere," he said to himself, vexed and surprised that he, whose plastic memories were always so precise, should not remember where; and then his pencil stopped. What he had really thought was: "Like the *effigy* of a young knight"—though he had instinctively changed the word as it formed itself. He leaned in the doorway, the sketch-book in hand, and continued to gaze at his son. It was the clinging sheet, no doubt, that gave him that look . . . and the white glare of the electric burner.

If war came, that was just the way a boy might lie on a battlefield—or afterward in a hospital bed. Not *his* boy, thank heaven; but very probably his boy's friends: hundreds and thousands of boys like his boy, the age of his boy, with a laugh like his boy's. . . The wicked waste of it! Well, that was what war meant . . . what tomorrow might bring to millions of parents like himself.

He stiffened his shoulders, and opened the sketch-book again. What watery stuff was he made of, he wondered? Just because the boy lay as if he were posing for a tombstone! . . . What of Signorelli, who had sat at his dead son's side and drawn him, tenderly, minutely, while the coffin waited?

Well, damn Signorelli—that was all! Campton threw down his book, turned out the sitting-room lights, and limped away to bed.

<hr>

V

The next morning he said to George, over coffee on the terrace: "I think I'll drop in at Cook's about our tickets."

George nodded, munching his golden roll.

"Right. I'll run up to see mother, then."

His father was silent. Inwardly he was saying to himself: "The chances are she'll be going back to Deauville this afternoon."

There had not been much to gather from the newspapers heaped at their feet. Austria had ordered general mobilisation; but while the tone of the despatches was nervous and contradictory that of the leading articles remained almost ominously reassuring. Campton absorbed the reassurance without heeding its quality: it was a drug he had to have at any price.

He expected the Javanese dancer to sit for him that afternoon, but he had not proposed to George to be present. On the chance that things might eventually take a wrong turn he meant to say a word to Fortin-Lescluze; and the presence of his son would have been embarrassing.

"You'll be back for lunch?" he called to George, who still lounged on the terrace in pyjamas.

"Rather.—This, unless mother makes a point . . . in case she's leaving."

"Oh, of course," said Campton with grim cordiality.

"You see, dear old boy, I've got to see Uncle Andy some time. . ." It was the grotesque name that George in his babyhood, had given to

Mr. Brant, and when he grew up it had been difficult to substitute another. "Especially now——" George added, pulling himself up out of his chair.

"Now?"

They looked at each other in silence, irritation in the father's eye, indulgent amusement in the son's.

"Why, if you and I are really off on this long trek——"

"Oh, of course," agreed Campton, relieved. "You'd much better lunch with them. I always want you to do what's decent." He paused on the threshold to add: "By the way, don't forget Adele."

"Well, rather not," his son responded. "And we'll keep the evening free for something awful."

As he left the room he heard George rapping on the telephone and calling out Miss Anthony's number.

Campton had to have reassurance at any price; and he got it, as usual, irrationally but irresistibly, through his eyes. The mere fact that the midsummer sun lay so tenderly on Paris, that the bronze dolphins of the fountains in the square were spraying the Nereids' Louis Philippe chignons as playfully as ever; that the sleepy Cities of France dozed as heavily on their thrones, and the Horses of Marly pranced as fractiously on their pedestals; that the glorious central setting of the city lay there in its usual mellow pomp—all this gave him a sense of security that no crisscrossing of Reuters and Havases could shake.

Nevertheless, he reflected that there was no use in battling with the silly hysterical crowd he would be sure to encounter at Cook's; and having left word with the hotel-porter to secure two "sleepings" on the Naples express, he drove to the studio.

On the way, as his habit was, he thought hard of his model: everything else disappeared like a rolled-up curtain, and his inner vision centred itself on the little yellow face he was to paint.

Peering through her cobwebby window, he saw old Mme. Lebel on the watch. He knew she wanted to pounce out and ask if there would be war; and composing his most taciturn countenance he gave her a preoccupied nod and hurried by.

The studio looked grimy and disordered, and he remembered that he had intended, the evening before, to come back and set it to rights. In pursuance of this plan, he got out a canvas, fussed with his brushes and colours, and then tried once more to make the place tidy. But his attempts at order always resulted in worse confusion; the fact had been one of Julia's grievances against him, and he had often thought that a reaction from his ways probably explained the lifeless neatness of the Anderson Brant drawing-room.

Campton had fled to Montmartre to escape a number of things: first of all, the possibility of meeting people who would want to talk about the European situation, then of being called up by Mrs. Brant, and lastly of having to lunch alone in a fashionable restaurant. In his morbid dread of seeing people he would have preferred an omelette in the studio, if only Mariette had been at hand to make it; and he decided, after a vain struggle with his muddled "properties," to cross over to the Luxembourg quarter and pick up a meal in a wine-shop.

He did not own to himself his secret reason for this decision; but it caused him, after a glance at his watch, to hasten his steps down the rue Montmartre and bribe a passing taxi to carry him to the Museum of the Luxembourg. He reached it ten minutes before the midday closing, and hastening past the serried statues, turned into a room halfway down the gallery. Whistler's Mother and the Carmencita of Sargent wondered at each other from its walls; and on the same wall with the Whistler hung the picture Campton had come for: his portrait of his son. He had given it to the Luxembourg the day after Mr. Brant had tried to buy it, with the object of inflicting the most cruel slight he could think of on the banker.

In the generous summer light the picture shone out on him with a communicative warmth: never had he seen so far into its depths. "No wonder," he thought, "it opened people's eyes to what I was trying for."

He stood and stared his own eyes full, mentally comparing the features before him with those of the firmer harder George he had left on the terrace of the Crillon, and noting how time, while fulfilling the rich promise of the younger face, had yet taken something from its brightness.

Campton, at that moment, found more satisfaction than ever in thinking how it must have humiliated Brant to have the picture given to France. "He could have understood my keeping it myself—or holding it for a bigger price—but *giving it*——!" The satisfaction was worth the sacrifice of the best record he would ever have of that phase of his son's youth. At various times afterward he had tried for the same George, but not one of his later studies had that magic light on it. Still, he was glad he had given the picture. It was safe, safer than it would have been with him. His great dread had always been that if his will were mislaid (and his things were always getting mislaid) the picture might be sold, and fall into Brant's hands after his death.

The closing signal drove him out of the Museum, and he turned into the first wine-shop. He had advised George to lunch with the Brants, but there was disappointment in his heart. Seeing the turn things were taking, he had hoped the boy would feel the impulse to remain with him. But, after all, at such a time a son could not refuse to go to his mother. Campton pictured the little party of three grouped about the luncheon-table in the high cool dining-room of the Avenue Marigny, with the famous Hubert Robert panels, and the Louis XV silver and Sèvres; while he, the father, George's father, sat alone at the soiled table of a frowsy wine-shop.

Well—it was he who had so willed it. Life was too crazy a muddle—and who could have foreseen that he might have been repaid for twenty-six years with such a wife by keeping an undivided claim on such a son?

His meal over, he hastened back to the studio, hoping to find the dancer there. Fortin-Lescluze had sworn to bring her at two, and Campton was known to exact absolute punctuality. He had put the final touch to his fame by refusing to paint the mad young Duchesse de la Tour Crenelée—who was exceptionally paintable—because she had kept him waiting three-quarters of an hour. But now, though it was nearly three, and the dancer and her friend had not come, Campton dared not move, lest he should miss Fortin-Lescluze.

"Sent for by a rich patient in a war-funk; or else hanging about in the girl's dressing-room while she polishes her toe-nails," Campton reflected; and sulkily sat down to wait.

He had never been willing to have a telephone. To him it was a live thing, a kind of Laocoon-serpent that caught one in its coils and dragged one struggling to the receiver. His friends had spent all their logic in trying to argue away this belief; but he answered obstinately: "Every one would be sure to call me up when Mariette was out." Even the Russian lady, during her brief reign, had pleaded in vain on this point.

He would have given a good deal now if he had listened to her. The terror of having to cope with small material difficulties, always strongest in him in moments of artistic inspiration—when the hushed universe seemed hardly big enough to hold him and his model—this dread anchored him to his seat while he tried to make up his mind to send Mme. Lebel to the nearest telephone-station.

If he called to her, she would instantly begin: "And the war, sir?" And he would have to settle that first. Besides, if he did not telephone himself he could not make sure of another appointment with Fortin-Lescluze. But the idea of battling alone with the telephone in a public place covered his large body with a damp distress. If only George had been in reach!

He waited till four, and then, furious, locked the studio and went down. Mme. Lebel still sat in her spidery den. She looked at him gravely, their eyes met, they exchanged a bow, but she did not move or speak. She was busy as usual with some rusty sewing—he thought it odd that she should not rush out to waylay him. Everything that day was odd.

He found all the telephone-booths besieged. The people waiting were certainly bad cases of war-funk, to judge from their looks; after scrutinizing them for a while he decided to return to his hotel, and try to communicate with Fortin-Lescluze from there.

To his annoyance there was not a taxi to be seen. He limped down the slope of Montmartre to the nearest métro-station, and just as he was preparing to force his lame bulk into a crowded train, caught sight of a solitary horse-cab: a vehicle he had not risked himself in for years.

The cab-driver, for gastronomic reasons, declined to take him farther than the Madeleine; and getting out there, Campton walked along the rue Royale. Everything still looked wonderfully as usual; and the fountains in the Place sparkled gloriously.

Comparatively few people were about: he was surprised to see how few. A small group of them, he noticed, had paused near the doorway of the Ministry of Marine, and were looking—without visible excitement—at a white paper pasted on the wall.

He crossed the street and looked too. In the middle of the paper, in queer Gothic-looking characters, he saw the words

" Les Armees de Terre et de Mer. . . ."

War had come——

He knew now that he had never for an instant believed it possible. Even when he had had that white-lipped interview with the Brants, even when he had planned to take Fortin-Lescluze by his senile infatuation, and secure a medical certificate for George; even then, he had simply been obeying the superstitious impulse which makes a man carry his umbrella when he goes out on a cloudless morning.

War had come.

He stood on the edge of the sidewalk, and tried to think—now that it was here—what it really meant: that is, what it meant to him. Beyond that he had no intention of venturing. "This is not our job anyhow," he muttered, repeating the phrase with which he had bolstered up his talk with Julia.

But abstract thinking was impossible: his confused mind could only snatch at a few drifting scraps of purpose. "Let's be practical," he said to himself.

The first thing to do was to get back to the hotel and call up the physician. He strode along at his fastest limp, suddenly contemptuous of the people who got in his way.

"War—and they've nothing to do but dawdle and gape! How like the French!" He found himself hating the French.

He remembered that he had asked to have his sleepings engaged for the following night. But even if he managed to secure his son's discharge, there could be no thought, now, of George's leaving the country; and he stopped at the desk to cancel the order.

There was no one behind the desk: one would have said that confusion prevailed in the hall, if its emptiness had not made the word incongruous. At last a waiter with rumpled hair strayed out of the restaurant, and of him, imperiously, Campton demanded the concierge.

"The concierge? He's gone."

"To get my places for Naples?"

The waiter looked blank. "Gone: mobilised—to join his regiment. It's the war."

"But look here, some one must have attended to getting my places, I suppose," cried Campton wrathfully. He invaded the inner office and challenged a secretary who was trying to deal with several unmanageable travellers, but who explained to him, patiently, that his sleeping had certainly not been engaged, as no trains were leaving Paris for the present. "Not for civilian travel," he added, still more patiently.

Campton had a sudden sense of suffocation. No trains leaving Paris "for the Present"? But then people like himself—people who had nothing on earth to do with the war—had been caught like rats in a trap! He reflected with a shiver that Mrs. Brant would not be able to return to Deauville, and would probably insist on his coming to see her every day. He asked: "How long is this preposterous state of things to last?"—but no one answered, and he stalked to the lift and had himself carried up-stairs.

He was confident that George would be there waiting; but the sitting-room was empty. He felt as if he were on a desert island, with the last sail disappearing over the dark rim of the world.

After much vain ringing he got into communication with Fortin's house, and heard a confused voice saying that the physician had already left Paris.

"Left—for where? For how long?"

And then the eternal answer: "The doctor is mobilised. *It's the war.*"

Mobilised—already? Within the first twenty-four hours? A man of Fortin's age and authority? Campton was terrified by the uncanny rapidity with which events were moving, he whom haste had always confused and disconcerted, as if there were a secret link between his lameness and the movements of his will. He rang up Dastrey, but no one answered. Evidently his friend was out, and his friend's *bonne* also. "I suppose *she's* mobilised: they'll be mobilising the women next."

At last, from sheer over-agitation, his fatigued mind began to move more deliberately: he collected his wits, laboured with his more immediate difficulties, and decided that he would go to Fortin-Lescluze's house, on the chance that the physician had not, after all, really started.

"Ten to one he won't go till tomorrow," Campton reasoned.

The hall of the hotel was emptier than ever, and no taxi was in sight down the whole length of the rue Royale, or the rue Boissy d'Anglas, or the rue de Rivoli: not even a horse-cab showed against the deserted distances. He crossed to the métro, and painfully descended its many stairs.

VI

Campton, proffering twenty francs to an astonished maid-servant, learned that, yes, to his intimates—and of course Monsieur was one?—the doctor *was* in, was in fact dining, and did not leave till the next morning.

"Dining—at six o'clock?"

"Monsieur's son, Monsieur Jean, is starting at once for his depot. That's the reason."

Campton sent in his card. He expected to be received in the so-called "studio," a lofty room with Chinese hangings, Renaissance choir-stalls, organ, grand piano, and post-impressionist paintings, where Fortin-Lescluze received the celebrities of the hour. Mme. Fortin never appeared there, and Campton associated the studio with amusing talk, hot-house flowers, and ladies lolling on black velvet divans. He supposed that the physician was separated from his wife, and that she had a home of her own.

When the maid reappeared she did not lead him to the studio, but into a small dining-room with the traditional Henri II sideboard of waxed walnut, a hanging table-lamp under a beaded shade, an India-rubber plant on a plush pedestal, and napkins that were just being restored to their bone rings by the four persons seated about the red-and-white checkered table-cloth.

These were: the great man himself, a tall large woman with grey hair, a tiny old lady, her face framed in a peasant's fluted cap, and a plain young man wearing a private's uniform, who had a nose like the doctor's and simple light blue eyes.

The two ladies and the young man—so much more interesting to the painter's eye than the sprawling beauties of the studio—were introduced by Fortin-Lescluze as his wife, his mother and his son. Mme. Fortin said, in a deep alto, a word or two about the privilege of meeting the famous painter who had portrayed her husband, and the old mother, in a piping voice, exclaimed: "Monsieur, I was at Sedan in 1870. I saw the Germans. I saw the Emperor sitting on a bench. He was crying."

"My mother's heard everything, she's seen everything. There's no one in the world like my mother!" the physician said, laying his hand on hers.

"You won't see the Germans again, *ma bonne mère!*" her daughter-in-law added, smiling.

Campton took coffee with them, bore with a little inevitable talk about the war, and then eagerly questioned the son. The young man was a chemist, a *préparateur* in the laboratory of the Institut Pasteur. He was also, it appeared, given to prehistoric archæology, and had written a "thesis" on the painted caves of the Dordogne. He seemed extremely serious, and absorbed in questions of science and letters. But it appeared to him perfectly simple to be leaving it all in a few hours to join his regiment. "The war had to come. This sort of thing couldn't go on," he said, in the words of Mme. Lebel.

He was to start in an hour, and Campton excused himself for intruding on the family, who seemed as happily united, as harmonious in their deeper interests, as if no musical studio-parties and exotic dancers had ever absorbed the master of the house.

Campton, looking at the group, felt a pang of envy, and thought, for the thousandth time, how frail a screen of activity divided him from depths of loneliness he dared not sound. "'For every man hath business and desire,'" he muttered as he followed the physician.

In the consulting-room he explained: "It's about my son——"

He had not been able to bring the phrase out in the presence of the young man who must have been just George's age, and who was leaving in an hour for his regiment. But between Campton and the father there were complicities, and there might therefore be accommodations. In the consulting-room one breathed a lower air.

It was not that Campton wanted to do anything underhand. He was genuinely anxious about George's health. After all, tuberculosis did not disappear in a month or even a year: his anxiety was justified. And then George, but for the stupid accident of his birth, would never have been mixed up in the war. Campton felt that he could make his request with his head high.

Fortin-Lescluze seemed to think so too; at any rate he expressed no surprise. But could anything on earth have surprised him, after thirty years in the confessional of a room?

The difficulty was that he did not see his way to doing anything—not immediately, at any rate.

"You must let the boy join his base. He leaves tomorrow? Give me the number of his regiment and the name of the town, and trust me to do what I can."

"But you're off yourself?"

"Yes: I'm being sent to a hospital at Lyons. But I'll leave you my address."

Campton lingered, unable to take this as final. He looked about him uneasily, and then, for a moment, straight into the physician's eyes.

"You must know how I feel; your boy is an only son, too."

"Yes, yes," the father assented, in the absent-minded tone of professional sympathy. But Campton felt that he felt the deep difference.

"Well, goodbye—and thanks."

As Campton turned to go the physician laid a hand on his shoulder and spoke with sudden fierce emotion. "Yes: Jean is an only son—an only child. For his mother and myself it's not a trifle—having our only son in the war."

There was no allusion to the dancer, no hint that Fortin remembered her; it was Campton who lowered his gaze before the look in the other father's eyes.

<hr>

VII

"A son in the war——"

The words followed Campton down the stairs. What did it mean, and what must it feel like, for parents in this safe denationalized modern world to be suddenly saying to each other with white lips: A son in the war?

He stood on the kerbstone, staring ahead of him and forgetting whither he was bound. The world seemed to lie under a spell, and its weight was on his limbs and brain. Usually any deep inward trouble made him more than ever alive to the outward aspect of things; but this new world in which people talked glibly of sons in the war had suddenly become invisible to him, and he did not know where he was, or what he was staring at. He noted the fact, and remembered a story of St. Bernard—he thought it was—walking beside a beautiful lake in supersensual ecstasy, and saying afterward: "Was there a lake? I didn't see it."

On the way back to the hotel he passed the American Embassy, and had a vague idea of trying to see the Ambassador and find out if the United States were not going to devise some way of evading the tyrannous regulation that bound young Americans to France. "And they call this a free country!" he heard himself exclaiming.

The remark sounded exactly like one of Julia's, and this reminded him that the Ambassador frequently dined at the Brants'. They had certainly not left his door untried; and since, to the Brant circles, Campton was still a shaggy Bohemian, his appeal was not likely to fortify theirs.

His mind turned to Jorgenstein, and the vast web of the speculator's financial relations. But, after all, France was on the verge of war, if not in it; and following up the threads of the Jorgenstein web was likely to land one in Frankfort or Vienna.

At the hotel he found his sitting-room empty; but presently the door opened and George came in laden with books, fresh yellow and grey ones in Flammarion wrappers.

"Hullo, Dad," he said; and added: "So the silly show is on."

"Mobilisation is not war——," said Campton.

"No——"

"What on earth are all those books?"

"Provender. It appears we may rot at the depot for weeks. I've just seen a chap who's in my regiment."

Campton felt a sudden relief. The purchase of the books proved that George was fairly sure he would not be sent to the front. His father went up to him and tapped him on the chest.

"How about this——?" He wanted to add: "I've just seen Fortin, who says he'll get you off"; but though George's eye was cool and unenthusiastic it did not encourage such confidences.

"Oh—lungs? I imagine I'm sound again." He paused, and stooped to turn over the books. Carelessly, he added: "But then the stethoscope may think differently. Nothing to do but wait and see."

"Of course," Campton agreed.

It was clear that the boy hated what was ahead of him; and what more could his father ask? Of course he was not going to confess to a desire to shirk his duty; but it was easy to see that his whole lucid intelligence repudiated any sympathy with the ruinous adventure.

"Have you seen Adele?" Campton enquired, and George replied that he had dropped in for five minutes, and that Miss Anthony wanted to see his father.

"Is she—nervous?"

"Old Adele? I should say not: she's fighting mad. *La Revanche* and all the rest of it. She doesn't realize—*sancta simplicitas!*"

"Oh, I can see Adele throwing on the faggots!"

Father and son were silent, both busy lighting cigarettes. When George's was lit he remarked: "Well, if we're not called at once it'll be a good chance to read 'The Golden Bough' right through."

Campton stared, not knowing the book even by name. What a queer changeling the boy was! But George's composure, his deep and genuine indifference to the whole political turmoil, once more fortified his father.

"Have they any news—?" he ventured. "They," in their private language, meant the Brants.

"Oh, yes, lots: Uncle Andy was stiff with it. But not really amounting to anything. Of course there's no doubt there'll be war."

"How about England?"

"Nobody knows; but the bankers seem to think England's all right."
George paused, and finally added: "Look here, dear old boy—before
she leaves I think mother wants to see you."

Campton hardened instantly. "She *has* seen me—yesterday."

"I know; she told me."

The son began to cut the pages of one of his books with a visiting-
card he had picked up, and the father stood looking out on the Place
de la Concorde through the leafy curtain of the terrace.

Campton knew that he could not refuse his son's request; in his
heart of hearts he was glad it had been made, since it might mean
that "they" had found a way—perhaps through the Ambassador.

But he could never prevent a stiffening of his whole self at any
summons or suggestion from the Brants. He thought of the seeming
unity of the Fortin-Lescluze couple, and of the background of peaceful
family life revealed by the scene about the checkered tablecloth. Perhaps that was one of the advantages of a social organization which
still, as a whole, ignored divorce, and thought any private condonation
better than the open breaking-up of the family.

"All right; I'll go——" he agreed. "Where are we dining?"

"Oh, I forgot—an awful orgy. Dastrey wants us at the Union. Louis
Dastrey is dining with him, and he let me ask Boylston——"

"Boylston——?"

"You don't know him. A chap who was at Harvard with me. He's
out here studying painting at the Beaux-Arts. He's an awfully good
sort, and he wanted to see me before I go."

The father's heart sank. Only one whole day more with his boy,
and this last evening but one was to be spent with poor embittered
Dastrey, and two youths, one unknown to Campton, who would
drown them in stupid war-chatter? But it was what George wanted;
and there must not be a shade, for George, on these last hours.

"All right! You promised me something awful for to-night," Campton grinned sardonically.

"Do you mind? I'm sorry."

"It's only Dastrey's damned chauvinism that I mind. Why don't you
ask Adele to join the chorus?"

"Well—you'll like Boylston," said George.

Dastrey, after all, turned out less tragic and aggressive than
Campton had feared. His irritability had vanished, and though he
was very grave he seemed preoccupied only with the fate of Europe,
and not with his personal stake in the affair.

But the older men said little. The youngsters had the floor, and

Campton, as he listened to George and young Louis Dastrey, was overcome by a sense of such dizzy unreality that he had to grasp the arms of his ponderous leather armchair to assure himself that he was really in the flesh and in the world.

What! Two days ago they were still in the old easy Europe, a Europe in which one could make plans, engage passages on trains and steamers, argue about pictures, books, theatres, ideas, draw as much money as one chose out of the bank, and say: "The day after tomorrow I'll be in Berlin or Vienna or Belgrade." And here they sat in their same evening clothes, about the same shining mahogany writing-table, apparently the same group of free and independent youths and elderly men, and in reality prisoners, every one of them, hand-cuffed to this hideous masked bully of "War"!

The young men were sure that the conflict was inevitable—the evening papers left no doubt of it—and there was much animated discussion between young Dastrey and George.

Already their views diverged; the French youth, theoretically at one with his friend as to the senselessness of war in general, had at once resolutely disengaged from the mist of doctrine the fatal necessity of this particular war.

"It's the old festering wound of Alsace-Lorraine: Bismarck foresaw it and feared it—or perhaps planned it and welcomed it: who knows? But as long as the wound was there, Germany believed that France would try to avenge it, and as long as Germany believed that, she had to keep up her own war-strength; and she's kept it up to the toppling-over point, ruining herself and us. That's the whole thing, as I see it. War's rot; but to get rid of war forever we've got to fight this one first."

It was wonderful to Campton that this slender learned youth should already have grasped the necessity of the conflict and its deep causes. While his own head was still spinning with wrath and bewilderment at the bottomless perversity of mankind, Louis Dastrey had analyzed and accepted the situation and his own part in it. And he was not simply resigned; he was trembling with eagerness to get the thing over. "If only England is with us we're safe—it's a matter of weeks," he declared.

"Wait a bit—wait a bit; I want to know more about a whole lot of things before I fix a date for the fall of Berlin," his uncle interposed; but Louis flung him a radiant look. "We've been there before, my uncle!"

"But there's Russia too——" said Boylston explosively. He had not spoken before.

"'Nous l'avons eu, votre Rhin allemand,'" quoted George, as he poured a golden Hock into his glass.

He was keenly interested, that was evident; but interested as a looker-on, a dilettante. He had neither Valmy nor Sedan in his blood, and it was as a sympathizing spectator that he ought by rights to have been sharing his friend's enthusiasm, not as a combatant compelled to obey the same summons. Campton, glancing from one to another of their brilliant faces, felt his determination harden to save George from the consequences of his parents' stupid blunder.

After dinner young Dastrey proposed a music-hall. The audience would be a curious sight: there would be wild enthusiasm, and singing of the Marseillaise. The other young men agreed, but their elders, after a tacitly exchanged glance, decided to remain at the club, on the plea that some one at the Ministry of War had promised to telephone if there were fresh news.

Campton and Dastrey, left alone, stood on the balcony watching the Boulevards. The streets, so deserted during the day, had become suddenly and densely populated. Hardly any vehicles were in sight: the motor omnibuses were already carrying troops to the stations, there was a report abroad that private motors were to be requisitioned, and only a few taxis and horse-cabs, packed to the driver's box with young men in spick-and-span uniforms, broke through the mass of pedestrians which filled the whole width of the Boulevards. This mass moved slowly and vaguely, swaying this way and that, as though it awaited a portent from the heavens. In the glare of electric lamps and glittering theatre-fronts the innumerable faces stood out vividly, grave, intent, slightly bewildered. Except when the soldiers passed no cries or songs came from the crowd, but only the deep inarticulate rumour which any vast body of people gives forth.

"Queer——! How silent they are: how do you think they're taking it?" Campton questioned.

But Dastrey had grown belligerent again. He saw the throngs before him bounding toward the frontier like the unchained furies of Rude's "Marseillaise"; whereas to Campton they seem full of the dumb wrath of an orderly and laborious people upon whom an unrighteous quarrel has been forced. He knew that the thought of Alsace-Lorraine still stirred in French hearts; but all Dastrey's eloquence could not convince him that these people wanted war, or would have sought it had it not been thrust on them. The whole monstrous injustice seemed to take shape before him, and to brood like a huge sky-filling dragon of the northern darknesses over his light-loving, pleasure-loving, labour-loving France.

George came home late.

It was two in the morning of his last day with his boy when Campton heard the door open, and saw a flash of turned-on light.

All night he had lain staring into the darkness, and thinking, thinking: thinking of George's future, George's friends, George and women, of that unknown side of his boy's life which, in this great upheaval of things, had suddenly lifted its face to the surface. If war came, if George were not discharged, if George were sent to the front, if George were killed, how strange to think that things the father did not know of might turn out to have been the central things of his son's life!

The young man came, and Campton looked at him as though he were a stranger.

"Hullo, Dad—any news from the Ministry?" George, tossing aside his hat and stick, sat down on the bed. He had a crumpled rose in his button-hole, and looked gay and fresh, with the indestructible freshness of youth.

"What do I really know of him?" the father asked himself.

Yes: Dastrey had had news. Germany had already committed acts of overt hostility on the frontier: telegraph and telephone communications had been cut, French locomotives seized, troops massed along the border on the specious pretext of the *"Kriegsgefahrzustand."* It was war.

"Oh, well," George shrugged. He lit a cigarette, and asked: "What did you think of Boylston?"

"Boylston——?"

"The fat brown chap at dinner."

"Yes—yes—of course." Campton became aware that he had not thought of Boylston at all, had hardly been aware of his presence. But the painter's registering faculty was always latently at work, and in an instant he called up a round face, shyly jovial, with short-sighted brown eyes as sharp as needles, and dark hair curling tightly over a wide watchful forehead.

"Why—I liked him."

"I'm glad, because it was a tremendous event for him, seeing you. He paints, and he's been keen on your things for years."

"I wish I'd known. . . Why didn't he say so? He didn't say anything, did he?"

"No: he doesn't, much, when he's pleased. He's the very best chap I know," George concluded.

VIII

That morning the irrevocable stared at him from the head-lines of the papers. The German Ambassador was recalled. Germany had declared war on France at 6:40 the previous evening; there was an unintelligible allusion, in the declaration, to French aeroplanes throwing bombs on Nuremberg and Wesel. Campton read that part of the message over two or three times.

Aeroplanes throwing bombs? Aeroplanes as engines of destruction? He had always thought of them as a kind of giant kite that fools went up in when they were tired of breaking their necks in other ways. But aeroplane bombardment as a cause for declaring war? The bad faith of it was so manifest that he threw down the papers half relieved. Of course there would be a protest on the part of the allies; a great country like France would not allow herself to be bullied into war on such a pretext.

The ultimatum to Belgium was more serious; but Belgium's gallant reply would no doubt check Germany on that side. After all, there was such a thing as international law, and Germany herself had recognized it. . . So his mind spun on in vain circles, while under the frail web of his casuistry gloomed the obstinate fact that George was mobilised, that George was to leave the next morning.

The day wore on: it was the shortest and yet most interminable that Campton had ever known. Paris, when he went out into it, was more dazzlingly empty than ever. In the hotel, in the hall, on the stairs, he was waylaid by flustered compatriots— "Oh, Mr. Campton, you don't know me, but of course all Americans know *you!*"—who appealed to him for the very information he was trying to obtain himself: how one could get money, how one could get hold of the concierge, how one could send cables, if there was any restaurant where the waiters had not all been mobilised, if he had any "pull" at the Embassy, or at any of the steamship offices, or any of the banks. One disordered beauty blurted out: "Of course, with your connection with Bullard and Brant"—and was only waked to her mistake by Campton's indignant stare, and his plunge past her while she called out excuses.

But the name acted as a reminder of his promise to go and see Mrs. Brant, and he decided to make his visit after lunch, when George would be off collecting last things. Visiting the Brants with George would have been beyond his capacity.

The great drawing-rooms, their awnings spread against the sun, their tall windows wide to the glow of the garden, were empty when he entered; but in a moment he was joined by a tall angular woman with a veil pushed up untidily above her pink nose. Campton reflected that he had never seen Adele Anthony in the daytime without a veil pushed up above a flushed nose, and dangling in irregular wisps from the back of a small hard hat of which the shape never varied.

"Julia will be here in a minute. When she told me you were coming I waited."

He was glad to have a word with her before meeting Mrs. Brant, though his impulse had been almost as strong to avoid the one as the other. He dreaded belligerent bluster as much as vain whimpering, and in the depths of his soul he had to own that it would have been easier to talk to Mr. Brant than to either of the women.

"Julia is powdering her nose," Miss Anthony continued. "She had an idea that if you see she's been crying you'll be awfully angry."

Campton made an impatient gesture. "If I were—much it would matter!"

"Ah, but you might tell George; and George is not to know." She paused, and then bounced round on him abruptly. She always moved and spoke in explosions, as if the wires that agitated her got tangled, and then were too suddenly jerked loose.

"*Does* George know?"

"About his mother's tears?"

"About this plan you're all hatching to have him discharged?"

Campton reddened under her lashless blue gaze, and the consciousness of doing so made his answer all the curter.

"Probably not—unless you've told him!"

The shot appeared to reach the mark, for an answering blush suffused her sallow complexion. "You'd better not put ideas into my head!" she laughed. Something in her tone reminded him of all her old dogged loyalties, and made him ashamed of his taunt.

"Anyhow," he grumbled, "his place is not in the French army."

"That was for you and Julia to decide twenty-six years ago, wasn't it? Now it's up to him."

Her capricious adoption of American slang, fitted anyhow into her old-fashioned and punctilious English, sometimes amused but oftener exasperated Campton.

"If you're going to talk modern slang you ought to give up those ridiculous stays, and not wear a fringe like a mid-Victorian royalty," he jeered, trying to laugh off his exasperation.

She let this pass with a smile. "Well, I wish I could find the language to make you understand how much better it would be to leave George alone. This war will be the making of him."

"He's made quite to my satisfaction as it is, thanks. But what's the use of talking? You always get your phrases out of books."

The door opened, and Mrs. Brant came in.

Her appearance answered to Miss Anthony's description. A pearly mist covered her face, and some reviving liquid had cleared her congested eyes. Her poor hands had suddenly grown so thin and dry that the heavy rings, slipping down to the joints, slid back into place as she shook hands with Campton.

"Thank you for coming," she said.

"Oh——" he protested, helpless, and disturbed by Miss Anthony's presence. At the moment his former wife's feelings were more intelligible to him than his friend's: the maternal fibre stirred in her, and made her more appealing than any elderly virgin on the war-path.

"I'm off, my dears," said the elderly virgin, as if guessing his thought. Her queer shallow eyes included them both in a sweeping glance, and she flung back from the threshold: "Be careful of what you say to George."

What they had to say to each other did not last many minutes. The Brants had made various efforts, but had been baffled on all sides by the general agitation and confusion. In high quarters the people they wanted to see were inaccessible; and those who could be reached lent but a distracted ear. The Ambassador had at once declared that he could no nothing; others vaguely promised they "would see"—but hardly seemed to hear what they were being asked.

"And meanwhile time is passing—and he's going!" Mrs. Brant lamented.

The reassurance that Campton brought from Fortin-Lescluze, vague though it was, came to her as a miraculous promise, and raised Campton suddenly in her estimation. She looked at him with a new confidence, and he could almost hear her saying to Brant, as he had so often heard her say to himself: "You never seem able to get anything done. I don't know how other people manage."

Her gratitude gave him the feeling of having been engaged in something underhand and pusillanimous. He made haste to take leave, after promising to pass on any word he might receive from the physician; but he reminded her that he was not likely to hear anything till George had been for some days at his base.

She acknowledged the probability of this, and clung to him with trustful eyes. She was much disturbed by the preposterous fact that the Government had already requisitioned two of the Brant motors, and Campton had an idea that, dazzled by his newly-developed capacity to "manage," she was about to implore him to rescue from the clutches of the authorities her Rolls-Royce and Anderson's Delaunay.

He was hastening to leave when the door again opened. A rumpled-looking maid peered in, evidently perplexed, and giving way doubtfully to a young woman who entered with a rush, and then paused as if she too were doubtful. She was pretty in an odd dishevelled way, and with her elaborate clothes and bewildered look she reminded Campton of a fashion-plate torn from its page and helplessly blown about the world. He had seen the same type among his compatriots any number of times in the last days.

"Oh, Mrs. Brant—yes, I know you gave orders that you were not in to anybody, but I just wouldn't listen, and it's not that poor woman's fault," the visitor began, in a plaintive staccato which matched her sad eyes and her fluttered veils.

"You see, I simply had to get hold of Mr. Brant, because I'm here without a penny—literally!" She dangled before them a bejewelled mesh-bag. "And in a hotel where they don't know me. And at the bank they wouldn't listen to me, and they said Mr. Brant wasn't there, though of course I suppose he was; so I said to the cashier: 'Very well, then, I'll simply go to the Avenue Marigny and batter in his door—unless you'd rather I jumped into the Seine?'"

"Oh, Mrs. Talkett——" murmured Mrs. Brant.

"Really: it's a case of my money or my life!" the young lady continued with a studied laugh. She stood between them, artificial and yet so artless, conscious of intruding but evidently used to having her intrusions pardoned; and her large eyes turned interrogatively to Campton.

"Of course my husband will do all he can for you. I'll telephone," said Mrs. Brant; then, perceiving that her visitor continued to gaze at Campton, she added: "Oh, no, *this* is not . . . this is Mr. Campton."

"John Campton? I knew it!" Mrs. Talkett's eyes became devouring and brilliant. "Of course I ought to have recognised you at once—from your photographs. I have one pinned up in my room. But I was so flurried when I came in." She detained the painter's hand. "Do forgive me! For *years* I've dreamed of your doing me . . . you see, I paint a little myself . . . but it's ridiculous to speak of such things now." She added, as if she were risking something: "I knew your son at St. Moritz. We saw a great deal of him there, and in New York last winter."

"Ah——" said Campton, bowing awkwardly.

"Cursèd fools—all women," he anathematized her on the way downstairs.

In the street, however, he felt grateful to her for reducing Mrs. Brant to such confusion that she had made no attempt to detain him. His way of life lay so far apart from his former wife's that they had hardly ever been exposed to accidents of the kind, and he saw that Julia's embarrassment kept all its freshness.

The fact set him thinking curiously of what her existence had been since they had parted. She had long since forgotten her youthful art-jargon to learn others more consonant to her tastes. As the wife of the powerful American banker she dispensed the costliest hospitality with the simple air of one who has never learnt that human life may be sustained without the aid of orchids and champagne. With guests either brought up in the same convictions or bent on acquiring them she conversed earnestly and unweariedly about motors, clothes and morals; but perhaps her most stimulating hours were those brightened by the weekly visit of the Rector of her parish. With happy untrammelled hands she was now free to rebuild to her own measure a corner of the huge wicked welter of Paris; and immediately it became as neat, as empty, as air-tight as her own immaculate drawing-room.

There he seemed to see her, throning year after year in an awful emptiness of wealth and luxury and respectability, seeing only dull people, doing only dull things, and fighting feverishly to defend the last traces of a beauty which had never given her anything but the tamest and most unprofitable material prosperity.

"She's never even had the silly kind of success she wanted—poor Julia!" he mused, wondering that she had been able to put into her life so few of the sensations which can be bought by wealth and beauty. "And now what will be left—how on earth will she fit into a war?"

He was sure all her plans had been made for the coming six months: her week-end sets of heavy millionaires secured for Deauville, and after that for the shooting at the big château near Compiègne, and three weeks reserved for Biarritz before the return to Paris in January. One of the luxuries Julia had most enjoyed after her separation from Campton (Adele had told him) had been that of planning things ahead: Mr. Brant, thank heaven, was not impulsive. And now here was this black bolt of war falling among all her carefully balanced arrangements with a crash more violent than any of Campton's inconsequences!

As he reached the Place de la Concorde a newsboy passed with the three o'clock papers, and he bought one and read of the crossing of Luxembourg and the invasion of Belgium. The Germans were arrogantly acting up to their menace: heedless of international law, they were driving straight for France and England by the road they thought the most accessible. . .

In the hotel he found George, red with rage, devouring the same paper: the boy's whole look was changed.

"The howling blackguards! The brigands! This isn't war—it's simple murder!"

The two men stood and stared at each other. "Will England stand it?" sprang to their lips at the same moment.

Never—never! England would never permit such a violation of the laws regulating the relations between civilized peoples. They began to say both together that after all perhaps it was the best thing that could have happened, since, if there had been the least hesitation or reluctance in any section of English opinion, this abominable outrage would instantly sweep it away.

"They've been too damned clever for once!" George exulted. "France is saved—that's certain anyhow!"

Yes; France was saved if England could put her army into the field at once. But could she? Oh, for the Channel tunnel at this hour! Would this lesson at last cure England of her obstinate insularity? Belgium had announced her intention of resisting; but what was that gallant declaration worth in face of Germany's brutal assault? A poor little country pledged to a guaranteed neutrality could hardly be expected to hold her frontiers more than forty-eight hours against the most powerful army in Europe. And what a narrow strip Belgium was, viewed as an outpost of France!

These thoughts, racing through Campton's mind, were swept out of it again by his absorbing preoccupation. What effect would the Belgian affair have on George's view of his own participation in the war? For the first time the boy's feeling were visibly engaged; his voice shook as he burst out: "Louis Dastrey's right: this kind of thing has got to stop. We shall go straight back to cannibalism if it doesn't.— God, what hounds!"

Yes, but—Campton pondered, tried to think up Pacifist arguments, remembered his own discussion with Paul Dastrey three days before. "My dear chap, hasn't France perhaps gone about with a chip on her shoulder? Saverne, for instance: some people think——"

"Damn Saverne! Haven't the Germans shown us what they are now? Belgium sheds all the light *I* want on Saverne. They're not fit to live with white people, and the sooner they're shown it the better."

"Well, France and Russia and England are here to show them."

George laughed. "Yes, and double quick."

Both were silent again, each thinking his own thoughts. They were apparently the same, for just as Campton was about to ask where George had decided that they should take their last dinner, the young man said abruptly: "Look here, Dad; I'd planned a little tête-à-tête for us this evening."

"Yes——?"

"Well—I can't. I'm going to chuck you." He smiled a little, his colour rising nervously. "For some people I've just run across—who were awfully kind to me at St. Moritz—and in New York last winter. I didn't know they were here till . . . till just now. I'm awfully sorry; but I've simply got to dine with them."

There was a silence. Campton stared out over his son's shoulder at the great sunlit square. "Oh, all right," he said briskly.

This—on George's last night!

"You don't mind *much,* do you? I'll be back early, for a last pow-wow on the terrace." George paused, and finally brought out: "You see, it really wouldn't have done to tell mother that I was deserting her on my last evening because I was dining with you!"

A weight was lifted from Campton's heart, and he felt ashamed of having failed to guess the boy's real motive.

"My dear fellow, naturally . . . quite right. And you can stop in and see your mother on the way home. You'll find me here whenever you turn up."

George looked relieved. "Thanks a lot—you always know. And now for my adieux to Adele."

He went off whistling the waltz from the Rosenkavalier, and Campton returned to his own thoughts.

He was still revolving them when he went upstairs after a solitary repast in the confused and servantless dining-room. Adele Anthony had telephoned to him to come and dine—after seeing George, he supposed; but he had declined. He wanted to be with his boy, or alone.

As he left the dining-room he ran across Adamson, the American newspaper correspondent, who had lived for years in Paris and was reputed to have "inside information." Adamson was grave but confident. In his opinion Russia would probably not get to Berlin before November (he smiled at Campton's astonished outcry); but if England—oh, they were sure of England!—could get her army over without delay, the whole business would very likely be settled before that, in one big battle in Belgium. (Yes—poor Belgium, indeed!) Anyhow, in the opinion of the military experts the war was not likely to last more than three or four months; and of course, even if things went badly on the western front, which was highly unlikely, there was Russia to clench the business as soon as her huge forces got in motion. Campton drew much comfort from this sober view of the situation, midway between that of the optimists who knew Russia would be in Berlin in three weeks, and of those who saw the Germans in Calais even sooner. Adamson was a level-headed fellow, who weighed what he said and pinned his faith to facts.

Campton managed to evade several people whom he saw lurking for him, and mounted to his room. On the terrace, alone with the serene city, his confidence grew, and he began to feel more and more sure that, whatever happened, George was likely to be kept out of the fighting till the whole thing was over. With such formidable forces closing in on her it was fairly obvious that Germany must succumb before half or even a quarter of the allied reserves had been engaged. Sustained by the thought, he let his mind hover tenderly over George's future, and the effect on his character of this brief and harmless plunge into a military career.

IX

George was gone.

When, with a last whistle and scream, his train had ploughed its way out of the clanging station; when the last young figures clinging to the rear of the last carriage had vanished, and the bare rails again glittered up from the cindery tracks, Campton turned and looked about him.

All the platforms of the station were crowded as he had seldom seen any place crowded, and to his surprise he found himself taking in every detail of the scene with a morbid accuracy of observation. He had discovered, during these last days, that his artist's vision had been strangely unsettled. Sometimes, as when he had left Fortin's house, he saw nothing: the material world, which had always tugged at him with a thousand hands, vanished and left him in the void. Then again, as at present, he saw everything, saw it too clearly, in all its superfluous and negligible reality, instead of instinctively selecting, and disregarding what was not to his purpose.

Faces, faces—they swarmed about him, and his overwrought vision registered them one by one. Especially he noticed the faces of the women, women of all ages, all classes. These were the wives, mothers, grandmothers, sisters, mistresses of all those heavily laden trainfuls of French youth. He was struck with the same strong cheerfulness in all: some pale, some flushed, some serious, but all firmly and calmly smiling.

One young woman in particular his look dwelt on—a dark girl in a becoming dress—both because she was so pleasant to see, and because there was such assurance in her serenity that she did not have to constrain her lips and eyes, but could trust them to be what she wished. Yet he saw by the way she clung to the young artilleryman from whom she was parting that hers were no sisterly farewells.

An immense hum of voices filled the vast glazed enclosure. Campton caught the phrases flung up to the young faces piled one above another in the windows—words of motherly admonishment, little jokes, tender names, mirthful allusions, last callings out: "Write often! Don't forget to wrap up your throat. . . Remember to send a line to Annette. . . Bring home a Prussian helmet for the children! *On les aura, pas, mon vieux?*" It was all bright, brave and confident. "If Berlin could only see it!" Campton thought.

He tried to remember what his own last words to George had been, but could not; yet his throat felt dry and thirsty, as if he had talked a great deal. The train vanished in a roar, and he leaned against a pier to let the crowd flood by, not daring to risk his lameness in such a turmoil.

Suddenly he heard loud sobs behind him. He turned, and recognized the hat and hair of the girl whose eyes had struck him. He could not see them now, for they were buried in her hands and her whole body shook with woe. An elderly man was trying to draw her away— her father, probably.

"Come, come, my child——"

"Oh—oh—oh," she hiccoughed, following blindly.

The people nearest stared at her, and the faces of other women grew pale. Campton saw tears on the cheeks of an old body in a black bonnet who might have been his own Mme. Lebel. A pale lad went away weeping.

But they were all afraid, then, all in immediate deadly fear for the lives of their beloved! The same fear grasped Campton's heart, a very present terror, such as he had hardly before imagined. Compared to it, all that he had felt hitherto seemed as faint as the sensations of a looker-on. His knees failed him, and he grasped a transverse bar of the pier.

People were leaving the station in groups of two or three who seemed to belong to each other; only he was alone. George's mother had not come to bid her son goodbye; she had declared that she would rather take leave of him quietly in her own house than in a crowd of dirty people at the station. But then it was impossible to conceive of her being up and dressed and at the Gare de l'Est at five in the morning—and how could she have got there without her motor? So Campton was alone, in that crowd which seemed all made up of families.

But no—not all. Ahead of him he saw one woman moving away alone, and recognized, across the welter of heads, Adele Anthony's adamantine hat and tight knob of hair.

Poor Adele! So she had come too—and had evidently failed in her quest, not been able to fend a way through the crowd, and perhaps not even had a glimpse of her hero. The thought smote Campton with compunction: he regretted his sneering words when they had last met, regretted refusing to dine with her. He wished the barrier of people between them had been less impenetrable; but for the moment it was useless to try to force a way through it. He had to wait till the crowd shifted to other platforms, whence other trains were starting, and by that time she was lost to sight.

At last he was able to make his way through the throng, and as he came out of a side entrance he saw her. She appeared to be looking for a taxi—she waved her sunshade aimlessly. But no one who knew the Gare de l'Est would have gone around that corner to look for a taxi; least of all the practical Adele. Besides, Adele never took taxis: she travelled in the bowels of the earth or on the dizziest omnibus tops.

Campton knew at once that she was waiting for him. He went up to her and a guilty pink suffused her nose.

"You missed him after all——?" he said.

"I—oh, no, I didn't."

"You didn't? But I was with him all the time. We didn't see you——"

"No, but *I* saw—distinctly. That was all I went for," she jerked back.

He slipped his arm through hers. "This crowd terrifies me. I'm glad you waited for me," he said.

He saw her pleasure, but she merely answered: "I'm dying of thirst, aren't you?"

"Yes—or hunger, or something. Could we find a *laiterie?*"

They found one, and sat down among early clerks and shop-girls, and a few dishevelled women with swollen faces whom Campton had noticed in the station. One of them, who sat opposite an elderly man, had drawn out a pocket mirror and was powdering her nose.

Campton hated to see women powder their noses—one of the few merits with which he credited Julia Brant was that of never having adopted these dirty modern fashions, of continuing to make her toilet in private "like a lady," as people used to say when he was young. But now the gesture charmed him, for he had recognized the girl who had been sobbing in the station.

"How game she is! I like that. But why is she so frightened?" he wondered. For he saw that her chocolate was untouched, and that the smile had stiffened on her lips.

Since his talk with Adamson he could not bring himself to be seriously alarmed. Fear had taken him by the throat for a moment in the station, at the sound of the girl's sobs; but already he had thrown it off. Everybody agreed that the war was sure to be over in a few weeks; even Dastrey had come round to that view; and with Fortin's protection, and the influences Anderson Brant could put in motion, George was surely safe—as safe at his depot as anywhere else in the precarious world. Campton poured out Adele's coffee, and drank off his own as if it had been champagne.

"Do you know anything about the people George was dining with last night?" he enquired abruptly.

Miss Anthony knew everything and everybody in the American circle in Paris; she was a clearing-house of Franco-American gossip, and it was likely enough that if George had special reasons for wishing to spend his last evening away from his family she would know why. But the chance of her knowing what had been kept from him made Campton's question, as soon as it was put, seem indiscreet, and he added hastily: "Not that I want——"

She looked surprised. "No: he didn't tell me. Some young man's affair, I suppose. . ." She smirked absurdly, her lashless eyes blinking under the pushed-back veil.

Campton's mind had already strayed from the question. Nothing bored him more than Adele doing the "sad dog," and he was vexed at having given her such a chance to be silly. What he wanted to know was whether George had spoken to his old friend about his future—about his own idea of his situation, and his intentions and wishes in view of the grim chance which people, with propitiatory vagueness, call "anything happening." Had the boy left any word, any message with her for any one? But it was useless to speculate, for if he had, the old goose, true as steel, would never betray it by as much as a twitch of her lids. She could look, when it was a question of keeping a secret, like such an impenetrable idiot that one could not imagine any one's having trusted a secret to her.

Campton had no wish to surprise George's secrets, if the boy had any. But their parting had been so hopelessly Anglo-Saxon, so curt and casual, that he would have liked to think his son had left, somewhere, a message for him, a word, a letter, in case . . . in case there was anything premonitory in the sobbing of that girl at the next table.

But Adele's pink nose confronted him, as guileless as a rabbit's, and he went out with her unsatisfied. They parted at the door of the restaurant, and Campton went to the studio to see if there were any news of his maid-servant Mariette. He meant to return to sleep there that night, and even his simple housekeeping was likely to be troublesome if Mariette should not arrive.

On the way it occurred to him that he had not yet seen the morning papers, and he stopped and bought a handful.

Negotiations, hopes, fears, conjectures—but nothing new or definite, except the insolent fact of Germany's aggression, and the almost-certainty of England's intervention. When he reached the studio he found Mme. Lebel in her usual place, paler than usual, but with firm lips and bright eyes. Her three grandsons had left for their depots the day before: one was in the *Chasseurs Alpins,* and probably already on his way to Alsace, another in the infantry, the third in the heavy artillery; she did not know where the two latter were likely to be sent. Her eldest son, their father, was dead; the second, a man of fifty, and a cabinetmaker by trade, was in the territorials, and was not to report for another week. He hoped, before leaving, to see the return of his wife and little girl, who were in the Ardennes with the wife's people. Mme. Lebel's mind was made up and her philosophy ready for immediate application.

"It's terribly hard for the younger people; but it had to be. I come from Nancy, Monsieur: I remember the German occupation. I understand better than my daughter-in-law. . ."

There was no news of Mariette, and small chance of having any for some days, much less of seeing her. No one could tell how long civilian travel would be interrupted. Mme. Lebel, moved by her lodger's plight, promised to "find some one"; and Campton mounted to the studio.

He had left it only two days before, on the day when he had vainly waited for Fortin and his dancer; and an abyss already divided him from that vanished time. Then his little world still hung like a straw above an eddy; now it was spinning about in the central vortex.

The pictures stood about untidily, and he looked curiously at all those faces which belonged to the other life. Each bore the mark of its own immediate passions and interests; not one betrayed the least consciousness of coming disaster except the face of poor Madame de Dolmetsch, whose love had enlightened her. Campton began to think of the future from the painter's point of view. What a modeller of faces a great war must be! What would the people who came through it look like, he wondered.

His bell tinkled, and he turned to answer it. Dastrey, he supposed . . . he had caught a glimpse of his friend across the crowd at the Gare de l'Est, seeing off his nephew, but had purposely made no sign. He still wanted to be alone, and above all not to hear war-talk. Mme. Lebel, however, had no doubt revealed his presence in the studio, and he could not risk offending Dastrey.

When he opened the door it was a surprise to see there, instead of Dastrey's anxious face, the round rosy countenance of a well-dressed youth with a shock of fair hair above eyes of childish candour.

"Oh—come in," Campton said, surprised, but divining a compatriot in a difficulty.

The youth obeyed, blushing his apologies.

"I'm Benny Upsher, sir," he said, in a tone modest yet confident, as if the name were an introduction.

"Oh——" Campton stammered, cursing his absentmindedness and his unfailing faculty for forgetting names.

"You're a friend of George's, aren't you?" he risked.

"Yes—tremendous. We were at Harvard together—he was two years ahead of me."

"Ah—then you're still there?"

Mr. Upsher's blush became a mask of crimson. "Well—I thought I was, till this thing happened."

"What thing?"

The youth stared at the older man with a look of celestial wonder. "This war.—George has started already, hasn't he?"

"Yes. Two hours ago."

"So they said—I looked him up at the Crillon. I wanted most awfully to see him; if I had, of course I shouldn't have bothered you."

"My dear young man, you're not bothering me. But what can I do?"

Mr. Upsher's composure seemed to be returning as the necessary preliminaries were cleared away. "Thanks a lot," he said. "Of course what I'd like best is to join his regiment."

"Join his regiment—*you!*" Campton exclaimed.

"Oh, I know it's difficult; I raced up from Biarritz quick as I could to catch him." He seemed still to be panting with the effort. "I want to be in this," he concluded.

Campton contemplated him with helpless perplexity. "But I don't understand—there's no reason, in your case. With George it was obligatory—on account of his being born here. But I suppose you were born in America?"

"Well, I guess so: in Utica. My mother was Madeline Mayhew. I think we're a sort of cousins, sir, aren't we?"

"Of course—of course. Excuse my not recalling it—just at first. But, my dear boy, I still don't see——"

Mr. Upsher's powers of stating his case were plainly limited. He pushed back his rumpled hair, looked hard again at his cousin, and repeated doggedly: "I want to be *in* this."

"This war?"

He nodded.

Campton groaned. What did the boy mean, and why come to him with such tomfoolery? At that moment he felt even more unfitted than usual to deal with practical problems, and in spite of the forgotten cousinship it was no affair of his what Madeline Mayhew's son wanted to be in.

But there was the boy himself, stolid, immovable, impenetrable to hints, and with something in his wide blue eyes like George—and yet so childishly different.

"Sit down—have a cigarette, won't you?—You know, of course," Campton began, "that what you propose is almost insuperably difficult?"

"Getting into George's regiment?"

"Getting into the French army at all—for a foreigner, a neutral. . . I'm afraid there's really nothing I can do."

Benny Upsher smiled indulgently. "I can fix that up all right; getting into the army, I mean. The only thing that might be hard would be getting into his regiment."

"Oh, as to that—out of the question, I should think." Campton was conscious of speaking curtly: the boy's bland determination was beginning to get on his nerves.

"Thank you no end," said Benny Upsher, getting up. "Sorry to have butted in," he added, holding out a large brown hand.

Campton followed him to the door perplexedly. He knew that something ought to be done—but what? On the threshold he laid his hand impulsively on the youth's shoulder. "Look here, my boy, we're cousins, as you say, and if you're Madeline Mayhew's boy you're an only son. Moreover you're George's friend—which matters still more to me. I can't let you go like this. Just let me say a word to you before——"

A gleam of shrewdness flashed through Benny Upsher's inarticulate blue eyes. "A word or two *against,* you mean? Why, it's awfully kind, but not the least earthly use. I guess I've heard all the arguments. But all I see is that hulking bully trying to do Belgium in. England's coming in, ain't she? Well, then why ain't we?"

"England? Why—why, there's no analogy——"

The young man groped for the right word. "I don't know. Maybe not. Only in tight places we always *do* seem to stand together."

"You're mad—this is not our war. Do you really want to go out and butcher people?"

"Yes—this kind of people," said Benny Upsher cheerfully. "You see, I've had all this talk from Uncle Harvey Mayhew a good many times on the way over. We came out on the same boat: he wanted me to be his private secretary at the Hague Congress. But I was pretty sure I'd have a job of my own to attend to."

Campton still contemplated him hopelessly. "Where is your uncle?" he wondered.

Benny grinned. "On his way to the Hague, I suppose."

"He ought to be here to look after you—some one ought to!"

"Then you don't see your way to getting me into George's regiment?" Benny simply replied.

An hour later Campton still seemed to see him standing there, with obstinate soft eyes repeating the same senseless question. It cost him an effort to shake off the vision.

He returned to the Crillon to collect his possessions. On his table was a telegram, and he seized it eagerly, wondering if by some mad chance George's plans were changed, if he were being sent back, if Fortin had already arranged something. . .

He tore open the message, and read: "Utica July thirty-first. No news from Benny please do all you can to facilitate his immediate return to America dreadfully anxious your cousin Madeline Upsher."

"Good Lord!" Campton groaned—"and I never even asked the boy's address!"

Book
Two

X

The war was three months old—three centuries. By virtue of some gift of adaptation which seemed forever to discredit human sensibility, people were already beginning to live into the monstrous idea of it, acquire its ways, speak its language, regard it as a thinkable, endurable, arrangeable fact; to eat it by day, and sleep on it—yes, and soundly—at night.

The war went on; life went on; Paris went on. She had had her great hour of resistance, when, alone, exposed and defenceless, she had held back the enemy and broken his strength. She had had, afterward, her hour of triumph, the hour of the Marne; then her hour of passionate and prayerful hope, when it seemed to the watching nations that the enemy was not only held back but thrust back, and victory finally in reach. That hour had passed in its turn, giving way to the grey reality of the trenches. A new speech was growing up in this new world. There were trenches now, there was a "Front"—people were beginning to talk of their sons at the front.

The first time John Campton heard the phrase it sent a shudder through him. Winter was coming on, and he was haunted by the vision of the youths out there, boys of George's age, thousands and thousands of them, exposed by day in reeking wet ditches and sleeping at night under the rain and snow. People were talking calmly of victory in the spring—the spring that was still six long months away! And meanwhile, what cold and wet, what blood and agony, what shattered bodies out on that hideous front, what shattered homes in all the lands it guarded!

Campton could bear to think of these things now. *His* son was not at the front—was safe, thank God, and likely to remain so!

During the first awful weeks of silence and uncertainty, when every morning brought news of a fresh disaster, when no letters came from the army and no private mesages could reach it—during those weeks, while Campton, like other fathers, was without news of his son, the war had been to him simply a huge featureless mass crushing him earthward, blinding him, letting him neither think nor move nor breathe.

But at last he had got permission to go to Chalons, whither Fortin, who chanced to have begun his career as a surgeon, had been hastily transferred. The physician, called from his incessant labours in a roughly-improvised operating-room, to which Campton was led between rows of stretchers laden with livid blood-splashed men, had said kindly, but with a shade of impatience, that he had not forgotten, had done what he could; that George's health did not warrant his being discharged from the army, but that he was temporarily on a staff-job at the rear, and would probably be kept there if such and such influences were brought to bear. Then, calling for hot water and fresh towels, the surgeon vanished and Campton made his way back with lowered eyes between the stretchers.

The "influences" in question were brought to bear—not without Anderson Brant's assistance—and now that George was fairly certain to be kept at clerical work a good many miles from the danger-zone Campton felt less like an ant under a landslide, and was able for the first time to think of the war as he might have thought of any other war: objectively, intellectually, almost dispassionately, as of history in the making.

It was not that he had any doubt as to the rights and wrongs of the case. The painfully preserved equilibrium of the neutrals made a pitiful show now that the monstrous facts of the first weeks were known: Germany's diplomatic perfidy, her savagery in the field, her premeditated and systematized terrorizing of the civil populations. Nothing could efface what had been done in Belgium and Luxembourg, the burning of Louvain, the bombardment of Rheims. These successive outrages had roused in Campton the same incredulous wrath as in the rest of mankind; but being of a speculative mind—and fairly sure now that George would never lie in the mud and snow with the others—he had begun to consider the landslide in its universal relations, as well as in its effects on his private ant-heap.

His son's situation, however, was still his central thought. That this lad, who was meant to have been born three thousand miles away in his own safe warless country, and who was regarded by the government of that country as having been born there, as subject to her laws and entitled to her protection—that this lad, by the most idiotic of blunders, a blunder perpetrated before he was born, should have been dragged into a conflict in which he was totally unconcerned, should become temporarily and arbitrarily the subject of a foreign state, exposed to whatever catastrophes that state might draw upon itself, this fact dawned on him that his boy's very life might hang on some tortuous secret negotiation between the cabinets of Europe.

He still refused to admit that France had any claim on George, any right to his time, to his suffering or to his life. He had argued it out a hundred times with Adele Anthony. "You say Julia and I were to blame for not going home before the boy was born—and God knows I agree with you! But suppose we'd meant to go? Suppose we'd made every arrangement, taken every precaution, as my parents did in my case, got to Havre or Cherbourg, say, and been told the steamer had broken her screw—or been prevented ourselves, at the last moment, by illness or accident, or any sudden grab of the Hand of God? You'll admit we shouldn't have been to blame for that; yet the law would have recognized no difference. George would still have found himself a French soldier on the second of last August because, by the same kind of unlucky accident, he and I were born on the wrong side of the Atlantic. And I say that's enough to prove it's an iniquitous law, a travesty of justice. Nobody's going to convince me that, because a steamer may happen to break a phlange of her screw at the wrong time, or a poor woman be frightened by a thunderstorm, France has the right to force an American boy to go and rot in the trenches."

"In the trenches—is George in the trenches?" Adele Anthony asked, raising her pale eyebrows.

"No," Campton thundered, his fist crashing down among her tea things; "and all your word-juggling isn't going to convince me that he ought to be there." He paused and stared furiously about the little lady-like drawing-room into which Miss Anthony's sharp angles were so incongruously squeezed. She made no answer, and he went on: "George looks at the thing exactly as I do."

"Has he told you so?" Miss Anthony enquired, rescuing his teacup and putting sugar into her own.

"He has told me nothing to the contrary. You don't seem to be aware that military correspondence is censored, and that a solider can't always blurt out everything he thinks."

Miss Anthony followed his glance about the room, and her eyes paused with his on her own portrait, now in the place of honour over the mantelpiece, where it hung incongruously above a menagerie of china animals and a collection of trophies for the Marne.

"I dropped in at the Luxembourg yesterday," she said. "Do you know whom I saw there? Anderson Brant. He was looking at George's portrait, and turned as red as a beet. You ought to do him a sketch of George some day—after this."

Campton's face darkened. He knew it was partly through Brant's influence that George had been detached from his regiment and given a staff job in the Argonne; but Miss Anthony's reminder annoyed him. The Brants had acted through sheer selfish cowardice, the desire to safeguard something which belonged to them, something they valued as they valued their pictures and tapestries, though of course in a greater degree; whereas he, Campton, was sustained by a principle which he could openly avow, and was ready to discuss with any one who had the leisure to listen.

He had explained all this so often to Miss Anthony that the words rose again to his lips without an effort. "If it had been a national issue I should have wanted him to be among the first: such as our having to fight Mexico, for instance——"

"Yes; or the moon. For my part, I understand Julia and Anderson better. They don't care a fig for national issues; they're just animals defending their cub."

"*Their*—thank you!" Campton exclaimed.

"Well, poor Anderson really *was* a dry-nurse to the boy. Who else was there to look after him? You were painting Spanish beauties at the time." She frowned. "Life's a puzzle. I see perfectly that if you'd let everything else go to keep George you'd never have become the great John Campton: the *real* John Campton you were meant to be. And it wouldn't have been half as satisfactory for you—or for George either. Only, in the meanwhile, somebody had to blow the child's nose, and pay his dentist and doctor; and you ought to be grateful to Anderson for doing it. Aren't there bees or ants, or something, that are kept for such purposes?"

Campton's lips were opened to reply when her face changed, and he saw that he had ceased to exist for her. He knew the reason. That look came over everybody's face nowadays at the hour when the evening paper came. The old maid-servant brought it in, and lingered to hear the *communiqué*. At that hour, everywhere over the globe, business and labour and pleasure (if it still existed) were suspended for a moment while the hearts of all men gathered themselves up in a question and prayer.

Miss Anthony sought for her *lorgnon* and failed to find it. With a shaking hand she passed the newspaper over to Campton.

"Violent enemy attacks in the region of Dixmude, Ypres, Armentières, Arras, in the Argonne, and on the advanced slopes of the Grand Couronné de Nancy, have been successfully repulsed. We have taken back the village of Soupir, near Vailly (Aisne); we have taken Maucourt and Mogeville, to the northeast of Verdun. Progress has been made in the region of Vermelles (Pas-de-Calais), south of Aix Noulette. Enemy attacks in the Hauts-de-Meuse and southeast of Saint-Mihiel have also been repulsed.

"In Poland the Austrian retreat is becoming general. The Russians are still advancing in the direction of Kielce-Sandomir and have progressed beyond the San in Galicia. Mlawa has been reoccupied, and the whole railway system of Poland is now controlled by the Russian forces."

A good day—oh, decidedly a good day. At this rate, what became of the gloomy forecasts of the people who talked of a winter in the trenches, to be followed by a spring campaign? True, the Serbian army was still retreating before superior Austrian forces—but there too the scales would soon be turned if the Russians continued to progress. That day there was hope everywhere: the old maid-servant went away smiling, and Miss Anthony poured out another cup of tea.

Campton had not lifted his eyes from the paper. Suddenly they lit on a short paragraph: "Fallen on the Field of Honour." One had got used to that with the rest; used even to the pang of reading names one knew, evoking familiar features, young faces blotted out in blood, young limbs convulsed in the fires of that hell called "the Front." But this time Campton turned pale and the paper fell to his knee.

"Fortin-Lescluze; Jean-Jacques-Marie, lieutenant of *Chasseurs à Pied,* gloriously fallen for France. . ." There followed a ringing citation.

Fortin's son, his only son, was dead.

Campton saw before him the honest *bourgeois* dining-room, so strangely out of keeping with the rest of the establishment; he saw the late August sun slanting in on the group about the table, on the ambitious and unscrupulous great man, the two quiet women hidden under his illustrious roof, and the youth who had held together these three dissimilar people, making an invisible home in the heart of all that publicity. Campton remembered his brief exchange of words with Fortin on the threshold, and the father's uncontrollable outburst: "For his mother and myself it's not a trifle—having our only son in the war."

Campton shut his eyes and leaned back, sick with the memory. This man had had a share in saving George; but his own son he could not save.

"What's the matter?" Miss Anthony asked, her hand on his arm.

Campton could not bring the name to his lips. "Nothing—nothing. Only this room's rather hot—and I must be off anyhow." He got up, escaping from her solicitude, and made his way out. He must go at once to Fortin's for news. The physician was still at Chalons; but there would surely be some one at the house, and Campton could at least leave a message and ask where to write.

Dusk had fallen. His eyes usually feasted on the beauty of the new Paris, the secret mysterious Paris of veiled lights and deserted streets; but to-night he was blind to it. He could see nothing but Fortin's face, hear nothing but his voice when he said: "Our only son in the war."

He groped along the pitch-black street for the remembered outline of the house (since no house-numbers were visible), and rang several times without result. He was just turning away when a big mud-splashed motor drove up. He noticed a soldier at the steering-wheel, then three people got out stiffly: two women smothered in crape and a haggard man in a dirty uniform. Campton stopped, and Fortin-Lescluze recognized him by the light of the motor-lamp. The four stood and looked at each other. The old mother, under her crape, appeared no bigger than a child.

"Ah—you know?" the doctor said. Campton nodded.

The father spoke in a firm voice. "It happened three days ago—at Suippes. You've seen his citation? They brought him in to me at

Chalons without a warning—and too late. I took off both legs, but gangrene had set in. Ah—if I could have got hold of one of our big surgeons. . . Yes, we're just back from the funeral. . . My mother and my wife . . . they had that comfort. . ."

The two women stood beside him like shrouded statues. Suddenly Mme. Fortin's deep voice came through the crape: "You saw him, Monsieur, that last day . . . the day you came about your own son, I think?"

"I . . . yes . . ." Campton stammered in anguish.

The physician intervened. "And, now, *ma bonne mère,* you're not to be kept standing. You're to go straight in and take your *tisane* and go to bed." He kissed his mother and pushed her into his wife's arms. "Good-bye, my dear. Take care of her."

The women vanished under the porte-cochère, and Fortin turned to the painter.

"Thank you for coming. I can't ask you in—I must go back immediately."

"Back?"

"To my work. Thank God. If it were not for that——"

He jumped into the motor, called out *"En route,"* and was absorbed into the night.

XI

Campton went home to his studio.

He still lived there, shiftlessly and uncomfortably—for Mariette had never come back from Lille. She had not come back, and there was no news of her. Lille had become a part of the "occupied provinces," from which there was no escape; and people were beginning to find out what that living burial meant.

Adele Anthony had urged Campton to go back to the hotel, but he obstinately refused. What business had he to be living in expensive hotels when, for the Lord knew how long, his means of earning a livelihood were gone, and when it was his duty to save up for George—George, who was safe, who was definitely out of danger, and whom he longed more than ever, when the war was over, to withdraw from the stifling atmosphere of his stepfather's millions?

He had been so near to having the boy to himself when the war broke out! He had almost had in sight the proud day when he should be able to say: "Look here: this is your own bank-account. Now you're independent—for God's sake stop and consider what you want to do with your life."

The war had put an end to that—but only for a time. If victory came before long, Campton's reputation would survive the eclipse, his chances of money-making would be as great as ever, and the new George, the George matured and disciplined by war, would come back with a finer sense of values, and a soul steeled against the vulgar opportunities of wealth.

Meanwhile, it behoved his father to save every penny. And the simplest way of saving was to go on camping in the studio, taking his meals at the nearest wine-shop, and entrusting his bed-making and dusting to old Mme. Lebel. In that way he could live for a long time without appreciably reducing his savings.

Mme. Lebel's daughter-in-law, Mme. Jules, who was in the Ardennes with the little girl when the war broke out, was to have replaced Mariette. But, like Mariette, Mme. Jules never arrived, and no word came from her or the child. They too were in an occupied province. So Campton jogged on without a servant. It was very uncomfortable, even for his lax standards; but the dread of letting a stranger loose in the studio made him prefer to put up with Mme. Lebel's intermittent services.

So far she had borne up bravely. Her orphan grandsons were all at the front (how that word had insinuated itself into the language!) but she continued to have fairly frequent reassuring news of them. The *Chasseur Alpin,* slightly wounded in Alsace, was safe in hospital; and the others were well, and wrote cheerfully. Her son Jules, the cabinet-maker, was guarding a bridge at St. Cloud, and came in regularly to see her; but Campton noticed that it was about him that she seemed most anxious.

He was a silent industrious man, who had worked hard to support his orphaned nephews and his mother, and had married in middle age, only four or five years before the war, when the lads could shift for themselves, and his own situation was secure enough to permit the luxury of a wife and baby.

Mme. Jules had waited patiently for him, though she had other chances; and finally they had married and the baby had been born, and blossomed into one of those finished little Frenchwomen who, at four or five, seem already to be musing on the great central problems of love and thrift. The parents used to bring the child to see Campton, and he had made a celebrated sketch of her, in her Sunday bonnet, with little earrings and a wise smile. And these two, mother and child, had disappeared on the second of August as completely as if the earth had opened and swallowed them.

As Campton entered he glanced at the old woman's den, saw that it was empty, and said to himself: "She's at St. Cloud again." For he knew that she seized every chance of being with her eldest.

He unlocked his door and felt his way into the dark studio. Mme. Lebel might at least have made up the fire! Campton lit the lamp, found some wood, and knelt down stiffly by the stove. Really, life was getting too uncomfortable. . .

He was trying to coax a flame when the door opened and he heard Mme. Lebel.

"Really, you know——" he turned to rebuke her; but the words died on his lips. She stood before him, taking no notice; then her shapeless black figure doubled up, and she sank down into his own armchair. Mme. Lebel, who, even when he offered her a seat, never did more than rest respectful knuckles on its back!

"What's the matter? What's wrong?" he exclaimed.

She lifted her aged face. "Monsieur, I came about your fire; but I am too unhappy. I have more than I can bear." She fumbled vainly for a handkerchief, and wiped away her tears with the back of her old laborious hand.

"Jules has enlisted, Monsieur; enlisted in the infantry. He has left for the front without telling me."

"Good Lord. Enlisted? At his age—is he crazy?"

"No, Monsieur. But the little girl—he's had news——"

She waited to steady her voice, and then fishing in another slit of her multiple skirts, pulled out a letter. "I got that at midday. I hurried to St. Cloud—but he left yesterday."

The letter was grim reading. The poor father had accidentally run across an escaped prisoner who had regained the French lines near the village where Mme. Jules and the child were staying. The man, who knew the wife's family, had been charged by them with a message to the effect that Mme. Jules, who was a proud woman, had got into trouble with the authorities, and been sent off to a German prison on the charge of spying. The poor little girl had cried and clung to her mother, and had been so savagely pushed aside by the officer who made the arrest that she had fallen on the stone steps of the "Kommandantur" and fractured her skull. The fugitive reported her as still alive, but unconscious, and dying.

Jules Lebel had received this news the previous day; and within twenty-four hours he was at the front. Guard a bridge at St. Cloud after that? All he asked was to kill and be killed. He knew the name and the regiment of the officer who had denounced his wife. "If I live long enough I shall run the swine down," he wrote. "If not, I'll kill as many of his kind as God lets me."

Mme. Lebel sat silent, her head bowed on her hands; and Campton stood and watched her. Presently she got up, passed the back of her hand across her eyes, and said: "The room is cold. I'll fetch some coal."

Campton protested. "No, no, Mme Lebel. Don't worry about me.

Make yourself something warm to drink, and try to sleep——"

"Oh, Monsieur, thank God for the work! If it were not for that——" she said, in the same words as the physician.

She hobbled away, and presently he heard her bumping up again with the coal.

When his fire was started, and the curtains drawn, and she had left him, the painter sat down and looked about the studio. Bare and untidy as it was, he did not find the sight unpleasant: he was used to it, and being used to things seemed to him the first requisite of comfort. But to-night his thoughts were elsewhere: he saw neither the tattered tapestries with their huge heroes and kings, nor the blotched walls hung with pictures, nor the canvases stacked against the chair-legs, nor the long littered table at which he wrote and ate and mixed his colours. At one moment he was with Fortin-Lescluze, speeding through the night toward fresh scenes of death; at another, in the *loge* downstairs, where Mme. Lebel, her day's work done, would no doubt sid down as usual by her smoky lamp and go on with her sewing. "Thank God for the work——" they had both said.

And here Campton sat with idle hands, and did nothing——

It was not exactly his fault. What was there for a portrait-painter to do? He was not a portrait-painter only, and on his brief trip to Chalons some of the scenes by the way—gaunt unshorn faces of territorials at railway bridges, soldiers grouped about a provision-lorry, a mud-splashed company returning to the rear, a long grey train of "seventy-fives" ploughing forward through the rain—at these sights the old graphic instinct had stirred in him. But the approaches of the front were sternly forbidden to civilians, and especially to neutrals (Campton was beginning to wince at the word); he himself, who had been taken to Chalons by a high official of the Army Medical Board, had been given only time enough for his interview with Fortin, and brought back to Paris the same night. If ever there came a time for art to interpret the war, as Raffet, for instance, had interpreted Napoleon's campaigns, the day was not yet; the world in which men lived at present was one in which the word "art" had lost its meaning.

And what was Campton, what had he ever been, but an artist? . . . A father; yes, he had waked up to the practice of that other art, he was learning to be a father. And now, at a stroke, his only two reasons for living were gone: since the second of August he had had no portraits to paint, no son to guide and to companion.

Other people, he knew, had found jobs: most of his friends had been drawn into some form of war-work. Dastrey, after vain attempts to enlist, thwarted by an untimely sciatica, had found a post near the front, on the staff of a Red Cross Ambulance. Adele Anthony was working eight or nine hours a day in a Depot which distributed food and clothing to refugees from the invaded provinces; and Mrs. Brant's name figured on the committees of most of the newly-organized war charities. Among Campton's other friends many had accepted humbler tasks. Some devoted their time to listing and packing hospital supplies, keeping accounts in ambulance offices, sorting out refugees at the railway-stations, and telling them where to go for food and help; still others spent their days, and sometimes their nights, at the bitter-cold suburban sidings where the long train-loads of wounded stopped on the way to the hospitals of the interior. There was enough misery and confusion at the rear for every civilian volunteer to find his task.

Among them all, Campton could not see his place. His lameness put him at a disadvantage, since taxicabs were few, and it was difficult for him to travel in the crowded métro. He had no head for figures, and would have thrown the best-kept accounts into confusion; he could not climb steep stairs to seek out refugees, nor should he have known what to say to them when he reached their attics. And so it would have been at the railway canteens; he choked with rage and commiseration at all the suffering about him, but found no word to cheer the sufferers.

Secretly, too, he feared the demands that would be made on him if he once let himself be drawn into the network of war charities. Tiresome women would come and beg for money, or for pictures for bazaars: they were already getting up bazaars.

Money he could not spare, since it was his duty to save it for George; and as for pictures—why, there were a few sketches he might give, but here again he was checked by his fear of establishing a precedent. He had seen in the papers that the English painters were already giving blank canvases to be sold by auction to millionaires in quest of a portrait. But that form of philanthropy would lead to his having to paint all the unpaintable people who had been trying to bribe a picture out of him since his sudden celebrity. No artist had a right to cheapen his art in that way: it could only result in his turning out work that would injure his reputation and reduce his sales after the war.

So far, Campton had not been troubled by many appeals for help; but that was probably because he had kept out of sight, and thrown into the fire the letters of the few ladies who had begged a sketch for their sales, or his name for their committees.

One appeal, however, he had not been able to avoid. About two months earlier he had had a visit from George's friend Boylston, the youth he had met at Dastrey's dinner the night before war was declared. In the interval he had entirely forgotten Boylston; but as soon as he saw the fat brown young man with a twinkle in his eyes and his hair, Campton recalled him, and held out a cordial hand. Had not George said the Boylston was the best fellow he knew?

Boylston seemed much impressed by the honour of waiting on the great man. In spite of his cool twinkling air he was evidently full of reverence for the things and people he esteemed, and Campton's welcome sent the blood up to the edge of his tight curls. It also gave him courage to explain his visit.

He had come to beg Campton to accept the chairmanship of the American Committee of "The Friends of French Art," an international group of painters who proposed to raise funds for the families of mobilised artists. The American group would naturally be the most active, since Americans had, in larger numbers than any other foreigners, sought artistic training in France; and all the members agreed that Campton's name must figure at their head. But Campton was known to be inaccessible, and the committee, aware that Boylston was a friend of George's, had asked him to transmit their request.

"You see, sir, nobody else represents. . ."

Campton thought as seldom as possible of what followed: he hated the part he had played. But, after all, what else could he have done? Everything in him recoiled from what acceptance would bring with it: publicity, committee meetings, speechifying, writing letters, seeing troublesome visitors, hearing harrowing stories, asking people for money—above all, having to give his own; a great deal of his own.

He stood before the young man, abject, irresolute, chinking a bunch of keys in his trouser-pocket, and remembering afterward that the chink must have sounded as if it were full of money. He remembered too, oddly enough, that as his own embarrassment increased Boylston's vanished. It was as though the modest youth, taking his host's measure, had reluctantly found him wanting, and from that moment had felt less in awe of his genius. Illogical, of course, and unfair—but there it was.

The talk had ended by Campton's refusing the chairmanship, but agreeing to let his name figure on the list of honorary members, where he hoped it would be overshadowed by rival glories. And, having reached this conclusion, he had limped to his desk, produced a handful of notes, and after a moment's hesitation held out two hundred francs with the stereotyped: "Sorry I can't make it more. . ."

He had meant it to be two hundred and fifty; but, with his usual luck, all his fumbling had failed to produce a fifty-franc note; and he could hardly ask Boylston to "make the change."

On the threshold the young man paused to ask for the last news of George; and on Campton's assuring him that it was excellent, added, with evident sincerity: "Still hung up on that beastly staff-job? I do call that hard luck——" And now, of all the unpleasant memories of the visit, that phrase kept the sharpest sting.

Was it in fact hard luck? And did George himself think so? There was nothing in his letters to show it. He seemed to have undergone no change of view as to his own relation to the war; he had shown no desire to "be in it," as that mad young Upsher said.

For the first time since he had seen George's train pull out of the Gare de l'Est Campton found himself wondering at the perfection of his son's moral balance. So many thing had happened since; war had turned out to be so immeasurably more hideous and abominable than those who most abhorred war had dreamed it could be; the issues at stake had become so glaringly plain, right and wrong, honour and dishonour, humanity and savagery faced each other so squarely across the trenches, that it seemed strange to Campton that his boy, so eager, so impressionable, so quick on the uptake, should not have felt some such burst of wrath as had driven even poor Jules Lebel into the conflict.

The comparison, of course, was absurd. Lebel had been parted from his dearest, his wife dragged to prison, his child virtually murdered: any man, in his place, must have felt the blind impulse to kill. But what was Lebel's private plight but a symbol of the larger wrong? This war could no longer be compared to other wars: Germany was conducting it on methods that civilization had made men forget. The occupation of Luxembourg; the systematic destruction of Belgium; the savage treatment of the people of the invaded regions; the outrages of Louvain and Rheims and Ypres; the voice with which these offences cried to heaven had waked the indignation of humanity. Yet George, in daily contact with all this woe and ruin, seemed as unmoved as though he had been behind a desk in the New York office of Bullard and Brant.

If there were any change in his letters it was rather that they were more indifferent. His reports of himself became drier, more stereotyped, his comments on the situation fewer: he seemed to have been subdued to the hideous business he worked in. It was true that his letters had never been expressive: his individuality seemed to dry up in contact with pen and paper. It was true also that letters from the front were severely censored, and that it would have been foolish to put in them anything likely to prevent their delivery. But George had managed to send several notes by hand, and these were as colourless as the others; and so were his letters to his mother, which Mrs. Brant always sent to Miss Anthony, who privately passed them on to Campton.

Besides, there were other means of comparison. People with sons at the front were beginning to hand about copies of their letters; a few passages, strangely moving and beautiful, had found their way into the papers. George, God be praised, was not at the front; but he was in the war zone, far nearer the sights and sounds of death than his father, and he had comrades and friends in the trenches. Strange that what he wrote was still so cold to the touch. . .

"It's the scientific mind, I suppose," Campton reflected. "These youngsters are all rather like beautifully made machines. . ." Yet it had never before struck him that his son was like a beautifully made machine.

He remembered that he had not dined, and got up wearily. As he passed out he noticed on a pile of letters and papers a brand-new card: he could always tell the new cards by their whiteness, which twenty-four hours of studio-dust turned to grey.

Campton held the card to the light. It was large and glossy, a beautiful thick pre-war card; and on it was engraved:

HARVEY MAYHEW

Délégué des Etats Unis au Congrès de la Paix

with a pen-stroke through the lower line. Beneath was written an imperative "p.t.o."; and reversing the card, Campton read, in an agitated hand: "Must see you at once. Call up Nouveau Luxe"; and, lower down: "Excuse ridiculous card. Impossible get others under six weeks."

So Mayhew had turned up! Well, it was a good thing: perhaps he might bring news of that mad Benny Upsher whose doings had caused Campton so much trouble in the early days that he could never recall the boy's obstinate rosy face without a stir of irritation.

"I want to be *in* this thing——" Well, young Upsher had apparently been in it with a vengeance; but what he had cost Campton in cables to his distracted family, and in weary pilgrimages to the War Office, the American Embassy, the Consulate, the Prefecture of Police, and diverse other supposed sources of information, the painter meant some day to tell his young relative in no measured terms. That is, if the chance ever presented itself; for, since he had left the studio that morning four months ago, Benny had so completely vanished that Campton sometimes wondered, with a little shiver, if they were ever likely to exchange words again in this world.

"Mayhew will know; he wants to tell me about the boy, I suppose," he mused.

Harvey Mayhew—Harvey Mayhew with a pen-stroke through the title which, so short a time since, it had been his chief ambition to display on his cards! No wonder it embarrassed him now. But where on earth had he been all this time? As Campton pondered on the card a memory flashed out. Mayhew? Mayhew? Why, wasn't it Mayhew who had waylaid him in the Crillon a few hours before war was declared, to ask his advice about the safest way of travelling to the Hague? And hadn't he, Campton, in all good faith, counselled him to go by Luxembourg "in order to be out of the way of trouble"?

The remembrance swept away the painter's sombre thoughts, and he burst into a laugh that woke the echoes of the studio.

XII

Not having it in his power to call up his cousin on the telephone, Campton went the next morning to the Nouveau Luxe.

It was the first time that he had entered the famous hotel since the beginning of the war; and at sight of the long hall his heart sank as it used to whenever some untoward necessity forced him to run its deadly blockade.

But the hall was empty when he entered, empty not only of the brilliant beings who filled his soul with such dismay, but also of the porters, footmen and lift-boys who, even in its unfrequented hours, lent it the lustre of their liveries.

A tired concierge sat at the desk and near the door a boy scout, coiling his bare legs about a high stool, raised his head languidly from his book. But for these two, the world of the Nouveau Luxe had disappeared.

As the lift was not running there was nothing to disturb their meditations; and when Campton had learned that Mr. Mayhew would receive him he started alone up the deserted stairs.

Only a few dusty trunks remained in the corridors where luggage used to be piled as high as in the passages of the great liners on sailing-day; and instead of the murmur of ladies'-maids' skirts, and explosions of laughter behind glazed service-doors, the swish of a charwoman's mop alone broke the silence.

"After all," Campton thought, "if war didn't kill people how much pleasanter it might make the world!"

This was evidently not the opinion of Mr. Harvey Mayhew, whom he found agitatedly pacing a large room hung in shrimp-pink brocade, which opened on a vista of turquoise tiling and porcelain tub.

Mr. Mayhew's round countenance, composed of the same simple curves as his nephew's, had undergone a remarkable change. He was still round, but he was ravaged. His fringe of hair had grown greyer, and there were crow's-feet about his blue eyes, and wrathful corrugations in his benignant forehead.

He seized Campton's hands and glared at him through indignant eye-glasses.

"My dear fellow, I looked you up as soon as I arrived. I need you—we all need you—we need your powerful influence and your world-wide celebrity. Campton, the day for words has gone by. We must *act!*"

Campton let himself down into an armchair. No verb in the language terrified him as much as that which his cousin had flung at him. He gazed at the ex-Delegate with dismay. "I didn't know you were here. Where have you come from?" he asked.

Mr. Mayhew, resting a manicured hand on the edge of a gilt table, looked down awfully on him.

"I come," he said, "from a German prison."

"Good Lord—*you?*" Campton gasped.

He continued to gaze at his cousin with terror, but of a new kind. Here at last was someone who had actually been in the jaws of the monster, who had seen, heard, suffered—a witness who could speak of that which he knew! No wonder Mr. Mayhew took himself seriously— at last he had something to be serious about! Campton stared at him as if he had risen from the dead.

Mr. Mayhew cleared his throat and went on: "You may remember our meeting at the Crillon—on the 31st of last July it was—and my asking you the best way of getting to the Hague, in view of impending events. At that time" (his voice took a note of irony) "I was a Delegate to the Peace Congress at the Hague, and conceived it to be my duty to carry out my mandate at whatever personal risk. You advised me—as you may also remember—in order to be out of the way of trouble, to travel by Luxembourg," (Campton stirred uneasily). "I followed your advice; and, not being able to go by train, I managed, with considerable difficulty, to get permission to travel by motor. I reached Luxembourg as the German army entered it—the next day I was in a German prison."

The next day! Then this pink-and-white man who stood there with his rimless eye-glasses and neatly trimmed hair, and his shining nails reflected in the plate glass of the table-top, this perfectly typical, usual sort of harmless rich American, had been for four months in the depths of the abyss that men were beginning to sound with fearful hearts!

"It is a simple miracle," said Mr. Mayhew, "that I was not shot as a spy."

Campton's voice choked in his throat. "Where were you imprisoned?"

"The first night, in the Police commissariat, with common thieves and vagabonds—with—" Mr. Mayhew lowered his voice and his eyes: "With prostitutes, Campton. . ."

He waited for this to take effect, and continued: "The next day, in consequence of the energetic intervention of our consul—who behaved extremely well, as I have taken care to let them know in Washington—I was sent back to my hotel on parole, and kept there, kept there, Campton—*I,* the official representative of a friendly country—

under strict police surveillance, like . . . like an unfortunate woman . . . for eight days: a week and one day over!"

Mr. Mayhew sank into a chair and passed a scented handkerchief across his forehead. "When I was finally released I was without money, without luggage, without my motor or my wretched chauffeur—a Frenchman, who had been instantly carried off to Germany. In this state of destitution, and without an apology, I was shipped to Rotterdam and put on a steamer sailing for America." He wiped his forehead again, and the corners of his agitated lips. "Peace, Campton—*Peace?* When I think that I believed in a thing called Peace! That I left Utica—always a difficult undertaking for me—because I deemed it my duty, in the interests of *Peace*," (the word became a hiss) "to travel to the other side of the world, and use the weight of my influence and my experience in such a cause!"

He clenched his fist and shook it in the face of an invisible foe.

"My influence, if I have any; my experience—ha, I *have* had experience now, Campton! And, my God, sir, they shall both be used till my last breath to show up these people, to proclaim to the world what they really are, to rouse public opinion in America against a nation of savages who ought to be hunted off the face of the globe like vermin—like the vermin in their own prison cells! Campton—if I may say so without profanity—I come to bring not Peace but a Sword!"

It was some time before the flood of Mr. Mayhew's wrath subsided, or before there floated up from its agitated depths some fragments of his subsequent history and present intentions. Eventually, however, Campton gathered that after a short sojourn in America, where he found opinion too lukewarm for him, he had come back to Europe to collect the experiences of other victims of German savagery. Mr. Mayhew, in short, meant to devote himself to Atrocities; and he had sought out Campton to ask his help, and especially to be put in contact with persons engaged in refugee-work, and likely to have come across flagrant offences against the law of nations.

It was easy to comply with the latter request. Campton scribbled a message to Adele Anthony at her refugee Depot; and he undertook also to find out from what officials Mr. Mayhew might obtain leave to visit the front.

"I know it's difficult——" he began; but Mr. Mayhew laughed. "I am here to surmount difficulties—after what I've been through!"

It was not until then that Mr. Mayhew found time to answer an enquiry about his nephew.

"Benny Upsher? Ha—I'm proud of Benny! He's a hero, that nephew of mine—he was always my favourite."

He went on to say that the youth, having failed to enlist in the French army, had managed to get back to England, and there, passing himself off as a Canadian ("Born at Murray Bay, sir—wasn't it lucky?") had joined an English regiment, and, after three months' training, was now on his way to the front. His parents had made a great outcry—moved heaven and earth for news of him—but the boy had covered up his tracks so cleverly that they had had no word till he was starting for Boulogne with his draft. Rather high-handed—and poor Madeline had nearly gone out of her mind; but Mr. Mayhew confessed he had no patience with such feminine weakness. "Benny's a man, and must act as a man. That boy, Campton, saw things as they were from the first."

Campton took leave, dazed and crushed by the conversation. It was all one to him if Harvey Mayhew chose to call on America to avenge his wrongs; Campton himself was beginning to wish that his country would wake up to what was going on in the world; but that he, Campton, should be drawn into the affair, should have to write letters, accompany the ex-Delegate to Embassies and Red Crosses, languish with him in ministerial antechambers, and be deafened with appeals to his own celebrity and efficiency; that he should have ascribed to himself that mysterious gift of "knowing the ropes" in which his whole blundering career had proved him to be cruelly lacking: this was so dreadful to him as to obscure every other question.

"Thank the Lord," he muttered, "I haven't got the telephone anyhow!"

He glanced cautiously down the wide stairs of the hotel to assure himself of a safe retreat; but in the hall an appealing voice detained him.

"Dear Master! Dear great Master! I've been lying in wait for you!"

A Red Cross nurse advanced: not the majestic figure of the Crimean legend, but the new version evolved in the rue de la Paix: short skirts, long ankles, pearls and curls. The face under the coif was young, wistful, haggard with the perpetual hurry of the aimless. Where had he seen those tragic eyes, so full of questions and so invariably uninterested in the answers?

"I'm Madge Talkett—I saw you at—I saw you the day war was declared," the young lady corrected herself. Campton remembered their meeting at Mrs. Brant's, and was grateful for her evident embarrassment. So few of the new generation seemed aware that there were any privacies left to respect! He looked at Mrs. Talkett more kindly.

"You *must* come," she continued, laying her hand on his arm (her imperatives were always in italics).

"Just a step from here—to my hospital. There's someone asking for you."

"For me? Someone wounded?" What if it were Benny Upsher? A cold fear broke over Campton.

"Someone dying," Mrs. Talkett said. "Oh, nobody you know—a poor young French soldier. He was brought here two days ago . . . and he keeps on repeating your name. . ."

"My name? Why my name?"

"We don't know. We don't think he knows you . . . but he's shot to pieces and half delirious. He's a painter, and he's seen pictures of yours, and keeps talking about them, and saying he wants you to look at his. . . You *will* come? It's just next door, you know."

He did not know—having carefully avoided all knowledge of hospitals in his dread of being drawn into war-work, and his horror of coming as a mere spectator to gaze on agony he could neither comfort nor relieve. Hospitals were for surgeons and women; if he had been rich he would have given big sums to aid them; being unable to do even that, he preferred to keep aloof.

He followed Mrs. Talkett out of the hotel and around the corner. The door of another hotel, with a big Red Cross above it, admitted them to a marble vestibule full of the cold smell of disinfectants. An orderly sat reading a newspaper behind the desk, and nurses whisked backward and forward with trays and pails. A lady with a bunch of flowers came down the stairs drying her eyes.

Campton's whole being recoiled from what awaited him. Since the poor youth was delirious, what was the use of seeing him? But women took a morbid pleasure in making one do things that were useless!

On an upper floor they paused at a door where there was a moment's parleying.

"Come," Mrs. Talkett said; "he's a little better."

The room contained two beds. In one lay a haggard elderly man with closed eyes and lips drawn back from his clenched teeth. His legs stirred restlessly, and one of his arms was in a lifted sling attached to a horrible kind of gallows above the bed. It reminded Campton of Juan de Borgoña's pictures of the Inquisition, in the Prado.

"Oh, *he's* all right; he'll get well. It's the other. . ."

The other lay quietly in his bed. No gallows overhung him, no visible bandaging showed his wound. There was a flush on his young cheeks and his eyes looked out, large and steady, from their hollow brows. But he was the one who would not get well.

Mrs. Talkett bent over him: her voice was sweet when it was lowered.

"I've kept my promise. Here he is."

The eyes turned in the lad's immovable head, and he and Campton looked at each other. The painter had never seen the face before him: a sharp irregular face, prematurely hollowed by pain, with thick chestnut hair tumbled above the forehead.

"It's you, Master!" the boy said.

Campton sat down beside him. "How did you know? Have you seen me before?"

"Once—at one of your exhibitions." He paused and drew a hard breath. "But the first thing was the portrait at the Luxembourg . . . your son. . ."

"Ah, you look like him!" Campton broke out.

The eyes of the young soldier lit up. "Do I? . . . Someone told me he was your son. I went home from seeing that and began to paint. After the war, would you let me come and work with you? My things . . . wait . . . I'll show you my things first." He tried to raise himself. Mrs. Talkett slipped her arm under his shoulders, and resting against her he lifted his hand and pointed to the bare wall facing him.

"There—there; you see? Look for yourself. The brushwork . . . not too bad, eh? I was . . . getting it. . . There, that heard of my grandfather, eh? And my lame sister. . . Oh, I'm young . . ." he smiled . . . "never had any models. . . But after the war you'll see. . ."

Mrs. Talkett let him down again, and feverishly, vehemently, he began to describe, one by one, and over and over again, the pictures he saw on the naked wall in front of him.

A nurse had slipped in, and Mrs. Talkett signed to Campton to follow her out. The boy seemed aware that the painter was going, and interrupted his enumeration to say: "As soon as the war's over you'll let me come?"

"Of course I will," Campton promised.

In the passage he asked "Can nothing save him? Has everything possible been done?"

"Everything. We're all so fond of him—the biggest surgeons have seen him. It seems he had great talent—but he never could afford models, so he has painted his family over and over again." Mrs. Talkett looked at Campton with a good deal of feeling in her changing eyes. "You see, it *did* help, your coming. I know you thought it tiresome of me to insist." She led him downstairs and into the office, where a lame officer with the Croix de Guerre sat at the desk. The officer wrote out the young soldier's name—René Davril—and his family's address.

"They're quite destitute, Monsieur. An old infirm grandfather, a lame sister who taught music, a widowed mother and several younger children. . ."

"I'll come back, I'll come back," Campton again promised as he parted from Mrs. Talkett.

He had not thought it possible that he would ever feel so kindly toward her as at that moment. And then, a second later, she nearly spoiled it by saying: "Dear Master—you see the penalty of greatness!"

The name of René Davril was with Campton all day. The boy had believed in him—his eyes had been opened by the sight of George's portrait! And now, in a day or two more, he would be filling a three-

by-six ditch in a crowded graveyard. At twenty—and with eyes like
George's.

What could Campton do? No one was less visited by happy inspira-
tions; the "little acts of kindness" recommended to his pious infancy
had always seemed to him far harder to think of than to perform. But
now some instinct carried him straight to the corner of his studio
where he remembered having shoved out of sight a half-finished
study for George's portrait. He found it, examined it critically, scribbled his signature in one corner, and set out with it for the hospital.
On the way he had to stop at the Ministry of War on Mayhew's tiresome business, and was delayed there till too late to proceed with his
errand before luncheon. But in the afternoon he passed in again
through the revolving plate glass, and sent up his name. Mrs. Talkett
was not there, but a nurse came down, to whom, with embarrassment, he explained himself.

"Poor little Davril? Yes—he's still alive. Will you come up? His family are with him."

Campton shook his head and held out the parcel. "It's a picture he
wanted——"

The nurse promised it should be given. She looked at Campton
with a vague benevolence, having evidently never heard his name;
and the painter turned away with a cowardly sense that he ought to
have taken the picture up himself. But to see the death-change on a
face so like his son's, and its look reflected in other anguished faces,
was more than he could endure. He turned away.

The next morning Mrs. Talkett wrote that René Davril was better,
that the fever had dropped, and that he was lying quietly looking at
the sketch. "The only thing that troubles him is that he realized now
that you have not seen his pictures. But he is very happy, and blesses
you for your goodness."

His goodness! Campton, staring at the letter, could only curse himself for his stupidity. He saw now that the one thing which might
have comforted the poor lad would have been to have his own pictures
seen and judged; and that one thing, he, Campton, so many years
vainly athirst for the approbation of the men he revered—that one
thing he had never thought of doing! The only way of atoning for his
negligence was instantly to go out to the suburb where the Davril
family lived. Campton, without a scruple, abandoned Mr. Mayhew,
with whom he had an appointment at the Embassy and another at
the War Office, and devoted the rest of the day to the expedition. It
was after six when he reached the hospital again; and when Mrs.
Talkett came down he went up to her impetuously.

"Well—I've seen them; I've seen his pictures, and he's right.
They're astonishing! Awkward, still, and hesitating; but with such a

sense of air and mass. He'll do things—May I go up and tell him?"
He broke off and looked at her.

"He died an hour ago. If only you'd seen them yesterday!" she said.

XIII

The killing of René Davril seemed to Campton one of the most senseless crimes the war had yet perpetrated. It brought home to him, far more vividly than the distant death of poor Jean Fortin, what an incalculable sum of gifts and virtues went to make up the monster's daily meal.

"Ah, you want genius, do you? Mere youth's not enough . . . and health and gaiety and courage; you want brains in the bud, imagination and poetry, ideas all folded up in their sheath! It takes that, does it, to temp your jaded appetite?" He was reminded of the rich vulgarians who will eat only things out of season. "That's what war is like," he muttered savagely to himself.

The next morning he went to the funeral with Mrs. Talkett—between whom and himself the tragic episode had created a sort of improvised intimacy—walking at her side through the November rain, behind the poor hearse with the tricolour over it.

At the church, while the few mourners shivered in a damp side chapel, he had time to study the family: a poor sobbing mother, two anæmic little girls, and the lame sister who was musical—a piteous group, smelling of poverty and tears. Behind them, to his surprise, he saw the curly brown head and short-sighted eyes of Boylston. Campton wondered at the latter's presence; then he remembered "The Friends of French Art," and concluded that the association had probably been interested in poor Davril.

With some difficulty he escaped from the thanks of the mother and sisters, and picked up a taxi to take Mrs. Talkett home.

"No—back to the hospital," she said. "A lot of bad cases have come in, and I'm on duty again all day." She spoke as if it were the most natural thing in the world; and he shuddered at the serenity with which women endure the unendurable.

At the hospital he followed her in. The Davril family, she told him, had insisted that they had no claim on his picture, and that it must be returned to him. Mrs. Talkett went up to fetch it; and Campton waited in one of the drawing-rooms. A step sounded behind him, and another nurse came in—but was it a nurse, or some haloed nun from an Umbrian triptych, her pure oval framed in white, her long fingers clasping a book and lily?

"Mme. de Dolmetsch!" he cried; and thought: "A new face again—what an artist!"

She seized his hands.

"I heard from dear Madge Talkett that you were here, and I've asked her to leave us together." She looked at him with ravaged eyes, as if just risen from a penitential vigil.

"Come, please, into my little office: you didn't know that I was the *Infirmière-Major?* My dear friend, what upheavals, what cataclysms! I see no one now: all my days and nights are given to my soldiers."

She glided ahead on noiseless sandals to a little room where a bowl of jade filled with gardenias, and a tortoise-shell box of gold-tipped cigarettes, stood on a desk among torn and discoloured *livrets militaires.* The room was empty, and Mme. de Dolmetsch, closing the door, drew Campton to a seat at her side. So close to her, he saw that the perfect lines of her face were flawed by marks of suffering. "The woman really has a heart," he thought, "or the war couldn't have made her so much handsomer."

Mme. de Dolmetsch leaned closer: a breath of incense floated from her conventual draperies.

"I know why you came," she continued; "you were good to that poor little Davril." She clutched Campton suddenly with a blue-veined hand. "My dear friend, can anything justify such horrors? Isn't it abominable that boys like that should be murdered? That some senile old beast of a diplomatist should decree, after a good dinner, that all we love best must be offered up?" She caught his hands again, her liturgical scent enveloping him. "Campton, I know you feel as I do." She paused, pressing his fingers hard, her beautiful mouth trembling. "For God's sake tell me," she implored, "how you've managed to keep your son from the front!"

Campton drew away, red and inarticulate. "I—my son? Those things depend on the authorities. My boy's health . . ." he stammered.

"Yes, yes; I know. Your George is delicate. But so is my Ladislas—dreadfully. The lungs too. I've trembled for him for so long; and now, at any moment . . ." Two tears gathered on her long lashes and rolled down . . . "at any moment he may be taken from the War Office, where he's doing invaluable work, and forced into all that blood and horror; he may be brought back to me like those poor creatures up-stairs, who are hardly men any longer . . . mere vivisected animals, without eyes, without faces." She lowered her voice and drew her lids together, so that her very eyes seemed to be whispering. "Ladislas has enemies who are jealous of him (I could give you their names); at the moment someone who ought to be at the front is intriguing to turn him out and get his place. Oh, Campton, you've known their terror—you know what one's nights are like! Have pity—tell me how you managed!"

He had no idea of what he answered, or how he finally got away.

Everything that was dearest to him, the thought of George, the vision of the lad dying upstairs, was defiled by this monstrous coupling of their names with that of the supple middle-aged adventurer safe in his spotless uniform at the War Office. And beneath the boiling-up of Campton's disgust a new fear lifted its head. How did Mme. de Dolmetsch know about George? And what did she know? Evidently there had been foolish talk somewhere. Perhaps it was Mrs. Brant—or perhaps Fortin himself. All these great doctors forgot the professional secret with some one woman, if not with many. Had not Fortin revealed to his own wife the reason of Campton's precipitate visit? The painter escaped from Mme. de Dolmetsch's scented lair, and from the sights and sounds of the hospital, in a state of such perturbation that for a while he stood in the street wondering where he had meant to go next.

He had his own reasons for agreeing to the Davrils' suggestion that the picture should be returned to him; and presently these reasons came back. "They'd never dare to sell it themselves; but why shouldn't I sell it for them?" he had thought, remembering their denuded rooms, and the rusty smell of the women's mourning. It cost him a pang to part with a study of his boy; but he was in a superstitious and expiatory mood, and eager to act on it.

He remembered having been told by Boylston that "The Friends of French Art" had their office in the Palais Royal, and he made his way through the deserted arcades to the door of a once-famous restaurant.

Behind the plate-glass windows young women with rolled-up sleeves and straw in their hair were delving in packing-cases, while, divided from them by an improvised partition, another group were busy piling on the cloak-room shelves garments such as had never before dishonoured them.

Campton stood fascinated by the sight of the things these young women were sorting: pink silk combinations, sporting ulsters in glaring black and white checks, straw hats wreathed with last summer's sunburnt flowers, high-heeled satin shoes split on the instep, and fringed and bugled garments that suggested obsolete names like "dolman" and "mantle," and looked like the costumes dug out of a country-house attic by amateurs preparing to play "Caste." Was it possible that "The Friends of French Art" proposed to clothe the families of fallen artists in these prehistoric properties?

Boylston appeared, flushed and delighted (and with straw in his hair also), and led his visitor up a corkscrew stair. They passed a room where a row of people in shabby mourning like that of the Davril family sat on restaurant chairs before a *caissière*'s desk; and at the desk Campton saw Miss Anthony, her veil pushed back and a card-catalogue at her elbow, listening to a young woman who was dramatically stating her case.

Boylston saw Campton's surprise, and said: "Yes, we're desperately short-handed, and Miss Anthony has deserted her refugees for a day or two to help me to straighten things out."

His own office was in a faded *cabinet particulier* where the dinner-table had been turned into a desk, and the weak-springed divan was weighed down under suits of ready-made clothes bearing the label of a wholesale clothier.

"These are the things we really give them; but they cost a lost of money to buy," Boylston explained. On the divan sat a handsomely dressed elderly lady with a long emaciated face and red eyes, who rose as they entered. Boylston spoke to her in an undertone and led her into another *cabinet,* where Campton saw her tragic figure sink down on the sofa, under a glass scrawled with amorous couplets.

"That was Mme. Beausite. . . You didn't recognize her? Poor thing! Her youngest boy is blind: his eyes were put out by a shell. She is very unhappy, and she comes here and helps now and then. Beausite? Oh no, we never see *him*. He's only our Honorary President."

Boylston, obviously spoke without afterthought; but Campton felt the sting. He too was on the honorary committee.

"Poor woman! What? The young fellow who did Cubist things? I hadn't heard. . ." He remembered the cruel rumour that Beausite, when his glory began to wane, had encouraged his three sons in three different lines of art, so that there might always be a Beausite in the fashion. . . "You must have to listen to pretty ghastly stories here," he said.

The young man nodded, and Campton, with less embarrassment than he had expected, set forth his errand. In that atmosphere it seemed natural to be planning ways of relieving misery, and Boylston at once put him at his ease by looking pleased but not surprised.

"You mean to sell the sketch, sir? That will put the Davrils out of anxiety for a long time; and they're in a bad way, as you saw." Boylston undid the parcel, with a respectful: "May I?" and put the canvas on a chair. He gazed at it for a few moments, the blood rising sensitively over his face till it reached his tight ridge of hair. Campton remembered what George had said of his friend's silent admirations; he was glad the young man did not speak.

When he did, it was to say with a businesslike accent: "We're trying to get up an auction of pictures and sketches—and if we could lead off with this. . ."

It was Campton's turn to redden. The possibility was one he had not thought of. If the picture were sold at auction, Anderson Brant would be sure to buy it! But he could not say this to Boylston. He hesitated, and the other, who seemed quick at feeling his way, added at once: "But perhaps you'd rather sell it privately? In that case we should get the money sooner."

It was just the right thing to say: and Campton thanked him and picked up his sketch. At the door he hesitated, feeling that it became a member of the honorary committee to add something more.

"How are you getting on? Getting all the help you need?"

Boylston smiled. "We need such a lot. People have been very generous: we've had several big sums. But look at those ridiculous clothes down-stairs—we get boxes and boxes of such rubbish! And there are so many applicants, and such hard cases. Take those poor Davrils, for instance. The lame Davril girl has a talent for music: plays the violin. Well, what good does it do her now? The artists are having an awful time. If this war goes on much longer, it won't be only at the front that they'll die."

"Ah——" said Campton. "Well, I'll take this to a dealer——"

On the way down he turned in to greet Miss Anthony. She looked up in surprise, her tired face haloed in tumbling hairpins; but she was too busy to do more than nod across the group about her desk.

At his offer to take her home she shook her head. "I'm here till after seven. Mr. Boylston and I are nearly snowed under. We've got to go down presently and help unpack and after that I'm due at my refugee canteen at the Nord. It's my night shift."

Campton, on the way back to Montmartre, fell to wondering if such excesses of altruism were necessary, or a mere vain overflow of energy. He was terrified by his first close glimpse of the ravages of war, and the efforts of the little band struggling to heal them seemed pitifully ineffectual. No doubt they did good here and there, made a few lives less intolerable; but how the insatiable monster must laugh at them as he spread his red havoc wider!

On reaching home, Campton forgot everything at sight of a letter from George. He had not had one for two weeks, and this interruption, just as the military mails were growing more regular, had made him anxious. But it was the usual letter: brief, cheerful, inexpressive. Apparently there was no change in George's situation, nor any wish on his part that there should be. He grumbled humorously at the dulness of his work and the monotony of life in a war-zone town; and wondered whether, if this sort of thing went on, there might not soon be some talk of leave. And just at the end of this affectionate and unsatisfactory two pages, Campton lit on a name that roused him.

"I saw a fellow who'd seen Benny Upsher yesterday on his way to the English front. The young lunatic looked very fit. You know he volunteered in the English army when he found he couldn't get into the French. He's likely to get all the fighting he wants." It was a relief to know that someone had seen Benny Upsher lately. The letter was but four days old, and he was then on his way to the front. Probably he was not yet in the fighting he wanted, and one could, without remorse, call up an unmutilated face and clear blue eyes.

Campton, re-reading the postscript, was struck by a small thing. George had originally written: "I saw Benny Upsher yesterday," and had then altered the phrase to "I saw a fellow who'd seen Benny Upsher." There was nothing out of the way in that: it simply showed that he had written in haste and revised the sentence. But he added: "The young lunatic looked very fit." Well: that too was natural. It was "the fellow" who reported Benny as looking fit; the phrase was rather elliptic, but Campton could hardly have said why it gave him the impression that it was George himself who had seen Upsher. The idea was manifestly absurd, since there was the length of the front between George's staff-town and the fiery pit yawning for his cousin. Campton laid aside the letter with the distinct wish that his son had not called Benny Upsher a young lunatic.

XIV

When Campton took his sketch of George to Léonce Black, the dealer who specialized in "Camptons," he was surprised at the magnitude of the sum which the great picture-broker, lounging in a glossy War Office uniform among his Gauguins and Vuillards, immediately offered.

Léonce Black noted his surprise and smiled. "You think there's nothing doing nowadays? Don't you believe it, Mr. Campton. Now that the big men have stopped painting, the collectors are all the keener to snap up what's left in their portfolios." He placed the cheque in Campton's hand, and drew back to study the effect of the sketch, which he had slipped into a frame against a velvet curtain. "Ah——" he said, as if he were tasting an old wine.

As Campton turned to go the dealer's enthusiasm bubbled over. "Haven't you got anything more? Remember me if you have."

"I don't sell my sketches," said Campton. "This was exceptional— for a charity..."

"I know, I know. Well, you're likely to have a good many more calls of the same sort before we get *this* war over," the dealer remarked philosophically. "Anyhow, remember I can place anything you'll give me. When people want a Campton it's to me they come. I've got standing orders from two clients . . . both given before the war, and both good today."

Campton paused in the doorway, seized by his old fear of the painting's passing into Anderson Brant's possession.

"Look here: where is this one going?"

The dealer cocked his handsome grey head and glanced archly

through plump eyelids. "Violation of professional secrecy? Well . . . Well . . . under constraint I'll confess it's to a young lady: great admirer, artist herself. Had her order by cable from New York a year ago. Been on the lookout ever since."

"Oh, all right," Campton answered, repocketing the money.

He set out at once for "The Friends of French Art," and Léonce Black, bound for the Ministry of War, walked by his side, regaling him alternately with the gossip of the Ministry and with racy anecdotes of the dealers' world. In M. Black's opinion the war was an inexcusable blunder, since Germany was getting to be the best market for the kind of freak painters out of whom the dealers who "know how to make a man 'foam'" can make a big turn-over. "I don't know what on earth will become of all those poor devils now: Paris cared for them only because she knew Germany would give any money for their things. Personally, as you know, I've always preferred sounder goods: I'm a classic, my dear Campton, and I can feel only classic art," said the dealer, swelling out his uniformed breast and stroking his Assyrian nose as though its handsome curve followed the pure Delphic line. "But, as long as things go on as they are at present in *my* department of the administration, the war's not going to end in a hurry," he continued. "And now we're in for it, we've got to see the thing through."

Campton found Boylston, as usual, in his melancholy *cabinet particulier*. He was listening to the tale of a young woman with streaming eyes and an extravagant hat. She was so absorbed in her trouble that she did not notice Campton's entrance, and behind her back the painter made a sign to say that she was not to be interrupted.

He was as much interested in the suppliant's tale as in watching Boylston's way of listening. That modest and commonplace-looking young man was beginning to excite a lively curiosity in Campton. It was not only that he remembered George's commendation, for he knew that the generous enthusiasms of youth may be inspired by trifles imperceptible to the older. It was Boylston himself who interested the painter. He knew no more of the young man than the scant details Miss Anthony could give. Boylston, it appeared, was the oldest hope of a well-to-do Connecticut family. On his leaving college a place had been reserved for him in the paternal business; but he had announced good-humouredly that he did not mean to spend his life in an office, and one day, after a ten minutes' conversation with his father, as to which details were lacking, he had packed a suitcase and sailed for France. There he had lived ever since, in shabby rooms in the rue de Verneuil, on the scant allowance remitted by an irate parent: apparently never running into debt, yet always ready to help a friend.

All the American art-students in Paris knew Boylston; and though he was still in the early thirties, they all looked up to him. For Boylston had one quality which always impresses youth: Boylston knew every-body. Whether you went with him to a smart restaurant in the rue Royale, or to a wine-shop of the Left Bank, the *patron* welcomed him with the same cordiality, and sent the same emphatic instructions to the cook. The first fresh peas and the tenderest spring chicken were always for this quiet youth, who, when he was alone, dined cheerfully on veal and *vin ordinaire*. If you wanted to know where to get the best Burgundy, Boylston could tell you; he could also tell you where to buy an engagement ring for your girl, a Ford run-about going at half-price, or the *papier timbré* on which to address a summons to a recalcitrant laundress.

If you got into a row with your landlady you found that Boylston knew her, and that at sight of him she melted and withdrew her claim; or, failing this, he knew the solicitor in whose office her son was a clerk, or had other means of reducing her to reason. Boylston also knew a man who could make old clocks go, another who could clean flannels without their shrinking, and a third who could get you old picture-frames for a song; and, best of all, when any inexperienced American youth was caught in the dark Parisian cobweb (and the people at home were on no account to hear about it) Boylston was found to be the friend and familiar of certain occult authorities who, with a smile and a word of warning, could break the mesh and free the victim.

The mystery was, how and why all these people did what Boylston wanted; but the reason began to dawn on Campton as he watched the young woman in the foolish hat deliver herself of her grievance. Boylston was simply a perfect listener—and most of his life was spent in listening. Everything about him listened: his round forehead and peering screwed-up eyes, his lips twitching responsively under the close-clipped moustache, and every crease and dimple of his sagacious and humorous young countenance; even the attitude of his short fat body, with elbows comfortably bedded in heaped-up papers, and fingers plunged into his crinkled hair. There was never a hint of hurry or impatience about him: having once asserted his right to do what he liked with his life, he was apparently content to let all his friends prey on it. You never caught his eye on the clock, or his lips shaping an answer before you had turned the last corner of your story. Yet when the story was told, and he had surveyed it in all its bearings, you could be sure he would do what he could for you, and do it before the day was over.

"Very well, Mademoiselle," he said, when the young woman had finished. "I promise you I'll see Mme. Beausite, and try to get her to recognize your claim."

"Mind you, I don't ask charity—I won't *take* charity from your committee!" the young lady hissed, gathering up a tawdry hand-bag.

"Oh, we're not forcing it on any one," smiled Boylston, opening the door for her.

When he turned back to Campton his face was flushed and frowning. "Poor thing! She's a nuisance, but I'll fight to the last ditch for her. The chap she lives with was Beausite's secretary and understudy, and devilled for him before the war. The poor fellow has come back from the front a complete wreck, and can't even collect the salary Beausite owes him for the last three months before the war. Beausite's plea is that he's too poor, and that the war lets him out of paying. Of course he counts on our doing it for him."

"And you're not going to?"

"Well," said Boylston humorously, "I shouldn't wonder if he beat us in the long run. But I'll have a try first; and anyhow the poor girl needn't know. She used to earn a little money doing fashion-articles, but of course there's no market for that now, and I don't see how the pair can live. They have a little boy, and there's an infirm mother, and they're waiting to get married till the girl can find a job."

"Good Lord!" Campton groaned, with a sudden vision of the countless little trades and traffics arrested by the war, and all the industrious thousands reduced to querulous pauperism or slow death.

"How *do* they live—all these people?"

"They don't—always. I could tell you——"

"Don't, for God's sake; I can't stand it." Campton drew out the cheque. "Here: this is what I've got for the Davrils."

"Good Lord!" said Boylston, staring with round eyes.

"It will pull them through, anyhow, won't it?"

"Well——" said Boylston. "It will if you'll endorse it," he added, smiling. Campton laughed and took up a pen.

A day or two later Campton, returning home one afternoon, overtook a small black-veiled figure with a limp like his own. He guessed at once that it was the lame Davril girl, come to thank him; and his dislike of such ceremonies caused him to glance about for a way of escape. But as he did so the girl turned with a smile that put him to shame. He remembered Adele Anthony's saying, one day when he had found her in her refugee office patiently undergoing a like ordeal: "We've no right to refuse the only coin they can repay us in."

The Davril girl was a plain likeness of her brother, with the same hungry flame in her eyes. She wore the nondescript black that Campton had remarked at the funeral; and knowing the importance which the French attach to every detail of conventional mourning, he wondered that mother and daughter had not laid out part of his gift in crape. But doubtless the equally strong instinct of thrift had caused Mme. Davril to put away the whole sum.

Mlle. Davril greeted Campton pleasantly, and assured him that she had not found the long way from Villejuif to Montmartre too difficult.

"I would have gone to you," the painter protested; but she answered that she wanted to see with her own eyes where her brother's friend lived.

In the studio she looked about her with a quick searching glance, said "Oh, a piano——" as if the fact were connected with the object of her errand—and then, settling herself in an armchair, unclasped her shabby hand-bag.

"Monsieur, there has been a misunderstanding; this money is not ours." She laid Campton's cheque on the table.

A flush of annoyance rose to the painter's face. What on earth had Boylston let him in for? If the Davrils were as proud as all that it was not worth while to have sold a sketch it had cost him such a pang to part with. He felt the exasperation of the would-be philanthropist when he first discovers that nothing complicates life as much as doing good.

"But, Mademoiselle——"

"This money is not ours. If René had lived he would never have sold your picture; and we would starve rather than betray his trust."

When stout ladies in velvet declare that they would starve rather than sacrifice this or that principle, the statement has only the cold beauty of rhetoric; but on the drawn lips of a thinly-clad young woman evidently acquainted with the process, it becomes a fiery reality.

"Starve—nonsense! My dear young lady, you betray him when you talk like that," said Campton, moved.

She shook her head. "It depends, Monsieur, which things matter most to one. We shall never—my mother and I—do anything that René would not have done. The picture was not ours: we brought it back to you——"

"But if the picture's not yours it's mine," Campton interrupted; "and I'd a right to sell it, and a right to do what I choose with the money."

His visitor smiled. "That's what we feel; it was what I was coming to." And clasping her threadbare glove-tips about the arms of the chair Mlle. Davril set forth with extreme precision the object of her visit.

It was to propose that Campton should hand over the cheque to "The Friends of French Art," devoting one-third to the aid of the families of combatant painters, the rest to young musicians and authors. "It doesn't seem right that only the painters' families should benefit by what your committee are doing. And René would have thought so too. He knew so many young men of letters and journalists who, before the war, just managed to keep their families alive; and in my profession I could tell you of poor music-teachers and accompanists whose work stopped the day war broke out, and who have been living ever since on the crusts their luckier comrades could spare them. René would have let us accept from you help that was shared with others: he would have been so glad, often, of a few francs to relieve the misery we see about us. and this great sum might be the beginning of a co-operative work for artists ruined by the war."

She went on to explain that in the families of almost all the young artists at the front there was at least one member at home who practised one of the arts, or who was capable of doing some kind of useful work. The value of Campton's gift, Mlle. Davril argued, would be tripled if it were so employed as to give the artists and their families occupation: producing at least the illusion that those who could were earning their living, or helping their less fortunate comrades. "It's not only a question of saving their dignity: I don't believe much in that. You have dignity or you haven't—and if you have, it doesn't need any saving," this clear-toned young woman remarked. "The real question, for all of us artists, is that of keeping our hands in, and our interest in our work alive; sometimes, too, of giving a new talent its first chance. At any rate, it would mean work and not stagnation; which is all that most charity produces."

She developed her plan: for the musicians, concerts in private houses (hence her glance at the piano); for the painters, small exhibitions in the rooms of the committee, where their pictures would be sold with the deduction of a percentage, to be returned to the general fund; and for the writers—well, their lot was perhaps the hardest to deal with; but an employment agency might be opened, where those who chose could put their names down and take such work as was offered. Above all, Mlle. Davril again insisted, the fund created by Campton's gift was to be spent only in giving employment, not for mere relief.

Campton listened with growing attention. Nothing hitherto had been less in the line of his interests than the large schemes of general amelioration which were coming to be classed under the transatlantic term of "Social Welfare." If questioned on the subject a few months earlier he would probably have concealed his fundamental indifference under the profession of an extreme individualism, and the assertion of every man's right to suffer and starve in his own way. Even since René Davril's death had brought home to him the boundless havoc of the war, he had felt no more than the impulse to ease his own pain by putting his hand in his pocket when a particular case was too poignant to be ignored.

Yet here were people who had already offered their dearest to France, and were now pleading to be allowed to give all the rest; and who had had the courage and wisdom to think out in advance the form in which their gift would do most good. Campton had the awe of the unpractical man for anyone who knows how to apply his ideas. He felt that there was no use in disputing Mlle. Davril's plan: he must either agree to it or repocket his cheque.

"I'll do as you want, of course; but I'm not much good about details. Hadn't you better consult some one else?" he suggested.

Oh, that was already done: she had outlined her project to Miss Anthony and Mr. Boylston, who approved. All she wanted was Campton's consent; and this he gave the more cordially when he learned that, for the present at least, nothing more was expected of him. First steps in beneficence, he felt, were unspeakably terrifying; yet he was already aware that, resist as he might, he would never be able to keep his footing on the brink of the abyss.

Into it, as the days went by, his gaze was oftener and oftener plunged. He had begun to feel that pity was his only remaining link with his kind, the one barrier between himself and the dreadful solitude which awaited him when he returned to his studio. What would there have been to think of there, alone among his unfinished pictures and his broken memories, if not the wants and woes of people more bereft than himself? His own future was not a thing to dwell on. George was safe: but what George and he were likely to make of each other after the ordeal was over was a question he preferred to put aside. He was more and more taking George and his safety for granted, as a solid standing-ground from which to reach out a hand to the thousands struggling in the depths. As long as the world's fate was in the balance it was every man's duty to throw into that balance his last ounce of brain and muscle. Campton wondered how he had ever thought that an accident of birth, a remoteness merely geographical, could justify, or even make possible, an attitude of moral aloofness. Harvey Mayhew's reasons for wishing to annihilate Germany began to seem less grotesque than his own for standing aside.

In the heat of his conversion he no longer grudged the hours given to Mr. Mayhew. He patiently led his truculent relative from one government office to another, everywhere laying stress on Mr. Mayhew's sympathy with France and his desire to advocate her cause in the United States, and trying to curtail his enumeration of his grievances by a glance at the clock, and the reminder that they had another Minister to see. Mr. Mayhew was not very manageable. His adventure had grown with repetition, and he was increasingly disposed to feel that the retaliation he called down on Germany could best be justified by telling every one what he had suffered from her. Intensely aware of the value of time in Utica, he was less sensible of it in Paris, and seemed to think that, since he had left a flourishing business to preach the Holy War, other people ought to leave their affairs to give him a hearing. But his zeal and persistence were irresistible, and doors which Campton had seen barred against the most reasonable appeals flew open at the sound of Mr. Mayhew's trumpet. His pink face and silvery hair gave him an apostolic air, and circles to which America had hitherto been a mere speck in space suddenly discovered that he represented that legendary character, the Typical American.

The keen Boylston, prompt to note and utilize the fact, urged Campton to interest Mr. Mayhew in "The Friends of French Art," and with considerable flourish the former Peace Delegate was produced at a committee meeting and given his head. But his interest flagged when he found that the "Friends" concerned themselves with Atrocities only in so far as any act of war is one, and that their immediate task was the humdrum one of feeding and clothing the families of the combatants and sending "comforts" to the trenches. He served up, with a somewhat dog-eared eloquence, the usual account of his own experiences, and pressed a modest gift upon the treasurer; but when he departed, after wringing everybody's hands, and leaving the French members bedewed with emotion, Campton had the conviction that their quiet weekly meetings would not often be fluttered by his presence.

Campton was spending an increasing amount of time in the Palais Royal restaurant, where he performed any drudgery for which no initiative was required. Once or twice, when Miss Anthony was submerged by a fresh influx of refugees, he lent her a hand too; and on most days he dropped in late at the office, waited for her to sift and dismiss the last applicants, and saw her home through the incessant rain. It interested him to note that the altruism she had so long wasted on pampered friends was developing into a wise and orderly beneficence. He had always thought of her as an eternal schoolgirl; now she had grown into a woman. Sometimes he fancied the change dated from the moment when their eyes had met across the station, the day they had seen George off. He wondered whether it might not be interesting to paint her new face, if ever painting became again thinkable.

"Passion—I suppose the great thing is a capacity for passion," he mused.

In himself he imagined the capacity to be quite dead. He loved his son: yes—but he was beginning to see that he loved him for certain qualities he had read into him, and the perhaps after all——. Well, perhaps after all the sin for which he was now atoning in loneliness was that of having been too exclusively an artist, of having cherished George too egotistically and self-indulgently, too much as his own most beautiful creation. If he had loved him more humanly, more tenderly and recklessly, might he have not put into his son the tenderness and recklessness which were beginning to seem to him the qualities most supremely human?

XV

A week or two later, coming home late from a long day's work at the office, Campton saw Mme. Lebel awaiting him.

He always stopped for a word now; fearing each time that there was bad news of Jules Lebel, but not wishing to seem to avoid her.

Today, however, Mme. Lebel, though mysterious, was not anxious.

"Monsieur will find the studio open. There's a lady: she insisted on going up."

"A lady? Why did you let her in? What kind of a lady?"

"A lady—well, a lady with such magnificent furs that one couldn't keep her out in the cold," Mme. Lebel answered with simplicity.

Campton went up apprehensively. The idea of unknown persons in possession of his studio always made him nervous. Whoever they were, whatever errands they came on, they always—especially women—disturbed the tranquil course of things, faced him with unexpected problems, unsettled him in one way or another. Bouncing in on people suddenly was like dynamiting fish: it left him with his mind full of fragments of dismembered thoughts.

As he entered he perceived from the temperate atmosphere that Mme. Lebel had not only opened the studio but made up the fire. The lady's furs must indeed be magnificent.

She sat at the farther end of the room, in a high-backed chair near the stove, and when she rose he recognized his former wife. The long sable cloak, which had slipped back over the chair, justified Mme. Lebel's description, but the dress beneath it appeared to Campton simpler than Mrs. Brant's habitual raiment. The lamplight, striking up into her powdered face, puffed out her underlids and made harsh hollows in her cheeks. She looked frightened, ill and yet determined.

"John——" she began, laying her hand on his sleeve.

It was the first time she had ever set foot in his shabby quarters, and in his astonishment he could only stammer out: "Julia——"

But as he looked at her he saw that her face was wet with tears. "Not—bad news?" he broke out.

She shook her head and, drawing a handkerchief from a diamond-monogrammed bag, wiped away the tears and the powder. Then she pressed the handkerchief to her lips, gazing at him with eyes as helpless as a child's.

"Sit down," said Campton.

As they faced each other across the long table, with papers and paint-rags and writing materials pushed aside to make room for the threadbare napkin on which his plate and glass, and bottle of *vin ordinaire*, were set out, he wondered if the scene woke in her any memory of their first days of gaiety and poverty, or if she merely pitied him for still living in such squalor. And suddenly it occurred to him that when the war was over, and George came back, it would be pleasant to hunt out a little apartment in an old house in the Faubourg St. Germain, put some good furniture in it, and oppose the discreeter charm of such an interior to the heavy splendours of the Avenue Marigny. How could he expect to hold a luxury-loving youth if he had only this dingy studio to receive him in?

Mrs. Brant began to speak.

"I came here to see you because I didn't wish any one to know; not Adele, nor even Anderson." Leaning toward him she went on in short breathless sentences: "I've just left Madge Talkett: you know her, I think? She's at Mme. de Dolmetsch's hospital. Something dreadful has happened . . . too dreadful. It seems that Mme. de Dolmetsch was very much in love with Ladislas Isador; a writer, wasn't he? I don't know his books, but Madge tells me they're wonderful . . . and of course men like that ought not to be sent to the front. . ."

"Men like what?"

"Geniuses," said Mrs. Brant. "He was dreadfully delicate besides, and was doing admirable work on some military commission in Paris; I believe he knew any number of languages. And poor Mme. de Dolmetsch—you know I've never approved of her; but things are so changed nowadays, and at any rate she was madly attached to him, and had done everything to keep him in Paris: medical certificates, people at Headquarters working for her, and all the rest. But it seems there are no end of officers always intriguing to get staff-jobs: strong able-bodied young men who ought to be in the trenches, and are fit for nothing else, but who are jealous of the others. And last week, in spite of all she could do, poor Isador was ordered to the front."

Campton made an impatient movement. It was even more distasteful to him to be appealed to by Mrs. Brant in Isador's name than by Mme. de Dolmetsch in George's. His gorge rose at the thought that people should associate in their minds cases as different as those of his son and Mme. de Dolmetsch's lover.

"I'm sorry," he said. "But if you've come to ask me to do something more about George—take any new steps—it's no use. I can't do the sort of thing to keep my son safe that Mme. de Dolmetsch would do for her lover."

Mrs. Brant stared. "Safe? He was killed the day after he got to the front."

"Good Lord—Isador?"

Ladislas Isador killed at the front! The words remained unmeaning; by no effort could Campton relate them to the fat middle-aged philanderer with his Jewish eyes, his Slav eloquence, his Levantine gift for getting on, and for getting out from under. Campton tried to picture the clever contriving devil drawn in his turn into that merciless red eddy, and gulped down the Monster's throat with the rest. What a mad world it was, in which the same horrible and magnificent doom awaited the coward and the hero!

"Poor Mme. de Dolmetsch!" he muttered, remembering with a sense of remorse her desperate appeal and his curt rebuff. Once again the poor creature's love had enlightened her, and she had foreseen what no one else in the world would have believed: that her lover was to die like a hero.

"Isador was nearly forty, and had a weak heart; and she'd left nothing, literally nothing, undone to save him." Campton read in his wife's eyes what was coming. "It's impossible *now* that George should not be taken," Mrs. Brant went on.

The same thought had tightened Campton's own heart-strings; but he had hoped she would not say it.

"It may be George's turn any day," she insisted.

They sat and looked at each other without speaking; then she began again imploringly: "I tell you there's not a moment to be lost!"

Campton picked up a palette-knife and began absently to rub it with an oily rag. Mrs. Brant's anguished voice still sounded on. "Unless something is done immediately. . . It appears there's a regular hunt for *embusqués,* as they're called. As if it was everybody's business to be killed! How's the staff-work to be carried on if they're all taken? But it's certain that if we don't act at once . . . act energetically. . ."

He fixed his eyes on hers. "Why do you come to *me?*" he asked.

Her lids opened wide. "But he's our child."

"Your husband knows more people—he has ways, you've often told me——"

She reddened faintly and seemed about to speak; but the reply died on her lips.

"Why did you say," Campton pursued, "that you had come here because you wanted to see me without Brant's knowing it?"

She lowered her eyes and fixed them on the knife he was still automatically rubbing.

"Because Anderson thinks . . . Anderson won't . . . He says he's done all he can."

"Ah——" cried Campton, drawing a deep breath. He threw back his shoulders, as if to shake off a weight. "I—feel exactly as Brant does," he declared.

"You—you feel as he does? You, George's father? But a father has never done all he can for his son! There's always something more that he can do!"

The words, breaking from her in a cry, seemed suddenly to change her from an ageing doll into a living and agonized woman. Campton had never before felt as near to her, as moved to the depths by her. For the length of a heart-beat he saw her again with a red-haired baby in her arms, the light of morning on her face.

"My dear—I'm sorry." He laid his hand on hers.

"Sorry—sorry? I don't want you to be sorry. I want you to do something—I want you to save him!"

He faced her with bent head, gazing absently at their interwoven fingers: each hand had forgotten to release the other.

"I can't do anything more," he repeated.

She started up with a despairing exclamation. "What's happened to you? Who has influenced you? What has changed you?"

How could he answer her? He hardly knew himself: had hardly been conscious of the change till she suddenly flung it in his face. If blind animal passion be the profoundest as well as the fiercest form of attachment, his love for his boy was at that moment as nothing to hers. Yet his feeling for George, in spite of all the phrases he dressed it in, had formerly in its essence been no other. That his boy should survive—survive at any price—that had been all he cared for or sought to achieve. It had been convenient to justify himself by arguing that George was not bound to fight for France; but Campton now knew that he would have made the same effort to protect his son if the country engaged had been his own.

In the careless pre-war world, as George himself had once said, it had seemed unbelievable that people should ever again go off and die in a ditch to oblige anybody. Even now, the automatic obedience of the millions of the untaught and the unthinking, though it had its deep pathetic significance, did not move Campton like the clear-eyed sacrifice of the few who knew why they were dying. Jean Fortin, René Davril, and such lads as young Louis Dastrey, with his reasoned horror of butchery and waste in general, and his instant grasp of the necessity of this particular sacrifice: it was they who had first shed light on the dark problem.

Campton had never before, at least consciously, thought of himself and the few beings he cared for as part of a greater whole, component elements of the immense amazing spectacle. But the last four months had shown him man as a defenceless animal suddenly torn from his shell, stripped of all the interwoven tendrils of association, habit, background, daily ways and words, daily sights and sounds, and flung out of the human habitable world into naked ether, where nothing breathes or lives. That was what war did; that was why those who best understood it in all its farthest-reaching abomination willingly gave their lives to put an end to it.

He heard Mrs. Brant crying.

"Julia," he said, "Julia, I wish you'd try to see . . ."

She dashed away her tears. "See what? All I see is *you,* sitting here safe and saying you can do nothing to save him! But to have the right to say that you ought to be in the trenches yourself! What do you suppose those young men out there think of their fathers, safe at home, who are too high-minded and conscientious to protect them?"

He looked at her compassionately. "Yes," he said, "that's the bitterest part of it. But for that, there would hardly be anything in the worst war for us old people to lie awake about."

Mrs. Brant had stood up and was feverishly pulling on her gloves: he saw that she no longer heard him. He helped her to draw her furs about her, and stood waiting while she straightened her veil and tapped the waves of hair into place, her eyes blindly seeking for a mirror. There was nothing more that either could say.

He lifted the lamp, and went out of the door ahead of her.

"You needn't come down," she said in a sob; but leaning over the rail into the darkness he answered: "I'll give you a light: the concierge has forgotten the lamp on the stairs."

He went ahead of her down the long greasy flights, and as they reached the ground floor he heard a noise of feet coming and going, and frightened voices exclaiming. In the doorway of the porter's lodge Mrs. Brant's splendid chauffeur stood looking on compassionately at a group of women gathered about Mme. Lebel.

The old woman sat in her den, her arms stretched across the table, her sewing fallen at her feet. On the table lay an open letter. The grocer's wife from the corner stood by, sobbing.

Mrs. Brant stopped, and Campton, sure now of what was coming, pushed his way through the neighbours about the door. Mme. Lebel's eyes met his with the mute reproach of a tortured animal. "Jules," she said, "last Wednesday . . . through the heart."

Campton took her old withered hand. The women ceased sobbing and a hush fell upon the stifling little room. When Campton looked up again he saw Julia Brant, pale and bewildered, hurrying toward her motor, and the vault of the porte-cochère sent back the chauffeur's answer to her startled question: "Poor old lady—yes, her only son's been killed at the front."

XVI

Campton sat with his friend Dastrey in the latter's pleasant little *entresol* full of Chinese lacquer and Venetian furniture.

Dastrey, in the last days of January, had been sent home from his ambulance with an attack of rheumatism; and when it became clear that he could no longer be of use in the mud and cold of the army zone he had reluctantly taken his place behind a desk at the Ministry of War. The friends had dined early, so that he might get back to his night-shift; and they sat over coffee and liqueurs, the mist of their cigars floating across lustrous cabinet-fronts and the worn gilding of slender consoles.

On the other side of the hearth young Boylston, sunk in an armchair, smoked and listened.

"It always comes back to the same thing," Campton was saying nervously. "What right have useless old men like me, sitting here with my cigar by this good fire, to preach blood and butchery to boys like George and your nephew?"

Again and again, during the days since Mrs. Brant's visit, he had turned over in his mind the same torturing question. How was he to answer that last taunt of hers?

Not long ago, Paul Dastrey would have seemed the last person to whom he could have submitted such a problem. Dastrey, in the black August days, starting for the front in such a frenzy of baffled bloodlust, had remained for Campton the type of man with whom it was impossible to discuss the war. But three months of hard service in *Postes de Secours* and along the awful battle-edge had sent him home with a mind no longer befogged by personal problems. He had done his utmost, and knew it; and the fact gave him the professional calm which keeps surgeons and nurses steady through all the horrors they are compelled to live among. Those few months had matured and mellowed him more than a lifetime of Paris.

He leaned back with half-closed lids, quietly considering his friend's difficulty.

"I see. Your idea is that, being unable to do even the humble kind of job that I've been assigned to, you've no right *not* to try to keep your boy out of it if you can?"

"Well—by any honourable means."

Dastrey laughed faintly, and Campton reddened. "The word's not happy, I admit."

"I wasn't thinking of that: I was considering how the meaning had evaporated out of lots of our old words, as if the general smash-up had broken their stoppers. So many of them, you see," said Dastrey smiling, "we'd taken good care not to uncork for centuries. Since I've been on the edge of what's going on fifty miles from here a good many of my own words have lost their meaning, and I'm not prepared to say where honour lies in a case like yours." He mused a moment, and then went on: "What would George's view be?"

Campton did not immediately reply. Not so many weeks ago he would have welcomed the chance of explaining that George's view, thank God, had remained perfectly detached and objective, and that the cheerful acceptance of duties forcibly imposed on him had not in the least obscured his sense of the fundamental injustice of his being mixed up in the thing at all.

But how could he say this now? If George's view were still what his father had been in the habit of saying it was, then he held that view alone: Campton himself no longer thought that any civilized man could afford to stand aside from such a conflict.

"As far as I know," he said, "George hasn't changed his mind."

Boylston stirred in his armchair, knocked the ash from his cigar, and looked up at the ceiling.

"Whereas *you*——" Dastrey suggested.

"Yes," said Campton. "I feel differently. You speak of the difference of having been in contact with what's going on out there. But how can anybody *not* be in contact, who has any imagination, any sense of right and wrong? Do these pictures and hangings ever shut it out from you—or those books over there, when you turn to them after your day's work? Perhaps they do, because you've got a real job, a job you've been ordered to do, and can't not do. But for a useless drifting devil like me—my God, the sights and the sounds of it are always with me!"

"There are a good many people who wouldn't call you useless, Mr. Campton," said Boylston.

Campton shook his head. "I wish there were any healing in the kind of thing I'm doing; perhaps there is to you, to whom it appears to come naturally to love your kind." (Boylston laughed.) "Service is of no use without conviction: that's one of the uncomfortable truths this stir-up has brought to the surface. I was meant to paint pictures in a world at peace, and I should have more respect for myself if I could go on unconcernedly doing it, instead of pining to be in all the places where I'm not wanted, and should be of no earthly use. That's why——" he paused, looked about him, and sought understanding in Dastrey's friendly gaze: "That's why I respect George's opinion, which really consists in not having any, and simply doing without comment the work assigned to him. The whole thing is so far beyond human measure that one's individual rage and revolt seem of no more use than a woman's scream at an accident she isn't in."

Even while he spoke, Campton knew he was arguing only against himself. He did not in the least believe that any individual sentiment counted for nothing at such a time, and Dastrey really spoke for him in rejoining: "Every one can at least contribute an attitude: as you have, my dear fellow. Boylston's here to confirm it."

Boylston grunted his assent.

"An attitude—an attitude?" Campton retorted. "The word is revolting to me! Anything a man like me can do is too easy to be worth doing. And as for anything one can *say:* how dare one say anything, in the face of what is being done out there to keep this room and this fire, and this ragged end of life, safe for such survivals as you and me?" He crossed to the table to take another cigar. As he did so he laid an apologetic pressure on his host's shoulder. "Men of our age are the chorus of the tragedy, Dastrey; we can't help ourselves. As soon as I open my lips to blame or praise I see myself in white petticoats, with a long beard held on by an elastic, goading on the combatants in a cracked voice from a safe corner of the ramparts. On the whole I'd sooner be spinning among the women."

"Well," said Dastrey, getting up, "I've got to get back to my spinning at the Ministry; where, by the way, there are some very pretty young women at the distaff. It's extraordinary how much better pretty girls type than plain ones; I see now why they get all the jobs."

The three went out into the winter blackness. They were used by this time to the new Paris: to extinguished lamps, shuttered windows, deserted streets, the almost total cessation of wheeled traffic. All through the winter, life had seemed in suspense everywhere, as much on the battle-front as in the rear. Day after day, week after week, of vague non-committal news from west and east; everywhere the enemy baffled but still menacing, everywhere death, suffering, destruction, without any perceptible oscillation of the scales, any compensating hope of good to come out of the long slow endless waste. The benumbed and darkened Paris of those February days seemed the visible image of a benumbed and darkened world.

Down the empty asphalt sheeted with rain the rare street lights stretched interminable reflections. The three men crossed the bridge and stood watching the rush of the Seine. Below them gloomed the vague bulk of deserted bath-houses, unlit barges, river-steamers out of commission. The Seine too had ceased to live: only a single orange gleam, low on the water's edge, undulated on the jetty waves like a streamer of seaweed.

The two Americans left Dastrey at his Ministry, and the painter strolled on to Boylston's lodging before descending to the underground railway. He, whom his lameness had made so heavy and indolent, now limped about for hours at a time over wet pavements and under streaming skies: these midnight tramps had become a sort of expiatory need to him. "Out there—out there, if they had these wet stones under them they'd think it was the floor of heaven," he used to muse, driving on obstinately through rain and darkness.

The thought of "Out there" besieged him day and night, the phrase was always in his ears. Wherever he went he was pursued by visions of that land of doom: visions of fathomless mud, rat-haunted trenches,

freezing nights under the sleety sky, men dying in the barbed wire between the lines or crawling out to save a comrade and being shattered
to death on the return. His collaboration with Boylston had brought
Campton into close contact with these things. He knew by heart the
history of scores and scores of young men of George's age who were
doggedly suffering and dying a few hours away from the Palais Royal
office where their records were kept. Some of these histories were so
heroically simple that the sense of pain was lost in beauty, as though
one were looking at suffering transmuted into poetry. But others were
abominable, unendurable, in their long-drawn useless horror: stories
of cold and filth and hunger, of ineffectual effort, of hideous mutilation, of men perishing of thirst in a shell-hole, and half-dismembered
bodies dragging themselves back to shelter only to die as they reached
it. Worst of all were the perpetually recurring reports of military
blunders, medical neglect, carelessness in high places: the torturing
knowledge of the lives that might have been saved if this or that officer's brain, this or that surgeon's hand, had acted more promptly. An
impression of waste, confusion, ignorance, obstinacy, prejudice, and
the indifference of selfishness or of mortal fatigue, emanated from
these narratives written home from the front, or faltered out by white
lips on hospital pillows.

"The Friends of French Art," especially since they had enlarged
their range, had to do with young men accustomed to the freest exercise of thought and criticism. A nation in arms does not judge a war
as simply as an army of professional soldiers. All these young intelli-
gences were so many subtly-adjusted instruments for the testing of
the machinery of which they formed a part; and not one accepted the
results passively. Yet in one respect all were agreed: the "had to be" of
the first day was still on every lip. The German menace must be met:
chance willed that theirs should be the generation to meet it; on that
point speculation was vain and discussion useless. The question that
stirred them all was how the country they were defending was helping them to carry on the struggle. There the evidence was cruelly
clear, the comment often scathingly explicit; and Campton, bending
still lower over the abyss, caught a shuddering glimpse of what might
be—must be—if political blunders, inertia, tolerance, perhaps even
evil ambitions and connivance, should at last outweigh the effort of
the front. There was no logical argument against such a possibility.
All civilizations had their orbit; all societies rose and fell. Some day,
no doubt, by the action of that law, everything that made the world
livable to Campton and his kind would crumble in new ruins above
the old. Yes—but woe to them by whom such things came; woe to the
generation that bowed to such a law! The Powers of Darkness were always watching and seeking their hour; but the past was a record of

their failures as well as of their triumphs. Campton, brushing up his history, remembered the great turning-points of progress, saw how the liberties of England had been born of the ruthless discipline of the Norman conquest, and how even out of the hideous welter of the French Revolution and the Napoleonic wars had come more freedom and a wiser order. The point was to remember that the efficacy of the sacrifice was always in proportion to the worth of the victims; and there at least his faith was sure.

He could not, he felt, leave his former wife's appeal unnoticed; after a day or two he wrote to George, telling him of Mrs. Brant's anxiety, and asking in vague terms if George himself thought any change in his situation probable. His letter ended abruptly: "I suppose it's hardly time yet to ask for leave——"

XVII

Not long after his midnight tramp with Boylston and Dastrey the post brought Campton two letters. One was postmarked Paris, the other bore the military frank and was addressed in his son's hand: he laid it aside while he glanced at the first. It contained an engraved card:

Mrs. Anderson Brant

At Home on February 20th at 4 o'clock

Mr. Harvey Mayhew will give an account of his captivity in Germany

Mme. de Dolmetsch will sing

For the benefit of the "Friends of French Art Committee"

Tickets 100 francs

Enclosed was the circular of the sub-committee in aid of Musicians at the Front, with which Campton was not directly associated. It bore the names of Mrs. Talkett, Mme. Beausite and a number of other French and American ladies.

Campton tossed the card away. He was not annoyed by the invitation: he knew that Miss Anthony and Mlle. Davril were getting up a series of drawing-room entertainments for that branch of the charity, and that the card had been sent to him as a member of the Honorary Committee. But any reminder of the sort always gave a sharp twitch to the Brant nerve in him. He turned to George's letter.

It was no longer than usual; but in other respects it was unlike his son's previous communications. Campton read it over two or three times.

"Dear Dad, thanks for yours of the tenth, which must have come to me on skis, the snow here is so deep." (There had, in fact, been a heavy snow-fall in the Argonne.) "Sorry mother is bothering about things again; as you've often reminded me, they always have a way of 'being as they will be,' and even war doesn't seem to change it. Nothing to worry her in my case—but you can't expect her to believe that, can you? Neither you nor I can help it I suppose.

"There's one thing that might help, though; and that is, your letting her feel that you're a little nearer to her. War makes a lot of things look differently, especially this sedentary kind of war: it's rather like going over all the old odds-and-ends in one's cupboards. And some of them do look so foolish.

"I wish you'd see her now and then—just naturally, as if it had happened. You know you've got one Inexhaustible Topic between you. The said I.T. is doing well, and has nothing new to communicate up to now except a change of address. Hereafter please write to my Base instead of directing here, as there's some chance of a shift of H.Q. The precaution is probably just a new twist of the old red tape, signifying nothing; but Base will always reach me if we *are* shifted. Let mother know, and explain, please; otherwise she'll think the unthinkable.

"Interrupted by big drive—quill-drive, of course!
"As ever
"GEORGIUS SCRIBLERIUS.

"P.S. Don't be too savage to Uncle Andy either.
"No. 2.—I *had* thought of leave; but perhaps you're right about that."

It was the first time George had written in that way of his mother. His smiling policy had always been to let things alone, and go on impartially dividing his devotion between his parents, since they refused to share even that common blessing. But war gave everything a new look; and he had evidently, as he put it, been turning over the old things in his cupboards. How was it possible, Campton wondered, that after such a turning-over he was still content to write "Nothing new to communicate," and to make jokes about another big quill-drive? Glancing at the date of the letter, Campton saw that it had been written on the day after the first ineffectual infantry assault on Vauquois. And George was sitting a few miles off, safe in headquarters at Sainte-Menehould, with a stout roof over his head and a beautiful brown gloss on his boots, scribbling punning letters while his comrades fell back from that bloody summit. . .

Suddenly Campton's eyes filled. No; George had not written that letter for the sake of the joke: the joke was meant to cover what went before it. Ah, how young the boy was to imagine that his father would not see! Yes, as he said, war made so many of the old things look foolish. . .

Campton set out for the Palais Royal. He felt happier than for a long time past: the tone of his boy's letter seemed to correspond with his own secret change of spirit. He knew the futility of attempting to bring the Brants and himself together, but was glad that George had made the suggestion. He resolved to see Julia that afternoon.

At the Palais Royal he found the indefatigable Boylston busy with an exhibition of paintings sent home from the front, and Mlle. Davril helping to catalogue them. Lamentable pensioners came and went, bringing fresh tales of death, fresh details of savagery; the air was dark with poverty and sorrow. In the background Mme. Beausite flitted about, tragic and ineffectual. Boylston had not been able to extract a penny from Beausite for his secretary and the latter's left-handed family; but Mme. Beausite had discovered a newly-organized charity which lent money to "temporarily embarrassed" war-victims; and with an artless self-satisfaction she had contrived to obtain a small loan for the victim of her own thrift. "For what other purpose are such charities founded?" she said, gently disclaiming in advance the praise which Miss Anthony and Boylston had no thought of offering her. Whenever Campton came in she effaced herself behind a desk, where she bent her beautiful white head over a card-catalogue without any perceptible results.

The telephone rang. Boylston, after a moment, looked up from the receiver.

"Mr. Campton!"

The painter glanced apprehensively at the instrument, which still seemed to him charged with explosives.

"Take the message, do. The thing always snaps at me."

There was a listening pause: then Boylston said: "It's about Upsher——"

Campton started up. "Killed——?"

"Not sure. It's Mr. Brant. The news was wired to the bank; they want you to break it to Mr. Mayhew."

"Oh, Lord," the painter groaned, the boy's face suddenly rising before his blurred eyes. Miss Anthony was not at the office that morning, or he would have turned to her; at least she might have gone with him on his quest. He could not ask Boylston to leave the office, and he felt that curious incapacity to deal with the raw fact of sorrow which had often given an elfin unreality to the most poignant moments of his life. It was as though experience had to enter into the very substance of his soul before he could even feel it.

"Other people," he thought, "would know what to say, and I shan't. . ."

Some one, meanwhile, had fetched a cab, and he drove to the Nouveau Luxe, though with little hope of finding Mr. Mayhew. But Mr. Mayhew had grown two secretaries, and turned the shrimp-pink drawing-room into an office. One of the secretaries was there, hammering at a typewriter. She was a competent young woman, who instantly extracted from her pocket-diary the fact that her chief was at Mrs. Anderson Brant's, rehearsing.

"Rehearsing——?"

"Why, yes; he's to speak at Mrs. Brant's next week on Atrocities," she said, surprised at Campton's ignorance.

She suggested telephoning; but in the shrunken households of the rich, where but one or two servants remained, telephoning had become as difficult as in the under-staffed hotels; and after one or two vain attempts Campton decided to go to the Avenue Marigny. He felt that to get hold of Mayhew as soon as possible might still in some vague way help poor Benny—since it was not yet sure that he was dead. "Or else it's just the need to rush about," he thought, conscious that the only way he had yet found of dealing with calamity was a kind of ant-like agitation.

On the way the round pink face of Benny Upsher continued to float before him in its very substance, with the tangibility that only a painter's visions wear. "I want to be *in* this thing," he heard the boy repeating, as if impelled by some blind instinct flowing down through, centuries and centuries of persistent childish minds.

"If he or his forebears had ever thought things out he probably would have been alive and safe today," Campton mused, "like George. . . The average person is always just obeying impulses stored up thousands of years ago, and never re-examined since." But this consideration, though drawn from George's own philosophy, did not greatly comfort his father.

At the Brants' a bewildered concierge admitted him and rang a bell which no one answered. The vestibule and the stairs were piled with bales of sheeting, bulging jute-bags, stacked-up hospital supplies. A boy in scout's uniform swung inadequate legs from the lofty porter's arm-chair beside the table with its monumental bronze inkstand. Finally, from above, a maid called to Campton to ascend.

In the drawing-room pictures and tapestries, bronzes and *pâtes ten-dres,* had vanished, and a plain moquette replaced the priceless Savonnerie across whose pompous garlands Campton had walked on the day of his last visit.

The maid led him to the ball-room. Through double doors of glass Mr. Mayhew's oratorical accents, accompanied by faint chords on the piano, reached Campton's ears: he paused and looked. At the far end of the great gilded room, on a platform backed by velvet draperies, stood Mr. Mayhew, a perfect pearl in his tie and a perfect crease in his trousers. Beside him was a stage-property tripod surmounted by a classical perfume-burner; and on it Mme. de Dolmetsch, swathed in black, leaned in an attitude of affliction.

Beneath the platform a bushy-headed pianist struck an occasional chord from Chopin's Dead March; and near the door three or four Red Cross nurses perched on bales of blankets and listened. Under one of their coifs Campton recognized Mrs. Talkett. She saw him and made a sign to the lady nearest her; and the latter, turning, revealed the astonished eyes of Julia Brant.

Campton's first impression, while they shook hands under cover of Mr. Mayhew's rolling periods, was of his former wife's gift of adaptation. She had made herself a nurse's face; not a theatrical imitation of it like Mme. de Dolmetsch's, nor yet the face of a nurse on a war-poster, like Mrs. Talkett's. Her lovely hair smoothed away under her strict coif, her chin devoutly framed in linen, Mrs. Brant look serious, tender and efficient. Was it possible that she had found her vocation?

She gave him a glance of alarm, but his eyes must have told her that he had not come about George, for with a reassured smile she laid a finger on her lip and pointed to the platform; Campton noticed that her nails were as beautifully polished as ever.

Mr. Mayhew was saying: "All that I have to give, yes, all that is most precious to me, I am ready to surrender, to offer up, to lay down in the Great Struggle which is to save the world from barbarism. I, who was one of the first Victims of that barbarism. . .

He paused and looked impressively at the bales of blankets. The piano filled in the pause, and Mme. de Dolmetsch, without changing her attitude, almost without moving her lips, sang a few noted of lamentation.

"Of that hideous barbarism——" Mr. Mayhew began again. "I repeat that I stand here ready to give up everything I hold most dear——"

"Do stop him," Campton whispered to Mrs. Brant.

Little Mrs. Talkett, with the quick intuition he had noted in her, sprang up and threaded her way to the stage. Mme. de Dolmetsch flowed from one widowed pose into another, and Mr. Mayhew, majestically descending, approached Mrs. Brant.

"You agree with me, I hope? You feel that anything more than Mme. de Dolmetsch's beautiful voice—anything in the way of a choral accompaniment—would only weaken my effect? Where the facts are so overwhelming it is enough to state them; that is," Mr. Mayhew added modestly, "if they are stated vigorously and tersely—as I hope they are."

Mme. do Dolmetsch, with the gesture of a marble mourner torn from her cenotaph, glided up behind him and laid her hand in Campton's.

"Dear friend, you've heard? . . . You remember our talk? I am Cassandra, cursed with the hideous gift of divination." Tears rained down her cheeks, washing off the paint like mud swept by a shower. "My only comfort," she added, fixing her perfect eyes on Mr. Mayhew, "is to help our great good friend in the crusade against the assassins of my Ladislas."

Mrs. Talkett had said a word to Mr. Mayhew. Campton saw his complacent face go to pieces as if it had been vitrioled.

"Benny—Benny——" he screamed, "Benny hurt? My Benny? It's some mistake! What makes you think——?" His eyes met Campton's. "Oh, my God! Why, he's my sister's child!" he cried, plunging his face into his soft manicured hands.

In the cab to which Campton led him, he continued to sob with the full-throated sobs of a large invertebrate distress, beating his breast for an unfindable handkerchief, and, when he found it, immediately weeping it into pulp.

Campton had meant to leave him at the bank; but when the taxi stopped Mr. Mayhew was in too pitiful a plight for the painter to resist his entreaty.

"It was you who saw Benny last—you can't leave me!" the poor man implored; and Campton followed him up the majestic stairway.

Their names were taken in to Mr. Brant, and with a motion of wonder at the unaccountable humours of fate, Campton found himself for the first time entering the banker's private office.

Mr. Brant was elsewhere in the great glazed labyrinth, and while the visitors waited, the painter's registering eye took in the details of the room, from the Barye *cire-perdue* on a peach-coloured marble mantel to the blue morocco armchairs about a giant writing-table. On the table was an electric lamp in a celadon vase, and just the right number of neatly folded papers lay under a paper-weight of Chinese crystal. The room was as tidy as an expensive stage-setting or the cage of a well-kept canary: the only object marring its order was a telegram lying open on the desk.

Mr. Brant, grey and glossy, slipped in on noiseless patent leather. He shook hands with Mr. Mayhew, bowed stiffly but deprecatingly to

Campton, gave his usual cough, and said: "This is terrible."

And suddenly, as the three men sat there, so impressive and important and powerless, with that fatal telegram marring the tidiness of the desk, Campton murmured to himself: "If this thing were to happen to me I couldn't bear it. . . . I simply couldn't bear it. . . ."

Benny Upsher was not dead—at least his death was not certain. He had been seen to fall in a surprise attack near Neuve Chapelle; the telegram, from his commanding officer, reported him as "wounded and missing."

The words had taken on a hideous significance in the last months. Freezing to death between the lines, mutilation and torture, or weeks of slow agony in German hospitals: these were the alternative visions associated with the now familiar formula. Mr. Mayhew had spent a part of his time collecting details about the treatment of those who had fallen, alive but wounded, into German hands; and Campton guessed that as he sat there every one of these details, cruel, sanguinary, remorseless, had started to life, and that all their victims wore the face of Benny.

The wretched man sat speechless, so unhinged and swinging loose in his grief that Mr. Brant and Campton could only look on, following the thoughts he was thinking, seeing the sights he was seeing, and each avoiding the other's eye lest they should betray to one another the secret of their shared exultation at George's safety.

Finally Mr. Mayhew was put in charge of a confidential clerk, who was to go with him to the English Military Mission in the hope of getting further information. He went away, small and shrunken, with the deprecating smile of a man who seeks to ward off a blow; as he left the room Campton heard him say timidly to the clerk: "No doubt you speak French, sir? The words I want don't seem to come to me."

Campton had meant to leave at the same time; but some vague impulse held him back. He remembered George's postscript: "Don't be too savage to Uncle Andy," and wished he could think of some friendly phrase to ease off his leave-taking. Mr. Brant seemed to have the same wish. He stood, erect and tightly buttoned, one small hand resting on the arm of his desk-chair, as though he were posing for a cabinet size, with the photographer telling him to look natural. His lids twitched behind his protective glasses, and his upper lip, which was as straight as a ruler, detached itself by a hair's breadth from the lower; but no word came.

Campton glanced up and down the white-panelled walls, and spoke abruptly.

"There was no reason on earth," he said, "why poor young Upsher should ever have been in this thing."

Mr. Brant bowed.

"This sort of crazy impulse to rush into other people's rows," Campton continued with rising vehemence, "is of no more use to a civilized state than any other unreasoned instinct. At bottom it's nothing but what George calls the baseball spirit: just an ignorant passion for fisticuffs."

Mr. Brant looked at him intently. "When did—George say that?" he asked, with his usual cough before the name.

Campton coloured. "Oh—er—some time ago: in the very beginning, I think. It was the view of most thoughtful young fellows at that time."

"Quite so," said Mr. Brant, cautiously stroking his moustache.

Campton's eyes again wandered about the room.

"*Now,* of course——"

"Ah—*now*. . ."

The two men looked at each other, and Campton held out his hand. Mr. Brant, growing pink about the forehead, extended his dry fingers, and they shook hands in silence.

XVIII

In the street Campton looked about him with the same confused sense as when he had watched Fortin-Lescluze driving away to Chalous, his dead son's image in his eyes.

Each time that Campton came in contact with people on whom this calamity had fallen he grew more acutely aware of his own inadequacy. If he had been Fortin-Lescluze it would have been impossible for him to go back to Chalons and resume his task. If he had been Harvey Mayhew, still less could he have accommodated himself to the intolerable, the really inconceivable, thought that Benny Upsher had vanished into that fiery furnace like a crumpled letter tossed into a grate. Young Fortin was defending his country—but Upsher, in God's name what was Benny Upsher of Connecticut doing in a war between the continental powers?

Suddenly Campton remembered that he had George's letter in his pocket, and that he had meant to go back with it to Mrs. Brant's. He had started out that morning full of the good intentions the letter had inspired; but now he had no heart to carry them out. Yet George had said: "Let mother know, and explain, please"; and such an injunction could not be disregarded.

He was still hesitating on a street corner when he remembered that Miss Anthony was probably on her way home for luncheon, and that if he made haste he might find her despatching her hurried meal. It was instinctive with him, in difficult hours, to turn to her, less for counsel than for shelter; her simple unperplexed view of things was as comforting as his mother's solution of the dark riddles he used to propound in the nursery.

He found her in her little dining-room, with Delft plates askew on imitation Cordova leather, and a Death's Head Pennon and a Prussian helmet surmounting the nymph in cast bronze on the mantelpiece. In entering he faced the relentless light of a ground-glass window opening on an air-shaft; and Miss Anthony, flinging him a look, dropped her fork and sprang up crying: "George——"

"George—why George?" Campton recovered his presence of mind under the shock of her agitation. "What made you think of George?"

"Your—your face," she stammered, sitting down again. "So absurd of me. . . But you looked. . . A seat for monsieur, Jeanne," she cried over her shoulder to the pantry.

"Ah—my face? Yes, I suppose so. Benny Upsher has disappeared— I've just had to break it to Mayhew."

"Oh, that poor young Upsher? How dreadful!" Her own face grew instantly serene. "I'm so sorry—so very sorry. . . Yes, yes, you *shall* lunch with me—I know there's another cutlet," she insisted.

He shook his head. "I couldn't."

"Well, then, I've finished." She led the way into the drawing-room. There it was her turn to face the light, and he saw that her own features were as perturbed as she had apparently discovered his to be.

"Poor Benny, poor boy!" she repeated, in the happy voice she might have had if she had been congratulating Campton on the lad's escape. He saw that she was still thinking not of Upsher but of George, and her inability to fit her intonation to her words betrayed the violence of her relief. But why had she imagined George to be in danger?

Campton recounted the scene at which he had just assisted, and while she continued to murmur her sympathy he asked abruptly: "Why on earth should you have been afraid for George?"

Miss Anthony had taken her usual armchair. It was placed, as the armchairs of elderly ladies usually are, with its high back to the light, and Campton could no longer observe the discrepancy between her words and her looks. This probably gave her laugh its note of confidence. "My dear, if you were to cut me open George's name would run out of every vein," she said.

"But in that tone—it was your tone. You thought he'd been—that something had happened," Campton insisted. "How could it, where he is?"

She shrugged her shoulders in the "foreign" way she had picked up in her youth. The gesture was as incongruous as her slang, but it had become part of her physical self, which lay in a loose mosaic of incongruities over the solid crystal block of her character.

"Why, indeed? I suppose there are risks everywhere, aren't there?"

"I don't know." He pulled out the letter he had received that morning.

A sudden light had illuminated it, and his hand shook. "I don't even know where George is any longer."

She seemed to hesitate for a moment, and then asked calmly: "What do you mean?"

"Here—look at this. We're to write to his base. I'm to tell his mother of the change." He waited, cursing the faint winter light, and the protecting back of her chair. "What can it mean," he broke out, "except that he's left Sainte-Menehould, that he's been sent elsewhere, and that he doesn't want us to find out where?"

Miss Anthony bent her long nose over the page. Her hand held the letter steadily, and he guessed, as she perused it, that she had had one of the same kind, and had already drawn her own conclusions. What they were, that first startled "George!" seemed to say. But would she ever let Campton see as far into her thoughts again? He continued to watch her hands patiently, since nothing was to be discovered of her face. The hands folded the letter with precision, and handed it back to him.

"Yes: I see why you thought that—one might have," she surprised him by conceding. Then, darting at his unprotected face a gaze he seemed to feel though he could not see it: "If it had meant that George had been ordered to the front, how would you have felt?" she demanded.

He had not expected the question, and though in the last weeks he had so often propounded it to himself, it caught him in the chest like a blow. A sense of humiliation, a longing to lay his weakness bare, suddenly rose in him, and he bowed his head. "I couldn't . . . I couldn't bear it," he stammered.

She was silent for an interval; then she stood up, and laying her hand on his shaking shoulder crossed the room to a desk in which he knew she kept her private papers. Her key clinked, and a moment later she handed him a letter. It was in George's writing, and dated on the same day as his own.

"Dearest old girl, nothing new but my address. Hereafter please write to our Base. This order has just been lowered from the empyrean at the end of an endless reel of red tape. What it means nobody knows. It does not appear to imply an immediate change of Headquarters; but even if such a change comes, my job is likely to remain the same. I'm getting used to it, and no wonder, for one day differeth not from another, and I've had many of them now. Take care of Dad and mother, and of your matchless self. I'm writing to father today. Your George the First—and Last (or I'll know why)."

The two letters bore one another out in a way which carried conviction. Campton saw that his sudden doubts must have been produced (since he had not felt them that morning) by the agonizing experience he had undergone: the vision of Benny Upsher had unmanned him. George was safe, and asked only to remain so: that was evident from both letters. And as the certainty of his son's acquiescence once more penetrated Campton it brought with it a fresh reaction of shame. Ashamed—yes, he had begun to be ashamed of George as well as of himself. Under the touch of Adele Anthony's implacable honesty his last pretenses shrivelled up, and he longed to abase himself. He lifted his head and looked at her, remembering all she would be able to read in his eyes.

"You're satisfied?" she enquired.

"Yes. If that's the word." He stretched his hand toward her, and then drew it back. "But it's *not:* it's not the word any longer." He laboured with the need of self-expression, and the opposing instinct of concealing feelings too complex for Miss Anthony's simple gaze. How could he say: "I'm satisfied; but I wish to God that George were not"? And was he satisfied, after all? And how could he define, or even be sure that he was actually experiencing, a feeling so contradictory that it seemed to be made up of anxiety for his son's safety, shame at that anxiety, shame at George's own complacent acceptance of his lot, and terror of a possible change in that lot? There were hours when it seemed to Campton that the Furies were listening, and ready to fling their awful answer to him if he as much as whispered to himself: "Would to God that George were not satisfied!"

The sense of their haunting presence laid its clutch on him, and caused him, after a pause, to finish his phrase in another tone. "No; satisfied's not the word; I'm *glad* George is out of it!" he exclaimed.

Miss Anthony was folding away the letter as calmly as if it had been a refugee record. She did not appear to notice the change in Campton's voice.

"I don't pretend to your sublime detachment: you've never had a child," he sneered. (Certainly, if the Furies were listening, they would put that down to his credit!)

"Oh, my poor John," she said; then she locked the desk, took her hat from the lamp-chimney on which it had been hanging, jammed it down on her head like a helmet, and remarked: "We'll go together, shall we? It's time I got back to the office."

On the way downstairs both were silent. Campton's ears echoed with his stupid taunt, and he glanced at her without daring to speak. On the last landing she paused and said: "I'll see Julia this evening about George's change of address. She may be worried; and I can explain—I can take her my letter."

"Oh, do" he assented. "And tell her—tell her—if she needs me——"

It was as much of a message as he found courage for. Miss Anthony nodded.

XIX

One day Mme. Lebel said: "The first horse-chestnuts are in bloom. And monsieur must really buy himself some new shirts."

Campton looked at her in surprise. She spoke in a different voice; he wondered if she had had good news of her grandchildren. Then he saw that the furrows in her old face were as deep as ever, and that the change in her voice was simply an unconscious response to the general stirring of sap, the spring need to go on living, through everything and in spite of everything.

On se fait une raison, as Mme. Lebel would have said. Life had to go on, and new shirts had to be bought. No one knew why it was necessary, but every one felt that it was; and here were the horse-chestnuts once more actively confirming it. Habit laid its compelling grasp on the wires of the poor broken marionettes with which the Furies had been playing, and they responded, though with feebler flappings, to the accustomed jerk.

In Campton the stirring of the sap had been a cold and languid process, chiefly felt in his reluctance to go on with his relief work. He had tried to close his ears to the whispers of his own lassitude, vexed, after the first impulse of self-dedication, to find that no vocation declared itself, that his task became each day more tedious as well as more painful. Theoretically, the pain ought to have stimulated him: perpetual immersion in that sea of anguish should have quickened his effort to help the poor creatures sinking under its waves. The woe of the war had had that effect on Adele Anthony, on young Boylston, on Mlle. Davril, on the greater number of his friends. But their ardour left him cold. He wanted to help, he wanted it, he was sure, as earnestly as they; but the longing was not an inspiration to him, and he felt more and more that to work listlessly was to work ineffectually.

"I give the poor devils so many boots and money-orders a day; you give them yourself, and so does Boylston," he complained to Miss Anthony; who murmured: Ah, *Boylston*——" as if that point of the remark were alone worth noticing.

"At his age too; it's extraordinary, the way the boy's got out of himself."

"Or into himself, rather. He *was* a pottering boy before—now he's a man, with a man's sense of things."

"Yes; but his patience, his way of getting into their minds, their prejudices, their meannesses, their miseries! He doesn't seem to me like the kind who was meant to be a missionary."

"Not a bit of it. . . But he's burnt up with shame at our not being in the war—as all the young Americans are."

Campton made an impatient movement. "Benny Upsher again——! Can't we let our government decide all that for us? What else did we elect it for, I wonder?"

"I wonder," echoed Miss Anthony.

Talks of this kind were irritating and unprofitable, and Campton did not again raise the question. Miss Anthony's vision was too simplifying to penetrate far into his doubts, and after nearly a year's incessant contact with the most savage realities her mind still seemed at ease in its old formulas.

Simplicity, after all, was the best safeguard in such hours. Mrs. Brant was as absorbed in her task as Adele Anthony. Since the Brant villa at Deauville had been turned into a hospital she was always on the road, in a refulgent new motor emblazoned with a Red Cross, carrying supplies, rushing down with great surgeons, hurrying back to committee meetings and conferences with the Service de Santé (for she and Mr. Brant were among the leaders in American relief work in Paris), and throwing open the Avenue Marigny drawing-rooms for concerts, lectures and such sober philanthropic gaieties as society was beginning to countenance.

On the day when Mme. Lebel told Campton that the horse-chestnuts were in blossom and he must buy some new shirts he was particularly in need of such incentives. He had made up his mind to go to see Mrs. Brant about a concert for "The Friends of French Art" which was to be held in her house. Ever since George had asked him to see something of his mother Campton had used the pretext of charitable collaboration as the best way of getting over their fundamental lack of anything to say to each other.

The appearance of the Champs Elysées confirmed Mme. Lebel's announcement. Everywhere the punctual rosy spikes were rising above unfolding green; and Campton, looking up at them, remembered once thinking how Nature had adapted herself to the scene in overhanging with her own pink lamps and green fans the lamps and fans of the *cafés chantants* beneath. The latter lights had long since been extinguished, the fans folded up; and as he passed the bent and broken arches of electric light, the iron chairs and dead plants in paintless boxes, all heaped up like the scenery of a bankrupt theatre, he felt the pang of Nature's obstinate renewal in a world of death. Yet he also felt the stir of the blossoming trees in the form of a more restless discontent, a duller despair, a new sense of inadequacy. How could war go on when spring had come?

Mrs. Brant, having reduced her household and given over her drawing-rooms to charity, received in her boudoir, a small room contrived by a clever upholsterer to simulate a seclusion of which she have never felt the need. Photographs strewed the low tables; and facing the door Campton saw George's last portrait, in uniform, enclosed in an expensive frame. Campton had received the same photograph, and thrust it into a drawer; he thought a young man on a safe staff job rather ridiculous in uniform, and at the same time the sight filled him with a secret dread.

Mrs. Brant was bidding good-bye to a lady in mourning whom Campton did not know. His approach through the carpeted antechamber had been unnoticed, and as he entered the room he heard Mrs. Brant say in French, apparently in reply to a remark of her visitor: "Bridge, *chère Madame?* No; not yet. I confess I haven't the courage to take up my old life. We mothers with sons at the front . . ."

"Ah," exclaimed the other lady, "there I don't agree with you. I think one owes it to them to go on as if one were as little afraid as *they* are. That is what all my sons prefer. . . Even," she added, lowering her voice but lifting her head higher, "even, I'm sure, the one who is buried by the Marne." With a flush on her handsome face she pressed Mrs. Brant's hand and passed out.

Mrs. Brant had caught sight of Campton as she received the rebuke. Her colour rose slightly, and she said with a smile: "So many women can't get on without amusement."

"No," he agreed. There was a pause, and then he asked: "Who was it?"

"The Marquise de Tranlay—the widow."

"Where are the sons she spoke of?"

"There are three left: one in the *Chasseurs à Pied;* the youngest, who volunteered at seventeen, in the artillery in the Argonne; the third, badly wounded, in hospital at Compiègne. And the eldest killed. I simply can't understand. . ."

"Why," Campton interrupted, "did you speak as if George were at the front? Do you usually speak of him in that way?"

Her silence and her deepening flush made him feel the unkindness of the question. "I didn't mean . . . forgive me," he said. "Only sometimes, when I see women like that I'm——"

"Well?" she questioned.

He was silent in his turn, and she did not insist. They sat facing each other, each forgetting the purpose of their meeting. For the hundredth time he felt the uselessness of trying to carry out George's filial injunction: between himself and George's mother these months of fiery trial seemed to have loosed instead of tightened the links.

He wandered back to Montmartre through the bereft and beautiful city. The light lay on it in wide silvery washes, harmonizing the grey stone, the pale foliage, and a sky piled with clouds which seemed to rebuild in translucid masses the monuments below. He caught himself once more viewing the details of the scene in the terms of his trade. River, pavements, terraces heavy with trees, the whole crowded sky-line from Notre Dame to the Panthéon, instead of presenting themselves in their bare reality, were transposed into a painter's vision. And the faces around him became again the starting-point of rapid incessant combinations of line and colour, as if the visible world were once more at its old trick of weaving itself into magic designs.

The reawakening of this instinct deepened Campton's sense of unrest, and made him feel more than ever unfitted for a life in which such things were no longer of account, in which it seemed a disloyalty even to think of them.

He returned to the studio, having promised to deal with some office work which he had carried home the night before. The papers lay on the table; but he turned to the window and looked out over his budding lilacs at the new strange Paris. He remembered that it was almost a year since he had leaned in the same place, gazing down on the wise and frivolous old city in her summer dishabille while he planned his journey to Africa with George; and something George had once quoted from Faust came drifting through his mind: "Take care! You've broken my beautiful world! There'll be splinters. . ." Ah, yes, splinters, splinters . . . everybody's hands were red with them! What retribution devised by man could be commensurate with the crime of destroying his beautiful world? Campton sat down to the task of collating office files.

His bell rang, and he started up, as much surprised as if the simplest events had become unusual. It would be natural enough that Dastrey or Boylston should drop in—or even Adele Anthony—but his heart beat as if it might be George. He limped to the door, and found Mrs. Talkett.

She said: "May I come in?" and did so without waiting for his answer. The rapidity of her entrance surprised him less than the change in her appearance. But for the one glimpse of her dishevelled elegance, when she had rushed into Mrs. Brant's drawing-room on the day after war was declared, he had seen her only in a nursing uniform, as absorbed in her work as if it had been a long-thwarted vocation. Now she stood before him in raiment so delicately springlike that it seemed an emanation of the day. Care had dropped from her with her professional garb, and she smiled as though he must guess the reason.

In ordinary times he would have thought: "She's in love——" but that explanation was one which seemed to belong to other days. It reminded him, however, how little he knew of Mrs. Talkett, who, after René Davril's death, had vanished from his life as abruptly as she had entered it. Allusions to "the Talketts," picked up now and again at Adele Anthony's, led him to conjecture an invisible husband in the background; but all he knew of Mrs. Talkett was what she had told him of her "artistic" yearnings, and what he had been able to divine from her empty questioning eyes, from certain sweet inflections when she spoke of her wounded soldiers, and from the precise and finished language with which she clothed her unfinished and unprecise thoughts. All these indications made up an image not unlike that of the fashion-plate torn from its context of which she had reminded him at their first meeting; and he looked at her with indifference, wondering why she had come.

With an abrupt gesture she pulled the pin from her heavily-plumed hat, tossed it on the divan, and said: "Dear Master, I just want to sit with you and have you talk to me." She dropped down beside her hat, clasped her thin hands about her thin knee, and broke out, as if she had already forgotten that she wanted him to talk to her: "Do you know, I've made up my mind to begin to live again—to live my own life, I mean, to be my real *me,* after all these dreadful months of exile from myself. I see now that *that* is my real duty—just as it is yours, just as it is that of every artist and every creator. Don't you feel as I do? Don't you agree with me? We *must* save Beauty for the world; before it is too late we must save it out of this awful wreck and ruin. It sounds ridiculously presumptuous, doesn't it, to say 'we' in talking of a great genius like you and a poor little speck of dust like me? But after all there is the same instinct in us, the same craving, the same desire to realize Beauty, though you do it so magnificently and so—so objectively, and I . . ." she paused, unclasped her hands, and lifted her lovely bewildered eyes, "I do it only by a ribbon in my hair, a flower in a vase, a way of looping a curtain, or placing a lacquer screen in the right light. But I oughtn't to be ashamed of my limitations, do you think I ought? Surely every one ought to be helping to save Beauty; every one is needed, even the humblest and most ignorant of us, or else the world will be all death and ugliness. And after all, ugliness is the only *real* death, isn't it?" She drew a deep breath and added: "It has done me good already to sit here and listen to you."

Campton, a few weeks previously, would have been amused, or perhaps merely irritated. But in the interval he had become aware in himself of the same irresistible craving to "live," as she put it, and as he had heard it formulated, that very day, by the mourning mother who had so sharply rebuked Mrs. Brant. The spring was stirring them all in their different ways, secreting in them the sap which craved to burst into bridge-parties, or the painting of masterpieces, or a consciousness of the need for new shirts.

"But what am I in all this?" Mrs. Talkett rushed on, sparing him the trouble of a reply. "Nothing but the match that lights the flame! Sometimes I imagine that I might put what I mean into poetry . . . I *have* scribbled a few things, you know . . . but that's not what I was going to tell you. It's you, dear Master, who must set us the example of getting back to our work, our real work, whatever it is. What have you done in all these dreadful months—the real You? Nothing! And the World will be the poorer for it ever after. Master, you must paint again—you must begin today!"

Campton gave an uneasy laugh. "Oh—paint!" He waved his hand toward the office files of "The Friends of French Art." "There's my work."

"Not the real you. It's your dummy's work—just as my nursing has been mine. Oh, one did one's best—but all the while beauty and art and the eternal things were perishing! And what will the world be like without them?"

"I shan't be here," Campton growled.

"But your son will." She looked at him profoundly. "You know I know your son—we're friends. And I'm sure he would feel as I feel—he would tell you to go back to your painting."

For months past any allusion to George had put Campton on his guard, stiffening him with improvised defences. But this appeal of Mrs. Talkett's found him unprepared, demoralized by the spring sweetness, and by his secret sense of his son's connivance with it. What was war—any war—but an old European disease, an ancestral blood-madness seizing on the first pretext to slake its frenzy? Campton reminded himself again that he was the son of free institutions, of a country in no way responsible for the centuries of sinister diplomacy which had brought Europe to ruin, and was now trying to drag down America. George was right, the Brants were right, this young woman through whose lips Campton's own secret instinct spoke was right.

He was silent so long that she rose with the anxious frown that appeared to be her way of blushing, and faltered out: "I'm boring you—I'd better go."

She picked up her hat and held its cataract of feathers poised above her slanted head.

"Wait—let me do you like that!" Campton cried. It had never before occurred to him that she was paintable; but as she stood there with uplifted arm the long line flowing from her wrist to her lip suddenly wound itself about him like a net.

"Me?" she stammered, standing motionless, as if frightened by the excess of her triumph.

"Do you mind?" he queried; and hardly hearing her faltered-out: "Mind? When it was what I came for!" he dragged forth an easel, flung on it the first canvas he could lay hands on (though he knew it was the wrong shape and size), and found himself instantly transported into the lost world which was the only real one.

XX

For a month Campton painted on in transcendent bliss.

His first stroke carried him out of space and time, into a region where all that had become numbed and atrophied in him could expand and breathe. Lines, images, colours were again the sole facts: he plunged into their whirling circles like a stranded sea-creature into the sea. Once more every face was not a vague hieroglyph, a curtain drawn before an invisible aggregate of wants and woes, but a work of art, a flower in a pattern, to be dealt with on its own merits, like a bronze or a jewel. During the first day or two his hand halted; but the sense of insufficiency was a goad, and he fought with his subject till he felt a strange ease in every renovated muscle, and his model became like a musical instrument on which he played with careless mastery.

He had transferred his easel to Mrs. Talkett's apartment. It was an odd patchwork place, full of bold beginnings and doubtful pauses, rash surrenders to the newest fashions and abrupt insurrections against them, where Louis-Philippe mahogany had entrenched itself against the aggression of *art nouveau* hangings, and the frail grace of eighteenth-century armchairs shed derision on lumpy modern furniture painted like hobby-horses at a fair. It amused Campton to do Mrs. Talkett against such a background: her thin personality needed to be filled out by the visible results of its many quests and cravings. There were people one could sit down before a blank wall, and all their world was there, in the curves of their faces and the way their hands lay in their laps; others, like Mrs. Talkett, seemed to be made out of the reflection of what surrounded them, as if they had been born of a tricky grouping of looking-glasses, and would vanish if it were changed.

At first Campton was steeped in the mere sensual joy of his art; but after a few days the play of the mirrors began to interest him. Mrs. Talkett had abandoned her hospital work, and was trying, as she said, to "recreate herself." In this she was aided by a number of people who struck Campton as rather too young not to have found some other job, or too old to care any longer for that particular one. But all this did not trouble his newly recovered serenity. He seemed to himself, somehow, like a drowned body—but drowned in a toy aquarium—still staring about with living eyes, but aware of the other people only as shapes swimming by with a flash of exotic fins. They were enclosed together, all of them, in an unreal luminous sphere, mercifully screened against the reality from which a common impulse of horror had driven them; and since he was among them it was not his business to wonder at the others. So, through the cloud of his art, he looked out on them impartially.

The high priestess of the group was Mme. de Dolmetsch, with Harvey Mayhew as her acolyte. Mr. Mayhew was still in pursuit of Atrocities: he was in fact almost the only member of the group who did not rather ostentatiously disavow the obligation to "carry on." But he had

discovered that to discharge this sacred task he must vary it by frequent intervals of relaxation. He explained to Campton that he had
found it to be "his duty to rest"; and he was indefatigable in the performance of duty. He had therefore, with an expenditure of eloquence
which Campton thought surprisingly slight, persuaded Boylston to
become his understudy, and devote several hours a day to the
whirling activities of the shrimp-pink Bureau of Atrocities at the Nouveau Luxe. Campton, at first, could not understand how the astute
Boylston had allowed himself to be drawn into the eddy; but it turned
out that Boylston's astuteness had drawn him in. "You see, there's an
awful lot of money to be got out of it, one way and another, and I
know a use for every penny—that it, Miss Anthony and I do," the
young man modestly explained; adding, in response to the painter's
puzzled stare, that Mr. Mayhew's harrowing appeals were beginning
to bring from America immense sums for the Victims, and that Mr.
Mayhew, while immensely gratified by the effect of his eloquence, and
the prestige it was bringing him in French social and governmental
circles, had not the cloudiest notion how the funds should be used,
and had begged Boylston to advise him. It was owing to this that the
ex-Delegate to the Hague was able, with a light conscience, to seek
the repose of Mrs. Talkett's company and, with a smile of the widest
initiation, to listen to the subversive conversation of her familiars.

"Subversive" was the motto of the group. Every one was engaged in
attacking some theory of art or life or letters which nobody in particular defended. Even Mr. Talkett—a kindly young man with eyeglasses
and glossy hair, who roamed about straightening the furniture, like a
gentlemanly detective watching the presents at a wedding—owned to
Campton that *he* was subversive; and on the painter's pressing for a
definition, added: "Why, I don't believe in anything *she* doesn't believe
in," while his eye-glasses shyly followed his wife's course among the
teacups.

Mme. de Dolmetsch, though obviously anxious to retain her hold on
Mr. Mayhew, did not restrict herself to such mild fare, but exercised
her matchless eyes on a troop of followers: the shock-haired pianist
who accompanied her recitations, a straight-backed young American
diplomatist whose collars seemed a part of his career, a lustrous
South American millionaire, and a short squat Sicilian who designed
the costumes for the pianist's unproduced ballets.

All these people appeared to believe intensely in each other's reality and importance; but it gradually came over Campton that all of
them, excepting their host and hostess, knew that they were merely
masquerading.

To Campton, used to the hard-working world of art, this playing at
Bohemia seemed a nursery-game; but the scene acquired an unexpected

solidity from the appearance in it, one day, of the banker Jorgenstein, who strolled in as naturally as if he had been dropping into Campton's studio to enquire into the progress of his own portrait.

"I must come and look you up, Campton—get you to finish me," he said jovially, tapping his fat boot with a malacca stick as he looked over the painter's head at the canvas on which Mrs. Talkett's restless image seemed to flutter like a butterfly impaled.

"You'll owe it to *me* if he does you," the sitter declared, smiling back at the leer which Campton divined behind his shoulder; and he felt a sudden pity for her innocence.

"My wife made Campton come back to his real work—doing his bit, you know," said Mr. Talkett, straightening a curtain and disappearing again, like a diving animal; and Mrs. Talkett turned her plaintive eyes on Campton. "That kind of idiocy is all I've ever had," they seemed to say; and he nearly cried back to her: "But, you poor child, it's the only honest thing anywhere near you!"

Absorbed in his picture, he hardly stopped to wonder at Jorgenstein's reappearance, at his air of bloated satisfaction or his easy allusions to Cabinet Ministers and eminent statesmen. The atmosphere of the Talkett house was so mirage-like that even the big red bulk of the international financier became imponderable in it.

But one day Campton, on his way home, ran across Dastrey, and remembered that they had not met for weeks. The ministerial drudge looked worn and preoccupied, and Campton was abruptly recalled to the world he had been trying to escape from.

"You seem rather knocked-up—what's wrong with you?"

Dastrey stared. "Wrong with me? Well—did you like the communiqué this morning?"

"I didn't read it," said Campton curtly. They walked along a few steps in silence.

"You see," the painter continued, "I've gone back to my job—my painting. I suddenly found I had to."

Dastrey glanced at him with surprising kindness. "Ah, that's good news, my dear fellow!"

"You think so?" Campton half-sneered.

"Of course—why not? What are you painting? May I come and see?"

"Naturally." Campton paused. "The fact is, I was bitten the other day with a desire to depict that little will-o'-the-wisp of a Mrs. Talkett. Come to her house any afternoon and I'll show you the thing."

"To her house?" Dastrey paused with a frown. "Then the picture's finished?"

"No—not by a long way. I'm doing it there—in her *milieu,* among her crowd. It amuses me; they amuse me. When will you come?" He shot out the sentences like challenges; and his friend took them up in the same tone.

"To Mrs. Talkett's—to meet her crowd? Thanks—I'm too much tied down by my job."

"No; you're not. You're too disapproving," said Campton quarrelsomely. "You think we're all a lot of shirks, of drones, of international loafers—I don't know what you call us. But I'm one of them, so whatever name you give them I must answer to. Well, I'll tell you what they are, my dear fellow—and I'm not ashamed to be among them: they're people who've resolutely, unanimously, unshakeably decided, for a certain number of hours each day, to forget the war, to ignore it, to live as if it were not and never had been, so that——"

"So that?"

"So that beauty shall not perish from the earth!" Campton shouted, bringing his stick down with a whack on the pavement.

Dastrey broke into a laugh. "*Allons donc!* Decided to forget the war? Why, bless your heart, they've never, not one of 'em, ever been able to remember it for an hour together; no, not from the first day, except as it interfered with their plans or cut down their amusements or increased their fortunes. You're the only one of them, my dear chap, (since you class yourself among them) of whom what you've just said is true; and if you can forget the war while you're at your work, so much the better for you and for us and for posterity; and I hope you'll paint all Mrs. Talkett's crowd, one after another. Though I doubt if they're as good subjects now as when you caught them last July with the war-funk on." He held out his hand with a dry smile. "Good-bye. I'm off to meet my nephew, who's here on leave."

He hastened away, leaving Campton in a crumbled world. Louis Dastrey on leave? But that was because he was at the front, the real front, in the trenches, had already had a slight wound and a fine citation. Staff-officers, as George had wisely felt, were not asking for leave just yet. . .

The thoughts excited by this encounter left Campton more than ever resolved to drug himself with work and frivolity. It was none of his business to pry into the consciences of the people about him, not even into Jorgenstein's—into which one would presumably have had to be let down in a diver's suit, with oxygen pumping at top pressure. If the government tolerated Jorgenstein's presence in France, probably on the ground that he could be useful—so the banker himself let it be known—it was silly of people like Adele Anthony and Dastrey to wince at the mere mention of his name. There woke in Campton all the old spirit of aimless random defiance—revolt for revolt's sake— which had marked the first period of his life after his separation from his wife. He had long since come to regard it as a crude and juvenile phase—yet here he was reliving it.

Though he knew of the intimacy between Mrs. Talkett and the Brants he had no fear of meeting Julia: it was impossible to picture her neat head battling with the blasts of that dishevelled drawing-room. But though she did not appear there, he heard her more and more often alluded to, in terms of startling familiarity, by Mrs. Talkett's visitors. It was clear that they all saw her, chiefly in her own house, that they thought her, according to their respective vocabularies, "a perfect dear," *"une femme exquise"* or *"une bonne vieille"* (ah, poor Julia!); and that their sudden enthusiasm for her was not uninspired by the fact that she had got her marvellous *chef* demobilised, and was giving little "war-dinners" followed by a quiet turn at bridge.

Campton remembered Mme. de Tranlay's rebuke to Mrs. Brant on the day when he had last called in the Avenue Marigny; then he remembered also that it was on that very day that he had returned to his painting.

"After all, she held out longer than I did—poor Julia!" he mused, annoyed at the idea of her being the complacent victim of all the voracities he saw about him, and yet reflecting that she was at last living her life, as they called it at Mrs. Talkett's. After all, the fact that George was not at the front seemed to exonerate his parents—unless, indeed, it did just the opposite.

One day, coming earlier than usual to Mrs. Talkett's to put in a last afternoon's work on her portrait, Campton, to his surprise, found his wife in front of it. Equally to his surprise he noticed that she was dressed with a juvenility quite new to her; and for the first time he thought she looked old-fashioned and also old. She met him with her usual embarrassment.

"I didn't know you came as early as this. Madge told me I might just run in——" She waved her hand toward the portrait.

"I hope you like it," he said, suddenly finding that he didn't.

"It's marvellous—marvellous." She looked at him timidly. "It's extraordinary, how you've caught her rhythm, her *tempo*," she ventured in the jargon of the place. Campton, to hide a smile, turned away to get his brushes. "I'm so glad," she continued hastily, "that you've begun to paint again. We all need to . . . to . . ."

"Oh, not you and I, do we?" he rejoined with a scornful laugh.

She evidently caught the allusion, for she blushed all over her uncovered neck, up through the faintly wrinkled cheeks to the roots of her newly dyed hair; then he saw her eyes fill.

"What's she crying for? Because George is *not* in danger?" he wondered, busying himself with his palette.

Mrs. Talkett hurried in with surprise and apologies; and one by one

the habitués followed, with cheery greetings for Mrs. Brant and a moment of constraint as they noted Campton's presence, and the relation
between the two was mutely passed about. Then the bridge-tables
were brought, Mr. Talkett began to straighten the cards nervously,
and the guests broke up into groups, forgetting everything but their
own affairs. As Campton turned back to his work he was aware of a
last surprise in the sight of Mrs. Brant serene and almost sparkling,
waving her adieux to the bridge-tables, and going out followed by
Jorgenstein, with whom she seemed on terms of playful friendliness.
Of all strange war promiscuities, Campton thought this the strangest.

<hr />

XXI

The next time Campton saw Mrs. Brant was in his own studio.

He was preparing, one morning, to leave the melancholy place,
when the bell rang and his *bonne* let her in. Her dress was less
frivolous than at Mrs. Talkett's, and she wore a densely patterned
veil, like the ladies in cinema plays when they visit their seducers or
their accomplices.

Through the veil she looked at him agitatedly, and said: "George is
not at Sainte-Menehould."

He stared.

"No. Anderson was there the day before yesterday."

"Brant? At Sainte-Menehould?" Campton felt the blood rush to his
temples. What! He, the boy's father, had not so much as dared to ask
for the almost unattainable permission to go into the war-zone; and
this other man, who was nothing to George, absolutely nothing, who
had no right whatever to ask for leave to visit him, had somehow obtained the priceless favour, and instead of passing it on, instead of offering at least to share it with the boy's father, had sneaked off secretly to feast on the other's lawful privilege!

"How the devil——?" Campton burst out.

"Oh, he got a Red Cross mission; it was arranged very suddenly—
through a friend. . ."

"Yes—well?" Campton stammered, sitting down lest his legs should
fail him, and signing to her to take a chair.

"Well—he was not there!" she repeated excitedly. "It's what we
might have known—since he's changed his address."

"Then he didn't see him?" Campton interrupted, the ferocious joy of
the discovery crowding out his wrath and wonder.

"Anderson didn't? No. He wasn't there, I tell you!"

"The H.Q. has been moved?"

"No, it hasn't. Anderson saw one of the officers. He said George had been sent on a mission."

"To another H.Q.?"

"That's what they said. I don't believe it."

"What do you believe?"

"I don't know. Anderson's sure they told him the truth. The officer he saw is a friend of George's, and he said George was expected back that very evening."

Campton sat looking at her uncertainly. Did she dread, or did she rather wish, to disbelieve the officer's statement? Where did she hope or fear that George had gone? And what were Campton's own emotions? As confused, no doubt, as hers—as undefinable. The insecurity of his feelings moved him to a momentary compassion for hers, which were surely pitiable, whatever else they were. Then a savage impulse swept away every other, and he said: "Wherever George was, Brant's visit will have done him no good."

She grew pale. "What do you mean?"

"I wonder it never occurred to you—or to your husband, since he's so solicitous," Campton went on, prolonging her distress.

"Please tell me what you mean," she pleaded with frightened eyes.

"Why, in God's name, couldn't you both let well enough alone? Didn't you guess why George never asked for leave—why I've always advised him not to? Don't you know that nothing is as likely to get a young fellow into trouble as having his family force their way through to see him, use influence, seem to ask favours? I dare say that's how that fool of a Dolmetsch woman got Isador killed. No one would have noticed where he was if she hadn't gone on so about him. They *had* to send him to the front finally. And now the chances are——"

"Oh, no, no, no—don't say it!" She held her hands before her face as if he had flung something flaming at her. "It was I who made Anderson go!"

"Well—Brant ought to have thought of that—*I* did," he pursued sardonically.

Her answer disarmed him. "You're his father."

"I don't mean," he went on hastily, "that Brant's not right: of course there's nothing to be afraid of. I can't imagine why you thought there was."

She hung her head. "Sometimes when I hear the other women— other mothers—I feel as if our turn must come too. Even at Sainte-Menehould a shell might hit the house. Anderson said the artillery fire seemed so near."

He made no answer, and she sat silent, without apparent thought of leaving. Finally he said: "I was just going out——"

She stood up. "Oh, yes—that reminds me. I came to ask you to come with me."

"With you——?"

"The motor's waiting—you must." She laid her hand on his arm. "To see Olida, the new *clairvoyante*. Everybody goes to her—everybody who's anxious about anyone. Even the scientific people believe in her. She's told people the most extraordinary things—it seems she warned Daisy de Dolmetsch. . . Well, I'd *rather* know!" she burst out passionately.

Campton smiled. "She'll tell you that George is back at his desk."

"Well, then—isn't that worth it? Please don't refuse me!"

He disengaged himself gently. "My poor Julia, go by all means if it will reassure you."

"Ah, but you've got to come too. you can't say no: Madge Talkett tells me that if *the two nearest* go together Olida sees so much more clearly—especially a father and mother," she added hastily, as if conscious of the inopportune "nearest." After a moment she went on: "Even Mme. de Tranlay's been; Daisy de Dolmetsch met her on the stairs. Olida told her that her youngest boy, from whom she'd had no news for weeks, was all right, and coming home on leave. Mme. de Tranlay didn't know Daisy, except by sight, but she stopped her to tell her. Only fancy—the last person she would have spoken to in ordinary times! But she was so excited and happy! And two days afterward the boy turned up safe and sound. You must come!" she insisted.

Campton was seized with a sudden deep compassion for all these women groping for a ray of light in the blackness. It moved him to think of Mme. de Tranlay's proud figure climbing a *clairvoyante*'s stairs.

"I'll come if you want me to," he said.

They drove to the Batignolles quarter. Mrs. Brant's lips were twitching under her veil, and as the motor stopped she said childishly: "I've never been to this kind of place before."

"I should hope not," Campton rejoined. He himself, during the Russian lady's rule, had served an apprenticeship among the soothsayers, and come away disgusted with the hours wasted in their company. He suddenly remembered the Spanish girl in the little white house near the railway, who had told his fortune in the hot afternoons with cards and olive-stones, and had found, by irrefutable signs, that he and she would "come together" again. "Well, it was better than this pseudo-scientific humbug," he mused, "because it was picturesque—and so was she—and she believed in it."

Mrs. Brant rang, and Campton followed her into a narrow hall. A servant-woman showed them into a *salon* which was as commonplace as a doctor's waiting-room. On the mantelpiece were vases of pampas grass, and a stuffed monkey swung from the electrolier. Evidently Mme. Olida was superior to the class of fortune-tellers who prepare a special stage-setting, and no astrologer's robe or witch's kitchen was to be feared.

The maid led them across a plain dining-room into an inner room. The shutters were partly closed, and the blinds down. A voluminous woman in loose black rose from a sofa. Gold ear-rings gleamed under her oiled black hair—and suddenly, through the billows of flesh, and behind the large pale mask, Campton recognized the Spanish girl who used to read his fortune in the house by the railway. Her eyes rested a moment on Mrs. Brant; then they met his with the same heavy stare. But he noticed that her hands, which were small and fat, trembled a little as she pointed to two chairs.

"Sit down, please," she said in a low rough voice, speaking in French. The door opened again, and a young man with Levantine eyes and a showy necktie looked in. She said sharply: "No," and he disappeared. Campton noticed that a large emerald flashed on his manicured hand. Mme. Olida continued to look at her visitors.

Mrs. Brant wiped her dry lips and stammered: "We're his parents—a son at the front. . ."

Mme. Olida fell back in a trance-like attitude, let her lids droop over her magnificent eyes, and rested her head against a soiled sofa-pillow. Presently she held out both hands.

"You are his parents? Yes? Give me each a hand, please." As her cushioned palm touched Campton's he thought he felt a tremor of recognition, and saw, in the half-light, the tremor communicate itself to her lids. He grasped her hand firmly, and she lifted her eyes, looked straight into his with her heavy velvety stare, and said: "You should hold my hand more loosely; the currents must not be compressed." She turned her palm upward, so that his finger-tips rested on it as if on a keyboard; he noticed that she did not do the same with the hand she had placed in Mrs. Brant's.

Suddenly he remembered that one sultry noon, lying under the olives, she had taught him, by signals tapped on his own knee, how to say what he chose to her without her brothers' knowing it. He looked at the huge woman, seeking the curve of the bowed upper lip on which what used to be a faint blue shadow had now become a line as thick as her eyebrows, and recalling how her laugh used to lift the lip above her little round teeth while she threw back her head, showing the Agnus Dei in her neck. Now her mouth was like a withered flower, and in a crease of her neck a string of pearls was embedded.

"Take hands, please," she commanded. Julia gave Campton her ungloved hand, and he sat between the two women.

"You are the parents? You want news of your son—ah, like so many!" Mme. Olida closed her eyes again.

"To know where he is—whereabouts—that is what we want," Mrs. Brant whispered.

Mme. Olida sat as if labouring with difficult visions. The noises of the street came faintly through the closed windows and a smell of garlic and cheap scent oppressed Campton's lungs and awakened old associations. With a final effort of memory he fixed his eyes on the *clairvoyante*'s darkened mask, and tapped her palm once or twice. She neither stirred nor looked at him.

"I see—I see——" she began in the consecrated phrase. "A veil—a thick veil of smoke between me and a face which is young and fair, with a short nose and reddish hair: thick, thick, thick hair, exactly like this gentleman's when he was young. . ."

Mrs. Brant's hand trembled in Campton's. "It's true," she whispered, "before your hair turned grey it used to be as red as Georgie's."

"The veil grows denser—there are awful noises; there's a face with blood—but not that first face. This is a very young man, as innocent as when he was born, with blue eyes like flax-flowers, but blood, blood . . . why do I see that face? Ah, now it is on a hospital pillow—not your son's face, the other; there is no one near, no one but some German soldiers laughing and drinking; the lips move, the hands are stretched out in agony; but no one notices. It is a face that has something to say to the gentleman; not to you, Madame. The uniform is different—is it an English uniform? . . . Ah, now the face turns grey; the eyes shut, there is foam on the lips. Now it is gone—there's another man's head on the pillow. . . Now, now your son's face comes back; but not near those others. The smoke has cleared. . . I see a desk and papers; your son is writing. . ."

"Oh," gasped Mrs. Brant.

"If you squeeze my hands you arrest the current," Mme. Olida reminded her. There was another interval; Campton felt his wife's fingers beating between his like trapped birds. The heat and darkness oppressed him; beads of sweat came out on his forehead. Did the woman really see things, and was that face with the blood on it Benny Upsher's?

Mme. Olida droned on. "It is your son who is writing—the young man with the very thick hair. He is writing to you—trying to explain something. Perhaps you have hoped to see him lately? That is it; he is telling you why it could not be. He is sitting quietly in a room. There is no smoke." She released Mrs. Brant's hand and Campton's. "Go home, Madame. You are fortunate. Perhaps his letter will reach you tomorrow."

Mrs. Brant stood up sobbing. She found her gold bag and pushed it toward Campton. He had been feeling in his own pocket for money; but as he drew it forth Mme. Olida put back his hand. "No. I am superstitious; it's so seldom that I can give good news. *Bonjour, madame, bonjour, monsieur.* I commend your son to the blessed Virgin and to all the saints and angels."

Campton put Julia into the motor. She was still crying, but her tears were radiant. "Isn't she wonderful? Didn't you see how she seem to *recognize* George? There's no mistaking his hair! How could she have known what it was like? Don't think me foolish—I feel so comforted!"

"Of course; you'll hear from him tomorrow," Campton said. He was touched by her maternal passion, and ashamed of having allowed her so small a share in his jealous worship of his son. He walked away, thinking of a young man dying in a German hospital, and of the other man's face succeeding his on the pillow.

XXII

Two days later, to Campton's surprise, Anderson Brant appeared in the morning at the studio.

Campton, finishing a late breakfast in careless studio-garb, saw his visitor peer cautiously about, as though fearing undressed models behind the screens or empty beer-bottles under the tables. It was the first time that Mr. Brant had entered the studio since his attempt to buy George's portrait, and Campton guessed at once that he had come again about George.

He looked at the painter shyly, as if oppressed by the indiscretion of intruding at that hour.

"It was my—Mrs. Brant who insisted—when she got this letter," he brought out between precautionary coughs.

Campton looked at him tolerantly: a barrier seemed to have fallen between them since their brief exchange of words about Benny Upsher. The letter, as Campton had expected, was a line from George to his mother, written two days after Mr. Brant's visit to Sainte-Menehould. It expressed, in George's usual staccato style, his regret at having been away. "Hard luck, when one is riveted to the same square yard of earth for weeks on end, to have just happened to be somewhere else the day Uncle Andy broke through." It was always the same tone of fluent banter, in which Campton fancied he detected a lurking stridency, like the scrape of an overworked gramophone containing only comic disks.

"Ah, well—his mother must be satisfied," Campton said as he gave the letter back.

"Oh, completely. So much so that I've induced her to go off for a while to Biarritz. The doctor finds her overdone; she'd got it into her head that George had been sent to the front; I couldn't convince her to the contrary."

Campton looked at him. "You yourself never believed it?"

Mr. Brant, who had half risen, as though feeling that his errand was done, slid back into his seat and clasped his small hands on his agate-headed stick.

"Oh, never."

"It was not," Campton pursued, "with that idea that you went to Sainte-Menehould?"

Mr. Brant glanced at him in surprise. "No. On the contrary——"

"On the contrary?"

"I understood from—from his mother that, in the circumstances, you were opposed to his asking for leave; thought it unadvisable, that is. So, as it was such a long time since we'd seen him——" The "we," pulling him up short, spread a brick-red blush over his baldness.

"Not longer than since I have—but then I've not your opportunities," Campton retorted, the sneer breaking out in spite of him. Though he had grown kindly disposed toward Mr. Brant when they were apart, the old resentments still broke out in his presence.

Mr. Brant clasped and unclasped the knob of his stick. "I took the first chance that offered; I had his mother to think of." Campton made no answer, and he continued: "I was sorry to hear you thought I'd perhaps been imprudent."

"There's no perhaps about it," Campton retorted. "Since you say you were not anxious about the boy I can't imagine why you made the attempt."

Mr. Brant was silent. He seemed overwhelmed by the other's disapprobation, and unable to find any argument in his own defence. "I never dreamed it could cause any trouble," he said at length.

"That's the ground you've always taken in your interference with my son!" Campton had risen, pushing back his chair, and Mr. Brant stood up also. They faced each other without speaking.

"I'm sorry," Mr. Brant began, "that you should take such a view. It seemed to me natural . . ., when Mr. Jorgenstein gave me the chance——"

"Jorgenstein! It was Jorgenstein who took you to the front? Took you to see my son?" Campton threw his head back and laughed. "That's complete—that's really complete!"

Mr. Brant reddened as if the laugh had been a blow. He stood very erect, his lips as tightly closed as a shut penknife. He had the attitude of a civilian under fire, considerably perturbed, but obliged to set the example of fortitude.

Campton looked at him. At last he had Mr. Brant at a disadvantage. Their respective situations were reversed, and he saw that the banker was aware of it, and oppressed by the fear that he might have done harm to George. He evidently wanted to say all this and did not know how.

His distress moved Campton, in whose ears the sound of his own outburst still echoed unpleasantly. If only Mr. Brant would have kept out of his way he would have found it so easy to be fair to him!

"I'm sorry," he began in a quieter tone. "I dare say I'm unjust—perhaps it's in the nature of our relation. Can't you understand how I've felt, looking on helplessly all these years, while you've done for the boy everything I wanted to do for him myself? Haven't you guessed why I jumped at my first success, and nursed my celebrity till I'd got half the fools in Europe lining up to be painted?" His excitement was mastering him again, and he went on hurriedly: "Do you suppose I'd have wasted all these precious years over their stupid faces if I hadn't wanted to make my son independent of you? And he *would* have been, if the war hadn't come; been my own son again and nobody else's, leading his own life, whatever he chose it to be, instead of having to waste his youth in your bank, learning how to multiply your millions."

The futility of this retrospect, and the inconsistency of his whole attitude, exasperated Campton more than anything his visitor could do or say, and he stopped, embarrassed by the sound of his own words, yet seeing no escape save to bury them under more and more. But Mr. Brant had opened his lips.

"They'll be *his,* you know: the millions," he said.

Campton's anger dropped: he felt Mr. Brant at last too completely at his mercy. He waited for a moment before speaking.

"You tried to buy his portrait once—you remember I told you it was not for sale," he then said.

Mr. Brant stood motionless, grasping his stick in one hand and stroking his moustache with the other. For a while he seemed to be considering Campton's words without feeling their sting. "It was not the money . . ." he stammered out at length, from the depth of some unutterable plea for understanding; then he added: "I wish you a good morning," and walked out with his little stiff steps.

XXIII

Campton was thoroughly ashamed of what he had said to Mr. Brant, or rather of his manner of saying it. If he could have put the same facts quietly, ironically, without forfeiting his dignity, and with the added emphasis which deliberateness and composure give, he would scarcely have regretted the opportunity. He had always secretly accused himself of a lack of courage in accepting Mr. Brant's heavy benefactions for George when the boy was too young to know what they might pledge him to; and it had been a disappointment that George, on reaching the age of discrimination, had not appeared to find the burden heavy, or the obligations unpleasant.

Campton, having accepted Mr. Brant's help, could hardly reproach his son for feeling grateful for it, and had therefore thought it "more decent" to postpone disparagement of their common benefactor till his own efforts had set them both free. Even then, it would be impossible to pay off the past—but the past might have been left to bury itself. Now his own wrath had dug it up, and he had paid for the brief joy of casting its bones in Mr. Brant's face by a deep disgust at his own weakness.

All these things would have weighed on him even more if the outer weight of events had not been so much heavier. He had not returned to Mrs. Talkett's since the banker's visit; he did not wish to meet Jorgenstein, and his talk with the banker, and his visit to the *clairvoyante,* had somehow combined to send that whole factitious world tumbling about his ears. It was absurd to attach any importance to poor Olida's vaticinations; but the vividness of her description of the baby-faced boy dying in a German hospital haunted Campton's nights. If it were not the portrait of Benny Upsher it was at least that of hundreds and thousands of lads like him, who were thus groping and agonizing and stretching out vain hands, while in Mrs. Talkett's drawing-room well-fed men and expensive women heroically "forgot the war." Campton, seeking to expiate his own brief forgetfulness by a passion of renewed activity, announced to Boylston the next afternoon that he was coming back to the office.

Boylston hardly responded: he looked up from his desk with a face so strange that Campton broke off to cry out: "What's happened?"

The young man held out a newspaper. "They've done it—they've done it!" he shouted. Across the page the name of the *Lusitania* blazed out like the writing on the wall.

The Berserker light on Boylston's placid features transformed him into an avenging cherub. "Ah, now we're in it at last!" he exulted, as if the horror of the catastrophe were already swallowed up in its result. The two looked at each other without further words; but the older man's first thought had been for his son. Now, indeed, America was "in it": the gross tangible proof for which her government had forced her to wait was there in all its unimagined horror. Cant and cowardice in high places had drugged and stupefied her into the strange belief that she was too proud to fight for others; and here she was brutally forced to fight for herself. Campton waited with a straining heart for his son's first comment on the new fact that they were "in it."

But his excitement and Boylston's exultation were short-lived. Before many days it became apparent that the proud nation which had flamed up overnight at the unproved outrage of the *Maine* was lying supine under the flagrant provocation of the *Lusitania*. The days which followed were, to many Americans, the bitterest of the war: to Campton they seemed the ironic justification of the phase of indifference and self-absorption through which he had just passed. He could not go back to Mrs. Talkett and her group; but neither could he take up his work with even his former zeal. The bitter taste of the national humiliation was perpetually on his lips: he went about like a man dishonoured.

He wondered, as the days and the weeks passed, at having no word from George. Had he refrained from writing because he too felt the national humiliation too deeply either to speak of it or to leave it unmentioned? Or was he so sunk in security that he felt only a mean thankfulness that nothing was changed? From such thoughts Campton's soul recoiled; but they lay close under the surface of his tenderness, and reared their evil heads whenever they caught him alone.

As the summer dragged itself out he was more and more alone. Dastrey, cured of his rheumatism, had left the Ministry to resume his ambulance work. Miss Anthony was submerged under the ever-mounting tide of refugees. Mrs. Brant had taken a small house at Deauville (on the pretext of being near her hospital), and Campton heard of the Talketts' being with her, and others of their set. Mr. Mayhew appeared at the studio one day, in tennis flannels and a new straw hat, announcing that he "needed rest," and rather sheepishly adding that Mrs. Brant had suggested his spending "a quiet fortnight" with her. "I've *got* to do it, if I'm to see this thing through," Mr. Mayhew added in a stern voice, as if commanding himself not to waver.

A few days later, glancing over the *Herald,* Campton read that Mme. de Dolmetsch, "the celebrated *artiste,"* was staying with Mr. and Mrs. Anderson Brant at Deauville, where she had gone to give recitations for the wounded in hospital. Campton smiled, and then thought with a tightening heart of Benny Upsher and Ladislas Isador, so incredibly unlike in their lives, so strangely one in their death. Finally, not long afterward, he read that the celebrated financier, Sir Cyril Jorgenstein (recently knighted by the British Government) had bestowed a gift of a hundred thousand francs upon Mrs. Brant's hospital. It was rumoured, the paragraph ended, the Sir Cyril would soon receive the Legion of Honour for his magnificent liberalities to France.

And still the flood of war rolled on. Success here, failure there, the menace of disaster elsewhere—Russia retreating to the San, Italy declaring war on Austria and preparing to cross the Isonzo, the British advance at Anzac, and from the near East news of the new landing at Suvla. Through all this alternating of tragedy and triumph ran the million and million individual threads of hope, fear, fortitude, resolve, with which the fortune of the war was obscurely but fatally interwoven. Campton remembered his sneer at Dastrey's phrase: "One can at least contribute an attitude." He had begun to feel the force of that, to understand the need of every human being's "pulling his weight" in the struggle, had begun to scan every face in the street in the passionate effort to distinguish between the stones in the wall of resistance and the cracks through which discouragement might filter.

The shabby office of the Palais Royal again became his only haven. His portrait of Mrs. Talkett had brought him many new orders; but he refused them all, and declined even to finish the pictures interrupted by the war. One of his abrupt revulsions of feeling had flung him back, heart and brain, into the horror he had tried to escape from. "If thou ascend up into heaven I am there; if thou make thy bed in hell, behold I am there," the war said to him; and as the daily head-lines shrieked out the names of new battle-fields, from the Arctic shore to the Pacific, he groaned back like the Psalmist: "Whither shall I go from thee?"

The people about him—Miss Anthony, Boylston, Mlle. Davril, and all their band of tired resolute workers—plodded ahead, their eyes on their task, seeming to find in its fulfillment a partial escape from the intolerable oppression. The women especially, with their gift of living in the particular, appeared hardly aware of the appalling development of the catastrophe; and Campton felt himself almost as lonely among these people who thought of nothing but the war as among those who hardly thought of it at all. It was only when he and Boylston, after a hard morning's work, went out to lunch together, that what he called the *Lusitania look,* suddenly darkening the younger man's face, moved the painter with an anguish like his own.

Boylston, breaking through his habitual shyness, had one day remonstrated with Campton for not going on with his painting: but the latter had merely rejoined: "We've each of us got to worry through this thing in our own way—" and the subject was not again raised between them.

The intervals between George's letters were growing longer. Campton, who noted in his pocket-diary the dates of all that he received, as well as those addressed to Mrs. Brant and Miss Anthony, had not had one to record since the middle of June. And in that there was no allusion to the *Lusitania.*

"It's queer," he said to Boylston, one day toward the end of July; "I don't know yet what George thinks about the *Lusitania.*"

"Oh, yes, you do, sir!" Boylston returned, laughing; "but all the mails from the war-zone," he added, "have been very much delayed lately. When there's a big attack on anywhere they hold up everything along the line. And besides, no end of letters are lost."

"I suppose so," said Campton, pocketing the diary, and trying for the millionth time to call up a vision of his boy, seated at a desk in some still unvisualized place, his rumpled fair head bent above columns of figures or files of correspondence, while day after day the roof above him shook with the roar of the attacks which held up his letters.

Book
Three

XXIV

The gates of Paris were behind them, and they were rushing through an icy twilight between long lines of houses, factory chimneys and city-girt fields, when Campton at last roused himself and understood.

It was he, John Campton, who sat in that car—that noiseless swiftly-sliding car, so cushioned and commodious, so ingeniously fitted for all the exigencies and emergencies of travel, that it might have been a section of the Nouveau Luxe on wheels; and the figure next to him, on the extreme other side of the deeply upholstered seat, was that of Anderson Brant. This, for the moment, was as far as Campton's dazed perceptions carried him. . .

The motor was among real fields and orchards, and the icy half-light which might just as well have been dusk was turning definitely to dawn, when at last, disentangling his mind from a tight coil of passport and permit problems, he thought: "But this is the road north of Paris—that must have been St. Denis."

Among all the multiplied strangenesses of the last strange hours it had hardly struck him before that, now he was finally on his way to George, it was not to the Argonne that he was going, but in the opposite direction. The discovery held his floating mind for a moment, but for a moment only, before it drifted away again, to be caught on some other projecting strangeness.

Chief among these was Mr. Brant's presence at his side, and the fact that the motor they were sitting in was Mr. Brant's. But Campton felt that such enormities were not to be dealt with yet. He had neither slept nor eaten since the morning before, and whenever he tried to grasp the situation in its entirety his spirit fainted away again into outer darkness. . .

His companion presently coughed, and said, in a voice even more than usually colourless and expressionless: "We are at Luzarches already."

It was the first time, Campton was sure, that Mr. Brant had spoken since they had got into the car together, hours earlier as it seemed to him, in the dark street before the studio in Montmartre; the first, at least, except to ask, as the chauffeur touched the self-starter: "Will you have the rug over you?"

The two travellers did not share a rug: a separate one, soft as fur and light as down, lay neatly folded on the grey carpet before each seat; but Campton, though the early air was biting, had left his where it lay, and had not answered.

Now he was beginning to feel that he could not decently remain silent any longer; and with an effort which seemed as mechanical and external as the movements of the chauffeur whose back he viewed through the wide single sheet of plate-glass, he brought out, like a far-off echo: "Luzarches . . . ?"

It was not that there lingered in him any of his old sense of antipathy toward Mr. Brant. In the new world into which he had been abruptly hurled, the previous morning, by the coming of that letter which looked so exactly like any other letter—in this new world Mr. Brant was nothing more than the possessor of the motor and of the "pull" that were to get him, Campton, in the shortest possible time, to the spot of earth where his son lay dying. Once assured of this, Campton had promptly and indifferently acquiesced in Miss Anthony's hurried suggestion that it would be only decent to let Mr. Brant go to Doullens with him.

But the exchange of speech with any one, whether Mr. Brant or another, was for the time being manifestly impossible. The effort, to Campton, to rise out of his grief, was like that of a dying person struggling back from regions too remote for his voice to reach the ears of the living. He shrank into his corner, and tried once more to fix his attention on the flying landscape.

All that he saw in it, speeding ahead of him even faster than their own flight, was the ghostly vision of another motor, carrying a figure bowed like his, mute like his: the figure of Fortin-Lescluze, as he had seen it plunge away into the winter darkness after the physician's son had been killed. Campton remembered asking himself then, as he had asked himself so often since: "How should I bear it if it happened to me?"

He knew the answer to that now, as he knew everything else a man could know: so it had seemed to his astonished soul since the truth had flashed at him out of that fatal letter. Ever since then he had been turning about and about in a vast glare of initiation: of all the old crowded misty world which the letter had emptied at a stroke, nothing remained but a few memories of George's boyhood, like a closet of toys in a house knocked down by an earthquake.

The vision of Fortin-Lescluze's motor vanished, and in its place Campton suddenly saw Boylston's screwed-up eyes staring out at him under furrows of anguish. Campton remembered, the evening before, pushing the letter over to him across the office table, and stammering: "Read it—read it to me. I can't——" and Boylston's sudden sobbing explosion: "But I *knew,* sir—I've known all along . . ." and then the endless pause before Campton gathered himself up to falter out (like a child deciphering the words in a primer): "You *knew*—knew that George was wounded?"

"No, no, not that; but that he might be—oh, at any minute! Forgive me—oh, do forgive me! He wouldn't let me tell you that he was at the front," Boylston had faltered through his sobs.

"Let you tell me——?"

"You and his mother: he refused a citation last March so that you shouldn't find out that he'd exchanged into an infantry regiment. He was determined to from the first. He's been fighting for months; he's been magnificent; he got away from the Argonne last February; but you were none of you to know."

"But why—why—why?" Campton had flashed out; then his heart stood still, and he awaited the answer with lowered head.

"Well, you see, he was afraid: afraid you might prevent . . . use your influence . . . you and Mrs. Brant. . ."

Campton looked up again, challenging the other. "He imagined perhaps that we *had*—in the beginning?"

"Oh, yes"—Boylston was perfectly calm about it—"he knew all about that. And he made us swear not to speak; Miss Anthony and me. Miss Anthony knew. . . If this thing happened," Boylston ended in a stricken voice, "you were not to be unfair to her, he said."

Over and over again that short dialogue distilled itself syllable by syllable, pang by pang, into Campton's cowering soul. He had had to learn all this, this overwhelming unbelievable truth about his son; and at the same instant to learn that that son was grievously wounded, perhaps dying (what else, in such circumstances, did the giving of the Legion of Honour ever mean?); and to deal with it all in the wild minutes of preparation for departure, of intercession with the authorities, sittings at the photographer's, and a crisscross of confused telephone-calls from the Embassy, the Préfecture and the War Office.

From the welter of images Miss Anthony's face next detached itself: white and withered, yet with a look which triumphed over its own ruin, and over Campton's wrath.

"Ah—you knew too, did you? You were his other confidant? How you all kept it up—how you all lied to us!" Campton had burst out at her.

She took it firmly. "I showed you his letters."

"Yes: the letters he wrote to you to be shown."

She received this in silence, and he followed it up. "It was you who drove him to the front—it was you who sent my son to his death!"

Without flinching, she gazed back at him. "Oh, John—it was you!"

"I—I? What do you mean? I never as much as lifted a finger——"

"No?" She gave him a wan smile. "Then it must have been the old man who invented the Mangle!" she cried, and cast herself on Campton's breast. He held her there for a long moment, stroking her lank hair, and saying "Adele—Adele," because in that rush of understanding he could not think of anything else to say. At length he stooped and laid on her lips the strangest kiss he had ever given or taken; and it was then that, drawing back, she exclaimed: "That's for George, when you get to him. Remember!"

The image of George's mother rose last on the whirling ground of

Campton's thoughts: an uncertain image, blurred by distance, indistinct as some wraith of Mme. Olida's evoking.

Mrs. Brant was still at Biarritz; there had been no possibility of her getting back in time to share the journey to the front. Even Mr. Brant's power in high places must have fallen short of such an attempt; and it was not made. Boylston, despatched in haste to bear the news of George's wounding to the banker, had reported that the utmost Mr. Brant could do was to write at once to his wife, and arrange for her return to Paris, since telegrams to the frontier departments travelled more slowly than letters, and in nine cases out of ten were delayed indefinitely. Campton had asked no more at the time but in the last moment before leaving Paris he remembered having said to Adele Anthony: "You'll be there when Julia comes?" and Miss Anthony had nodded back: "At the station."

The word, it appeared, roused the same memory in both of them; meeting her eyes, he saw there the Gare de l'Est in the summer morning, the noisily manœuvring trains jammed with bright young heads, the flowers, the waving handkerchiefs, and everybody on the platform smiling fixedly till some particular carriage-window slid out of sight. The scene, at the time, had been a vast blur to Campton: would he ever again, he wondered, see anything as clearly as he saw it now, in all its unmerciful distinctness? He heard the sobs of the girl who had said such a blithe goodbye to the young *Chasseur Alpin,* he saw her going away, led by her elderly companion, and powdering her nose at the *laiterie* over the cup of coffee she could not swallow. And this was what her sobs had meant. . .

"This place," said Mr. Brant, with his usual preliminary cough, "must be——" He bent over a motor-map, trying to decipher the name; but after fumbling for his eye-glasses, and rubbing them with a beautifully monogrammed cambric handkerchief, he folded the map up again and slipped it into one of the many pockets which honeycombed the interior of the car. Campton recalled the deathlike neatness of the banker's private office on the day when the one spot of disorder in it had been the torn telegram announcing Benny Upsher's disappearance.

The motor lowered its speed to make way for a long train of army lorries. Close upon them clattered a file of gun-wagons, with unshaven soldiers bestriding the gaunt horses. Torpedo-cars carrying officers slipped cleverly in and out of the tangle, and motor-cycles, incessantly rushing by, peppered the air with their explosions.

"This is the sort of thing he's been living in—living in for months and months," Campton mused.

He himself had seen something of the same kind when he had gone to Châlons in the early days to appeal to Fortin-Lescluze; but at that time the dread significance of the machinery of war had passed almost unnoticed in his preoccupation about his boy. Now he realized that for a year that machinery had been the setting of his boy's life; for months past such sights and sounds as these had formed the whole of George's world; and Campton's eyes took in every detail with an agonized avidity.

"What's that?" he exclaimed.

A huge continuous roar, seeming to fall from the low clouds above them, silenced the puny rumble and clatter of the road. On and on it went, in a slow pulsating rhythm, like the boom of waves driven by a gale on some far-distant coast.

"That? The guns——" said Mr. Brant.

"At the front?"

"Oh, sometimes they seem much nearer. Depends on the wind."

Campton sat bewildered. Had he ever before heard that sinister roar? At Châlons? He would not be sure. But the sound had assuredly not been the same; now it overwhelmed him like the crash of the sea over a drowning head. He cowered back in his corner. Would it ever stop, he asked himself? Or was it always like this, day and night, in the hell of hells that they were bound for? Was that merciless thud forever in the ears of the dying?

A sentinel stopped the motor and asked for their pass. He turned it about and about, holding it upside-down in his horny hands, and wrinkling his brows in the effort to decipher the inverted characters.

"How can I tell——?" he grumbled doubtfully, looking from the faces of the two travellers to their unrecognizable photographs.

Mr. Brant was already feeling for his pocket, and furtively extracting a bank-note.

"For God's sake—not that!" Campton cried, bringing his hand down on the banker's. Leaning over, he spoke to the sentinel. "My son's dying at the front. Can't you see it when you look at me?"

The man looked, and slowly gave back the paper. "You can pass," he said, shouldering his rifle.

The motor shot on, and the two men drew back into their corners. Mr. Brant fidgeted with his eye-glasses, and after an interval coughed again. "I must thank you," he began, "for—for saving me just now from an inexcusable blunder. It was done mechanically . . . one gets into the habit. . ."

"Quite so," said Campton drily. "But there are cases——"

"Of course—of course."

Silence fell once more. Mr. Brant sat bolt upright, his profile detached against the wintry fields. Campton, sunk into his corner, glanced now and then at the neat grey silhouette, in which the perpendicular glint of the eye-glass nearest him was the only point of light. He said to himself that the man was no doubt suffering horribly; but

he was not conscious of any impulse of compassion. He and Mr. Brant
were like two strangers pinned down together in a railway-smash: the
shared agony did not bring them nearer. On the contrary, Campton,
as the hours passed, felt himself more and more exasperated by the
mute anguish at his side. What right had this man to be suffering as
he himself was suffering, what right to be here with him at all? It was
simply in the exercise of what the banker called his "habit"—the habit
of paying, of buying everything, people and privileges and possessions—that he had acquired this ghastly claim to share in an agony
which was not his.

"I shan't even have my boy to myself on his death-bed," the father
thought in desperation; and the mute presence at his side became
once more the symbol of his own failure.

The motor, with frequent halts, continued to crawl slowly on between lorries, field-kitchens, artillery wagons, companies of haggard
infantry returning to their cantonments, and more and more vanloads
of troops pressing forward; it seemed to Campton that hours elapsed
before Mr. Brant again spoke.

"This must be Amiens," he said, in a voice even lower than usual.

The father roused himself and looked out. They were passing
through the streets of a town swarming with troops—but he was still
barely conscious of what he looked at. He perceived that he had been
half-asleep, and dreaming of George as a little boy, when he used to
have such bad colds. Campton remembered in particular the day he
had found the lad in bed, in a scarlet sweater, in his luxurious overheated room, reading the first edition of Lavengro. It was on that day
that he and his son had first really got to know each other; but what
was it that had marked the date to George? The fact that Mr. Brant,
learning of his joy in the book, had instantly presented it to him—
with the price-label left inside the cover.

"And it'll be worth a lot more than that by the time you're grown up,"
Mr. Brant had told his step-son; to which George was recorded to have
answered sturdily: "No, it won't, if I find other stories I like better."

Miss Anthony had assisted at the conversation and reported it tri-
umphantly to Campton; but the painter, who had to save up to give
his boy even a simple present, could see in the incident only one more
attempt to rob him of his rights. "They won't succeed, though, they
won't succeed: they don't know how to go about it, thank the Lord," he
had said.

But they had succeeded after all; what better proof of it was there
than Mr. Brant's tacit right to be sitting here beside him today; than
the fact that but for Mr. Brant it might have been impossible for
Campton to get to his boy's side in time?

Oh, that pitiless incessant hammering of the guns! As the travellers advanced the noise grew louder, fiercer, more unbroken; the closely-fitted panes of the car rattled and danced like those of an old omnibus. Sentinels stopped the chauffeur more frequently; Mr. Brant had to produce the blue paper again and again. The day was wearing on—Campton began again to be aware of a sick weariness, a growing remoteness and confusion of mind. Through it he perceived that Mr. Brant, diving into deep recesses of upholstery, had brought out a silver sandwich-box, a flask and glasses. As by magic they stood on a shiny shelf which slid out of another recess, and Mr. Brant was proffering the box. "It's a long way yet; you'll need all your strength," he said.

Campton, who had half turned from the invitation, seized a sandwich and emptied one of the glasses. Mr. Brant was right; he must not let himself float away into the void, seductive as its drowsy shimmer was.

His wits returned, and with them a more intolerable sense of reality. He was all alive now. Every crash of the guns seemed to tear a piece of flesh from his body; and it was always the piece nearest the heart. The nurse's few lines had said: "A shell wound: the right arm fractured, fear for the lungs." And one of these awful crashes had done it: bursting in mystery from that innocent-looking sky, and rushing inoffensively over hundreds of other young men till it reached its destined prey, found George, and dug a red grave for him. Campton was convinced now that his son was dead. It was not only that he had received the Legion of Honour; it was the appalling all-destroying thunder of the shells as they went on crashing and bursting. What could they leave behind them but mismated fragments? Gathering up all his strength in the effort not to recoil from the vision, Campton saw his son's beautiful body like a carcass tumbled out of a butcher's cart. . .

"Doullens," said Mr. Brant.

They were in a town, and the motor had turned into the court of a great barrack-like building. Before them stood a line of empty stretchers such as Campton had seen at Châlons. A young doctor in a cotton blouse was lighting a cigarette and laughing with a nurse—laughing! At regular intervals the cannonade shook the windows; it seemed the heart-beat of the place. Campton noticed that many of the window-panes had been broken, and patched with paper.

Inside they found another official, who called to another nurse as she passed by laden with fresh towels. She disappeared into a room where heaps of bloody linen were being stacked into baskets, returned, looked at Campton and nodded. He looked back at her blunt tired features and kindly eyes, and said to himself that they had perhaps been his son's last sight on earth.

The nurse smiled.

"It's three flights up," she said; "he'll be glad."

Glad! He was not dead, then; he could even be glad! In the stagger-ing rush of relief the father turned instinctively to Mr. Brant; he felt that there was enough joy to be shared. But Mr. Brant, though he must have heard what the nurse had said, was moving away; he did not seem to understand.

"This way——" Campton called after him, pointing to the nurse, who was already on the first step of the stairs.

Mr. Brant looked slightly puzzled; then, as the other's meaning reached him, he coloured a little, bent his head stiffly, and waved his stick toward the door.

"Thanks," he said, "I think I'll take a stroll first . . . stretch my legs . . ." and Campton, with a rush of gratitude, understood that he was to be left alone with his son.

XXV

He followed his guide up the steep flights, which seemed to become buoyant and lift him like waves. It was as if the muscle that always dragged back his lame leg had suddenly regained its elasticity. He floated up as one mounts stairs in a dream. A smell of disinfectants hung in the cold air, and once, through a half-open door, a sickening odour came: he remembered it at Châlons, and Fortin's murmured: "Gangrene—ah, if only we could get them sooner!"

How soon had they got *his* boy, Campton wondered? The letter, mercifully sent by hand to Paris, had reached him on the third day af-ter George's arrival at the Doullens hospital; but he did not yet know how long before that the shell-splinter had done its work. The nurse did not know either. How could she remember? They had so many! The administrator would look up the files and tell him. Only there was no time for that now.

On a landing Campton heard a babble and scream: a nauseating scream in a queer bleached voice that might have been man, woman or monkey's. Perhaps that was what the French meant by "a white voice": this voice which was as featureless as some of the poor men's obliterated faces! Campton shot an anguished look at his companion, and she understood and shook her head. "Oh, no: that's in the big ward. It's the way they scream after a dressing. . ."

She opened a door, and he was in a room with three beds in it, wooden pallets hastily knocked together and spread with rough grey blankets. In spite of the cold, flies still swarmed on the unwashed panes, and there were big holes in the fly-net over the bed nearest the window. Under the net lay a middle-aged bearded man, heavily bandaged about the chest and left arm: he was snoring, his mouth open, his gaunt cheeks drawn in with the fight for breath. Campton said to himself that if his own boy lived he should like some day to do something for this poor devil who was his roommate. Then he looked about him and saw that the two other beds were empty.

He drew back.

The nurse was bending over the bearded man. "He'll wake presently—I'll leave you"; and she slipped out. Campton looked again at the stranger; then his glance travelled to the scarred brown hand on the sheet, a hand with broken nails and blackened finger-tips. It was George's hand, his son's, swollen, disfigured but unmistakable. The father knelt down and laid his lips on it.

"What was the first thing you felt?" Adele Anthony asked him afterward: and he answered: "Nothing."

"Yes—at the very first, I know: it's always like that. But the first thing *after* you began to feel anything?"

He considered, and then said slowly: "The difference."

"The difference in *him?*"

"In him—in life—in everything."

Miss Anthony, who understood as a rule, was evidently puzzled. "What kind of a difference?"

"Oh, a complete difference." With that she had to be content.

The sense of it had first come to Campton when the bearded man, raising his lids, looked at him from far off with George's eyes, and touched him, very feebly, with George's hand. It was in the moment of identifying his son that he felt the son he had known to be lost to him forever.

George's lips were moving, and the father laid his ear to them; perhaps these were last words that his boy was saying.

"Old Dad—in a motor?"

Campton nodded.

The fact seemed faintly to interest George, who continued to examine him with those distant eyes.

"Uncle Andy's?"

Campton nodded again.

"Mother——?"

"She's coming too—very soon."

George's lips were screwed into a whimsical smile. "I must have a shave first," he said, and drowsed off again, his hand in Campton's. . .

"The other gentleman—?" the nurse questioned the next morning. Campton had spent the night in the hospital, stretched on the floor at his son's threshold. It was a breach of rules, but for once the major had condoned it. As for Mr. Brant, Campton had forgotten all about him, and at first did not know what the nurse meant. Then he woke with a start to the consciousness of his fellow-traveller's nearness. Mr. Brant, the nurse explained, had come to the hospital early, and had been waiting below for the last two hours. Campton, almost as gaunt and unshorn as his son, pulled himself to his feet and went down. In the hall the banker, very white, but smooth and trim as ever, was patiently measuring the muddy flags.

"Less temperature this morning," Campton called from the last flight.

"Oh," stammered Mr. Brant, red and pale by turns.

Campton smiled haggardly and pulled himself together in an effort of communicativeness. "Look here—he's asked for you; you'd better go up. Only for a few minutes, please; he's awfully weak."

Mr. Brant, speechless, stood stiffly waiting to be conducted. Campton noticed the mist in his eyes, and took pity on him.

"I say—where's the hotel? Just a step away? I'll go around, then, and get a shave and a wash while you're with him," the father said, with a magnanimity which he somehow felt the powers might take account of in their subsequent dealings with George. If the boy was to live Campton could afford to be generous; and he had decided to assume that the boy would live, and to order his behaviour accordingly.

"I—thank you," said Mr. Brant, turning toward the stairs.

"Five minutes at the outside!" Campton cautioned him, and hurried out into the morning air through which the guns still crashed methodically.

When he got back to the hospital, refreshed and decent, he was surprised, and for a moment alarmed, to find that Mr. Brant had not come down.

"Sending up his temperature, of course—damn him!" Campton raged, scrambling up the stairs as fast as his stiff leg permitted. But outside of George's door he saw a small figure patiently mounting guard.

"I stayed with him less than five minutes; I was merely waiting to thank you."

"Oh, that's all right." Campton paused, and then made his supreme effort. "How does he strike you?"

"Hopefully—hopefully. He had his joke as usual," Mr. Brant said with a twitching smile.

"Oh, *that*——! But his temperature's decidedly lower. Of course they may have to take the ball out of the lung; but perhaps before they do it he can be moved from this hell."

The two men were silent, the same passion of anxiety consuming them, and no means left of communicating it to each other.

"I'll look in again later. Shall I have something to eat sent round to you from the hotel?" Mr. Brant suggested.

"Oh, thanks—if you would."

Campton put out his hand and crushed Mr. Brant's dry fingers. But for this man he might not have got to his son in time; and this man had not once made use of the fact to press his own claim on George. With pity in his heart, the father, privileged to remain at his son's bedside, watched Mr. Brant's small figure retreating alone. How ghastly to sit all day in that squalid hotel, his eyes on his watch, with nothing to do but to wonder and wonder about the temperature of another man's son!

The next day was worse; so much worse that everything disappeared from Campton's view but the present agony of watching, hovering, hanging helplessly on the words of nurse and doctor, and spying on the glances they exchanged behind his back.

There could be no thought yet of extracting the bullet; a great surgeon, passing through the wards on a hasty tour of inspection, had confirmed this verdict. Oh, to have kept the surgeon there—to have had him at hand to watch for the propitious moment and seize it without an instant's delay! Suddenly the vision which to Campton had been among the most hideous of all his crowding nightmares—that of George stretched naked on an operating-table, his face hidden by a chloroform mask, and an orderly hurrying away with a pile of red towels like those perpetually carried through the passages below— this vision became to the father's fevered mind as soothing as a glimpse of Paradise. If only George's temperature would go down—if only the doctors would pronounce him strong enough to have the bullet taken out! What would anything else matter then? Campton would feel as safe as he used to years ago, when after the recurring months of separation the boy came back from school, and he could take him in his arms and make sure that he was the same Geordie, only bigger, browner, with thicker curlier hair, and tougher muscles under his jacket.

What if the great surgeon, on his way back from the front, were to pass through the town again that evening, reverse his verdict, and perhaps even perform the operation then and there? Was there no way of prevailing on him to stop and take another look at George on the return? The idea took immediate possession of Campton, crowding out his intolerable anguish, and bringing such relief that for a few seconds he felt as if some life-saving operation had been performed on himself. As he stood watching the great man's retreat, followed by doctors and nurses, Mr. Brant suddenly touched his arm, and the eyes of the two met. Campton understood and gasped out: "Yes, yes; we must manage to get him back."

Mr. Brant nodded. "At all costs." He paused, again interrogated Campton's eyes, and stammered: "You authorize——?"

"Oh, God—anything!"

"He's dined at my house in Paris," Mr. Brant threw in, as if trying to justify himself.

"Oh, go—*go!*" Campton almost pushed him down the stairs. Ten minutes later he reappeared, modest but exultant.

"Well?"

"He wouldn't commit himself, before the others——"

"Oh——"

"But to me, as he was getting into the motor——"

"Well?"

"Yes: if possible. Somewhere about midnight."

Campton turned away, choking, and stumped off toward the tall window at the end of the passage. Below him lay the court. A line of stretchers was being carried across it, not empty this time, but each one with a bloody burden. Doctors, nurses, orderlies hurried to and fro. Drub, drub, drub, went the guns, shaking the windows, rolling their fierce din along the cloudy sky, down the corridors of the hospital and the pavement of the streets, like huge bowls crashing through story above story of a kind of sky-scraping bowling alley.

"Even the dead underground must hear them!" Campton muttered.

The word made him shudder superstitiously, and he crept back to George's door and opened it; but the nurse, within, shook her head.

"He must sleep after the examination. Better go."

Campton turned and saw Mr. Brant waiting. A bell rang twelve. The two, in silence, walked down the stairs, crossed the court (averting their eyes from the stretchers) and went to the hotel to get something to eat.

Midnight came. It passed. No one in the hurried confused world of the hospital had heard of the possibility of the surgeon's returning. When Campton mentioned it to the nurse she smiled her tired smile, and said "He could have done nothing."

Done nothing! How could she know? How could any one, but the surgeon himself? Would he have promised if he had not thought there was some chance? Campton, stretched out on a blanket and his rolled-up coat, lay through the long restless hours staring at the moonlit sky framed by the window of the corridor. Great clouds swept over that cold indifferent vault they seemed like the smoke from the guns which had not once ceased through the night. At last he got up, turned his back on the window, and lay down again facing the stairs. The moonlight un-

rolled a white strip along the stone floor. A church-bell rang one . . . two
. . . there were noises and movements below. Campton raised himself,
his heart beating all over his body. Steps came echoing up.

"Careful!" some one called. A stretcher rounded the stair-rail; another, and then another. An orderly with a lantern preceded them, followed by one of the doctors, an old bunched-up man in a muddy uniform, who stopped furtively to take a pinch of snuff. Campton could
not believe his eyes; didn't the hospital people know that every bed on
that floor was full? Every bed, that is, but the two in George's room;
and the nurse had given Campton the hope, the promise almost, that
as long as his boy was so ill she would keep those empty. "I'll manage
somehow," she had said.

For a mad moment Campton was on the point of throwing himself
in the way of the tragic procession, barring the threshold with his
arms. "What does this mean?" he stammered to the nurse, who had
appeared from another room with her little lamp.

She gave a shrug. "More casualties—every hospital is like this."

He stood aside, wrathful, impotent. At least if Brant had been
there, perhaps by some offer of money—but how, to whom? Of what
earthly use, after all, was Brant's boasted "influence"? These people
would only laugh at him—perhaps put them both out of the hospital!

He turned despairingly to the nurse. "You might as well have left
him in the trenches."

"Don't say that, sir," she answered; and the echo of his own words
horrified him like a sacrilege.

Two of the stretchers were carried into George's room. Campton
caught a glimpse of George, muttering and tossing; the moonlight lay
in the hollows of his bearded face, and again the father had the sense
of utter alienation from that dark delirious man who for brief intervals suddenly became his son, and then as suddenly wandered off into
strangeness.

The nurse slipped out of the room and signed to him.

"Both nearly gone . . . they won't trouble him long," she whispered.

The man on the third stretcher was taken to a room at the other end
of the corridor. Campton watched him being lifted in. He was to lie on
the floor, then? For in that room there was certainly no vacancy. But
presently he had the answer. The bearers did not come out empty-
handed; they carried another man whom they laid on the empty
stretcher. Lucky, lucky devil; going, no doubt, to a hospital at the rear!
As the procession reached the stairs the lantern swung above the lucky
devil's fact: his eyes stared ceilingward from black orbits. One arm,
swinging loose, dangled down, the hand stealthily counting the steps as
he descended—and no one troubled, for he was dead.

At dawn Campton, who must have been asleep, started up, again hearing steps. The surgeon? Oh, if this time it were the surgeon! But only Mr. Brant detached himself from the shadows accumulated in the long corridor: Mr. Brant, crumpled and unshorn, with blood-shot eyes, and gloves on his unconscious hands.

Campton glared at him resentfully.

"Well—how about your surgeon? I don't see him!" he exclaimed.

Mr. Brant shook his head despondently. "No—I've been waiting all night in the court. I thought if he came back I should be the first to catch him. But he has just sent his orderly for instruments; he's not coming. There's been terrible fighting——"

Campton saw two tears running down Mr. Brant's face: they did not move him.

The banker glanced toward George's door, full of the question he dared not put.

Campton answered it. "You want to know how he is? Well, how should he be, with that bullet in him, and the fever eating him inch by inch, and two more wounded men in his room? *That's* how he is!" Campton almost shouted.

Mr. Brant was trembling all over.

"Two more men—in his room?" he echoed shrilly.

"Yes—bad cases; dying." Campton drew a deep breath. "You see there are times when your money and your influence and your knowing everybody are no more use than so much sawdust——"

The nurse opened the door and looked out. "You're talking too loudly," she said.

She shut the door, and the two men stood silent, abashed; finally Mr. Brant turned away. "I'll go and try again. There must be other surgeons . . . other ways . . ." he whispered.

"Oh, your surgeons . . . oh, your ways!" Campton sneered after him, in the same whisper.

XXVI

From the room where he sat at the foot of George's glossy white bed, Campton, through the open door, could watch the November sun slanting down a white ward where, in the lane between other white beds, pots of chrysanthemums stood on white-covered tables.

Through the window his eyes rested incredulously on a court enclosed in monastic arches of grey stone, with squares of turf bordered by box hedges, and a fountain playing. Beyond the court sloped the faded foliage of a park not yet entirely stripped by Channel gales; and on days without wind, instead of the boom of the guns, the roar of the sea came faintly over intervening heights and hollows.

Campton's ears were even more incredulous than his eyes. He was gradually coming to believe in George's white room, the ward beyond, the flowers between the beds, the fountain in the court; but the sound of the sea still came to him, intolerably but unescapably, as the crash of guns. When the impression was too overwhelming he would turn away from the window and cast his glance on the bed; but only to find that the smooth young face on the pillow had suddenly changed into that of the haggard bearded stranger on the wooden pallet at Doullens. And Campton would have to get up, lean over, and catch the twinkle in George's eyes before the evil spell was broken.

Few words passed between them. George, after all these days, was still too weak for much talk; and silence had always been Campton's escape from feeling. He never had the need to speak in times of inward stress, unless it were to vent his anger—as in that hateful scene at Doullens between himself and Mr. Brant. But he was sure that George always knew what was passing through his mind; that when the sea boomed their thoughts flew back together to that other scene, but a few miles and a few days distant, yet already as far off, as much an affair they were both rid of, as a nightmare to a wakened sleeper; and that for a moment the same vision clutched them both, mocking their attempts at indifference.

Not that the sound, to Campton at any rate, suggested any abstract conception of war. Looking back afterward at this phase of his life he perceived that at no time had he thought so little of the war. The noise of the sea was to him simply the voice of the engine which had so nearly destroyed his son: that association, deeply imbedded in his half-dazed consciousness, left no room for others.

The general impression of unreality was enhanced by his not having yet been able to learn the details of George's wounding. After a week during which the boy had hung near death, the great surgeon—returning to Doullens just as Campton had finally ceased to hope for him—had announced that, though George's state was still grave, he might be moved to a hospital at the rear. So one day, miraculously, the perilous transfer had been made, in one of Mrs. Brant's own motor-ambulances; and for a week now George had lain in his white bed, hung over by white-gowned Sisters, in an atmosphere of sweetness and order which almost made it seem as if he were a child recovering from illness in his own nursery, or a red-haired baby sparring with dimpled fists at a new world.

In truth, Campton found his son as hard to get at as a baby; he looked at his father with eyes as void of experience, or at least of any means of conveying it. Campton, at first, could only marvel and wait; and the isolation in which the two were enclosed by George's weakness, and by his father's inability to learn from others what the boy was not yet able to tell him, gave a strange remoteness to everything but the things which count in an infant's world: food, warmth, sleep. Campton's nearest approach to reality was his daily scrutiny of the temperature-chart. He studied it as he used to study the *communiqués* which he now no longer even thought of.

Sometimes when George was asleep Campton would sit pondering on the days at Doullens. There was an exquisite joy in silently building up, on that foundation of darkness and anguish, the walls of peace that now surrounded him, a structure so transparent that one could peer through it at the routed Furies, yet so impenetrable that he sat there in a kind of god-like aloofness. For one thing he was especially thankful—and that was the conclusion of his unseemly wrangle with Mr. Brant; thankful that, almost at once, he had hurried after the banker, caught up with him, and stammered out, clutching his hand: "I know—I know how you feel."

Mr. Brant's reactions were never rapid, and the events of the preceding days had called upon faculties that were almost atrophied. He had merely looked at Campton in mute distress, returned his pressure, and silently remounted the hospital stairs with him.

Campton hated himself for his ill-temper, but was glad, even at the time, that no interested motive had prompted his apology. He should have hated himself even more if he had asked the banker's pardon because of Mr. Brant's "pull," and the uses to which it might be put; or even if he had associated his excuses with any past motives of gratitude, such as the fact that but for Mr. Brant he might never have reached George's side. Instead of that, he simply felt that once more his senseless violence had got the better of him, and he was sorry that he had behaved like a brute to a man who loved George, and was suffering almost as much as he was at the thought that George might die. . .

After that episode, and Campton's apology, the relations of the two men became so easy that each gradually came to take the other for granted; and Mr. Brant, relieved of a perpetual hostile scrutiny, was free to exercise his ingenuity in planning and managing. It was owing to him—Campton no longer minded admitting it—that the famous surgeon had hastened his return to Doullens, that George's translation to the sweet monastic building near the sea had been so rapidly effected, and that the great man, appearing there soon afterward, had extracted the bullet with his own hand. But for Mr. Brant's persistence even the leave to bring one of Mrs. Brant's motor-ambulances to Doullens would never have been given; and it might have been fatal to George to make the journey in a slow and jolting military train. But for Mr. Brant, again, he would have been sent to a crowded military hospital instead of being brought to this white heaven of rest. "And all that just because

I overtook him in time to prevent his jumping into his motor and going back to Paris in order to get out of my way!" Campton, at the thought, lowered his spirit into new depths of contrition.

George, who had been asleep, opened his eyes and looked at his father.

"Where's Uncle Andy?"

"Gone to Paris to get your mother."

"Yes. Of course. He told me——"

George smiled, and withdrew once more into his secret world.

But Campton's state of mind was less happy. As the time of Julia's arrival approached he began to ask himself with increasing apprehension how she would fit into the situation. Mr. Brant *had* fitted into it—perfectly. Campton had actually begun to feel a secret dependence on him, a fidgety uneasiness since he had left for Paris, sweet though it was to be alone with George. But Julia—what might she not do and say to unsettle things, break the spell, agitate and unnerve them all? Campton did not question her love for her son; but he was not sure what form it would take in conditions to which she was so unsuited. How could she ever penetrate into the mystery of peace which enclosed him and his boy? And if she felt them thus mysteriously shut off would she not dimly resent her exclusion? If only Adele Anthony had been coming too! Campton had urged Mr. Brant to bring her; but the banker had failed to obtain a permit for any one but the boy's mother. He had even found it difficult to get his own leave renewed; it was only after a first trip to Paris, and repeated efforts at the War Office, that he had been allowed to go to Paris and fetch his wife, who was just arriving from Biarritz.

Well—for the moment, at any rate, Campton had the boy to himself. As he sat there, trying to picture the gradual resurrection of George's pre-war face out of the delicately pencilled white mask on the pillow, he noted the curious change of planes produced by suffering and emaciation, and the altered relation of lights and shadows. Materially speaking, the new George looked like the old one seen in the bowl of a spoon, and through blue spectacles: peaked, narrow, livid, with elongated nose and sunken eye-sockets. But these altered proportions were not what had really changed him. There was something in the curve of the mouth that fever and emaciation could not account for. In that new line, and in the look of his eyes—the look travelling slowly outward through a long blue tunnel, like some mysterious creature rising from the depths of the sea—that was where the new George lurked, the George to be watched and lain in wait for, patiently and slowly puzzled out. . .

He reopened his eyes.

"Adele too?"

Campton had learned to bridge over the spaced between the questions. "No; not this time. We tried, but it couldn't be managed. A little later, I hope——"

"She's all right?"

"Rather! Blooming."

"And Boylston?"

"Blooming too."

George's lids closed contentedly, like doors shutting him away from the world.

It was the first time since his operation that he had asked about any of his friends, or had appeared to think they might come to see him. But his mind, like his stomach, could receive very little nutriment at a time; he liked to have one mouthful given to him, and then to lie ruminating it in the lengthening intervals between his attacks of pain.

Each time he asked for news of any one his father wondered what name would next come to his lips. Even during his delirium he had mentioned no one but his parents, Mr. Brant, Adele Anthony and Boylston; yet it was not possible, Campton thought, that these formed the circumference of his life, that some contracted fold of memory did not hold a nearer image, a more secret name. . . The father's heart beat faster, half from curiosity, half from a kind of shy delicacy, at the thought that at any moment that name might wake in George and utter itself.

Campton's thoughts again turned to his wife. With Julia there was never any knowing. Ten to one she would send the boy's temperature up. He was thankful that, owing to the difficulty of getting the news to her, and then of bringing her back from a frontier department, so many days had had to elapse.

But when she arrived, nothing, after all, happened as he had expected. She had put on her nurse's dress for the journey (he thought it rather theatrical of her, till he remembered how much easier it was to get about in any sort of uniform); but there was not a trace of coquetry in her appearance. As a frame for her haggard unpowdered face the white coif look harsh and unbecoming; she reminded him, as she got out of the motor, of some mortified Jansenist nun from one of Philippe de Champaigne's canvases.

Campton led her to George's door, but left her there; she did not appear to notice whether or not he was following her. He whispered: "Careful about his temperature; he's very weak," and she bent her profile silently as she went in.

XXVII

George, that evening, seemed rather better, and his temperature had not gone up: Campton had to repress a movement of jealousy at Julia's having done her son no harm. Her experience as a nurse, disciplining a vague gift for the sickroom, had developed in her the faculty of self-command: before the war, if George had met with a dangerous accident, she would have been more encumbering than helpful.

Campton had to admit the change, but it did not draw them any nearer. Her manner of loving their son was too different. Nowadays, when he and Anderson Brant were together, he felt that they were thinking of the same things in the same way; but Julia's face, even aged and humanized by grief, was still a mere mask to him. He could never tell what form her thoughts about George might be taking.

Mr. Brant, on his wife's arrival, had judged it discreet to efface himself. Campton hunted for him in vain in the park, and under the cloister; he remained invisible till they met at the early dinner which they shared with the staff. But the meal did not last long, and when it was over, and nurses and doctors scattered, Mr. Brant again slipped away, leaving his wife and Campton alone.

Campton glanced after him, surprised. "Why does he go?"

Mrs. Brant pursed her lips, evidently as much surprised by his question as he by her husband's withdrawal.

"I suppose he's going to bed—to be ready for his early start tomorrow."

"A start?"

She stared. "He's going back to Paris."

Campton was genuinely astonished. "Is he? I'm sorry."

"Oh——" She seemed unprepared for this. "After all, you must see—we can't very well . . . all three of us . . . especially with these nuns. . ."

"Oh, if it's only *that*——"

She did not take this up, and one of their usual silences followed. Campton was thinking that it was all nonsense about the nuns, and meditating on the advisability of going in pursuit of Mr. Brant to tell him so. He dreaded the prospect of a long succession of days alone between George and George's mother.

Mrs. Brant spoke again. "I was sorry to find that the Sisters have been kept on here. Are they much with George?"

"The Sisters? I don't know. The upper nurses are Red Cross, as you saw. But of course the others are about a good deal. What's wrong? They seem to me perfect."

She hesitated and coloured a little. "I don't want them to find out—about the Extreme Unction," she finally said.

Campton repeated her words blankly. He began to think that anxiety and fatigue had confused her mind.

She coloured more deeply. "Oh, I forgot—you don't know. I couldn't think of anything but George at first . . . and the whole thing is so painful to me. . . Where's my bag?"

She groped for her reticule, found it in the folds of the cloak she had kept about her shoulders, and fumbled in it with wrinkled jewelled fingers.

"Anderson hasn't spoken to you, then—spoken about Mrs. Talkett?" she asked suddenly.

"About Mrs. Talkett? Why should he? What on earth has happened?"

"Oh, I wouldn't see her myself . . . I couldn't . . . so he had to. She had to be thanked, of course . . . but it seems to me so dreadful, so very dreadful . . . *our* boy. . . that woman. . ."

Campton did not press her further. He sat dumbfounded, trying to take in what she was so obviously trying to communicate, and yet instinctively resisting the approach of the revelation he foresaw.

"George—*Mrs. Talkett?*" He forced himself to couple the two names, unnatural as their union seemed.

"I supposed you knew. Isn't it dreadful? A woman old enough——"

She drew a letter from her bag.

He interrupted her. "Is that letter what you want to show me?"

"Yes. She insisted on Anderson's keeping it—for you. She said it belonged to us, I believe. . . It seems there was a promise—made the night before he was mobilised—that if anything happened he would get word to her. . . No thought of *us!*" She began to whimper.

Campton reached out for the letter. Mrs. Talkett—Madge Talkett and George! That was where the boy had gone then, that last night when his father, left alone at the Crillon, had been so hurt by his desertion! That was the name which, in his hours of vigil in the little white room, Campton had watched for on his son's lips, the name which, one day, sooner or later, he would have to hear them pronounce. . . How little he had thought, as he sat studying the mysterious beauty of George's face, what a commonplace secret it concealed!

The writing was not George's, but that of an unlettered French soldier. Campton, glancing at the signature, recalled it as that of his son's orderly, who had been slightly wounded in the same attack as George, and sent for twenty-four hours to the same hospital at Doullens. He had been at George's side when he fell, and with the simple directness often natural to his class in France he told the tale of his lieutenant's wounding, in circumstances which appeared to have given George great glory in the eyes of his men. They thought the wound mortal; but the orderly and a stretcher-bearer had managed to get the young man into the shelter of a little wood. The stretcher-bearer, it turned out, was a priest. He had at once applied the consecrated oil, and George, still conscious, had received it "with a beautiful smile"; then the orderly, thinking all was over, had hurried back to the fighting, and been wounded. The next day he too had been carried to Doullens; and there, after many enquiries, he had found his lieutenant in the same hospital, alive, but too ill to see him.

He had contrived, however, to see the nurse, and had learned from her that the doctors had not given up hope. With that he had to be content; but before returning to his base he had hastened to fulfill his lieutenant's instructions (given "many months earlier") by writing to tell "his lady" that he was severely wounded, but still alive—"which is a good deal in itself," the orderly hopefully ended, "not to mention his receiving the Legion of Honour."

Campton laid the letter down. There was too much to be taken in all at once; and, as usual in moments of deep disturbance, he wanted to be alone, above all wanted to be away from Julia. But Julia held him with insistent eyes.

"Do you want this?" he asked finally, pushing the letter toward her.

She recoiled. "Want it? A letter written to that woman? No! I should have returned it at once—but Anderson wouldn't let me. . . Think of her forcing herself upon me as she did—and making you paint her portrait! I see it all now. Had you any idea this was going on?"

Campton shook his head, and perceived by her look of relief that what she had resented above all was the thought of his being in a secret of George's from which she herself was excluded.

"Adele didn't know either," she said, with evident satisfaction. Campton remembered that he had been struck by Miss Anthony's look of sincerity when he had asked her if she had any idea where George had spent his last evening, and she had answered negatively. This recollection made him understand Mrs. Brant's feeling of relief.

"Perhaps, after all, it's only a flirtation—a mere sentimental friendship," he hazarded.

"A flirtation?" Mrs. Brant's Mater Dolorosa face suddenly sharpened to worldly astuteness. "A sentimental friendship? Have you ever heard George mention her name—or make any sort of allusion to such a friendship?"

Campton considered. "No. I don't remember his ever speaking of her."

"Well, then——" Her eyes had the irritated look he had seen on the far-off day when he had thrown Beausite's dinner invitation into the fire. Once more, they seemed to say, she had taken the measure of his worldly wisdom.

George's silence—his care not even to mention that the Talketts were so much as known to him—certainly made it look as though the matter went deep with him. Campton, recalling the tone of the Talkett drawing-room and its familiars, had an even stronger recoil of indignation than Julia's; but he was silenced by a dread of tampering with his son's privacy, a sense of the sacredness of everything pertaining to that still-mysterious figure in the white bed upstairs.

Mrs. Brant's face had clouded again. "It's all so dreadful—and this Extreme Unction too! What is it exactly, do you know? A sort of baptism? Will the Roman Church try to get hold of him on the strength of it?"

Campton remembered with a faint inward amusement that, in spite of her foreign bringing-up, and all her continental affinities, Julia had remained as implacably and incuriously Protestant as if all her life she had heard the Scarlet Woman denounced from Presbyterian pulpits. At another time it would have amused him to ponder on this one streak in her of the ancestral iron; but now he wanted only to console her.

"Oh, no—it was just the accident of the priest's being there. One of our chaplains would have done the same kind of thing."

She looked at him mistrustfully. "The same kind of thing? It's never the same with them! Whatever they do reaches ahead. I've seen such advantage taken of the wounded when they were too weak to resist . . . didn't know what they were saying or doing. . ." Her eyes filled with tears. "A priest and a woman—I feel as if I'd lost my boy!"

The words went through Campton like a sword, and he sprang to his feet. "Oh, for God's sake be quiet—don't say it! What does anything matter but that he's alive?"

"Of course, of course. . . I didn't mean . . . But that he should have deceived us . . . about everything . . . everything. . ."

"Ah, don't say that either! Don't tempt Providence! If he deceived us, as you call it, we've no one but ourselves to blame; you and I, and—well, and Brant. Didn't we all do our best to make him deceive us—with our intriguing and our wire-pulling and our cowardice? How he despised us for it—yes, thank God, how he despised us from the first! He didn't hide the truth from Boylston or Adele, because they were the only two on a level with him. And *they* knew why he'd deceived us; they understood him, they abetted him from the first." He stopped, checked by Mrs. Brant's pale bewildered face, and the eyes imploringly lifted, as if to ward off unintelligible words.

"Ah, well, all this is no use," he said; "we've got him safe, and it's more than we deserve." He laid his hand on her shoulder. "Go to bed; you're dead-beat. Only don't say things—things that might wake up the Furies. . ."

He pocketed the letter and went out in search of Mr. Brant, followed by her gaze of perplexity.

The latter was smoking a last cigar as he paced up and down the cloister with upturned coat-collar. Silence lay on the carefully darkened building, crouching low under an icy sea-fog; at intervals, through the hush, the waves continued to mimic the booming of the guns.

Campton drew out the orderly's letter. "I hear you're leaving tomorrow early, and I suppose I'd better give this back," he said.

Mr. Brant had evidently expected him. "Oh, thanks. But Mrs. Talkett says she has no right to it."

"No right to it? That's a queer thing to say."

"So I thought. I suppose she meant, till you'd seen it. She was dreadfully upset . . . till she saw me she'd supposed he was dead."

Campton shivered. "She sent this to your house?"

"Yes; the moment she got it. It was waiting there when my—when Julia arrived."

"And you went to thank her?"

"Yes." Mr. Brant hesitated. "Julia disliked to keep the letter. And I thought it only proper to take it back myself."

"Certainly. And—what was your impression?"

Mr. Brant hesitated again. He had already, Campton felt, reached the utmost limit of his power of communicativeness. It was against all his habits to "commit himself." Finally he said, in an unsteady voice: "It was impossible not to feel sorry for her."

"Did she say—er—anything special? Anything about herself and——"

"No; not a word. She was—well, all broken up, as they say."

"Poor thing!" Campton murmured.

"Yes—oh, yes!" Mr. Brant held the letter, turning it thoughtfully about. "It's a great thing," he began abruptly, as if the words were beyond his control, "to have such a beautiful account of the affair. George himself, of course, would never——"

"No, never." Campton considered. "You must take it back to her, naturally. But I should like to have a copy first."

Mr. Brant put a hand in his pocket. "I supposed you would. And I took the liberty of making two—oh, privately, of course. I hope you'll find my writing fairly legible." He drew two folded sheets from his note-case, and offered one to Campton.

"Oh, thank you." The two men grasped hands through the fog.

Mr. Brant turned to continue his round, and Campton went up to the white-washed cell in which he was lodged. Screening his candle to keep the least light from leaking through the shutters, he re-read the story of George's wounding, copied out in the cramped tremulous writing of a man who never took pen in hand but to sign a daily batch of typed letters. The "hand-made" copy of a letter by Mr. Brant represented something like the pious toil expended by a monkish scribe on the page of a missal; and Campton was moved by the little man's devotion.

As for the letter, Campton had no sooner begun to re-read it than he entirely forgot that it was a message of love, addressed at George's request to Mrs. Talkett, and saw in it only the record of his son's bravery. And for the first time he understood that from the moment of George's wounding until now he had never really thought of him in relation to the war, never thought of his judgment on the war, of all the unknown emotions, resolves and actions which had drawn him so many months ago from his safe shelter in the Argonne.

These things Campton, unconsciously, had put out of his mind, or rather had lost out of his mind, from the moment when he had heard of George's bodily presence, with the physical signs of him, his weakness, his temperature, the pain in his arm, the oppression on his lung, all the daily insistent details involved in coaxing him slowly back to life.

The father could bear no more; he put the letter away, as a man might put away something of which his heart was too full to measure it. Later—yes; now, all he knew was that his son was alive.

But the hour of Campton's entering into glory came when, two or three days later, George asked with sudden smile: "When I exchanged regiments I did what you'd always hoped I would, eh, Dad?"

It was the first allusion, on the part of either, to the mystery of George's transit from the Argonne to the front. At Doullens he had been too weak to be questioned, and as he grew stronger, and entered upon the successive stages of his convalescence, he gave the impression of having travelled far beyond such matters, and of living his real life in some inconceivable region from which, with that new smile of his, he continued to look down unseeingly on his parents. "It's exactly as if he were dead," the father thought. "And if he were, he might go on watching us with just such a smile."

And then one morning as they were taking a few steps on a sunny terrace, Campton had felt the pressure of the boy's sound arm, and caught the old George in his look.

"I . . . good Lord . . . at any rate I'm glad you felt sure of me," Campton could only stammer in reply.

George laughed. "Well—rather!"

There was a long silence full of sea-murmurs, too drowsy and indolent, for once, to simulate the horror of the guns.

"I—I only wish you'd felt you could trust me about it from the first, as you did Adele and Boylston," the father continued.

"But, my dear fellow, I did feel it! I swear I did! Only, you see, there was mother. I thought it all over, and decided it would be easier for you both if I said nothing. And, after all, I'm glad now that I didn't—that is, if you really do understand."

"Yes; I understand."

"That's jolly." George's eyes turned from his and rested with a joyful gravity on the little round-faced Sister who hurried up to say that he'd been out long enough. Campton often caught him fixing this look of serene benevolence on the people who were gradually repeopling his world, a look which seemed to say that they were new to him, yet dimly familiar. He was like a traveller returning after incommunicable adventures to the place where he had lived as a child; and, as happens with such wanderers, the trivial and insignificant things, the things a newcomer would not have noticed, seemed often to interest him most of all.

He said nothing more about himself, but with the look of recovered humanness which made him more lovable if less remotely beautiful, began to question his father.

"Boylston wrote that you'd begun to paint again. I'm glad."

"Oh, I only took it up for a while last spring."

"Portraits?"

"A few. But I chucked it. I couldn't stand the atmosphere."

"What atmosphere?"

"Of people who could want to be painted at such a time. People who wanted to 'secure a Campton.' Oh, and then the dealers—God!"

George seemed unimpressed. "After all, life's got to go on."

"Yes—that's what they say! And the only result is to make me doubt if *theirs* has."

His son laughed, and then threw off: "You did Mrs. Talkett?"

"Yes," Campton snapped, off his guard.

"She's a pretty creature," said George; and at that moment his eyes, resting again on the little nurse, who was waiting at his door with a cup of cocoa, lit up with celestial gratitude.

"The *communiqué*'s good today," she cried; and he smiled at her boyishly. The war was beginning to interest him again: Campton was sure that every moment he could spare from that unimaginable region which his blue eyes guarded like a sword was spent among his comrades at the front.

As the day approached for the return to Paris, Campton began to penetrate more deeply into the meaning of George's remoteness. He himself, he discovered, had been all unawares in a far country, a country guarded by a wingèd sentry, as the old hymn had it: the region of silent incessant communion with his son. Just they two: everything else effaced; not discarded, destroyed, not disregarded even, but blotted out by a soft silver haze, as the brown slopes and distances were, on certain days, from the windows of the seaward-gazing hospital.

It was not that Campton had been unconscious of the presence of other suffering about them. As George grew stronger, and took his first steps in the wards, he and his father were inevitably brought into contact with the life of the hospital. George had even found a few friends, and two or three regimental comrades, among the officers perpetually coming and going, or enduring the long weeks of agony which led up to the end. But that was only toward the close of their sojourn, when George was about to yield his place to others, and be taken to Paris for the re-education of his shattered arm. And by that time the weeks of solitary communion had left such an imprint on Campton that, once the hospital was behind him, and no more than a phase of memory, it became to him as one of its own sea-mists, in which he and his son might have been peacefully shut away together from all the rest of the world.

XXVIII

"Preparedness!" cried Boylston in an exultant crow.

His round brown face with its curly crest and peering half-blind eyes beamed at Campton in the old way across the desk of the Palais Royal office; and from the corner where she had sunk down on one of the broken-springed divans, Adele Anthony echoed: "Preparedness!"

It was the first time that Campton had heard the word; but the sense of it had been in the air ever since he and George had got back to Paris. He remembered, on the very day of their arrival, noticing something different in both Boylston and Miss Anthony; and the change had shown itself in the same ways: both seemed more vivid yet more remote. It had struck Campton in the moment of first meeting them, in the Paris hospital near the Bois de Boulogne—Fortin-Lescluze's old Nursing-Home transformed into a House of Re-education—to which George had been taken. In the little cell crowded with flowers—almost too many flowers, his father thought, for the patient's aching head and tired eyes—Campton, watching the entrance of the two visitors, the first to be admitted after Julia and Mr. Brant, had instantly remarked the air they had of sharing something so secret and important that their joy at seeing George seemed only the over-flow of another deeper joy.

Their look had just such a vividness as George's own; as their glances crossed, Campton saw the same light in the eyes of all three. And now, a few weeks later, the clue to it came to him in Boylston's new word. *Preparedness!* America, it appeared, had caught it up from east to west, in that sudden incalculable way she had of flinging herself on a new idea; from a little group of discerning spirits the contagion had spread like a prairie fire, sweeping away all the other catchwords of the hour, devouring them in one great blaze of wrath and enthusiasm. America meant to be prepared! First had come the creation of the training camp at Plattsburg, for which, after long delays and much difficulty, permission had been wrung from a reluctant government; then, as candidates flocked to it, as the whole young manhood of the Eastern States rose to the call, other camps, rapidly planned, were springing up at Fort Oglethorpe in Georgia, at Fort Sheridan in Illinois, at The Presidio in California; for the idea was spreading through the West, and the torch kindled beside the Atlantic seaboard already flashed its light on the Pacific.

For hours at a time Campton heard Boylston talking about these training camps with the young Americans who helped him in his work, or dropped in to seek his counsel. More than ever, now, he was an authority and an oracle to these stray youths who were expending their enthusiasm for France in the humblest of philanthropic drudgery: students of the Beaux Arts or the University, or young men of leisure discouraged by the indifference of their country and the dilatoriness of their government, and fired by the desire to take part in a struggle in which they had instantly felt their own country to be involved in spite of geographical distance.

None of these young men had heard Benny Upsher's imperious call to be "in it" from the first, no matter how or at what cost. They were of the kind to wait for a lead—and now Boylston was giving it to them with his passionate variations on the great theme of Preparedness. George, meanwhile, lay there in his bed and smiled; and now and then Boylston brought one or two of the more privileged candidates to see him. One day Campton found young Louis Dastrey there, worn and haggard after a bad wound, and preparing to leave for America as instructor in one of the new camps. That seemed to bring the movement closer than ever, to bring it into their very lives. The thought flashed through Campton: "When George is up, we'll get him sent out too"; and once again a delicious sense of security crept through him.

George, as yet, was only sitting up for a few hours a day; the wound in the lung was slow in healing, and his fractured arm in recovering its flexibility. But in another fortnight he was to leave the hospital and complete his convalescence at his mother's.

The thought was bitter to Campton; he had had all kinds of wild plans—of taking George to the Crillon, or hiring an apartment for him, or even camping with him at the studio. But George had smiled all this away. He meant to return to the Avenue Marigny, where he always stayed when he came to Paris, and where it was natural that his mother should want him now. Adele Anthony pointed out to Campton how natural it was, one day as he and she left the Palais

Royal together. They were going to lunch at a near-by restaurant, as they often did on leaving the office, and Campton had begun to speak of George's future arrangements. He would be well enough to leave the hospital in another week, and then no doubt a staff-job could be obtained for him in Paris—"with Brant's pull, you know," Campton concluded, hardly aware that he had uttered the detested phrase without even a tinge of irony. But Adele was aware, as he saw by the faint pucker of her thin lips.

He shrugged her smile away indifferently. "Oh, well—hang it, yes! Everything's changed now, isn't if? After what the boy's been through I consider that we're more than justified in using Brant's pull in his favour—or anybody else's."

Miss Anthony nodded and unfolded her napkin.

"Well, then," Campton continued his argument, "as he's likely to be in Paris now till the war is over—which means some time next year, they all say—why shouldn't I take a jolly apartment somewhere for the two of us? Those pictures I did last spring brought me in a lot of money, and there's no reason——" His face lit up. "Servants, you say? Why, my poor Mariette may be back from Lille any time now. They tell me there's sure to be a big push in the spring. They're saving up for that all along the line. Ask Dastrey . . . ask. . ."

"You'd better let George go to his mother," said Miss Anthony concisely.

"Why?"

"Because it's natural—it's human. *You're* not always, you know," she added with another pucker.

"Not human?"

"I don't mean that you're inhuman. But you see things differently."

"I don't want to see anything but one; and that's my own son. How shall I ever see George if he's at the Avenue Marigny?"

"He'll come to you."

"Yes—when he's not at Mrs. Talkett's!"

Miss Anthony frowned. The subject had been touched upon between them soon after Campton's return, but Miss Anthony had little light to throw on it: George had been as mute with her as with every one else, and she knew Mrs. Talkett but slightly, and seldom saw her. Yet Campton perceived that she could not hear the young woman named without an involuntary contraction of her brows.

"I wish I liked her!" she murmured.

"Mrs. Talkett?"

"Yes—I should think better of myself if I did. And it might be useful. But I can't—I can't!"

Campton said within himself: "Oh, women——!" For his own resentment had died out long ago. He could think of the affair now as one of hundreds such as happen to young men; he was even conscious of regarding it, in some unlit secret fold of himself, as a probable guarantee of George's wanting to remain in Paris, another subterranean way of keeping him, should such be needed. Perhaps that was what Miss Anthony meant by saying that her liking Mrs. Talkett might be "useful."

"Why shouldn't he be with me?" the father persisted. "He and I were going off together when the war begun. I was defrauded of that—why shouldn't I have him now?"

Miss Anthony smiled. "Well, for one thing, because of that very 'pull' you were speaking of."

"Oh, the Brants, the Brants!" Campton glanced impatiently at the bill-of-fare, grumbled: "*Déjeuner du jour,* I suppose?" and went on: "Yes; I might have known it—he belongs to them. From the minute we got back, and I saw them at the station, with their motor waiting, and everything arranged as only money can arrange it, I knew I'd lost my boy again." He stared moodily before him. "And yet if the war hadn't come I should have got him back—I almost had."

His companion still smiled, a little wistfully. She leaned over and laid her hand on his, under cover of the bill-of-fare. "You did get him back, John, forever and always, the day he exchanged into the infantry. Isn't that enough?"

Campton answered her smile. "You gallant old chap, you!" he said; and they began to lunch.

George was able to be up now, able to drive out, and to see more people; and Campton was not surprised, on approaching his door a day or two later, to hear several voices in animated argument.

The voices (and this did surprise him) were all men's. In one he recognized Boylston's deep round notes; but the answering voice, flat, toneless and yet eager, puzzled him with a sense of something familiar but forgotten. He opened the door, and saw, at the tea-tray between George and Boylston, the smoothly-brushed figure of Roger Talkett.

Campton had not seen Mrs. Talkett's husband for months, and in the interval so much had happened that the young man, always somewhat faintly-drawn, had become as dim as a daguerreotype held at the wrong angle.

The painter hung back, slightly embarrassed; but Mr. Talkett did not seem in the least disturbed by his appearance, or by the fact of himself being where he was. It was evident that on whatever terms George might be with his wife, Mr. Talkett was determined to shed on him the same impartial beam as on all her other visitors.

His eye-glasses glinted blandly up at Campton. "Now I daresay I *am* subversive," he began, going on with what he had been saying, but in a tone intended to include the newcomer. "I don't say I'm not. We *are* a subversive lot at home, all of us—you must have noticed that, haven't you, Mr. Campton?"

Boylston emitted a faint growl. "What's that got to do with it?" he asked.

Mr. Talkett's glasses slanted in his direction. "Why—everything! Resistance to the herd-instinct (to borrow one of my wife's expressions) is really innate in me. And the idea of giving in now, of sacrificing my convictions, just because of all this deafening noise about America's danger and America's duties—well, *no,*" said Mr. Talkett, straightening his glasses, "Philistinism won't go down with me, in whatever form it tries to disguise itself." Instinctively, he stretched a neat hand toward the tea-cups, as if he had been rearranging the furniture at one of his wife's parties.

"But—but—but——" Boylston stuttered, red with rage.

George burst into a laugh. He seemed to take a boyish amusement in the dispute. "Tea, father?" he suggested, reaching across the tray for a cigarette.

Talkett jerked himself to his feet. "Take my chair, now do, Mr. Campton. You'll be more comfortable. Here, let me shake up this cushion for you——" (*"Cushion!"* Boylston interjected scornfully.) "A light, George? Now don't move!—I don't say, of course, old chap," Talkett continued, as he held the match deferentially to George's cigarette, "that this sort of talk would be safe—or advisable—just now in public; subversive talk never is. But when two or three of the Elect are gathered together—well, your father sees my point, I know. The Hero," he nodded at George, "has his job, and the Artist," with a slant at Campton, "his. In Germany, for instance, as we're beginning to find out, the creative minds, the Intelligentsia (to use another of my wife's expressions), have been carefully protected from the beginning, given jobs, vitally important jobs of course, but where their lives were not exposed. The country needs them too much in other ways; they would probably be wretched fighters, and they're of colossal service in their own line. Whereas in France and England——" he suddenly seemed to see his chance——"Well, look here, Mr. Campton, I appeal to you, I appeal to the great creative Artist: in any country but France and England, would a fellow of George's brains have been *allowed,* even at this stage of the war, to chuck an important staff job, requiring intellect, tact and *savoir faire,* and try to get himself killed like any unbaked boy—like your poor cousin Benny Upsher, for instance? Would he?"

"Yes—in America!" shouted Boylston; and Mr. Talkett's tallowy cheeks turned pink.

"George knows how I feel about these things," he stammered.

George still laughed in his remote impartial way, and Boylston asked with a grin: "Why don't you get yourself naturalized—a neutral?"

Mr. Talkett's pinkness deepened. "I have lived too much among Artists——" he began; and George interrupted gaily: "There's a lot to be said on Talkett's side too. Going, Roger? Well, I shall be able to look in on you now in a few days. Remember me to Madge. Good-bye."

Boylston rose also, and Campton remained alone with his son.

"Remember me to Madge!" That was the way in which the modern young man spoke of his beloved to his beloved's proprietor. There had not been a shadow of constraint in George's tone; and now, glancing at the door which had closed on Mr. Talkett, he merely said, as if apostrophizing the latter's neat back: "Poor devil! He's torn to pieces with it."

"With what?" asked Campton, startled.

"Why, with Boylston's Preparedness. Wanting to do the proper thing—and never before having had to decide between anything more vital than straight or turned-down collars. It's playing the very deuce with him."

His eyes grew thoughtful. Was he going to pronounce Mrs. Talkett's name—at last? But no; he wandered back to her husband. "Poor little ass! Of course he'll decide against." He shrugged his shoulders. "And Boylston's just as badly torn in the other direction."

"Boylston?"

"Yes. Knowing that he wouldn't be taken himself, on account of his bad heart and his blind eyes, and wondering if, in spite of his disabilities, he's got the right to preach to all these young chaps here who hang on his words like the gospel. One of them taunted him with it the other day."

"The cur!"

"Yes. And ever since, of course, Boylston's been twice as fierce, and overworking himself to calm his frenzy. The men who can't go are all like that, when they know it's their proper work. It isn't everybody's billet out there—I've learnt that since I've had a look at it—but it would be Boylston's if he had the health, and he knows it, and that's what drives him wild." George looked at his father with a smile. "You don't know how I thank my stars that there weren't any 'problems' for me, but just a plain job that picked me up by the collar, and dropped me down where I belonged." He reached for another cigarette. "Old Adele's coming presently. Do you suppose we could rake up some fresh tea?" he asked.

XXIX

Coming out of the unlit rainy March night, it was agreeable but almost startling to Campton to enter Mrs. Talkett's drawing-room. In the softness of shaded lamplight, against curtains closely drawn, young women dressed with extravagant elegance chatted with much-decorated officers in the new "horizon" uniform, with here and there among them an elderly civilian head, such as Harvey Mayhew's silvery thatch and the square rapacious skull of the newly-knighted patriot, Sir Cyril Jorgenstein.

Campton had gone to Mrs. Talkett's that afternoon because she had lent her apartment to "The Friends of French Art," who were giving a concert organized by Miss Anthony and Mlle. Davril, with Mme. de Dolmetsch's pianist as their leading performer. It would have been ungracious to deprive the indefatigable group of the lustre they fancied Campton's presence would confer; and he was not altogether sorry to be there. He knew that George had promised Miss Anthony to come; and he wanted to see his son with Mrs. Talkett.

An abyss seemed to divide this careless throng of people, so obviously assembled for their own pleasure, the women to show their clothes, the men to admire them, from the worn preoccupied audiences of the first war-charity entertainments. The war still raged; wild hopes had given way to dogged resignation; each day added to the sum of public anguish and private woe. But the strain had been too long, the tragedy too awful. The idle and the useless had reached their emotional limit, and once more they dressed and painted, smiled, gossiped, flirted as though the long agony were over.

On a sofa stacked with orange-velvet cushions Mme. de Dolmetsch reclined in a sort of serpent-coil of flexible grey-green hung with strange amulets. Her eyes, in which fabulous islands seemed to dream, were fixed on the bushy-haired young man at the piano. Close by, upright and tight-waisted, sat the Marquise de Tranlay, her mourning veil thrown back from a helmet-like hat. She had planted herself in a Louis Philippe armchair, as if appealing to its sturdy frame to protect her from the anarchy of Mrs. Talkett's furniture; and beside her was the daughter for whose sake she had doubtless come— a frowning beauty who, in spite of her dowdy dress and ugly boots, somehow declared herself as having already broken away from the maternal tradition.

Mme. de Tranlay's presence in that drawing-room was characteristic enough. It meant—how often one heard it nowadays!—that mothers had to take their daughters wherever there was a chance of their meeting young men, and that such chances were found only in the few "foreign" houses where, discreetly, almost clandestinely, entertaining had been resumed. You had to take them there, Mme. de Tranlay's look seemed to say, because they had to be married (the sooner the better in these wild times, with all the old barriers down), and because the young men were growing so tragically few, and the competition was so fierce, and because in such emergencies a French mother, whose first thought is always for her children, must learn to accept, even to seek, propinquities from which her inmost soul, and all the ancestral souls within her, would normally recoil.

Campton remembered her gallant attitude on the day when, under her fresh crape, she had rebuked Mrs. Brant's despondency. "But how she hates it here—how she must loathe sitting next to that woman!" he thought; and just then he saw her turn toward Mme. de Dolmetsch with a stiff bend from the waist, and heard her say in her most conciliatory tone: "Your great friend, the rich American, *chère Madame,* the benefactor of France—we should so like to thank him, Claire and I, for all he is doing for our country."

Beckoned to by Mme. de Dolmetsch, Mr. Mayhew, all pink and silver and prominent pearl scarf-pin, bowed before the Tranlay ladies, while the Marquise deeply murmured: "We are grateful—we shall not forget—" and Mademoiselle de Tranlay, holding him with her rich gaze, added in fluent English: "Mamma hopes you'll come to tea on Sunday—with no one but my uncle the Duc de Montlhéry—so that we may thank you better than we can here."

"Great women—great women!" Campton mused. He was still watching Mme. de Tranlay's dauntless mask when her glance deserted the gratified Mayhew to seize on a younger figure. It was that of George, who had just entered. Mme. de Tranlay, with a quick turn, caught Campton's eye, greeted him with her trenchant cordiality, and asked, in a voice like the pounce of talons: "The young officer who has the Legion of Honour—the one you just nodded to—with reddish hair and his left arm in a sling? French, I suppose, from his uniform; and yet——? Yes, talking to Mrs. Talkett. Can you tell me——?"

"My son," said Campton with satisfaction.

The effect was instantaneous, though Mme. de Tranlay kept her radiant steadiness. "How charming—charming—charming!" And, after a proper interval: "But, Claire, my child, we've not yet spoken to Mrs. Brant, whom I see over there." And she steered her daughter swiftly toward Julia.

Campton's eyes returned to his son. George was still with Mrs. Talkett, but they had only had time for a word or two before she was called away to seat an important dowager. In that moment, however, the father noted many things. George, as usual nowadays, kept his air of guarded kindliness, though the blue of his eyes grew deeper; but Mrs. Talkett seemed bathed in light. It was such a self-revelation that Campton's curiosity was lost in the artist's abstract joy. "If I could have painted her like that!" he thought, reminded of having caught Mme. de Dolmetsch transfigured by fear for her lover; but an instant later he remembered. "Poor little thing!" he murmured. Mrs. Talkett turned her head, as if his thought had reached her. "Oh, yes—oh, yes;

come and let me tell you all about it," her eyes entreated him. But Mayhew and Sir Cyril Jorgenstein were between them.

"George!" Mrs. Brant called; and across the intervening groups Campton saw his son bowing to the Marquise de Tranlay.

Mme. de Dolmetsch jumped up, her bracelets jangling like a prompter's call. "Silence!" she cried. The ladies squeezed into their seats, the men resigned themselves to door-posts and window-embrasures, and the pianist attacked Stravinsky. . .

"Dancing?" Campton heard his hostess answering some one. "N—no: not *quite* yet, I think. Though in London, already . . . oh, just for the officers on leave, of course. Poor darlings—why shouldn't they? But today, you see, it's for a charity." Her smile appealed to her hearer to acknowledge the distinction.

The music was over, and scanning the groups at the tea-tables, Campton saw Adele and Mlle. Davril squeezed away in the remotest corner of the room. He took a chair at their table, and Boylston presently blinked his way to them through the crowd.

They seemed, all four, more like unauthorized intruders on the brilliant scene than its laborious organizers. The entertainment, escaping from their control, had speedily reverted to its true purpose of feeding and amusing a crowd of bored and restless people; and the little group recognized the fact, and joked over it in their different ways. But Mlle. Davril was happy at the sale of tickets, which must have been immense to judge from the crowd (spying about the entrance, she had seen furious fine ladies turn away ticketless); and Adele Anthony was exhilarated by the nearness of people she did not know, or wish to know, but with whose names and private histories she was minutely and passionately familiar.

"That's the old Duchesse de Murols with Mrs. Talkett—there, she's put her at the Beausites' table! Well, of all places! Ah, but you're all too young to know about Beausite's early history. And now, of course, it makes no earthly difference to anybody. But there must be times when Mme. Beausite remembers, and grins. Now that she's begun to rouge again she looks twenty years younger than the Duchess.—— Ah," she broke off, abruptly signing to Campton.

He followed her glance to a table at which Julia Brant was seating herself with the Tranlay ladies and George. Mayhew joined them nobly deferential, and the elder ladies lent him their intensest attention, isolating George with the young girl.

"H'm," Adele murmured, "not such a bad thing! They say the girl will have half of old Montlhéry's money—he's her mother's uncle. And she's heaps handsomer than the other—not that *that* seems to count any more!"

Campton shrugged the subject away. Yes; it would be a good thing if George could be drawn from what his mother (with a retrospective pinching of the lips) called his "wretched infatuation." But the idea that the boy might be coaxed into a marriage—and a rich marriage—by the Brants, was even more distasteful to Campton. If he really loved Madge Talkett better stick to her than let himself be cajoled away for such reasons.

As the second part of the programme began, Campton and Boylston slipped out together. Campton was oppressed and disturbed. "It's queer," he said, taking Boylston's arm to steer him through the dense darkness of the streets; "all these people who've forgotten the war have suddenly made me remember it."

Boylston laughed. "Yes, I know." He seemed preoccupied and communicative, and the painter fancied he was going to lead the talk, as usual, to Preparedness and America's intervention; but after a pause he said: "You haven't been much at the office lately——"

"No," Campton interrupted. "I've shirked abominably since George got back. But now that he's gone to the Brants' you'll see——"

"Oh, I didn't mean it as a reproach, sir! How could you think it? We're running smoothly enough, as far as organization goes. That's not what bothers me——"

"You're bothered?"

Yes; he was—and so, he added, was Miss Anthony. The trouble was, he went on to explain, that Mr. Mayhew, after months of total indifference (except when asked to "represent" them on official platforms) had developed a disquieting interest in "The Friends of French Art." He had brought them, in the beginning, a certain amount of money (none of which came out of his own pocket), and in consequence had been imprudently put on the Financial Committee, so that he had a voice in the disposal of funds, though till lately he had never made it heard. But now, apparently, "Atrocities" were losing their novelty, and he was disposed to transfer his whole attention to "The Friends of French Art," with results which seemed incomprehensibly disturbing to Boylston, until he let drop the name of Mme. de Dolmetsch. Campton exclaimed at it.

"Well—yes. You must have noticed that she and Mr. Mayhew have been getting pretty chummy. You see, he's done such a lot of talking that people think he's at least an Oil King; and Mme. de Dolmetsch is dazzled. But she's got her musical prodigy to provide for——" and Boylston outlined the situation which his astuteness had detected while it developed unperceived under Campton's dreaming eyes. Mr. Mayhew was attending all their meetings now, finding fault, criticizing, asking to have the account investigated, though they had always been audited at regular intervals by expert accountants; and all this zeal originated in the desire to put Mme. de Dolmetsch in Miss Anthony's place, on the plea that her greater social experience, her gift of attracting and interesting, would bring in immense sums of money—whereas, Boylston grimly hinted, they already had a large balance in the bank, and it was with an eye to that balance that Mme. de Dolmetsch was forcing Mayhew to press her claim.

"You see, sir, Mr. Mayhew never turns out to be as liberal as they expect when they first hear him talk; and though Mme. de Dolmetsch has him in her noose she's not getting what she wants—by a long way. And so they've cooked this up between them—she and Mme. Beausite—without his actually knowing what they're after."

Campton stopped short, releasing Boylston's arm. "But what you suggest is abominable," he exclaimed.

"Yes. I know it." But the young man's voice remained steady. "Well, I wish you'd come to our meetings, now you're back."

"I will—I will! But I'm no earthly use on financial questions. You're much stronger there."

He felt Boylston's grin through the darkness. "Oh, they'll have me out too before long."

"You? Nonsense! What do you mean?"

"I mean that lots of people are beginning to speculate in war charities—oh, in all sorts of ways. Sometimes I'm sick to the point of chucking it all. But Miss Anthony keeps me going."

"Ah, she would!" Campton agreed.

As he walked home his mind was burdened with Boylston's warning. It was not merely the affair itself, but all it symbolized, that made his gorge rise, made him, as Boylston said, sick to the point of wanting to chuck it all—to chuck everything connected with this hideous world that was dancing and flirting and money-making on the great red mounds of dead. He grinned at the thought that he had once believed in the regenerative power of war—the salutary shock of great moral and social upheavals. Yet he *had* believed in it, and never more intensely than at George's bedside at Doullens, in that air so cleansed by passion and pain that mere living seemed a meaningless gesture compared to the chosen surrender of life. But in the Paris to which he had returned after barely four months of absence the instinct of self-preservation seemed to have wiped all meaning from such words. Poor fatuous Mayhew dancing to Mme. de Dolmetsch's piping, Jorgenstein sinking under the weight of his international honours, Mme. de Tranlay intriguing to push her daughter in such society, and Julia placidly abetting her—Campton hardly knew from which of these sorry visions he turned with a completer loathing. . .

There were still the others, to be sure, the huge obscure majority; out there in the night, the millions giving their lives for this handful of trivial puppets, and here in Paris, and everywhere, in every country, men and women toiling unweariedly to help and heal; but in Mrs. Talkett's drawing-room both fighters and toilers seemed to count as little in relation to the merry-makers as Miss Anthony and Mlle. Davril in relation to the brilliant people who had crowded their table into the obscurest corner of the room.

XXX

These thoughts continued to weigh on Campton; to shake them off he decided, with one of his habitual quick jerks of resolution, to get back to work. He knew that George would approve, and would perhaps be oftener with him if he had something interesting on his easel. Sir Cyril Jorgenstein had suggested that he would like to have his portrait finished—with the Legion of Honour added to his lapel, no doubt. And Harvey Mayhew, rosy and embarrassed, had dropped in to hint that, if Campton could find time to do a charcoal head—oh, just one of those brilliant sketches of his—of the young musical genius in whose career their friend Mme. de Dolmetsch was so much interested. . . But Campton had cut them both short. He was not working—he had no plans for the present. And in truth he had not thought even of attempting a portrait of George. The impulse had come to him, once, as he sat by the boy's bed; but the face was too incomprehensible. He should have to learn and unlearn too many things first——

At last, one day, it occurred to him to make a study of Mme. Lebel. He saw *her* in charcoal: her simple unquestioning anguish had turned her old face to sculpture. Campton set his canvas on the easel, and started to shout for her down the stairs; but as he opened the door he found himself face to face with Mrs. Talkett.

"Oh," she began at once, in her breathless way, "you're here? The old woman downstairs wasn't sure—and I couldn't leave all this money with her, could I?"

"Money? What money?" he echoed.

She was very simply dressed, and a veil, drooping low from her hat-brim, gave to her over-eager face a shadowy youthful calm.

"I *may* come in?" she questioned, almost timidly; and as Campton let her pass she added: "The money from the concert, of course—heaps and heaps of it! I'd no idea we'd made so much. And I wanted to give it to you myself."

She shook a bulging bag out of her immense muff, while Campton continued to stare at her.

"I didn't know you went out so early," he finally stammered, trying to push a newspaper over the disordered remains of his breakfast.

She lifted interrogative eye-brows. "That means that I'm in the way?"

"No. But why did you bring that money here?"

She looked surprised. "Why not? Aren't you the head—the real head of the committee? And wasn't the concert given in my house?" Her eyes rested on him with renewed timidity. "Is it—disagreeable to you to see me?" she asked.

"Disagreeable? My dear child, no." He paused, increasingly embarrassed. What did she expect him to say next? To thank her for having sent him the orderly's letter? It seemed to him impossible to plunge into the subject uninvited. Surely it was for her to give him the opening, if she wished to.

"Well, no!" she broke out. "I've never once pretended to you, have I? The money's a pretext. I wanted to see you—here, alone, with no one to disturb us."

Campton felt a confused stirring of relief and fear. All his old dread of scenes, commotions, disturbing emergencies—of anything that should upset his perpetually vibrating balance—was blent with the passionate desire to hear what his visitor had to say.

"You—it was good of you to think of sending us that letter," he faltered.

She frowned in her anxious way and looked away from him. "Afterward I was afraid you'd be angry."

"Angry? How could I?" He groped for a word. "Surprised—yes. I knew nothing . . . about you and . . ."

"Not even that it was I who bought the sketch of him—the one that Léonce Black sold for you last year?"

The blood rushed to Campton's face. Suddenly he felt himself trapped and betrayed. "You—*you?* You've got that sketch?" The thought was somehow intolerable to him.

"Ah, now you *are* angry," Mrs. Talkett murmured.

"No, no; but I never imagined——"

"I know. That was what frightened me—your suspecting nothing." She glanced about her, dropped to a corner of the divan, and tossed off her hat with the old familiar gesture. "Oh, can I talk to you?" she pleaded.

Campton nodded.

"I wish you'd light your pipe, then, and sit down too." He reached for his pipe, struck a match, and slowly seated himself. "You always smoke a pipe in the morning, don't you? *He* told me that," she went on; then she paused again and drew a long anxious breath. "Oh, he's so changed! I feel as if I didn't know him any longer—do *you?*"

Campton looked at her with deepening wonder. This was more surprising than discovering her to be the possessor of the picture; he had not expected deep to call unto deep in their talk. "I'm not sure that I do," he confessed.

Her fidgeting eyes deepened and grew quieter. "Your saying so makes me feel less lonely," she sighed, half to herself. "But has he told you nothing since he came back—really nothing?"

"Nothing. After all—how could he? I mean, without indiscretion?"

"Indiscretion? Oh——" She shrugged the word away with half a smile, as though such considerations belonged to a prehistoric order of things. "Then he hasn't even told you that he wants me to get a divorce?"

"A divorce?" Campton exclaimed. He sat staring at her as if the weight of his gaze might pin her down, keep her from fluttering away and breaking up into luminous splinters. George wanted her to get a divorce—wanted, therefore, to marry her! His passion went as deep for her as that—too deep, Campton conjectured, for the poor little ephemeral creature, who struck him as wriggling on it like a butterfly impaled.

"Please tell me," he said at length; and suddenly, in short inconsequent sentences, the confession poured from her.

George, it seemed, during the previous winter in New York, when they had seen so much of each other, had been deeply attracted, had wanted "everything," and at once—and there had been moments of tension and estrangement, when she had been held back by scruples she confessed she no longer understood (inherited prejudices, she supposed), and when her reluctance must have made her appear to be trifling, whereas, really it was just that she couldn't . . . couldn't. . . So they had gone on for several months, with the usual emotional ups-and-downs, till he had left for Europe to join his father; and when they had parted she had given him the half-promise that if they met abroad during the summer she would perhaps . . . after all . . .

Then came the war. George had been with her during those few last hours in Paris, and had dined with her and her husband (had Campton forgiven her?) the night before he was mobilised. And then, when he was gone, she had understood that only timidity, vanity, the phantom barriers of old terrors and traditions, had prevented her being to him all that he wanted. . .

She broke off abruptly, put in a few conventional words about an ill-assorted marriage, and never having been "really understood," and then, as if guessing that she was on the wrong tack, jumped up, walked to the other end of the studio, and turned back to Campton with the tears running down her ravaged face.

"And now—and now—he says he won't have me!" she lamented.

"Won't have you? But you tell me he wants you to be divorced."

She nodded, wiped away the tears, and in so doing stole an unconscious glance at the mirror above the divan. Then, seeing that the glance was detected, she burst into a sort of sobbing laugh. "My nose gets so dreadfully red when I cry," she stammered.

Campton took no notice, and she went on: "A divorce? Yes. And unless I do—unless I agree to marry him—we're never to be anything but friends."

"That's what he says?"

"Yes. Oh, we've been all in and out of it a hundred times."

She pulled out a gold-mesh bag and furtively restored her complexion, as Mrs. Brant had once done in the same place.

Campton sat still, considering. He had let his pipe go out. Nothing could have been farther from the revelation he had expected, and his own perplexity was hardly less great than his visitor's. Certainly it was not the way in which young men had behaved in his day—nor, evidently, had it been George's before the war.

Finally, he made up his mind to put the question: "And Talkett?"

She burst out at once: "Ah, that's what I say—it's not so simple!"

"What isn't?"

"Breaking up—all one's life." She paused with a deepening embarrassment. "Of course Roger has made me utterly miserable—but then I know he really hasn't meant to."

"Have you told George that?"

"Yes. But he says we must first of all be above-board. He says he sees everything differently now. That's what I mean when I say that I don't understand him. He says love's not the same kind of feeling to him that it was. There's something of Meredith's that he quotes—I wish I could remember it—something about a mortal lease."

"Good Lord," Campton groaned, not so much at the hopelessness of the case as at the hopelessness of quoting Meredith to her. After a while he said abruptly: "You must forgive my asking: but things change sometimes—they change imperceptibly. Do you think he's as much in love with you as ever?"

He had been half afraid of offending her: but she appeared to consider the question impartially, and without a shadow of resentment. "Sometimes I think more—because in the beginning it wasn't meant to last. And now—if he wants to marry me? Oh, I wish I knew what to do!"

Campton continued to ponder. "There's one more question, since we're talking frankly: what does Talkett know of all this?"

She looked frightened. "Oh, nothing, nothing!"

"And you've no idea how he would take it?"

She examined the question with tortured eye-brows, and at length, to Campton's astonishment, brought out: "Magnificently——"

"He'd be generous, you mean? But it would go hard with him?"

"Oh, dreadfully, dreadfully!" She seemed to need the assurance to restore her shaken self-approval.

Campton rose with a movement of pity and laid his hand on her shoulder. "My dear child, if your husband cares for you, give up my son."

Her face fell, and she drew back. "Oh, but you don't understand—not in the least! It's not possible—it's not moral——. You know I'm all for the new morality. First of all, we must be true to self." She paused, and then broke out: "You tell me to give him up because you think he's tired of me. But he's not—I know he's not! It's his ideas that you don't understand, any more than I do. It's the war that has changed him. He says he wants only things that last—that are permanent—things that hold a man fast. That sometimes he feels as if he were being swept away on a flood, and were trying to catch at things—at anything—as he's rushed along under the waves. . . He says he wants quiet, monotony . . . to be sure the same things will happen every day. When we go out together he sometimes stands for a quarter of an hour and stares at the same building, or at the Seine under the bridges. But he's happy, I'm sure. . . I've never seen him happier . . . only it's in a way I can't make out. . ."

"Ah, my dear, if it comes to that—I'm not sure that I can. Not sure enough to help you, I'm afraid."

She looked at him, disappointed. "You won't speak to him then?"

"Not unless he speaks to me."

"Ah, he frightens you—just as he does me!"

She pulled her hat down on her troubled brow, gathered up her furs, and took another sidelong peep at the glass. Then she turned toward the door. On the threshold she paused and looked back at Campton. "Don't you see," she cried, "that if I were to give George up he'd get himself sent straight back to the front?"

Campton's heart gave an angry leap; for a second he felt the impulse to strike her, to catch her by the shoulders and bundle her out of the room. With a great effort he controlled himself and opened the door.

"You don't understand—you don't understand!" she called back to him once again from the landing.

Madge Talkett had asked him to speak to his son: he had refused, and she had retaliated by planting that poisoned shaft in him. But what had retaliation to do with it? She had probably spoken the simple truth, and with the natural desire to enlighten him. If George wanted to marry her, it must be (since human nature, though it might change its vocabulary, kept its instincts), it must be that he was very much in love—and in that case her refusal would in truth go hard with him, and it would be natural that he should try to get himself sent away from Paris. . . From Paris, yes; but not necessarily to the front. After such wounds and such honours he had only to choose; a staff-appointment could easily be got. Or, no doubt, with his two languages, he might, if he preferred, have himself sent on a military mission to America. With all this propaganda talk, wasn't he the very type of officer they wanted for the neutral countries?

It was Campton's dearest wish that George should stay where he was; he knew his peace of mind would vanish the moment his son was out of sight. But he suspected that George would soon weary of staff-work, or of any form of soldiering at the rear, and try for the trenches if he left Paris; whereas, in Paris, Madge Talkett might hold him—as she had meant his father to see.

The first thing then, was to make sure of a job at the War Office.

Campton turned and tossed like a sick man on the hard bed of his problem. To plan, to scheme, to plot and circumvent—nothing was more hateful to him, there was nothing in which he was less skilled. If only he dared to consult Adele Anthony! But Adele was still incorrigibly warlike, and her having been in George's secret while his parents were excluded from it left no doubt as to the side on which her influence would bear. She loved the boy, Campton sometimes thought, even more passionately than his mother did; but—how did the old song go?—she loved honour, or her queer conception of it, more. Ponder as he would, he could not picture her, even now, lifting a finger to keep George back.

Campton struggled all the morning with these questions. After lunch he pocketed Mrs. Talkett's money-bag and carried it to the Palais Royal, where he discovered Harvey Mayhew in confabulation with Mme. Beausite, who still trailed her ineffectual beauty about the office. The painter thought he detected a faint embarrassment in the glance with which they both greeted him.

"Hallo, Campton! Looking for our good friend Boylston? He's off duty this afternoon, Mme. Beausite tells me; as he is pretty often in these days, I've noticed," Mr. Mayhew sardonically added. "In fact, the office has rather been left to run itself lately—eh? Of course our good Miss Anthony is absorbed with her refugees—gives us but a divided allegiance. And Boylston—well, young men, young men! Of course it's been a weary pull for him. By the way, my dear fellow," Mr. Mayhew continued, as Campton appeared about to turn away, "I called at Mrs. Talkett's just now to ask for the money from the concert—a good round sum, I hear it is—and she told me she'd given it to you. Have you brought it with you? If so, Mme. Beausite here would take charge of it——"

Mme. Beausite turned her great resigned eyes on the painter. "Mr. Campton knows I'm very careful. I will lock it up till his friend's return. Now that Mr. Boylston is so much away I very often have such responsibilities."

Campton's eyes returned her glance; but he did not waver. "Thanks so much; but as the sum is rather large it seems to me the bank's the proper place. Will you please tell Boylston I've deposited it?"

Mr. Mayhew's benevolent pink turned to an angry red. For a moment Campton thought he was about to say something foolish. But he merely bent his head stiffly, muttered a vague phrase about "irregular proceedings," and returned to his seat by Mme. Beausite's desk.

As for Campton, his words had decided his course: he would take the money at once to Bullard and Brant's and seize the occasion to see the banker. Mr. Brant was the only person with whom, at this particular juncture, he cared to talk of George.

XXXI

Mr. Brant's private office was as glitteringly neat as when Campton had entered it for the first time, and seen the fatal telegram about Benny Upsher marring the order of the desk.

Now he crossed the threshold with different feelings. To have Mr. Brant look up and smile, to shake hands with him, accept one of his cigars, and sink into one of the blue leather arm-chairs, seemed to be in the natural order of things. He felt only the relief of finding himself with the one person likely to understand.

"About George——" he began.

"Yes?" said Mr. Brant briskly. "It's curious—I was just thinking of looking you up. It's his birthday next Tuesday, you know."

"Oh——" said the father, slightly put off. He had not come to talk of birthdays; nor did he need to be reminded of his son's by Mr. Brant. He concluded that Mr. Brant would be less easy to get on with in Paris than at the front.

"And we thought of celebrating the day by a little party—a dinner, with perhaps the smallest kind of a dance: or just bridge—yes, probably just bridge," the banker added tentatively. "Opinions differ as to the suitability—it's for his mother to decide. But of course no evening clothes, and we hoped perhaps to persuade you. Our only object is to amuse him—to divert his mind from this wretched entanglement."

It was doubtful if Mr. Brant had ever before made so long a speech, except perhaps at a board meeting; and then only when he read the annual report. He turned pink and stared over Campton's shoulder at the panelled white wall, on which a false Reynolds hung.

Campton meditated. The blush was the blush of Mr. Brant, but the voice was the voice of Julia. Still, it was probable that neither husband nor wife was aware how far matters had gone with Mrs. Talkett.

"George is more involved than you think," Campton said.

Mr. Brant looked startled.

"In what way?"

"He means to marry her. He insists on her getting a divorce."

"A divorce? Good gracious," murmured Mr. Brant. He turned over a jade paper-cutter, trying its edge absently on his nail. "Does Julia——?" he began at length.

Campton shook his head. "No; I wanted to speak to you first."

Mr. Brant gave his quick bow. He was evidently gratified, and the sentiment stimulated his faculties, as it had when he found that Campton no longer resented his presence at the hospital. His small effaced features took on a business-like sharpness, and he readjusted his eye-glasses and straightened the paper-cutter, which he had put back on the desk a fraction of an inch out of its habitual place.

"You had this from George?" he asked.

"No; from her. She's been to see me. *She* doesn't want to divorce. She's in love with him; in her way, that is; but she's frightened."

"And that makes him the more eager?"

"The more determined, at any rate."

Mr. Brant appeared to seize the distinction. "George can be very determined."

"Yes. I think his mother ought to be made to understand that all this talk about a wretched entanglement isn't likely to make him any less so."

Mr. Brant's look seemed to say that making Julia understand had proved a no less onerous task for his maturity than for Campton's youth.

"If you don't object—perhaps the matter might, for the present, continue to be kept between you and me," he suggested.

"Oh, by all means. What I want," Campton pursued, "is to get him out of this business altogether. They wouldn't be happy—they couldn't be. She's too much like——" He broke off, frightened at what he had been about to say. "Too much," he emended, "like the usual fool of a woman that every boy of George's age thinks he wants simply because he can't get her."

"And you say she came to you for advice?"

"She came to me to persuade him to give up the idea of a divorce. Apparently she's ready for anything short of that. It's a queer business. She seems sorry for Talkett in a way."

Mr. Brant marked his sense of the weight of this by a succession of attentive nods. He put his hands in his pockets, leaned back, and tilted his dapper toes against the gold-trellised scrap-basket. The attitude seemed to change the pale panelling of his background into a glass-and-mahogany Wall Street office.

"Won't he be satisfied with—er—all the rest, so to speak; since you say she offers it?"

"No; he won't. There's the difficulty. It seems it's the new view. The way the young men feel since the war. He wants her for his wife. Nothing less."

"Ah, he respects her," murmured Mr. Brant, impressed; and Campton reflected that he had no doubt respected Julia.

"And what she wants is to get you to persuade him—to accept less?"

"Well—something of the sort."

Mr. Brant sat up and dropped his heels to the floor. "Well, then—don't!" he snapped.

"Don't—-?"

"Persuade her, on the contrary, to keep him hoping—to make him think she means to marry him. Don't you see?" Mr. Brant exclaimed, almost impatiently. "Don't you see that if she turns him down definitely he'll be scheming to get away, to get back to the front, the minute his leave is over? Tell her that—appeal to her on that ground. Make her do it. She will if she's in love with him. And we can't stop him from going back—not one of us. He's restless here already—I know that. Always talking about his men, saying he's got to get back to them. The only way is to hold him by this girl. She's the very influence we need!"

He threw it all out in sharp terse phrases, as a business man might try to hammer facts about an investment into the bewildered brain of an unpractical client. Campton felt the blood rising to his forehead, not so much in anger at Mr. Brant as at the sense of his own inward complicity.

"There's no earthly reason why George should ever go back to the front," he said.

"None whatever. We can get him any staff-job he chooses. His mother's already got the half-promise of a post for him at the War Office. But you'll see, you'll see! We can't stop him. Did we before? There's only this woman who can do it!"

Campton looked over the banker's head at the reflection of the false Reynolds in the mirror. That any one should have been fool enough to pay a big price for such a patent fraud seemed to him as incomprehensible as his own present obtuseness seemed to the banker.

"You do see, don't you?" argued Mr. Brant anxiously.

"Oh, I suppose so." Campton slowly got to his feet. The adroit brush-work of the forged picture fascinated him, and he went up to look at it more closely. Mr. Brant pursued him with a gratified glance.

"Ah, you're admiring my Reynolds. I paid a thumping price for it—but that's always my principle. Pay high, but get the best. It's a better investment."

"Just so," Campton assented dully. Mr. Brant seemed suddenly divided from him by the whole width of the gulf between that daub on the wall and a real Reynolds. They had nothing more to say to each other—nothing whatever. "Well, good-bye." He held out his hand.

"Think it over—think it over," Mr. Brant called out after him as he enfiladed the sumptuous offices, a medalled veteran holding back each door.

It was not until Campton was back at Montmartre, and throwing off his coat to get into his old studio clothes, that he felt in his pocket the weight of the forgotten concert-money. It was too late in the day to take it back to the bank, even if he had had the energy to retrace his steps; and he decided to hand the bag over to Boylston, with whom he was dining that night to meet the elder Dastrey, home on a brief leave from his ambulance.

"Think it over!" Mr. Brant's adjuration continued to echo in Campton's ears. As if he needed to be told to think it over! Once again the war-worn world had vanished from his mind, and he saw only George, himself and George, George and safety, George and peace. They blamed women who were cowards about their husbands, mistresses who schemed to protect their lovers! Well—he was as bad as any one of them, if it came to that. His son had bought his freedom, had once offered his life and nearly lost it. Brant was right: at all costs they must keep him from rushing back into that hell.

That Mrs. Talkett should be the means of securing his safety was bitter enough. This trivial barren creature to be his all—it seemed the parody of Campton's own youth! And Julia, after all, had been only a girl when he had met her, inexperienced and still malleable. A man less absorbed in his art, less oblivious of the daily material details of life, might conceivably have made something of her. But this little creature, with her farrago of false ideas, her vanity, her restlessness, her undisguised desire to keep George and yet not lose her world, had probably reached the term of her development, and would trip on through an eternal infancy of fads and frenzies.

Luckily, as Mr. Brant said, they could use her for the time; use her better, no doubt, than had she been a more finely tempered instrument. Campton was still pondering on these things as he set out for the restaurant where he had agreed to meet Boylston and Dastrey. At the foot of his own stairs he was surprised to run against Boylston under the porte-cochère. They gave each other a quick questioning look, as men did when they encountered each other unexpectedly in those days.

"Anything up? Oh, the money—you've come for the money?" Campton remembered that he had left the bag upstairs.

"The money? Haven't you heard? Louis Dastrey's killed," said Boylston.

They stood side by side in the doorway, while Campton's darkened

mind struggled anew with the mystery of fate. Almost every day now
the same readjustment had to be gone through: the cowering averted
mind dragged upward and forced to visualize a new gap in the ranks,
and summon the remaining familiar figures to fill it up and blot it
out. And today this cruel gymnastic was to be performed for George's
best friend, the elder Dastrey's sole stake in life! Only a few days ago
the lad had passed through Paris, just back from America, and in
haste to rejoin his regiment; alive and eager, throbbing with ideas,
with courage, mirth and irony—the very material France needed to
rebuild her ruins and beget her sons! And now, struck down as
George had been—not to rise like George. . .

Once more the inner voice in Campton questioned distinctly:
"Could you bear it?" and again he answered: "Less than ever!"

Aloud he asked: "Paul?"

"Oh, he went off at once. To break the news to Louis' mother in the
country."

"The boy was all Paul had left."

"Yes."

"What difference would it have made in the war, if he'd just stayed
on at his job in America?"

Boylston did not answer, and the two stood silent, looking out unseeingly at the black empty street. There was nothing left to say,
nowadays, when such blows fell; hardly anything left to feel, it sometimes seemed.

"Well, I suppose we must go and eat something," the older man
said; and arm in arm they went out into the darkness.

When Campton returned home that night he sat down and, with
the help of several pipes, wrote a note to Mrs. Talkett asking when
she would receive him.

Thereafter he tried to go back to his painting and to continue his
daily visits to the Palais Royal office. But for the time nothing seemed
to succeed with him. He threw aside his study of Mme. Lebel—he
hung about the office, confused and idle, and with the ever clearer
sense that there also things were disintegrating.

George's birthday party had been given up on account of young
Dastrey's death. Mrs. Brant evidently thought the postponement un-
necessary; since George's return she had gone over heart and soul to
the "business as usual" party. But Mr. Brant quietly sided with
George; and Campton was glad to be spared the necessity of celebrating the day in such a setting.

It was some time since Campton had seen his son; but the fault
was not his son's. The painter was aware of having voluntarily
avoided George. He said to himself: "As long as I know he's safe why

should I bother him?" But in reality he did not feel himself to be fit company for any one, and had even shunned poor Paul Dastrey on the latter's hurried passage through Paris, when he had come back from carrying the fatal news to young Dastrey's mother.

"What on earth could Paul and I have found to say to each other?" Campton argued with himself. "For men of our age there's nothing left to say nowadays. The only thing I can do is to try to work up one of my old studies of Louis. That might please him a little—later on."

But after one or two attempts he pushed away that canvas too.

At length one afternoon George came in. They had not met for over a week, and as George's blue uniform detached itself against the blurred tapestries of the studio, the north light modelling the fresh curves of his face, the father's heart gave a leap of pride. His son had never seemed to him so young and strong and vivid.

George, with a sudden blush, took his hand in a long pressure.

"I say, Dad—Madge has told me. Told me that you know about us and that you've persuaded her to see things as I do. She hadn't had a chance to speak to me of your visit till last night."

Campton felt his colour rising; but though his own part in the business still embarrassed him he was glad that the barriers were down.

"I didn't want," George continued, still flushed and slightly constrained, "to say anything to you about all this till I could say: 'Here's my wife.' And now she's promised."

"She's promised?"

"Thanks to you, you know. Your visit to her did it. She told me the whole thing yesterday. How she'd come here in desperation, to ask you to help her, to have her mind cleared up for her; and how you'd thought it all over, and then gone to see her, and how wise and perfect you'd been about it all. Poor child—if you knew the difference it's made to her!"

They were seated now, the littered table between them. Campton, his elbows on it, his chin on his hands, looked across at his son, who faced the light.

"The difference to you too?" he questioned.

George smiled: it was exactly the same detached smile which he used to shed on the little nurse who brought him his cocoa.

"Of course. Now I can go back without worrying." He let the words fall as carelessly as if there were nothing in them to challenge attention.

"Go back?" Campton stared at him with a blank countenance. Had he heard aright? The noise of a passing lorry suddenly roared in his ears like the guns of the front.

"Did you say: *go back?*"

George opened his blue eyes wide. "Why, of course; as soon as ever I'm patched up. You didn't think——?"

"I thought you had the sense to realize that you've done your share in one line, and that your business now is to do it in another."

The same detached smile again brushed George's lips. "But if I happen to have only one line?"

"Nonsense! You know they don't think that at the War Office."

"I don't believe the War Office will shut down if I leave it."

"What an argument! It sounds like——" Campton, breaking off on a sharp breath, closed his lids for a second. He had been gazing too steadily into George's eyes, and now at last he knew what that mysterious look in them meant. It was Benny Upsher's look, of course—inaccessible to reason, beyond reason, belonging to other spaces, other weights and measures, over the edge, somehow, of the tangible calculable world. . .

"A man can't do more than his duty: you've done that," he growled.

But George insisted with his gentle obstinacy: "You'll feel differently about it when America comes in."

Campton shook his head. "Never about your case."

"You will—when you see how we all feel. When we're all in it you wouldn't have me looking on, would you? And then there are my men—I've got to get back to my men."

"But you've no right to go now; no business," his father broke in violently. "Persuading that poor girl to wreck her life . . . and then leaving her, planting her there with her past ruined, and her future . . . George, you can't!"

George, in his long months of illness, had lost his old ruddiness of complexion. At his father's challenge the blood again rose the more visibly to his still-gaunt cheeks and white forehead: he was evidently struck.

"You'll kill her—and kill your mother!" Campton stormed.

"Oh, it's not for tomorrow. Not for a long time, perhaps. My shoulder's still too stiff. I was stupid," the young man haltingly added, "to put it as I did. Of course I've got to think of Madge now," he acknowledged, "as well as mother."

The blood flowed slowly back to Campton's heart. "You've got to think of—just the mere common-sense of the thing. That's all I ask. You've done your turn; you've done more. But never mind that. Now it's different. You're barely patched up: you're of use, immense use, for staff-work, and you know it. And you've asked a woman to tie up her future to yours—at what cost you know too. It's as much your duty to keep away from the front now as it was before—well, I admit it—to go there. You've done just what I should have wanted my son to do, up to this minute——"

George laid a hand on his a little wistfully. "Then just go on trusting me."

"I do—to see that I'm right! If I can't convince you, ask Boylston—
ask Adele!"

George sat staring down at the table. For the first time since they
had met at Doullens Campton was conscious of reaching his son's inner mind, and of influencing it.

"I wonder if you really love her?" he suddenly risked.

The question did not seem to offend George, scarcely to surprise
him. "Of course," he said simply. "Only—well, everything's different
nowadays, isn't it? So many of the old ideas have come to seem such
humbug. That's what I want to drag her out of—the coils and coils of
stale humbug. They were killing her."

"Well—take care *you* don't," Campton said, thinking that everything was different indeed, as he recalled the reasons young men had
had for loving and marrying in his own time.

A faint look of amusement came into George's eyes. "Kill her? Oh,
no. I'm gradually bringing her to life. But all this is hard to talk
about—yet. By-and-bye you'll understand; she'll show you, we'll show
you together. But at present nothing's to be said—to any one, please,
not even to mother. Madge thinks this is no time for such things.
There, of course, I don't agree; but I must be patient. The secrecy, the
underhandedness, are hateful to me; but for her it's all a part of the
sacred humbug."

He rose listlessly, as if the discussion had bled all the life out of
him, and took himself away.

When he had gone his father drew a deep breath. Yes—the boy
would stay in Paris; he would almost certainly stay; for the present,
at any rate. And people were still prophesying that in the spring
there would be a big push all along the line; and after that the nightmare might be over. Campton was glad he had gone to see Madge
Talkett. He was glad, above all, that if the thing had to be done it was
over, and that, by Madge's wish, no one was to know of what had
passed between them. It was a distinct relief, in spite of what he had
suggested to George, not to have to carry that particular problem to
Adele Anthony or Boylston.

A few days late George accepted a staff-appointment in Paris.

Book
Four

XXXII

Heavily the weeks went by.

The world continued to roar on through smoke and flame, and contrasted with that headlong race was the slow dragging lapse of hours and days to those who had to wait on events inactively.

When Campton met Paul Dastrey for the first time after the death of the latter's nephew, the two men exchanged a long hand-clasp and then sat silent. As Campton had felt from the first, there was nothing left for them to say to each other. If young men like Louis Dastrey must continue to be sacrificed by hundreds of thousands to save their country, for whom was the country being saved? Was it for the wasp-waisted youths in sham uniforms who hunted the reawakening hotels and restaurants, in the frequent intervals between their ambulance trips to safe distances from the front? Or for the elderly men like Dastrey and Campton, who could only sit facing each other with the spectre of the lost between them? Young Dastrey, young Fortin-Lescluze, René Davril, Benny Upsher—and how many hundreds more each day! And not even a child left by most of them to carry on the faith they had died for. . .

"If we're giving all we care for so that those little worms can reopen their dance-halls on the ruins, what in God's name *is* left?" Campton questioned.

Dastrey sat looking at the ground, his grey head bent between his hands. "France," he said.

"What's France, with no men left?"

"Well—I suppose, an Idea."

"Yes. I suppose so." Campton stood up heavily.

An Idea: they must cling to that. If Dastrey, from the depths of his destitution, could still feel it and live by it, why did it not help Campton more? An Idea: that was what France, ever since she had existed, had always been in the story of civilization; a luminous point about which striving visions and purposes could rally. And in that sense she had been as much Campton's spiritual home as Dastrey's; to thinkers, artists, to all creators, she had always been a second country. If France went, western civilization went with her; and then all they had believed in and been guided by would perish. That was what George had felt; it was what had driven him from the Argonne to the Aisne. Campton felt it too; but dully, through a fog. His son was safe; yes—but too many other men's sons were dying. There was no spot where his thoughts could rest: there were moments when the sight of George, intact and immaculate—his arm at last out of its sling—rose before his father like a reproach.

The feeling was senseless; but there it was. Whenever the young man entered the room Campton saw him attended by the invisible host of his comrades, the fevered, the maimed and the dying. The Germans had attacked at Verdun: horrible daily details of the struggle were pouring in. No one at the rear had really known, except in swift fitful flashes, about the individual suffering of the first months of the war; now such information was systematized and distributed everywhere, daily, with a cold impartial hand. And every night, when one laid one's old bones on one's bed, there were those others, the young in their thousands, lying down, perhaps never to rise again, in the mud and blood of the trenches.

Even Boylston's Preparedness was beginning to get on Campton's nerves. He tried to picture to himself how he should exult when his country at last fell into line; but he could realize only what his humiliation would be if she did not. It was almost a relief, at this time, to have his mind diverted to the dissensions among "The Friends of French Art," where, at a stormy meeting, Harvey Mayhew, as a member of the Finance Committee, had asked for an account of the money taken in at Mrs. Talkett's concert. This money, Mr. Mayhew stated, had passed through a number of hands. It should have been taken over by Mr. Boylston, as treasurer, at the close of the performance; but he had failed to claim it—had, in fact, been unfindable when the organizers of the concert brought their takings to Mrs. Talkett—and the money, knocking about from hand to hand, had finally been carried by Mrs. Talkett herself to Mr. Campton. The latter, when asked to entrust it to Mr. Mayhew, had refused on the ground that he had already deposited it in the bank; but a number of days later it was known to be still in his possession. All this time Mr. Boylston, treasurer, and chairman of the Financial Committee, appeared to think it quite in order that the funds should have been (as he assumed) deposited in the bank by a member who was not on that particular committee, and who, in reality, had forgotten that they were in his possession.

Mr. Mayhew delivered himself of this indictment amid an embarrassed silence. To Campton it had seemed as if a burst of protest must instantly clear the air. But after he himself had apologized for this negligence in not depositing the money, and Boylston had disengaged his responsibility in a few quiet words, there followed another blank interval. Then Mr. Mayhew suddenly suggested a complete reorganization of the work. He had something to criticize in every department. He, who so seldom showed himself at the office, now presented a list of omissions and commissions against which one after another of the active members rose to enter a mild denial. It was clear that some one belonging to the organization, and who was playing into his hands, had provided him with a series of cleverly falsified charges against the whole group of workers.

Presently Campton could stand it no longer, and, jumping up, suddenly articulate, he flung into his cousin's face a handful of home-truths under which he expected that glossy countenance to lost its lustre. But Mr. Mayhew bore the assault with urbanity. It did not behove him, he said, to take up the reproaches addressed to him by the most distinguished member of their committee—the most distinguished, he might surely say without offence to any of the others (a murmur of assent); it did not behove him, because one of the few occasions on which a great artist may be said to be at a disadvantage is when he is trying to discuss business matters with a man of business. He, Mr. Mayhew, was only that, nothing more; but he *was* that, and he had been trained to answer random abuse by hard facts. In no way did he intend to reflect on the devoted labours of certain ladies of the committee, nor on their sympathetic treasurer's gallant efforts to acquire, amid all his other pressing interests, the rudiments of business habits; but Miss Anthony had all along been dividing her time between two widely different charities, and Mr. Boylston, like his distinguished champion, was first of all an artist, with the habits of the studio rather than of the office. In the circumstances——

Campton jumped to his feet again. If he stayed a moment longer he felt he should knock Mayhew down. He jammed his hat on, shouted out "I resign," and limped out of the room.

It was the way in which his encounters with practical difficulties always ended. The consciousness of his inferiority in argument, the visionary's bewilderment when incomprehensible facts are thrust on him by fluent people, the helpless sense of not knowing what to answer, and of seeing his dream-world smashed in the rough-and-tumble of shabby motives—it all gave him the feeling that he was drowning, and must fight his way to the surface before they had him under.

In the street he stood in a cold sweat of remorse. He knew the charges of negligence against Miss Anthony and Boylston were trumped up. He knew there was an answer to be made, and that he was the man to make it; and his eyes filled with tears of rage and self-pity at his own incompetence. But then he took heart at the thought of Boylston's astuteness and Miss Anthony's courage. They would not let themselves be beaten—probably they would fight their battle better without him. He tried to protect his retreat with such arguments, and when he got back to the studio he called up Mme. Lebel, and plunged again into his charcoal study of her head. He did not remember having ever worked with such supernatural felicity: it was as if *that* were his victorious answer to all their lies and intrigues. . .

But the Mayhew party was victorious too. How it came about a mind like Campton's could not grasp. Mr. Mayhew, it appeared, had let fall that a very large gift of money from the world-renowned philanthropist, Sir Cyril Jorgenstein (obtained through the good offices of

Mmes. de Dolmetsch and Beausite) was contingent on certain immediate changes in the organization ("drastic changes" was Mr. Mayhew's phrase); and thereupon several hitherto passive members had suddenly found voice to assert the duty of not losing this gift. After that the way was clear. Adele Anthony and Boylston were offered ornamental posts which they declined, and within a week the Palais Royal saw them no more, and Paris drawing-rooms echoed with the usual rumours of committee wrangles and dark discoveries.

The episode left Campton with a bitter taste in his soul. It seemed to him like an ugly little allegory of Germany's manœuvring the world into war. The speciousness of Mr. Mayhew's arguments, the sleight-of-hand by which he had dislodged the real workers and replaced them by his satellites, reminded the painter of the neutrals who were beginning to say that there were two sides to every question, that war was always cruel, and how about the Russian atrocities in Silesia? As the month dragged on a breath of luke-warmness had begun to blow through the world, damping men's souls, confusing plain issues, casting a doubt on the worth of everything. People were beginning to ask what one knew, after all, of the secret motives which had impelled half-a-dozen self-indulgent old men ensconced in Ministerial offices to plunge the world in ruin. No one seemed to feel any longer that life is something more than being alive; apparently the only people not tired of the thought of death were the young men still pouring out to it in their thousands.

Still those thousands poured; still the young died; still, wherever Campton went, he met elderly faces, known and unknown, disfigured by grief, shrunken with renunciation. And still the months wore on without result.

One day in crossing the Tuileries he felt the same soft sparkle which, just about a year earlier, had abruptly stirred the sap in him. Yes—it was nearly a year since the day when he had noticed the first horse-chestnut blossoms, and been reminded by Mme. Lebel that he ought to buy some new shirts; and though today the horse-chestnuts were still leafless they were already misty with buds, and the tall white clouds above them full-uddered with spring showers. It was spring again, spring with her deluding promises—her gilding of worn stones and chilly water, the mystery of her distances, the finish and brilliance of her nearer strokes. Campton, in spite of himself, drank down the life-giving draught and felt its murmur in his veins. And just then, across the width of the gardens he saw, beyond a stretch of turf and clipped shrubs, two people, also motionless, who seemed to have the same cup at their lips. He recognized his son and Mrs. Talkett.

Their backs were toward him, and they stood close together, look-

ing with the same eyes at the same sight: an Apollo touched with flying sunlight. After a while they walked on again, slowly and close to
each other. George, as they moved, seemed now and then to point out
some beauty of sculpture, or the colour of a lichened urn; and once
they turned and took their fill of the great perspective tapering to the
Arch—the Arch on which Rude's Mænad-Marseillaise still yelled her
battalions on to death.

XXXIII

Campton finished his charcoal of Mme. Lebel; then attacked her in
oils. Now that his work at the Palais Royal was ended, painting was
once more his only refuge.

Adele Anthony had returned to her refugees; Boylston, pale and obstinate, toiled on at Preparedness. But Campton found it impossible
to take up any new form of work; his philanthropic ardour was exhausted. He could only shut himself up, for long solitary hours, in the
empty and echoing temple of his art.

George emphatically approved of his course: George was as insistent as Mrs. Brant on the duty of "business as usual." But on the
young man's lips the phrase had a different meaning; it seemed the
result of that altered perspective which Campton was conscious of
whenever, nowadays, he tried to see things as his son saw them.
George was not indifferent, he was not callous; but he seemed to feel
himself mysteriously set apart, destined to some other task for which
he was passively waiting. Even the split among "The Friends of
French Art" left him, despite his admiration for Boylston, curiously
unperturbed. He seemed to have taken the measure of all such
ephemeral agitations, and to regard them with an indulgent pity
which was worse than coldness.

"He feels that all we do is so useless," Campton said to Dastrey;
"he's like a gardener watching ants rebuild their hill in the middle of
a path, and knowing all the while that hill and path are going to be
wiped out by his pick."

"Ah, they're all like that," Dastrey murmured.

Mme. Lebel came up to the studio every afternoon. The charcoal
study had been only of her head; but for the painting Campton had
seated her in her own horsehair arm-chair, her smoky lamp beside
her, her sewing in her lap. More than ever he saw in the wise old face
something typical of its race and class: the obstinate French gift, as
some one had put it, of making one more effort after the last effort.

The old woman could not imagine why he wanted to paint her; but when one day he told her it was for her grandsons, her eyes filled, and she said: "For which one, sir? For they're both at Verdun."

One autumn afternoon he was late in getting back to the studio, where he knew she was waiting for him. He pushed the door open, and there, in the beaten-down attitude in which he had once before seen her, she lay across the table, her cap awry, her hands clutching her sewing, and George kneeling at her side. The young man's arm was about her, his head pressed against her breast; and on the floor lay the letter, the fatal letter which was always, nowadays, the key to such scenes.

Neither George nor the old woman had heard Campton enter; and for a moment he stood and watched them. George's face, so fair and ruddy against Mme. Lebel's rusty black, wore a look of boyish compassion which Campton had never seen on it. Mme. Lebel had sunk into his hold as if it soothed and hushed her; and Campton said to himself: "These two are closer to each other than George and I, because they've both seen the horror face to face. He knows what to say to her ever so much better than he knows what to say to his mother or me."

But apparently there was no need to say much. George continued to kneel in silence; presently he bent and kissed the old woman's cheek; then he got to his feet and saw his father.

"The *Chasseur Alpin,*" he merely said, picking up the letter and handing it to Campton. "It was the grandson she counted on most."

Mme. Lebel caught sight of Campton, smoothed herself and stood up also.

"I had found him a wife—a strong healthy girl with a good *dot.* There go my last great-grandchildren! For the other will be killed too. I don't understand any more, do you?" She made an automatic attempt to straighten the things on the table, but her hands beat the air and George had to head her downstairs.

It was that day that Campton said to himself: "We shan't keep him in Paris much longer." But the heavy weeks of spring and summer passed, the inconclusive conflict at the front went on with its daily toll of dead, and George still stuck to his job. Campton, during this time, continued to avoid the Brants as much as possible. His wife's conversation was intolerable to him; her obtuse optimism, now that she had got her son back, was even harder to bear than the guiltily averted glance of Mr. Brant, between whom and Campton their last talk had hung a lasting shadow of complicity.

But most of all Campton dreaded to meet the Talketts; the wife with her flushed cheek-bones and fixed eyes, the husband still affably and continuously arguing against Philistinism. One afternoon the painter stumbled on them, taking tea with George in Boylston's little flat; but he went away again, unable to bear the interminable discussion between Talkett and Boylston, and the pacifist's reiterated phrase: "To borrow one of my wife's expressions"—while George, with a closed brooding face, sat silent, laughing drily now and then. What a different George from the one his father had found, in silence also, kneeling beside Mme. Lebel!

Once again Campton was vouchsafed a glimpse of that secret George. He had walked back with his son after the funeral mass for young Lebel; and in the porter's lodge of the Avenue Marigny they found a soldier waiting—a young square-built fellow, with a shock of straw-coloured hair above his sunburnt rural face. Campton was turning from the door when George dashed past him, caught the young man by both shoulders, and shouted his name. It was that of the orderly who had carried him out of the firing-line and hunted him up the next day in the Doullens hospital. Campton saw the look the two exchanged: it lasted only for the taking of a breath; a moment later officer and soldier were laughing like boys, and the orderly was being drawn forth to shake hands with Campton. But again the glance was an illumination; it came straight from that far country, the Benny Upsher country, which Campton so feared to see in his son's eyes.

The orderly had been visiting his family, fugitives from the invaded regions who had taken shelter in one of Adele Anthony's suburban colonies. He had obtained permission to stop in Paris on his way back to the front; and for two joyful days he was lodged and feasted in the Avenue Marigny. Boylston provided him with an evening at Montmartre, George and Mrs. Brant took him to the theatre and the cinema, and on the last day of his leave Adele Anthony invited him to tea with Campton, Mr. Brant and Boylston. Mr. Brant, as they left this entertainment, hung back on the stairs to say in a whisper to Campton: "The family are provided for—amply. I've asked George to mention the fact to the young man; but not until just as he's starting."

Campton nodded. For George's sake he was glad; yet he could not repress a twinge of his dormant jealousy. Was it always to be Brant who thought first of the things to make George happy—always Brant who would alone have the power to carry them out?

"But he can't prevent that poor fellow's getting killed tomorrow," Campton thought almost savagely, as the young soldier beamed forth from the taxi in which George was hurrying him to the station.

It was not many days afterward that George looked in at the studio early one morning. Campton, over his breakfast, had been reading the *communiqué*. There was heavy news from Verdun; from east to west the air was dark with calamity; but George's face had the look it had worn when he greeted his orderly.

"Dad, I'm off," he said; and sitting down at the table, he unceremoniously poured himself some coffee into his father's empty cup.

"The battalion's been ordered back. I leave to-night. Let's lunch together somewhere presently, shall we?"

His eye was clear, his smile confident: a great weight seemed to have fallen from him, and he looked like the little boy sitting up in bed with his Lavengro. "After ten months of Paris——" he added, stretching his arms over his head with a great yawn.

"Yes—the routine——" stammered Campton, not knowing what he said. Yet he was glad too; yes, in his heart of hearts he knew he was glad; though, as always happened, his emotion took him by the throat and silenced him. But it did not matter, for George was talking.

"I shall have leave a good deal oftener nowadays," he said with animation. "And everything is ever so much better organized—letters and all that. I shan't seem so awfully far away. You'll see."

Campton still gazed at him struggling for expression. Their hands met. Campton said—or imagined he said: "I see—I do see, already——" though afterward he was not even sure that he had spoken.

What he saw, with an almost blinding distinctness, was the extent to which his own feeling, during the long months, had imperceptibly changed, and how his inmost impulse, now that the blow had fallen, was not of resistance to it, but of acquiescence, since it made him once more one with his son.

He would have liked to tell that to George; but speech was impossible. And perhaps, after all, it didn't matter; it didn't matter, because George understood. Their hand-clasp had made that clear, and an hour or two later they were lunching together almost gaily.

Boylston joined them and the three went on together to say good-bye to Adele Anthony. Adele, for once, was unprepared: it was almost a relief to Campton, who winced in advance at the thought her warlike attitude. The poor thing was far from warlike: her pale eyes clung to George's in a frightened stare, while her lips, a little stiffly, repeated the stock phrases of good cheer. "Such a relief . . . I congratulate you . . . getting out of all this *paperasserie* and red-tape. . . If I'd been you I couldn't have stood Paris another minute. . . The only hopeful people left are at the front. . ." It was the formula that sped every departing soldier.

The day wore on. To Campton its hours seemed as interminable yet as rapid as those before his son's first departure, nearly two years earlier. George had begged his father to come in the evening to the Avenue Marigny, where he was dining with the Brants. It was easier for Campton nowadays to fall in with such requests: during the months of George's sojourn in Paris a good many angles had had their edges rubbed off.

Besides, at that moment he would have done anything for his son—his son again at last! In their hand-clasp that morning the old George had come back to him, simple, boyish, just as he used to be; and Campton's dread of the future was lightened by a great glow of pride.

In the Avenue Marigny dining-room the Brants and George were still sitting together about the delicate silver and porcelain. There were no flowers: Julia, always correct, had long since banished them as a superfluity. But there was champagne for George's farewell, and a glimpse of rich fare being removed.

Mr. Brant rose to greet Campton. His concise features were drawn with anxiety, and with the effort to hide it; but his wife appeared to Campton curiously unperturbed, and the leave-taking was less painful and uselessly drawn out than he had expected.

George and his father were to be sent to the station in Mr. Brant's motor. Campton, as he got in, remembered with a shiver the grey morning, before daylight, when the same motor had stood at the studio door, waiting to carry him to Doullens; between himself and his son he seemed to see Mr. Brant's small suffering profile.

To shake off the memory he said: "Your mother's in wonderfully good form. I was glad to see she wasn't nervous."

George laughed. "No. Madge met her this morning at the new *clairvoyante*'s.— It does them all a lot of good," he added, with his all-embracing tolerance.

Campton shivered again. That universal smiling comprehension of George's always made him seem remoter than ever. "It makes him seem so old—a thousand years older than I am." But he forced an acquiescent laugh, and presently George went on: "About Madge—you'll be awfully good to her, won't you, if I get smashed?"

"My dear boy!"

There was another pause, and then Campton risked a question. "Just how do things stand? I know so little, after all."

For a moment George seemed to hesitate: his thick fair eyebrows were drawn into a puzzled frown. "I know—I've never explained it to you properly. I've tried to; but I was never sure that I could make you see." He paused and added quietly: "I know now that she'll never divorce Talkett."

"You know——?" Campton exclaimed with a great surge of relief.

"She thinks she will; but I see that the idea still frightens her. And I've kept on using the divorce argument only as a pretext."

The words thrust Campton back into new depths of perplexity. "A pretext?" he echoed.

"My dear old Dad—don't you guess? She's come to care for me awfully; if we'd gone all the lengths she wanted, and then I'd got killed, there would have been nothing on earth left for her. I hadn't the right, don't you see? We chaps haven't any futures to dispose of till this job we're in is finished. Of course, if I come back, and she can make up her mind to break with everything she's used to, we shall marry; but if things go wrong I'd rather leave her as she is, safe in her little old rut. So many people can't live out of one—and she's one of them, poor child, though she's so positive she isn't."

Campton sat chilled and speechless as the motor whirled them on through the hushed streets. It paralyzed his faculties to think that in a moment more they would be at the station.

"It's awfully fine: your idea," he stammered at length. "Awfully—magnanimous." But he still felt the chill down his spine.

"Oh, it's only that things look to us so different—so indescribably different—and always will, I suppose, even after this business is over. We seem to be sealed to it for life."

"Poor girl—poor girl!" Campton thought within himself. Aloud he said: "My dear chap, of course you can count on my being—my do-ing——"

"Of course, of course, old Dad."

They were at the station. Father and son got out and walked toward the train. Campton put both hands on George's shoulders.

"Look here," George broke out, "there's one thing more. I want to tell you that I know what a lot I owe to you and Adele. You've both been awfully fine: did you know it? You two first made me feel a lot of things I hadn't felt before. And you know this *is* my job; I've never been surer of it than at this minute."

They clasped hands in silence, each looking his fill of the other; then the crowd closed in, George exclaimed: "My kit-bag!" and somehow, in the confusion, the parting was over, and Campton, straining blurred eyes, saw his son's smile—the smile of the light-hearted lad of old days—flash out at him from the moving train. For an instant the father had the illusion that it was the goodbye look of the boy George, going back to school after the holidays.

Campton, as he came out of the station, stumbled, to his surprise, on Mr. Brant. The little man, as they met, flushed and paled, and sought the customary support from his eye-glasses.

"I followed you in the other motor," he said, looking away.

"Oh, I say——" Campton murmured; then, with an effort: "Shouldn't you like me to drive back with you?"

Mr. Brant shook his head. "Thank you. Thank you very much. But it's late and you'll want to be getting home. I'll be glad if you'll use my car." Together they strolled slowly across the station court to the place where the private motors waited; but there Campton held out his hand.

"Much obliged; I think I'll walk."

Mr. Brant nodded; then he said abruptly: "This *clairvoyante* business: is there anything to it, do you think? You saw how calm—er—Julia was just now: she wished me to tell you that Spanish woman she goes to—her name is Olida, I think—had absolutely reassured her about . . . about the future. The woman says she knows that George will come back soon, and never be sent to the front again. Those were the exact words, I believe. *Never be sent to the front again.* Julia put every kind of question, and couldn't trip her up; she wanted me to tell you so. It does sound . . . ? Well, at any rate, it's a help to the mothers."

XXXIV

The next morning Campton said to himself: "I can catch that good-bye look if I get it down at once——" and pulled out a canvas before Mme. Lebel came in with his coffee.

As sometimes happened to him, the violent emotions of the last twenty-four hours had almost immediately been clarified and transmuted into vision. He felt that he could think contentedly of George if he could sit down at once and paint him.

The picture grew under his feverish fingers—feverish, yet how firm! He always wondered anew at the way in which, at such hours, the inner flame and smoke issued in a clear guiding radiance. He saw—he saw; and the mere act of his seeing seemed to hold George safe in some pure impenetrable medium. His boy was there, sitting to him, the old George he knew and understood, essentially, vividly face to face with him.

He was interrupted by a ring. Mme. Lebel, tray in hand, opened the door, and a swathed and voluminous figure, sweeping in on a wave of musk, blotted her out. Campton, exasperated at the interruption, turned to face Mme. Olida.

So remote were his thoughts that he would hardly have recognized her had she not breathed, on the old familiar guttural: "Juanito!"

He was less surprised at her intrusion than annoyed at being torn from his picture. "Didn't you see a sign on the door? 'No admission before twelve'——" he growled.

"Oh, yes," she said; "that's how I knew you were in."

"But I'm *not* in; I'm working. I can't allow——"

Her large bosom rose. "I know, my heart! I remember how stern you always were. 'Work—work—my work!' It was always that, even in the first days. But I come to you on my knees: Juanito, imagine me there!" She sketched a plunging motion of her vast body, arrested it in time by supporting herself on the table, and threw back her head entreatingly, so that Campton caught a glint of the pearls in a crevasse of her quaking throat. He saw that her eyes were red with weeping.

"What can I do? You're in trouble?"

"Oh, such trouble, my heart—such trouble!" She leaned to him, absorbing his hands in her plump muscular grasp. "I must have news of my son; I must! The young man—you saw him that day you came with your wife? Yes—he looked in at the door: beautiful as a god, was he not? That was my son Pepito!" And with a deep breath of pride and anguish she unburdened herself of her tale.

Two or three years after her parting with Campton she had married a clever French barber from the Pyrenees. He had brought her to France, and they had opened a "Beauty Shop" at Biarritz and had prospered. Pepito was born there and soon afterward, alas, her clever husband, declaring that he "hated grease in cooking or in woman" ("and after my Pepito's birth I became as you now see me"), had gone off with the manicure and all their savings. Mme. Olida had had a struggle to bring up her boy; but she had kept on with the Beauty Shop, had made a success of it, and not long before the war had added fortune-telling to massage and hair-dressing.

"And my son, Juanito; was not my son an advertisement for a Beauty Shop, I ask you? Before he was out of petticoats he brought me customers; before he was sixteen all the ladies who came to me were quarreling over him. Ah, there were moments when he crucified me . . . but lately he had grown more reasonable, had begun to see where his true interests lay, and we had become friends again, friends and business partners. When the war broke out I came to Paris; I knew that all the mothers would want news of their sons. I have made a great deal of money; and I have had wonderful results—wonderful! I could give you instances—names that you know—where I have foretold everything! Oh, I have the gift, my heart, I have it!"

She pressed his hands with a smile of triumph; then her face clouded again.

"But six months ago my darling was called to his regiment—and for three months now I've had no news of him, none, none!" she sobbed, the tears making dark streaks through her purplish powder.

The upshot of it was that she had heard that Campton was "all-powerful"; that he knew Ministers and Generals, knew great financiers like Jorgenstein (who were so much more powerful than either Generals or Ministers), and could, if he chose, help her to trace her boy, who, from the day of his departure for the front, had vanished as utterly as if the earth had swallowed him.

"Not a word, not a sign—to me, his mother, who have slaved and slaved for him, who have made a fortune for him!"

Campton looked at her, marvelling. "But your gift as you call it . . . your powers . . . you can't use them for yourself?"

She returned his look with a tearful simplicity: she hardly seemed to comprehend what he was saying. "But my son! I want *news* of my son, real news; I want a letter; I want to see some one who has seen him! To touch a hand that has touched him! Oh, don't you understand?"

"Yes, I understand," he said; and she took up her desperate litany, clinging about him with soft palms like medusa-lips, till by dint of many promises he managed to detach himself and steer her gently to the door.

On the threshold she turned to him once more. "And your own son, Juanito—I know he's at the front again. His mother came the other day—she often comes. And I can promise you things if you'll help me. No, even if you don't help me—for the old days' sake, I will! I know secrets . . . magical secrets that will protect him. There's a Moorish salve, infallible against bullets . . . handed down from King Solomon . . . I can get it. . ."

Campton, guiding her across the sill, led her out and bolted the door on her; then he went back to his easel and stood gazing at the sketch of George. But the spell was broken: the old George was no longer there. The war had sucked him back into its awful whirlpool— once more he was that dark enigma, a son at the front. . .

In the heavy weeks which followed, a guarded allusion of Campton's showed him one day that Boylston was aware of there being "something between" George and Madge Talkett.

"Not that he's ever said anything—or even encouraged me to guess anything. But she's got a talking face, poor little thing; and not much gift of restraint. And I suppose it's fairly obvious to everybody—except perhaps to Talkett—that she's pretty hard hit."

"Yes. And George?"

Boylston's round face became remote and mysterious. "We don't really know—do we, sir?—exactly how any of them feel? Any more than if they were——" He drew up sharply on the word, but Campton faced it.

"Dead?"

"Transfigured, say; no, trans—— what's the word in the theology books? A new substance . . . somehow. . ."

"Ah, you feel that too?" the father exclaimed.

"Yes. They don't know it themselves, though—how far they are from us. At least I don't think they do."

Campton nodded. "But George, in the beginning, was—frankly indifferent to the war, wasn't he?"

"Yes; intellectually he was. But he told me that when he saw the first men on their way back from the front—with the first mud on them—he knew he belonged where they'd come from. I tried hard to persuade him when he was here that his real job was on a military mission to America—and it *was*. Think what he might have done out there! But it was no use. His orderly's visit did the trick. It's the thought of their men that pulls them all back. Look at Louis Das-trey—they couldn't keep him in America. There's something in all their eyes: I don't know what. *Dulce et decorum,* perhaps——"

"Yes."

There was a pause before Campton questioned: "And Talkett?"

"Poor little ass—I don't know. He's here arguing with me nearly every day. She looks over his shoulder, and just shrugs at me with her eyebrows."

"Can you guess what he thinks of George's attitude?"

"Oh, something different every day. I don't believe she's ever really understood. But then she loves him, and nothing else counts."

Mrs. Brant continued to face life with apparent serenity. She had returned several times to Mme. Olida's, and had always brought away the same reassuring formula: she thought it striking, and so did her friends, that the *clairvoyante*'s prediction never varied.

There was reason to believe that George's regiment had been sent to Verdun, and from Verdun the news was growing daily more hope-ful. This seemed to Mrs. Brant a remarkable confirmation of Olida's prophecy. Apparently it did not occur to her that, in the matter of hu-man life, victories may be as ruinous as defeats; and she triumphed in the fact—it had grown to be a fact to her—that her boy was at Ver-dun, when he might have been in the Somme, where things, though stagnant, were on the whole going less well. Mothers prayed for "a quiet sector"—and then, she argued, what happened? The men grew careless, the officers were oftener away; your son was ordered out to see to the repairs of a barbed-wire entanglement, and a sharp-shooter picked him off while you were sitting reading one of his letters, and thinking: "Thank God he's out of the fighting." And besides, Olida was *sure,* and all her predictions had been so wonderful. . .

Campton began to dread his wife's discovering Mme. Olida's fears for her own son. Every endeavour to get news of Pepito had been fruitless; finally Campton and Boylston concluded that the young man must be a prisoner. The painter had a second visit from Mme. Olida, in the course of which he besought her (without naming Julia) to be careful not to betray her private anxiety to the poor women who came to her for consolation; and she fixed her tortured velvet eyes on him reproachfully.

"How could you think it of me, Juanito? The money I earn is for my boy! That gives me the strength to invent a new lie every morning."

He took her fraudulent hand and kissed it.

The next afternoon he met Mrs. Brant walking down the Champs Elysées with her light girlish step. She lifted a radiant face to him. "A letter from George this morning! And, do you know, Olida prophesied it? I was there again yesterday; and she told me that he would soon be back, and that at that very moment she could see him writing to me. You'll admit it's extraordinary? So many mothers depend on her—I couldn't live without her. And her messages from her own son are so beautiful——"

"From her own son?"

"Yes: didn't I tell you? He says such perfect things to her. And she confessed to me, poor woman, that before the war he hadn't always been kind: he used to take her money, and behave badly. But now every day he sends her a thought-message—such beautiful things! She says she wouldn't have the courage to keep us all up if it weren't for the way that she's kept up by her boy. And now," Julia added gaily, "I'm going to order the cakes for my bridge-tea this afternoon. You know I promised Georgie I wouldn't give up my bridge-teas."

Now and then Campton returned to his latest portrait of his son; but in spite of George's frequent letters, in spite of the sudden drawing together of father and son during their last moments at the station, the vision of the boy George, the careless happy George who had ridiculed the thought of war and pursued his millennial dreams of an enlightened world—that vision was gone. Sometimes Campton fancied that the letters themselves increased this effect of remoteness. They were necessarily more guarded than the ones written, before George's wounding, from an imaginary H.Q.; but that did not wholly account for the difference. Campton, in the last analysis, could only say that as in the moment when George had comforted Mme. Lebel, or greeted his orderly, or when he had said those last few broken words at the station—he seemed nearer than ever, seemed part and substance of his father; or else he became again that beautiful distant apparition, the wingèd sentry guarding the Unknown.

The weeks thus punctuated by private anxieties rolled on dark with doom. At last, in December, came the victory of Verdun. Men took it reverently but soberly. The price paid had been too heavy for rejoicing; and the horizon was too ominous in other quarters. Campton had hoped that the New Year would bring his son back on leave; but still George did not speak of coming. Meanwhile Boylston's face grew rounder and more beaming. At last America was stirring in her sleep. "Oh, if only George were out there!" Boylston used to cry, as if his friend had been an army. His faith in George's powers of persuasion was almost mystical. And not long afterward Campton had the surprise of a visit which seemed, in the most unforeseen way, to confirm this belief. Returning to his studio one afternoon he found it tenanted by Mr. Roger Talkett.

The young man, as carefully brushed and equipped as usual, but pale with emotion, clutched the painter's hand in a moist grasp.

"My dear Master, I had to see you—to see you alone and immediately."

Campton looked at him with apprehension. What was the meaning of his "alone"? Had Mrs. Talkett lost her head, and betrayed her secret—or had she committed some act of imprudence of which the report had come back to her husband?

"Do sit down," said the painter weakly.

But his visitor, remaining sternly upright, shook his head and glanced at his wrist-watch. "My moments," he said, "are numbered—literally; all I have time for is to implore you to look after my wife." He drew a handkerchief from his glossy cuff, and rubbed his eyeglasses.

"Your wife?" Campton echoed, dismayed.

"My dear sir, haven't you guessed? It's George's wonderful example . . . his inspiration . . . I've been converted! We men of culture can't stand by while the ignorant and illiterate are left to die for us. We must leave that attitude to the Barbarian. Our duty is to set an example. I'm off to-night for America—for Plattsburg."

"Oh——" gasped Campton, wringing his hand.

Boylston burst into the studio the next day. "What did I tell you, sir? George's influence—it wakes up everybody. But Talkett—I'll be hanged if I should have thought it! And have you seen his wife? She's a war-goddess! I went to the station with them: their farewells were harrowing. At that minute, you know, I believe she'd forgotten that George ever existed!"

"Well, thank god for that," Campton cried.

"Yes. Don't you feel how we're all being swept into it?" panted Boylston breathlessly. His face had caught the illumination. "Sealed, as George says—we're sealed to the job every one of us! Even I feel that, sitting here at a stuffy desk. . ." He flushed crimson and his eyes filled. "We'll be in it, you know; America will—in a few weeks now, I believe! George was as sure of it as I am. And, of course, if the war goes on, our army will *have* to take short-sighted officers; won't they, sir? As England and France did from the first. They'll need the men; they'll need us all, sir!"

"They'll need *you,* my dear chap; and they'll have you, to the full, whatever your job is," Campton smiled; and Boylston, choking back a sob, dashed off again.

Yes, they were all being swept into it together—swept into the yawning whirlpool. Campton felt that as clearly as all these young men; he felt the triviality, the utter unimportance, of all their personal and private concerns, compared with this great headlong outpouring of life on the altar of conviction. And he understood why, for youths like George and Boylston, nothing, however close and personal to them, would matter till the job was over. "And not even for poor Talkett!" he reflected whimsically.

That afternoon, curiously appeased, he returned once more to his picture of his son. He had sketched the boy leaning out of the train window, smiling back, signalling, saying goodbye, while his destiny rushed him out into darkness as years ago the train used to rush him back to school. And while Campton worked he caught the glow again; it rested on brow and eyes, and spread in sure touches under his happy brush.

One day, as the picture progressed, he wavered over the remembrance of some little detail of the face, and went in search of an old portfolio into which, from time to time, he had been in the habit of thrusting his unfinished studies of George. He plunged his hand into the heap, and Georges of all ages looked forth at him: round baby-Georges, freckled schoolboys, a thoughtful long-faced youth (the delicate George of St. Moritz); but none seemed quite to serve his purpose and he rummaged on till he came to a page torn from an old sketch-book. It was the pencil study he had made of George as the lad lay asleep at the Crillon, the night before his mobilisation.

Campton threw the sketch down on the table; and as he sat staring at it he relived every phase of the emotion out of which it had been born. How little he had known then—how little he had understood! he could bear to look at the drawing now; could bear even to rethink the shuddering thoughts with which he had once flung it away from him. Was it only because the atmosphere was filled with a growing sense of hope? Because, in spite of everything, the victory of Verdun was there to show the inexhaustible strength of France, because people were more and more sure that America was beginning to waken . . . or just because, after too long and fierce a strain, human nature always instinctively contrives to get its necessary whiff of moral oxygen? Or was it that George's influence had really penetrated him, and that this strange renewed confidence in life and in ideals was his son's message of reassurance?

Certainly the old George was there, close to him, that morning; and somewhere else—in scenes how different—he was sure that the actual George, at that very moment, was giving out force and youth and hope to those about him.

"I couldn't be doing this if I didn't understand—at last," Campton thought as he turned back to the easel The little pencil sketch had given him just the hint he needed, and he took up his palette with a happy sigh.

A knock broke in on his rapt labour, and without turning he called out: "Damn it, who are you? Can't you read the sign? *Not in!*"

The door opened and Mr. Brant entered.

He appeared not to have heard the painter's challenge; his eyes, from the threshold, sprang straight to the portrait, and remained vacantly fastened there. Campton, long afterward, remembered thinking, as he followed the glance: "He'll be trying to buy this one too!"

Mr. Brant moistened his lips, and his gaze, detaching itself from George's face, moved back in the same vacant way to Campton's. The two men looked at each other, and Campton jumped to his feet.

"Not—not——?"

Mr. Brant tried to speak, and the useless effort contracted his mouth in a pitiful grimace.

"*My son?*" Campton shrieked, catching him by the arm. The little man dropped into a chair.

"Not dead . . . not dead. . . Hope . . . hope . . ." was shaken out of him in jerks of anguish.

The door burst open again, and Boylston dashed in beaming. He waved aloft a handful of morning papers.

"America! You've seen? They've sacked Bernstorff! Broken off diplomatic——"

His face turned white, and he stood staring incredulously from one of the two bowed men to the other.

XXXV

Campton once more stood leaning in the window of a Paris hospital.

Before him, but viewed at another angle, was spread that same great spectacle of the Place de la Concorde that he had looked down at from the Crillon on the eve of mobilisation; behind him, in a fresh white bed, George lay in the same attitude as when his father had stood in the door of his room and sketched him while he slept.

All day there had run through Campton's mind the *clairvoyante*'s promise to Julia: "Your son will come back soon, and will never be sent to the front again."

Ah, this time it was true—never, never would he be sent to the front again! They had him fast now, had him safe. That was the one certainty. Fast how, safe how?—the answer to that had long hung in the balance. For two weeks or more after his return the surgeons had hesitated. Then youth had seemed to conquer, and the parents had been told to hope that after a long period of immobility George's shattered frame would slowly re-knit, and he would walk again—or at least hobble. A month had gone by since then; and Campton could at last trust himself to cast his mind back over the intervening days, so like in their anguish to those at Doullens, yet so different in all that material aid and organization could give.

Evacuation from the base, now so systematically and promptly effected, had become a matter of course in all but the gravest cases; and even the delicate undertaking of deflecting George's course from the hospital near the front to which he had been destined, and bringing him to Paris, had been accomplished by a word in the right quarter from Mr. Brant.

Campton, from the first, had been opposed to the attempt to bring George to Paris; partly perhaps because he felt that in the quiet provincial hospital near the front he would be able to have his son to himself. At any rate, the journey would have been shorter; though, as against that, Paris offered more possibilities of surgical aid. His opposition had been violent enough to check his growing friendliness with the Brants; and at the hours when they came to see George, Campton now most often contrived to be absent. Well, at any rate, George was alive, he was there under his father's eye, he was going to live: there seemed to be no doubt about it now. Campton could think it all over slowly and even calmly, marvelling at the miracle and taking it in. . . So at least he had imagined till he first made the attempt; then the old sense of unreality enveloped him again, and he struggled vainly to clutch at something tangible amid the swimming mists. "George— George—George——" he used to say the name over and over below his breath, as he sat and watched at his son's bedside; but it sounded far off and hollow, like the voice of a ghost calling to another.

Who was "George"? What did the name represent? The father left his post in the window and turned back to the bed, once more searching the boy's face for enlightenment. But George's eyes were closed: sleep lay on him like an impenetrable veil. The sleep of ordinary men was not like that: the light of their daily habits continued to shine through the chinks of their closed faces. But with these others, these who had been down into the lower circles of the pit, it was different: sleep instantly and completely sucked them back into the unknown. There were times when Campton, thus watching beside his son, used to say to himself: "If he were dead he could not be farther from me"—so deeply did George seem plunged in secret traffic with things unutterable.

Now and then Campton, sitting beside him, seemed to see a little way into those darknesses; but after a moment he always shuddered back to daylight, benumbed, inadequate, weighed down with the weakness of the flesh and the incapacity to reach beyond his habitual limit of sensation. "No wonder they don't talk to us," he mused.

By-and-bye, perhaps, when George was well again, and the war over, the father might penetrate into his son's mind, and find some new ground of communion with him: now the thing was not to be conceived.

He recalled again Adele Anthony's asking him, when he had come back from Doullens: "What was the first thing you felt?" and his answering: "Nothing." . . Well, it was like that now: every vibration had ceased in him. Between himself and George lay the unbridgeable abyss of his son's experiences.

As he sat there, the door was softly opened a few inches and Boylston's face showed through the crack: light shot from it like the rays around a chalice. At a sign from him Campton slipped out into the corridor and Boylston silently pushed a newspaper into his grasp. He bent over it, trying with dazzled eyes to read sense into the staring head-lines: but "America—America—America——" was all that he could see.

A nurse came gliding up on light feet: the tears were running down her face. "Yes—I know, I know, I know!" she exulted. Up the tall stairs and through the ramifying of long white passages rose an unwonted rumour of sound, checked, subdued, invisibly rebuked, but ever again breaking out, like the noise of ripples on a windless beach. In every direction nurses and orderlies were speeding from one room to another of the house of pain with the message: "America has declared war on Germany."

Campton and Boylston stole back into George's room. George lifted his eyelids and smiled at them, understanding before they spoke.

"The sixth of April! Remember the date!" Boylston cried over him in a gleeful whisper.

The wounded man, held fast in his splints, contrived to raise his head a little. His eyes laughed back into Boylston's. "You'll be in uniform within a week!" he said; and Boylston crimsoned.

Campton turned away again to the window. The day had come—had come; and his son had lived to see it. So many of George's comrades had gone down to death without hope; and in a few months more George, leaning from that same window—or perhaps well enough to be watching the spectacle with his father from the terrace of the Tuileries—would look out on the first brown battalions marching across the Place de la Concorde, where father and son, in the early days of the war, had seen the young recruits of the Foreign Legion patrolling under improvised flags.

At the thought Campton felt a loosening of the tightness about his heart. Something which had been confused and uncertain in his relation to the whole long anguish was abruptly lifted, giving him the same sense of buoyancy that danced in Boylston's glance. At last, random atoms that they were, they seemed all to have been shaken into their places, pressed into the huge mysterious design which was slowly curving a new firmament over a new earth. . .

There was another knock; and a jubilant nurse appeared, hardly visible above a great bunch of lilacs tied with a starred and striped ribbon. Campton, as he passed the flowers over to his son, noticed an envelope with Mrs. Talkett's perpendicular scrawl. George lay smiling, the lilacs close to his pillow, his free hand fingering the envelope; but he did not unseal the letter, and seemed to care less than ever to talk.

After an interval the door opened again, this time to show Mr. Brant's guarded face. He drew back slightly at the sight of Campton; but Boylston, jumping up, passed close to the painter to breathe: "To-day, sir, just today—you must!"

Campton went to the door and signed silently to Mr. Brant to enter. Julia Brant stood outside, flushed and tearful, carrying as many orchids as Mrs. Talkett had sent lilacs. Campton held out his hand, and with an embarrassed hast she stammered: "we couldn't wait——" Behind her he saw Adele Anthony hurriedly coming up the stairs.

For a few minutes they all stood or sat about George's bed, while their voices, beginning to speak low, rose uncontrollably, interrupting one another with tears and laughter. Mr. Brant and Boylston were both brimming with news, and George, though he listened more than he spoke, now and then put a brief question which loosened fresh floods. Suddenly Campton noticed that the young man's face, which had been too flushed, grew pale; but he continued to smile, and his eyes to move responsively from one illuminated face to the other. Campton, seeing that the others meant to linger, presently rose and slipping out quietly walked across the Rue de Rivoli to the deserted terrace of the Tuileries. There he sat for a long time, looking out on the vast glittering spaces of the Place de la Concorde, and calling up, with his painter's faculty of vivid and precise visualization, a future vision of interminable lines of brown battalions marching past.

When he returned to the hospital after dinner the night-nurse met him. She was not quite as well satisfied with her patient that evening: hadn't he perhaps had too many visitors? Yes, of course—she knew it had been a great day, a day of international rejoicing, above all a blessed day for France. But the doctors, from the beginning, must have warned Mr. Campton that his son ought to be kept quiet—very quiet. The last operation had been a great strain on his heart. Yes, certainly, Mr. Campton might go in; the patient had asked for him.

Oh, there was no danger—no need for anxiety; only he must not stay too long; his son must try to sleep.

Campton nodded, and stole in.

George lay motionless in the shaded lamplight: his eyes were open, but they seemed to reflect his father's presence without any change of expression, like mirrors rather than like eyes. The room was doubly silent after the joyful hubbub of the afternoon. The nurse had put the orchids and lilacs where George's eyes could rest on them. But was it on the flowers that his gaze so tranquilly dwelt? Or did he see in their place the faces of their senders? Or was he again in that far country whither no other eyes could follow him?

Campton took his usual seat by the bed. Father and son looked at each other, and the old George glanced out for half a second between the wounded man's lids.

"There was too much talking today," Campton grumbled.

"Was there? I didn't notice," his son smiled.

No—he hadn't noticed; he didn't notice anything. He was a million miles away again, whirling into his place in the awful pattern of that new firmament. . .

"Tired, old man?" Campton asked under his breath.

"No; just glad," said George contentedly.

His father laid a hand on his and sat silently beside him while the spring night blew in upon them through the open window. The quiet streets grew quieter, the hush in their hearts seemed gradually to steal over the extinguished city. Campton kept saying to himself: "I must be off," and still not moving. The nurse was sure to come back presently—why should he not wait till she dismissed him?

After a while, seeing that George's eyes had closed, Campton rose, and crept across the room to darken the lamp with a newspaper. His movement must have roused his son, for he heard a light struggle behind him and the low cry: "Father!"

Campton turned and reached the bed in a stride. George, ashy-white, had managed to lift himself a little on his free elbow.

"Anything wrong?" the father cried.

"No; everything all right," George said. He dropped back, his lids closing again, and a single twitch ran through the hand that Campton had seized. After that he lay stiller than ever.

XXXVI

George's prediction had come true. At his funeral, three days afterward, Boylston, a new-fledged member of the American Military Mission, was already in uniform. . .

But through what perversity of attention did the fact strike Campton, as he stood, a blank unfeeling automaton, in the front pew behind that coffin draped with flags and flanked with candle-glitter? Why did one thing rather than another reach to his deadened brain, and mostly the trivial things, such as Boylston's being already in uniform, and poor Julia's nose, under the harsh crape, looking so blue-red without its powder, and the chaplain's asking "O grave, where is thy victory?" in the querulous tone of a schoolmaster reproaching a pupil who mislaid things? It was always so with Campton: when sorrow fell it left him insensible and dumb. Not till long afterward did he begin to feel its birth-pangs. . .

They first came to him, those pangs, on a morning of the following July, as he sat once more on the terrace of the Tuileries. Most of his time, during the months since George's death, had been spent in endless aimless wanderings up and down the streets of Paris: and that day, descending early from Montmartre, he had noticed in his listless way that all the buildings on his way were fluttering with American flags. The fact left him indifferent: Paris was always decorating nowadays for one ally or another. Then he remembered that it must be the Fourth of July; but the idea of the Fourth of July came to him, through the same haze of indifference, as a mere far-off childish memory of surreptitious explosions and burnt fingers. He strolled on toward the Tuileries, where he had got into the way of sitting for hours at a time, looking across the square at what had once been George's window.

He was surprised to find the Rue de Rivoli packed with people; but his only thought was the instinctive one of turning away to avoid them, and he began to retrace his steps in the direction of the Louvre. Then at a corner he paused again and looked back at the Place de la Concorde. It was not curiosity that drew him, heaven knew—he would never again be curious about anything—but he suddenly remembered the day three months earlier when, leaning from George's window in the hospital, he had said to himself "By the time our first regiments arrive he'll be up and looking at them from here, or sitting with me over there on the terrace"; and that decided him to turn back. It was as if he had felt the pressure of George's hand on his arm.

Though it was still so early he had some difficulty in pushing his way through the throng. No seats were left on the terrace, but he managed to squeeze into a corner near one of the great vases of the balustrade; and leaning there, with the happy hubbub about him, he watched and waited.

Such a summer morning it was—and such a strange grave beauty had fallen on the place! He seemed to understand for the first time— he who served Beauty all his days—how profoundly, at certain hours, it may become the symbol of things hoped for and things died for. All those stately spaces and raying distances, witnesses of so many memorable scenes, might have been called together just as the setting for this one event—the sight of a few brown battalions passing over them like a feeble trail of insects.

Campton, with a vague awakening of interest, glanced about him, studying the faces of the crowd. Old and young, infirm and healthy, civilians, and soldiers—ah, the soldiers!—all were exultant, confident, alive. Alive! The word meant something new to him now—something so strange and unnatural that his mind still hung and brooded over it. For now that George was dead, by what mere blind propulsion did all these thousands of human beings keep on mechanically living?

He became aware that a boy, leaning over intervening shoulders, was trying to push a folded paper into his hand. On it was pencilled, in Mr. Brant's writing: "There will be a long time to wait. Will you take the seat I have kept next to mine?" Campton glanced down the terrace, saw where the little man sat at its farther end, and shook his head. Then some contradictory impulse made him decide to get up, laboriously work his halting frame through the crowd, and insert himself into the place next to Mr. Brant. The two men nodded without shaking hands; after that they sat silent, their eyes on the empty square. Campton noticed that Mr. Brant wore his usual gray clothes, but with a mourning band on the left sleeve. The sight of that little band irritated Campton. . .

There was, as Mr. Brant had predicted, a long interval of waiting; but at length a murmur of jubilation rose far off, and gathering depth and volume came bellowing and spraying up to where they sat. The square, the Champs Elysées and all the leafy distances were flooded with it: it was as though the voice of Paris had sprung up in fountains out of her stones. Then a military march broke shrilly on the tumult; and there they came at last, in a scant swaying line—so few, so new, so raw; so little, in comparison with the immense assemblages familiar to the place, so much in meaning and in promise.

"How badly they march—there hasn't even been time to drill them properly!" Campton thought; and at the thought he felt a choking in his throat, and his sorrow burst up in him in healing springs. . .

It was after that day that he first went back to his work. He had not touched paint or pencil since George's death; now he felt the inspiration and the power returning, and he began to spend his days among the young American officers and soldiers, studying them, talking to them, going about with them, and then hurrying home to jot down his impressions. He had not, as yet, looked at his last study of George, or opened the portfolio with the old sketches; if any one had asked him, he would probably have said that they no longer interested him. His whole creative faculty was curiously, mysteriously engrossed in the recording of the young faces for whose coming George had yearned.

"It's their marching so badly—it's their not even having had time to be drilled!" he said to Boylston, half-shamefacedly, as they sat together one August evening in the studio window.

Campton seldom saw Boylston nowadays. All the young man's time was taken up by his job with the understaffed and inexperienced Military Mission; but fagged as he was by continual overwork and heavy responsibilities, his blinking eyes had at last lost their unsatisfied look, and his whole busy person radiated hope and encouragement.

On the day in question he had turned up unexpectedly, inviting himself to dine with Campton and smoke a cigar afterward in the quiet window overhanging Paris. Campton was glad to have him there; no one could tell him more than Boylston about the American soldiers, their numbers, the accommodations prepared for their reception, their first contact with the other belligerents, and their own view of the business they were about. And the two chatted quietly in the twilight till the young man, rising, said it was time to be off.

"Back to your shop?"

"Rather! There's a night's work ahead. But I'm as good as new after our talk."

Campton looked at him wistfully. "You know I'd like to paint you some day."

"Oh——" cried Boylston, suffused with blushes; and added with a laugh: "It's my uniform, not me."

"Well, your uniform *is* you—it's all of you young men."

Boylston stood in the window twisting his cap about undecidedly. "Look here, sir—now that you've got back to work again——"

"Well?" Campton interrupted suspiciously.

The young man cleared his throat and spoke with a rush. "His mother wants most awfully that something should be decided about the monument."

"Monument? What monument? I don't want my son to have a monument," Campton exploded.

But Boylston stuck to his point. "It'll break her heart if something isn't put on the grave before long. It's five months now—and they fully recognize your right to decide——"

"Damn what they recognize! It was they who brought him to Paris; they made him travel when he wasn't fit; they killed him."

"Well—supposing they did: judge how much more they must be suffering!"

"Let 'em suffer. He's my son—my son. He isn't Brant's."

"Miss Anthony thinks——"

"And he's not hers either, that I know of!"

Boylston seemed to hesitate. "Well, that's just it, isn't it, sir? You've had him; you have him still. Nobody can touch that fact, or take it from you. Every hour of his life was yours. But they've never had anything, those two others, Mr. Brant and Miss Anthony; nothing but a reflected light. And so every outward sign means more to them. I'm putting it badly, I know——"

Campton held out his hand. "You don't mean to, I suppose. But better not put it at all. Good night," he said. And on the threshold he called out sardonically: "And who's going to pay for a monument, I'd like to know?"

A monument—they wanted a monument! Wanted him to decide about it, plan it, perhaps design it—good Lord, he didn't know! No doubt it all seemed simple enough to them: anything did, that money could buy. . . When he couldn't yet bear to turn that last canvas out from the wall, or look into the old portfolio even. . . Suffering, suffering! What did they any of them know about suffering? Going over old photographs, comparing studies, recalling scenes and sayings, discussing with some sculptor or other the shape of George's eyelids, the spring of his chest-muscles, the way his hair grew and his hands, moved—why, it was like digging him up again out of that peaceful corner of the Neuilly cemetery where at last he was resting, like dragging him back to the fret and the fever, and the senseless roar of the guns that still went on.

And then: as he'd said to Boylston, who was to pay for their monument? Even if the making of it had struck him as a way of getting nearer to his boy, instead of building up a marble wall between them—even if the idea had appealed to him, he hadn't a penny to spare for such an undertaking. In the first place, he never intended to paint again for money; never intended to do anything but these gaunt and serious or round and babyish young American faces above their stiff military collard, and when their portraits were finished to put them away, locked up for his own pleasure; and what he had earned in the last years was to be partly for these young men—for their reading-rooms, clubs, recreation centres, whatever was likely to give them temporary rest and solace in the grim months to come; and partly for such of the protégés of "The Friends of French Art" as had been deprived of aid under the new management. Tales of private jealousy and petty retaliation came to Campton daily, now that Mme. Beausite administered the funds; Adele Anthony and Mlle. Davril, bursting with the wrongs of their pensioners, were always appealing to him for help. And then, hidden behind these more or less valid reasons, the old instinctive dread of spending had reasserted itself, he couldn't tell how or why, unless through some dim opposition to the Brants' perpetual outpouring; their hospitals, their motors, their bribes, their orchids, and now their monument—*their* monument!

He sought refuge from it all with his soldiers, haunting for hours every day one of the newly-opened Soldiers' and Sailors' Clubs. Adele Anthony had already found a job there, and was making a success of it. She looked twenty years older since George was gone, but she stuck to her work with the same humorous pertinacity; and with her mingled heartiness and ceremony, her funny resuscitation of obsolete American slang, and her ability to answer all their most disconcerting questions about Paris and France (Montmartre included), she easily eclipsed the ministering angels who twanged the home-town chord and called them "boys."

The young men appeared to return Campton's liking; it was as if they had guessed that he needed them, and wanted to offer him their shy help. He was conscious of something rather protecting in their attitude, of his being to them a vague unidentified figure, merely "the old gentleman" who was friendly to them; but he didn't mind. It was enough to sit and listen to their talk, to try and clear up a few of the countless puzzles which confronted them, to render them such fatherly services as he could, and in the interval to jot down notes of their faces—their inexhaustibly inspiring faces. Sometimes to talk with them was like being on the floor in George's nursery, among the blocks and the tin soldiers; sometimes like walking with young archangels in a cool empty heaven; but wherever he was he always had the sense of being among his own, the sense he had never had since George's death.

To think of them all as George's brothers, to study out the secret likeness to him in their young dedicated faces: that was now his one passion, his sustaining task; it was at such times that his son came back and sat among them. . .

Gradually, as the weeks passed, the first of his new friends, officers and soldiers, were dispersed throughout the training camps, and new faces succeeded to those he had tried to fix on his canvas; an endless line of Benny Upshers, baby-Georges, schoolboy Boylstons, they seemed to be. Campton saw each one go with a fresh pang, knowing that every move brought them so much nearer to the front, that everravening and inexorable front. They were always happy to be gone; and that only increased his pain. Now and then he attached himself more particularly to one of the young men, because of some look of the eyes or some turn of the mind like George's; and then the parting became anguish.

One day a second lieutenant came to the studio to take leave. He had been an early recruit of Plattsburg, and his military training was so far advanced that he counted on being among the first officers sent to the fighting line. He was a fresh-coloured lad, with fair hair that stood up in a defiant crest.

"There are so few of us, and there's so little time to lose; they can't afford to be too particular," he laughed.

It was just the sort of thing that George would have said, and the laugh was like an echo of George's. At the sound Campton suddenly burst into tears, and was aware of his visitor's looking at him with eyes of dismay and compassion.

"Oh, don't, sir, *don't*," the young man pleaded, wringing the painter's hand, and making what decent haste he could to get out of the studio.

Campton, left alone, turned once more to his easel. He sat down before a canvas on which he had blocked out a group of soldiers playing cards at their club; but after a stroke or two he threw aside his brush, and remained with his head bowed on his hands, a lonely tired old man.

He had kept a cheerful front at his son's going; and now he could not say goodbye to one of these young fellow without crying. Well—it was because he had no one left of his own, he supposed. Loneliness like his took all a man's strength from him. . .

The bell rang, but he did not move. It rang again; then the door was pushed timidly open, and Mrs. Talkett came in. He had not seen her since the day of George's funeral, when he had fancied he detected her in a shrunken black-veiled figure hurrying past in the meaningless line of mourners.

In her usual abrupt fashion she began, without a greeting: "I've come to say goodbye; I'm going to America."

He looked at her remotely, hardly hearing what she said. "To America?"

"Yes; to join my husband."

He continued to consider her in silence, and she frowned in her perplexed and fretful way. "He's at Plattsburg, you know." Her eyes wandered unseeingly about the studio. "There's nothing else to do, is there—now—here or anywhere? So I sail tomorrow; I mean to take a house somewhere near him. He's not well, and he writes that he misses me. The life in camp is so unsuited to him——"

Campton still listened absently. "Oh, you're right to go," he agreed at length, supposing it was what she expected of him.

"Am I?" She half-smiled. "What's right and what's wrong? I don't know any longer. I'm only trying to do what I suppose George would have wanted." She stood uncertainly in front of Campton. "All I *do* know," she cried, with a sharp break in her voice, "is that I've never in my life been happy enough to be so unhappy!" And she threw herself down on the divan in a storm of desolate sobbing.

After he had comforted her as best he could, and she had gone away, Campton continued to wander up and down the studio forlornly. That cry of hers kept on echoing in his ears: "I've never in my life been happy enough to be so unhappy!" It associated itself suddenly with a phrase of Boylston's that he had brushed away unheeding: "You've had your son—you have him still; but those others have never had anything."

Yes; Campton saw now that it was true of poor Madge Talkett, as it was of Adele Anthony and Mr. Brant, and even in a measure of Julia. They had never—no, not even George's mother—had anything, in the close inextricable sense in which Campton had had his son. And it was only now, in his own hour of destitution, that he understood how much greater the depth of their poverty had been. He recalled the frightened embarrassed look of the young lieutenant whom he had discountenanced by his tears; and he said to himself: "The only thing that helps is to be able to do things for people. I suppose that's why Brant's always trying——"

Julia too: it was strange that his thoughts should turn to her with such peculiar pity. It was not because the boy had been born of her body: Campton did not see her now, as he once had in a brief moment of compassion, as the young mother bending illumined above her baby. He saw her as an old empty-hearted woman, and asked himself how such an unmanageable monster as grief was to fill the room up of her absent son.

What did such people as Julia do with grief, he wondered, how did they make room for it in their lives, get up and lie down every day with its taste on their lips? Its elemental quality, that awful sense it communicated of a whirling earth, a crumbling Time, and all the cold stellar spaces yawning to receive us—these feelings which he was beginning to discern and to come to terms with in his own way (and with the sense that it would have been George's way too), these feelings could never give their stern appeasement to Julia. . . Her religion? Yes, such as it was no doubt it would help, talking with the Rector would help; giving more time to her church-charities, her wounded soldiers, imagining that she was paying some kind of tax on her affliction. But the vacant evenings, at home, face to face with Brant! Campton had long since seen that the one thing which had held the two together was their shared love of George; and if Julia discovered, as she could hardly fail to do, how much more deeply Brant had loved her son than she had, and how much more inconsolably he mourned him, that would only increase her sense of isolation. And so, in sheer self-defence, she would gradually, stealthily, fill up the void with the old occupations, with bridge and visits and secret consultations at the dressmaker's about the width of crape on her dresses; and all the while the object of life would be gone for her. Yes; he pitied Julia most of all.

But Mr. Brant too—perhaps in a different way it was he who suffered most. For the stellar spaces were not exactly Mr. Brant's native climate, and yet voices would call to him from them, and he would not know. . .

There were moments when Campton looked about him with astonishment at the richness of his own denuded life; when George was in the sunset, in the voices of young people, or in any trivial joke that father and son would have shared; and other moments when he was nowhere, utterly lost, extinct and irrecoverable; and others again when the one thing which could have vitalized the dead business of living would have been to see him shove open the studio door, stalk in, pour out some coffee for himself in his father's cup, and diffuse through the air the warm sense of his bodily presence, the fresh smell of his clothes and his flesh and his hair. But through all these moods, Campton began to see, there ran the life-giving power of a reality embraced and accepted. George had been; George was; as long as his father's consciousness lasted, George would be as much a part of it as the closest, most actual of his immediate sensations. He had missed nothing of George, and here was his harvest, his golden harvest.

Such states of mind were not constant with Campton; but more and more often, when they came, they swept him on eagle wings over the next desert to the next oasis; and so, gradually, the meaningless days became linked to each other in some kind of intelligible sequence.

Boylston, after the talk which had so agitated Campton, did not turn up again at the studio for some time; but when he next appeared the painter, hardly pausing to greet him, began at once, as if they had just parted: "That monument you spoke about the other day . . . you know. . ."

Boylston glanced at him in surprise.

"If they want me to do it, I'll do it," Campton went on, jerking the words out abruptly and walking away toward the window. He had not known, till he began, that he had meant to utter them, or how difficult they would be to say; and he stood there a moment struggling with the unreasoning rebellious irritability which so often lay in wait for his better impulses. At length he turned back, his hands in his pockets, clinking his change as he had done the first time that Boylston had come to him for help. "But as I plan the thing," he began again, in a queer growling tone, "it's going to cost a lot—everything of the sort does nowadays, especially in marble. It's hard enough to get any one to that kind of work at all. And prices have about tripled, you know."

Boylston's eyes filled, and he nodded, still without speaking.

"That's just what Brant'll like though, isn't it?" Campton said, with an irrepressible sneer in his voice. He saw Boylston redden and look away, and he too flushed to the forehead and broke off ashamed. Suddenly he had the vision of Mr. Brant effacing himself at the foot of the hospital-stairs when they had arrived at Doullens; Mr. Brant drawing forth the copy of the orderly's letter in the dark fog-swept cloister; Mr. Brant always yielding, always holding back, yet always remembering to do or to say the one thing the father's lacerated soul could bear.

"And he's had nothing—nothing—nothing!" Campton thought.

He turned again to Boylston, his face still flushed, his lips twitching. "Tell them—tell Brant—that I'll design the thing; I'll design it, and he shall pay for it. He'll want to—I understand that. Only, for God's sake, don't let him come here and thank me—at least not for a long time!"

Boylston again nodded silently, and turned to go.

After he had gone the painter moved back to his long table. He had always had a fancy for modelling—had always had lumps of clay lying about within reach. He pulled out all the sketches of his son from the old portfolio, spread them before him on the table, and began.

PARIS, 1918—*Saint Brice-sous-Forêt, 1922*

THE END